debt
of my soul

K.P. HAVEN

ISBN (Paperback): 979-8-98881 12-5-1

ISBN (Ebook): 979-8-98881 12-4-4

Edited by: Lawerence Editing

Proofreading by: Little Red Herring

Cover Design by: Emily Wittig Designs

Chapter Ornaments: iStock/Bitter & iStock/sabelskaya

ALSO BY K.P. HAVEN

<u>Blood Ties & Legacies Duet</u>

Heritage of Blood

Heritage of Fire

<u>Standalone Novels</u>

Debt of My Soul

Broken Blood Ties—coming spring 2025

Author's Note

Debt of My Soul is a gritty adult novel with a fade-to-black romance. That said, there are adult themes throughout this book. Moderate language, kidnapping, attempted SA, death/violence, drug abuse, organized crime, self-harm, and cheating (not by MCs).

While many of these are not key themes in this story, if any are triggering to you, please practice self-love and set the book aside.

Debt of My Soul

K.P. HAVEN

To my husband,
thank you for dragging me to Mississippi.

You are my home.

HE WHO IS QUICK TO BORROW IS SLOW TO PAY.

—GERMAN PROVERB

Chapter 1
Fleur

Standing here in the plumbing aisle, I've come to realize two things: first, I have no idea what I'm doing renovating an old farmhouse, and second, I'm not sure running away to the southern half of the country was a good idea.

I snatch a P trap off the shelf and stare at it. It *looks* like what I need for the kitchen sink, but to be sure, I roam the aisle riddled with different-sized PVC pipes and couplings. Whole shelves are filled with small bins of plumbing parts I never knew existed. And half of them are blocked with a metal stair contraption used for stocking items—making it nearly impossible to view the overcomplicated selections.

Back at my house, water is currently dripping from underneath my sink into the plastic Tupperware container I shoved under there. I've given myself an hour to fix the issue before it's overflowing with gag-inducing well water. And, glancing at my watch, I have twenty-five minutes left.

The breath full of lumber and paint thinner I inhaled seconds ago turns my stomach. I peer up and down the empty aisle, willing an employee to meander down here long enough that I can ask a question. The thought of searching out said employee though ... terrifying.

After squinting at some one-inch pipe, I pull up the photo of the space under my sink on my phone and mentally compare the two like the genuine novice I am. I should've measured. If I'm being honest, I should've picked another house to move into altogether. Unfortunately, my hurried departure from Michigan didn't lend itself to a particularly relaxing relocation or house hunt.

I knew I wanted a simple, secluded place. So when I discovered this tiny town, without a single stoplight—I knew this was it.

However, real estate is limited. There aren't any apartments for rent or many houses for sale. I hadn't planned to buy this soon, but when I passed the dilapidated old farmhouse, I called the number on the FOR SALE sign right away. Apparently, it'd been on the market for a while. Even so, when I made them a lowball cash offer, I fully expected a flat-out rejection. But, a few days later, I was the proud owner of twelve acres, a run-down home, and an online vision board miles long.

Since depleting my funds, the pitiful amount in my bank account doesn't afford me the luxury of hiring a contractor to tackle this disaster. So I've become a DIY homeowner. And I'm failing at it already. I can't even fix the kitchen sink.

I toss the P trap I'm holding into the cart and scroll through my recent calls to find my dad's number.

"Hello?" His voice is groggy, and he sounds half asleep. It makes my stomach clench—gosh, I miss home. I probably woke him from his afternoon nap. The kind you earn after retiring from forty years in the education system.

"Hey, Dad," I say, unable to hide my smile. "I'm sorry to call *again*, but I'm in the home improvement store, and I'm not sure what else I need to fix the kitchen sink issue I messaged you about."

"It's never a bother, Fleur. Make sure you get a P trap. One-half inch is the standard size for kitchen sinks. You'll want to get some PVC pipe of the same diameter and a few couplings. They might have a replacement kit that works for your situation."

He continues listing items, and I scramble to keep up, hunting for everything he mentions, right down to the plumber's tape. I'm overwhelmed already, and I haven't even tried to fix the leak yet.

A sting prickles behind my eyelids, and I massage my temple with the hand not holding the phone to my shoulder. I'm irritated with myself, and apparently—I scuff my shoe on the tile—this tacky floor.

After hanging up with my dad, I tuck my phone back in my crossbody bag and discreetly wipe beneath my eyes, hoping to hide the few tears that escaped down my cheeks at the realization I've overcommitted.

Scrubbing my palms against my torn and tattered work jeans, I set my gaze back on the endless options. Then I rummage through the tubs of items, sorting through what my father mentioned I needed. At this rate, I'll be finished renovating the farmhouse in twenty years.

While crouching down to pick through a bin of couplings, I sniffle as another wave of anxiety ripples through me. Trying to make it on my own wasn't in my plans.

But I guess neither was the twenty-one-year-old college student.

I aggressively rip a clear package from its spot on the shelf sending the whole bin, plumbing parts and all, skidding across the sticky floor. I tilt my head back at the fluorescent lights above and let out a less than ladylike groan. *My luck—always my luck.*

"Excuse me, ma'am?"

Rattled, I snap my head straight, then crane it to the left to see a handsome man standing there. In dark blue jeans, with a flannel button-up, he's everything I'd picture the men in this town look like. His head is topped with short dark brown hair, and his cleanly shaved face offers a view of his rounded chin.

I blink, processing, before diving to the floor to pick up the couplings I dropped. "Uh, sorry. Did you need to get in here? I'll just pick these up and be on my way." My arms flail around the dirt-caked tile, trying to reach each package and shove them back in the bin.

The man steps closer, and I catch a whiff of a woodsy scent as he bends down to help pick up some of my mess.

"Are you okay?" he asks.

I stop snatching and glance up at him. His eyes are a soft brown that seem to twinkle as he smiles at me. Sharp lips come together, curling up as he takes in my disheveled state.

"I, uh, yeah," I mumble.

"I couldn't help but overhear you on the phone ..."

His words cut out as the sudden rush of embarrassment burns my cheeks. *Great.* The first person I interact with in this town besides the realtor, and I'm already making a terrible impression.

"Yeah. Trying to figure out what I need for a small project." I offer a flat smile, secretly wishing this floor would open up and swallow me whole. His face lights up when I engage him, and my heart picks up its already fast pace.

"Small project?" The man crosses his arms, letting the bulk of his biceps rest on full display, and he casually leans against the plumbing shelf I'm sick of staring at.

"Well," I say, standing. "More like a massive undertaking,

and I have no idea what I'm doing." I motion to the cart full of plumbing items.

"Do you want me to get someone to help you?"

"No!" I blurt out. "I mean ... no, thank you. I'll figure it out."

He smirks at me but doesn't say anything else as he strolls to my cart and lifts out the items my father told me to get. "Kitchen sink trouble?"

I pick at a loose thread on my holed pants. "Actually, yeah."

He extends his hand to me. "I'm Adam."

"Fleur," I say as I meet his calloused hand and give it a slight squeeze.

His eyebrows rise. "Are you new in town, Fleur?" He grins with the question, but the smile is lost on someone like me. Moving here wasn't *really* a choice. More like a necessity.

"For now."

"Well," Adam says, reaching into his back pocket, "I'm in the business of helping people with projects around their homes. I'd be more than happy to give you a hand."

He passes me a business card. It names him the local handyman, with his number attached. Heat licks my cheeks, and I flick my eyes to his before staring back at the card again. I don't have money to pay someone, especially since I haven't started working at the bed-and-breakfast yet.

"Thank you. I-I unfortunately don't have a ton of extra cash right now. I'm planning to do most of the renovations to the farmhouse myself."

He blinks. "Farmhouse?"

Dang. Oversharing again, Fleur.

"Uh, yeah. It's outside of town. Anyway, I appreciate your—"

"You mean that old farmhouse right on Highway twelve? Across from the Mason Farm's cornfields?" he asks, brows drawn together. His face is smooth, but the wrinkles from his confusion make him look older than he probably is. Maybe in his thirties?

I study his expression, my gaze drawn to his bare chest peeking out from behind the partially unbuttoned blue and green flannel, forming a tempting V shape. Despite myself, there's a flicker of attraction.

I don't know who the Masons are. Honestly, I wasn't even aware someone owned the acres of field across from my new place. But I nod, acknowledging the place as mine, and move to pocket his card.

"Wow," he says, raising his eyebrows. "I didn't realize anyone had bought that. I've always wished someone would restore the place. If I had the money, I'd definitely do it." He moves across the aisle to pick a few items off the shelf.

I smile at his enthusiasm for my project—the excitement in his voice confirming my impulsive decision to purchase the property.

"I have big dreams." I grin. "But the know-how is a bit lacking."

He transfers the items he plucked from the shelf into my cart, rearranging a few pieces before taking others out and returning them.

He stands from his hunched position and brings a hand up to the back of his neck, rubbing it while his eyes rake over my attire.

I don't look cute, and Adam has probably noticed. The ripped jeans I put on to work, coupled with the bulldog mascot shirt I stole from Chris before I ran, all look like they've been plucked from a trash bag. My hair is braided over my shoulder, with one of my dad's pale-yellow bandanas folded up over my head. Although it basically blends into my blond hair, so much so that it isn't even noticed.

"Listen, I've been wanting to see the inside of that place forever. How about I follow you back to your house and fix your sink in exchange for a tour?" His eyes sparkle with his request, and I can't seem to look away.

I'm pretty sure there's a horror movie in the making here. A random guy offers to come back to my house to fix my sink for free. I look down the empty aisle, then glance at my cart with almost all new items I don't recognize. Desperation must make my judgment questionable because my heart pounds with anticipation. The idea he would work on my sink is ... beyond helpful. I've been doing dishes with gallon water jugs, refilling them at the local grocery store every day since I've been here. For a week.

As quickly as the joyful prospect of a working kitchen sink enters my mind, so does the realization that I'm going to have to show this man my current living conditions.

When I bought the place, I knew I'd have to resort to living in construction. I cleaned out the master bedroom and the kitchen the best I could, intending to only utilize those two rooms. My first project to tackle is the guest bathroom. It's a compact powder room with a toilet, a small vintage vanity, and a tiny shower. My plan is to get that renovated first so I have a facility to use while I upgrade the master bed and bath.

"Or, if you're uncomfortable—"

Adam's voice snaps me out of my worrisome thoughts, and I shake my head. "No, no. It would be helpful if you took a look, but let me pay you, please."

"Nah," he says, the twinge of his Southern accent making itself known. "I'll take a look at it for free and you can show me some of the other projects you're taking on. I'll give you a quote, with the *recently moved-here* discount, as well as your own labor factored in."

I take a quick breath to tell him that's okay and inform him I *can* figure it out on my own, but he continues.

"Plus, you'd be helping me out, too. It's been a bit slow for me around here." Adam shifts on his feet and glances down at his brown work boots.

I know the feeling of insecurity all too well, and I recognize it in his expression.

Not wanting to embarrass him further, I offer him a smile. "I'd like that."

When I anxiously chew on my bottom lip, it captures his attention, and he clears his throat, stepping toward me. "Let me grab a few things and I'll meet you out at the house after you check out."

I nod, crossing my arms in front of myself to avoid plucking the rubber bands on my wrist. He extends his hand to me again. I reach to take it and the warmth of his large hand engulfs mine.

"Welcome to Ruin, Mississippi, Fleur."

Chapter 2
Fleur

By the time I check out and load my jeep, the sun is already starting to set. I take off down Main Street, passing by the local bank and coffee shop.

The roar of a motorcycle alarms me, and I squint in my rearview mirror to see a sleek bike on my tail revving its engine like I'm the slowest person in town.

Jerk.

It's only thirty-five—I'm not speeding up. I hover at thirty-four to prove a point, and the motorcycle darts around me over the double-yellow line. As they pass, the pitch-black helmet turns to study me through my driver's side window before speeding past and cutting me off.

I slam on my brakes and throw my hands up. I thought small towns were supposed to be the epitome of charm and kindness.

Huffing out a sigh, I come to a four-way stop where a modest thrift store sits on the corner. Its awning droops to one side and the signage is rusty, but a gorgeous oak dresser with potential sits out front. It's a tall, six-drawer piece in desperate need of love. Nothing a good sanding and fresh stain couldn't fix.

I pull over, hoping to catch the employee before they close up for the evening. That's one thing I had to learn quickly upon moving to this sparse Southern town—they close their shops before 5:00 p.m. around here.

I push open the door, and the bell attached above jingles while the smell of antiques wafts up my nose. Shelves are filled to the brim with household items, and the nostalgia of hitting the once-a-month flea market with my mom invades my thoughts. The first Saturday of each month, in the three bearable seasons of the year, my mom would take me with her. At first, when I was younger, I'd tag along with her and her friends. But as I got older, it became something we did—just the two of us.

I pull out my phone and snap a photo to send to her. She'll be impressed. I've already found the jackpot in this town.

"Be right there!" A sweet, feminine voice with a thick accent rings out from the back. Although boxes are piled high near the rear of the store, so I can't exactly tell where the voice is coming from.

I head over to a section with multiple lamps, hoping to find a small one for my kitchen counter, and bring up my digital inspiration board for the house while perusing the few they have on the shelves.

"Hi, what can I do for you?"

A woman, perhaps late twenties, with brunette hair piled on top of her head, approaches. Beads of sweat collect above her upper lip and her breathing is heavy. I stare at her for a minute too long, my awkwardness compounded by her distractingly bright blue dress.

"Sorry, I was moving a bunch of donations in the back," she adds.

I shake my head. "It's not a problem. I wanted to ask about the dresser sitting out front. Is it still available? I didn't see a price."

"Oh my," she says, her Southern drawl growing deeper. "I meant to put a price on it this morning. I think it's fifty dollars. Let me grab my books and I'll tell you for sure. I'm River, by the way."

"Fleur." I follow her up to the hoarded counter. Three different types of Ruin, MS stickers are stacked high next to postcards that don't have a dent in them. She grabs two books from underneath the checkout and flips them open. Huh. No computer.

"I know," she says, probably reading the confusion in my expression. "This shop was my grandmother's before she died. She never upgraded things around here, and I haven't gotten around to it yet. Oh, here it is. Fifty dollars." She slams the books shut, dust kicking up into her brown eyes, and she rapidly blinks. "Did you want it?"

"Yes, please." I pause, wondering how I'm going to get this home. "Could I pay for it now and pick it up some other time? I only have my jeep, and I'm not sure it's going to fit in the back."

"Of course! Actually, I can deliver it to you for free. Anything to make room for all the other items I have yet to put out." She chucks a thumb over her shoulder, pointing toward where she was rustling around when I walked in.

"That would be great. Thank you." I pull out cash and hand it over.

River takes my number and address, commenting how excited she is that someone's finally going to "make that farmhouse shine," and she details plans to deliver the dresser sometime next week.

I dart out of the thrift store, trying to make up for lost time. The drive out of the small downtown is peaceful and quiet.

The summer days are hot, but the evenings are blissful, and I roll down the windows, letting the fresh air flick my braid in the wind.

The sky has transformed into a breathtaking view of oranges and yellows. The soft hues of pale yellow remind me of freshly bloomed daffodils. Even the wisps of clouds gradually stretch into a seamless blend of tangerine and apricot as the sun's dwindling rays glow behind them.

The drive to the farmhouse is mesmerizing. The landscape of cornfields and hay bales appears like a golden mirage with highlights that brush the entire canvas of this town. More people should take advantage of living in small towns like these —even if only for a brief time.

I turn onto the dirt road leading to my property, passing an old crumbling chimney on the corner of the street. Vines and ivy have found purchase in all the crevices and gaps of mortar. And the ground around it supports heaps of broken bricks. Each time I pass by, I wonder what happened to the house it once belonged to.

A long wooden and barbwire fence lines the road, and large cedar trees shadow sections of the red dirt as I drive. It's the first time in the week I've been here that I don't freeze with anxiety over uprooting my life. I'm looking forward to the renovations, and happiness actually feels within reach. A happiness I never thought I'd get to see again after my nine-year relationship shattered.

I never thought twenty-six was too old, but apparently, he did.

I was going to marry him. To say "I do" and have *the* life.

But that idea was flushed away in favor of a twenty-one-year-old college student.

To say I left Michigan to start over and find myself is a lie— one I have no problem telling when the alternative is reality.

And, well, reality sucks. I ran—hightailed it out of our shared life, crushed and embarrassed.

He's called a few times since I left. Logically, I should block him. Unfortunately, though, a sliver of teasing hope dangles in my mind. Maybe he'll tell me to come home, or perhaps he'll call to confess he misses me.

But so far, every voicemail he leaves asks where I am or if I'm coming home—it's humiliating.

Nausea curdles in my stomach, and the fried chicken sandwich I ate for lunch before my endless home improvement shopping threatens to make an appearance. I roll my shoulders and allow the crunch of the gravel dirt road to keep me from screaming. Then, reaching for the rubber bands on my wrist, I pull back twice, letting the sting of each snap bring me out of the shame-induced ache.

I'm not good enough. I was never good enough.

Rolling up my windows, I reach the long driveway leading to my new home.

The old farmhouse sits on a vast, sprawling property with a delicate charm that drew me in, despite my ignorance of remodeling. And even with all the land it sits on, the house still exudes a cozy, quaint feel.

It's traditional architecture—according to the realtor—with a steep-pitched gable roof. Time has faded any shingles that aren't missing, and the whitewashed wooden siding is worn but simple and beautiful.

A wide, wraparound porch hugs the front and sides of the house. Aged wooden columns and weathered railings run parallel to the space, but many of the boards are warped and in need of replacement. It's my first priority after the inside of the house is done.

The farmhouse is full of windows, framed by rustic wooden shutters, letting in picturesque natural light, but many are cloudy and need to be replaced. Thankfully, there's one stained glass transom window above the front door in good shape, and I plan to keep it original to the home.

Adam's red truck is parked in front of the fallen detached garage, and I linger, watching him walk around inspecting the house surrounded by untamed bushes. What does he see? Potential? More work than it's worth?

After turning the car off, the rustling of the oak tree leaves filters in through the cracked window, and I take a deep breath.

Here goes nothing.

"Rough, huh?" I say, shutting my car door and folding my arms in front of my chest. I'm trying to see the home through a contractor's eyes and not my own overzealous and unrealistic perspective.

Adam smiles at me, giving a quick kick to the few rows of blocks. "Foundation is solid. Definitely needs a hefty renovation, but she's beautiful." He rubs both of his hands in front of him while his gaze travels from the first to the second story.

Good. He gets it. He's drawn to this house the same way I am, and if his expression is any indication, he understands my vision.

"I was hoping you'd say that." I move toward him, digging my keys out of my purse, and unlock the front door.

I hold it open for him, studying his face to gauge his reaction. As he steps in, the creaking floor sings and the dust motes dance in the air. Faded floral wallpaper lines the entryway hall —most of it peeling. And when he doesn't balk at the splintered floorboards, I smile.

"Through here is the living room." I follow him as he moves into the living space with a brick fireplace and several hanging lights that have lost their luster. The ceilings are high, but the paint and plaster are chipped.

We continue through the country-style kitchen, master bed

and bath, and a downstairs bathroom before making our way up to the two other wallpapered guestrooms.

Every step on the stairs creaks to a tune that sounds like "Twinkle Twinkle Little Star," but Adam gazes around the space with awe and determination.

With the tour over, we head back to the kitchen, and I pour us each a glass of lemonade.

Adam raises his glass to me. "To breathing new life into this place."

I meet his glass with a quiet clink and smile over my glass at him. "I was worried you might give me the sad news that this was too much of a project."

He grins at me, tossing a thumb over his shoulder. "Nah, this old thing. She has great potential. Maybe a bit much for a first-time DIYer, though."

I huff out a laugh. "How do you know it's my first time?"

"I could tell by the way you were looking at the plumbing section at the store like it wronged you."

I nod and set my glass on the counter next to the sink. Adam moves over to open the cabinets below and I catch a whiff of his earthy masculine scent, letting my eyes close for a second too long in appreciation.

"Is it just leaking?"

I jolt, blinking at him. "Yeah. I think the P trap needs to be replaced."

He smirks at me and gestures below the sink. "I'd say most of this drainage system needs to be replaced. Are you planning to replace the sink during the renovation?"

The vintage porcelain glimmers under the golden hour sun creeping through the window above it. I had every intention of restoring it and using it in my final kitchen.

"No. I'd like to keep it. But I plan to replace the counter-tops, so it'll have to come out, right?"

"Yeah. How about this?" He withdraws his head out from under the sink and bangs it against the underside of the counter. I grimace, but he doesn't seem fazed. "Why don't I get the sink working for you to use? I'll save swapping out everything until the new counters are down and the sink is ready to be permanently in place."

It sounds like a plan. It sounds like he knows what he's doing and needs a project. But ...

"I, uh, I don't have the money for a contractor right now. I start my new job on Monday and would be happy to pay you to fix the sink, but I'm not sure I can commit to the large-scale project." I dip my face, trying to avoid his eyes.

Bulky work boots enter where I stare at the floor and his foot taps mine until my gaze lifts to meet his. Dark blue circles I hadn't noticed before line underneath his eyes. His dark hair is tussled after running a hand through it, and a spark of defeat flickers in his expression.

"I'm trying to make some extra money right now. Some ... things have come up, and I'm having trouble getting work. I can work out a payment plan with you, and I'll be willing to help anytime you need. Call if you get stuck on a particular part." He chuckles, then drags both of his hands over his thigh before he shoves them into his pockets and backpedals away.

"Oh, uh, okay," I say, trying to gauge my minor discomfort at his assertiveness. Flashes of a contractor burying his victims in drywall flicker in my mind, and I mentally slap myself for going back to the horror movie delusion.

He probably *is* in desperate need of a job and seeing how there aren't too many renovations in this dusty small town, he's probably trying to snag the job before I search for anyone else.

My parents always told me I was the opposite of assertive. A doormat through and through, apparently—thank you, Chris. *Jerk.*

Salespeople fluster me, and I'm always the "yes" person. Never quite figured out how to say no. But leaving Michigan ... that was putting my foot down.

Anxiety squeezes my stomach and I fiddle with the rubber bands at my wrist.

"How does next Saturday sound?" Adam prompts me with a wide grin as we walk toward the door.

"Uh, sure."

Only I'm not sure. I'm unsure what I'm agreeing to. But I know I need my sink fixed, and this man seems competent and nice enough to handle it for me. I can always use my credit card for a while.

"Great. I'll get everything and be by around nine next weekend." He offers me a wink and heads to the door. I lean against the patched-up doorframe as he strides to his truck and pulls away.

"Looks like we might get you fixed up yet," I say, rubbing a hand on the rough exterior of the threshold. I hope I'm talking about more than just the house.

Chapter 3
Him

There's an unfamiliar jeep driving slowly around town. Small towns aren't supposed to be tourist attractions.

Chapter 4
Fleur

Thirty minutes into my training, and I've already inhaled three buttermilk biscuits smothered with tomato gravy. Mr. and Mrs. Northgate are the sweetest elderly couple running this multigenerational bed-and-breakfast. The Old Hillside B&B is an anomaly in this small town. A well-preserved Victorian home with intricate gingerbread trim and an ivy-covered entrance.

The parlor, with plush vintage furniture, chandeliers, and a detailed fireplace, is ancient yet inviting. Built in the nineteenth century, the house has five rooms, each with its own mix of antique furniture and modern comforts. My favorite room, as seen on their website, has a four-poster bed with an embroidered canopy, and the bathroom has a large claw-foot soaking tub that I immediately added to my farmhouse master bath wish list.

My new employers have spent the last half an hour telling me stories of family gatherings, romantic weekends, and wandering travelers blowing through unencumbered. And, of course, feeding me.

Now I'm following Mrs. Northgate around the house for the essential introduction to the place. She's a plump older woman, with glasses that hang from a beaded chain. Her silver hair is pulled back into a low-set bun, and the fine lines around her pursed lips crease even further as she shows me the right way to enter one of the rooms with a finicky lock.

Technically, I've been hired as a housekeeper, but I've already been informed I'll be needed for other duties as well.

We continue with the tour.

"This is the supply closet. You'll find all the fresh linens and sheets you need. We also have travel toiletries that need to be replaced each day." She gestures to a metal door in the wall. "The laundry chute. Just toss all the used linens down here."

I open the chute, curious about how it looks, but the smell of old dryer sheets wafts up my nose as I stare into the black void. It's actually kind of creepy.

Mrs. Northgate chuckles at my scrunched nose and closes the door for me. "You'll get used to it."

I'm not sure if she's talking about the smell or the fact that I've never been a housekeeper before. It must show.

I completed two years of community college out of high school before I went to work for Chris's parents' family-run business. I thought I'd be marrying the love of my life, working the family business, and starting one of my own. Didn't think I'd need additional years of schooling, but what do you know—I did. Now, in a new town, with little education—and work experience I don't care to replicate—I'm limited on ways to make money.

The remainder of the orientation goes by relatively quickly, and I finish before check in at 3:00 p.m.

"Where you off to now?" Mrs. Northgate asks, pouring a cup of tea in the kitchen.

I smile. "The bank. Not overly exciting, but the one I used before doesn't have a branch here." Plus, I figure it's not starting over if I don't fully commit. That means new accounts.

"Well, have a good rest of your afternoon—Oh! Wait. Don't forget your schedule." Mrs. Northgate hands me a generic calendar printout with all the days I'm set to work, the times handwritten in cursive on each box. It's old school, but I like it.

"Thank you. I'll see you tomorrow then."

"Bye, Fleur. We're really glad you're here."

Her words stick with me on the way to open my new account.

* * *

The bank is a quaint brick building with two old teller windows. The woman at the first one points me to the seating area outside the account manager's office and I wait, people watching. Several local business owners come in, and a few mothers usher children in and out while juggling their deposit slips.

Smiling, I take out my phone to answer a couple messages from my mom, then one from River about a new table she got in, when—

Another message.

> So, you left?

I freeze, my gaze glued to the screen and the man's name.

Chris. He's messaged this exact message before, and I've ignored each one. Of course I left. Did he think I wouldn't?

Nine devoted years were swept away by a fling with a younger woman.

I toy with the rubber bands through my sleeve and chew my lip, trying to convince myself to block him and be done with it. The sound of a door opening jolts me from my internal debate, and I quickly tuck my phone away in my purse.

Standing, I come face to face with a middle-aged woman with brown hair beaming a smile in my direction.

"Hello, I'm Pam, the account manager here. Let's get you set up with a checking and savings," she says, extending her hand to me.

I take it, giving it a brief shake before she pushes open the door to her office and leads us in. It's small but ample for an account manager. Three large glass windows provide a perfect view of the lobby, and another window on the opposite side offers a view of the drive-through's brick pillars.

Pam slides into her gray plush chair behind a well-organized desk and types at her computer. I slide out the chair across from her and plop down.

"What brings you to Ruin?" Pam continues to type furiously, eyes popping between her screen and me. Would it be rude to tell her I did an internet search for small off-the-map towns far away from Michigan in a matter of five minutes and started driving?

"Looking for something different." My lips curl up when she narrows her eyes at me, like she knows I'm full of it.

"Well, we're always happy to have new residents. The rumor mill says you purchased the old farmhouse outside of town?"

I blink. That was fast. I haven't met many people, let alone told them I was renovating the farmhouse. She must sense my hesitation.

"I know." She nods. "Gossip moves fast in this town. Tell a local some news at breakfast, the whole town knows by lunch."

"I *did* want somewhere different." I chuckle. Pam joins in with a timid laugh and pulls some paperwork from her drawer.

"If you could fill these out and give me your license, then I can get these two accounts finalized." She gives me a pen with a pink puff on top of it, and I set out to fill in the few lines of information required.

The office falls into silence for a few minutes. The lobby bank chatter from the open door and the clicking of Pam's pink nails on the keyboard are the only sounds. My mind wanders back to the message Chris sent. *Is he sad I left? Does he realize what he threw away?*

I scribble my signature at the end of the last page in frustration and chuck the pen down, startling Pam from her computer.

"Oops, sorry. Got distracted," she says, eyes lowering down to the desk.

Great. I'm going to manage to alienate all the locals with my behavior.

"You're fine. It was the pen giving me grief," I lie, trying to justify why the single thought of a man I devoted my life to causes me to throw a mini tantrum.

I hand her the papers, and she tilts her head to the side, studying me before accepting them.

This woman can see right through me. I'm sure of it.

"Okay, well, let's get this information in the ..." Her words die, eyes widening before she squints through the windows into the lobby.

Four large men, each dressed in black pants and white T-shirts, strut in. However, each man is wearing a black leather vest or jacket lined with patches and skull prints. The whole lobby has gone quiet, and several tellers stiffen behind their windows. The men look around before settling on Pam's office.

"Excuse me for a moment." She jolts up from her desk and scurries out of the room.

While I should look away, I can't help but watch as she approaches them with a finger raised. Her cheeks are flushed, and I can only assume she's giving one of them a scolding. A young bald man lifts a large leather bag and grins while handing it to her. I scan the rest of the lobby, where people divert their eyes or play on their phones. Some even hurry out of the bank.

Huh.

I slide my perusal back to the men, but I'm greeted with a cold stare that steals the breath from my lungs. A bulky man with shoulder-length blond hair glares in my direction. Embarrassed, I yank my gaze away, choosing to jerk all the way around in favor of the other window and pulling my neck in the process.

I rub my aching muscle while counting the bricks outside. Breathing in and out slowly, I'm unable to place the thrill in my pounding heart. I fumble for my rubber bands, pulling back three times to finally snap myself out of it.

Slowly, I turn back toward the lobby but find the bustle of the day has resumed and the men are nowhere in sight. Exhaling a deep breath, I lean into my uncomfortable chair just as Pam flies back into her office.

"I apologize for that. I'll get you out of here in a few minutes."

"It's okay," I say, turning back again to the lobby—the lingering cold stare I was given eats away at me. My mouth goes dry as I contemplate the nosy question I'm about to ask. "So, uh, is that the local motorcycle club?"

Pam's face goes ashen. "No," she hisses. Her friendly, warm demeanor is washed away with the color in her face.

My gaze darts from side to side, unable to decide where to

land after that. I chew on my bottom lip. Pam sighs, her hand coming to rub her chest and fiddle with a gold cross necklace hanging low on her white blouse.

"No," she tries again, softer. "They're not a motorcycle club. It's best you steer clear of these guys around town."

I open my mouth, wanting to fan the flames of curiosity, but she cuts off any other questions.

"All right. You're all set. Here's your information. If you decide you want to set up a direct deposit for your paychecks, let me know." She shoves a bunch of paperwork across the desk and extends a shaky hand at me.

"Thank you." I take her hand, offering her a reprieve from the jitters clearly coursing through her body. She nods and bolts from the room.

This town was supposed to be safe, and all of a sudden, I'm feeling uneasy, my mind wrestling with the memorable internet information about Ruin. Family friendly, community focused, town events—nowhere did it mention a motorcycle club, er, whatever.

Wind blows strands of hair into my face as I head back to my car, and I brush them away to get a better look across the street.

Several shops line the sidewalk and people mill about abnormally for late afternoon on a workday. Planter boxes filled with red and shell-pink flowers sit along the curb next to each village-style lamppost with attached banners declaring a happy summer.

But that's not what snags my attention; it's the blond-haired man from the bank.

He stands there, muscular arms crossed over his chest—a rigid statue between the wind-whipped flowers and moving locals. Several tattoos climb one of his forearms, the dark ink matching the black attire he's wearing.

He stares at me, and I hold his gaze, panic rising in my chest. I scramble for my keys in my purse, stepping back a few paces before bumping into my car.

A semitruck stops at the only crosswalk in town, obscuring my view, and when it finally passes, he's gone.

Chapter 5
Fleur

An unfamiliar sound has me tossing the covers off myself and jolting out of bed before my sleep-induced brain finally comprehends it's loud banging on the screen door.

"Who in the world ..." I say to myself, but my voice dies as I realize what day it is.

Saturday.

Adam mentioned he'd be back on Saturday to work on the kitchen sink, and I completely forgot. Yesterday was a long day at the bed-and-breakfast. Mr. Northgate had outdoor work he needed help with, so after I finished cleaning the rooms and restocking the front entry snack area, I went to help pull weeds in their flower beds for far too long. How a man in his seventies can spend hours bent over like that is beyond me. I'm exhausted.

Another loud knock on the front door drags me out of bed, and I wrap my silk robe around my lacey pajama set. The air conditioning in this house only works fifty percent of the time, and it being summertime in Mississippi, my continued choice of what I wear to bed has dwindled down to fewer and fewer clothes.

Each step down the narrow hallway is an indecisive one. Accentuated by the obnoxious wooden floor creaking with every step. Answer the door. Don't answer the door. The wooden planks speak to me the entire trip to the front entrance.

When I reach the front door, I freeze, hand midway to the tarnished bronze knob I have zero intention of replacing. Adam stands on the other side of the door. And while meeting him was like a breath of fresh air in a new town, my traitorous heart sinks thinking about my inability to trust anyone.

More like men.

Disloyal, cheating ones.

At least he's been more than willing to help me with this massive undertaking of a project. And maybe this is what my heart needs to move on.

I shake my head. *You're getting ahead of yourself.*

I step close to the old mirror that hangs to the left of the door. It's gold and gaudy, not my taste for décor at all. But I stare blankly in it. I study the dark circles under my eyes above the dusting of freckles on my cheeks. What used to be my biggest insecurity has now become my most unique feature. My dirty-blond hair and cloudy gray eyes are average. Nothing special. Apparently, not enough for Chris to keep it in his pants.

I sigh, and the air released creates a puff of fog that blurs my reflection.

It's now or never.

Gripping the handle, I pull open the door.

"Hey!" Adam says, holding out a coffee cup to me. A black coffee bean inside a thin square is stamped on the side of the cup, and I briefly remember seeing that logo on a cozy-looking shop in town.

"Uh, hi," I say, tucking a piece of hair behind my ear. The smell of hay catches on the breeze and tickles my nose.

"I'm sorry. We did say Saturday, right?"

Adam's face is bright and awfully chipper for 7:00 a.m. *Didn't we say 9:00 a.m.?* He's smiling at me, his gaze lingering on my bare legs and climbing to my pajamas. I follow his perusal and shove my robe back together where it's open.

Putting on a show for the contractor this morning. Lovely.

"We did. I'm sorry. I overslept." I eyeball the coffee still hovering in my face, and he nods at me.

"You know you want it." His grin grows wider at my confused expression. Both work boots step into my view, closer than before and right at the threshold. My heart picks up speed at his charming smile, and I'm baffled by my own reaction.

"Uh, sure. Thank you so much. Come in. Let me just go get dressed quickly. I'm so sorry, again." I step back, holding the torn screen door open for him.

He sets his toolbox and materials down in the kitchen while I scurry back to my bedroom, nearly face-planting as I trip over the broken floorboard I dodge daily.

Fortunately, this room is the only space semi put together. I found a white oak bed frame at a yard sale in a nearby wealthy neighborhood. After three separate trips to bring it home, I still slept on the floor for a few nights, waiting for my boxed mattress to arrive. Now it's my sanctuary for all things sleep and grief. Because that's all I've done in it. Sleep and cry.

After hauling out my suitcase from the closet missing both doors, I dig through, looking for some gym shorts and a T-shirt. I definitely need to get some more work clothes. Looks like another trip to Double Lucky's thrift store is in order.

Clangs and clicks sound from underneath my closed door as I rip off my shirt and shove on a bra.

Beside the closet is the entrance to the small en suite. Unfortunately, all the tile work needs to be redone. A new toilet is also needed because, apparently, the plumbing is stopped up somewhere in the line, according to my dad—who I had to FaceTime in order to diagnose it.

For now, I use the hallway bathroom, and I dart out of my master bedroom to use it. Green and yellow tiles adorn the floor, and it looks like someone threw up in the square box, but it works. And that's what counts.

I brush my teeth and toss my hair into a messy ponytail. I linger, looking over my clear face in the mirror, then glance at the door while listening to Adam work in the kitchen. *What the hell.* I yank out my makeup and do a quick application. Some concealer, blush, and mascara. I'd hate to scare the man away before he's started.

Chris never cared if I wore makeup, or at least I thought he didn't. Many weekends at our home together we'd work tirelessly outdoors. Mini home improvement projects or work in the raised garden bed I attempted for several years. I'd roll out of bed without makeup and go the whole day in ragged clothes and frizzy hair. He was never deterred. We'd laugh and argue, casually making up throughout the day, then go on a dinner date in the evening.

I don't know what I did wrong.

After I compose myself, I pad into the kitchen. The entire cast iron bowl has been removed and Adam is on his back under the sink. His shirt rides up, and his muscular abs peek out, a faint patch of hair leading down to—

I blink and turn away, busying myself with the coffee he brought for me. A vanilla latte, from the taste of it.

"Thank you for the coffee. It's good!"

Adam tilts his chin to his chest, eyeing me. Another grin widens across his mouth, his eyes glistening with what looks like humor. I lift the cup in appreciation and offer him a smile over it before taking another sip.

"My good friend and his wife own the shop. I'm sure they'd love it if you stopped by. Everyone's been wondering about the new woman in town."

My cheeks heat. Thankfully, he doesn't notice from the dark void of my cabinets.

This is a small town. I knew the possibility of being discussed and gossiped about was there. Heck, even in my town back home, four times this size, news spread fast about Chris's indiscretions. Leaving quickly prevented anyone from talking me out of it. I'm sure the rumor mill has sprouted wings and fully taken off by now, but I'm miles away.

"Wondering, huh? Maybe more like questioning?" I snort.

His smile doesn't quite reach his eyes. "Trust me. People wonder. New folks around these parts are the talk of the town. Especially here in Ruin."

Flashes of my time in the bank yesterday occupy my thoughts—that man. *Especially here in Ruin.* Maybe that's why the man was glaring at me from across the street. He doesn't like outsiders.

"Yeah. In the bank yesterday I met with a woman named Pam—"

"Oh, she's a sweetheart. You'll love her," Adam interjects.

"Yeah. She was. A few men came in, though. They looked like part of a motorcycle club. But … when I asked, she said no. Told me to leave it alone." I bite my lip, looking at my teal nail polish, then lift my eyes ever so slightly.

Adam's face has fallen. A pale color replaces the sun-kissed golden cheeks he came in with. "I'd listen to her, Fleur. They aren't people you want to mess with."

You see, that right there is why I want to know. Who are these people who have the whole town spooked?

"I see."

Adam sighs and pulls himself out from under the sink, a pipe in hand. He holds my gaze while grabbing a greasy rag from under his armpit. Wiping his hands, he takes several steps toward me.

"They deal in drugs and run an underground gambling circuit. They're dangerous. You don't bother them; they won't bother you."

Drugs? Gambling? What the hell *is* this town I've moved to? Worry seeps into his expression, it tensing with—shame? He shakes his head, backing up and smirking.

"Wouldn't want to run you out of Ruin just yet." He winks at me, and I offer a shy laugh. "Now I've got your pipes replaced. But if you're planning to refinish this sink, we'll need to wait on it before moving forward."

"What do you think?" I ask. Because I don't know. I'd love to refinish it, but this is not my forte.

"I think ..." Adam pads over to me, hands shoved inside his jean pockets. "I think you should do whatever you want, Fleur."

My breath hitches at his tone, but giddiness jolts through me at his words. He's right. Nine years of decisions made together. This is *my* time.

"I'd like to refinish it."

✵ ✵ ✵

Scrubbing toilets is part of the job, but this particular bathroom toilet is full and gross. The work today is not as fun as it was three days ago with Adam.

He stayed for another five hours on Saturday to help me gut more of the kitchen. We talked the entire time. He filled me in on how long he's lived here, which is all his life. Both of his parents moved here from Tennessee after college, setting down roots with him and his siblings, and they haven't left since. Adam mentioned that after he graduated from high school, he made the choice to stick around town, working odd jobs before starting his own business.

I laughed more with Adam than I had in the past month, and it was cathartic. I needed that; to laugh without restraint. To have a reprieve from the hurt.

It may be bold to presume, but I think he had a nice time too. I almost forgot we were working until I had to hand over the cash advance I took out to pay him. Hopefully, in another week, I'll have my first paycheck.

I'm supposed to meet Adam at the home improvement store later this afternoon to look at cabinets and countertops. Last night, while curled up in bed scrolling through old high school photos of Chris and me, Adam messaged over several options to consider. His text came at the perfect time. Right before I was going to snap.

I smile, thinking about the weekend as I unload half of a spray can of cleaner onto this porcelain seat, gloves squeaking as I wipe it down.

Once the toilet has new life, I move on to the vanity and floors, scrubbing the white tile and making all the brushed nickel shine. Two hours later, I pack up the supplies. Then I return everything to the supply closet and toss the linens and towels down the laundry chute like a pro.

Skipping down the stairs, I fly into the kitchen where the

scent of cinnamon blankets everything. Mrs. Northgate is bent over the oven and using a spatula to flip pecans.

"I've finished the north and south rooms. They're all set for check-in. What are you making?"

"Oh good. And candied pecans. Here, try one." She wipes her hands on her blue checkered apron and moves a plastic container to the island while I scrub my hands practically raw at the sink. She extends the bowl to me, and I pop a couple in my mouth. My eyes go wide, utterly moved by the explosion of sweet, nutty flavor on my tongue.

She laughs. "I knew you'd love it. I should send some home with you. You need some more meat on those bones."

I chuckle along with her, but inside I deflate. Between my rapid dodge out of Michigan, my emotional state, and the busy renovations here—I haven't had much time to focus on fueling my body properly. Yesterday, the jeans I pulled out of my newly delivered dresser were a size too big.

I chew the inside of my cheek.

Hope feels so far off, yet so close at the same time. Something big is coming. I can feel it. This state of despair and pain won't last forever. The past several days have proven that.

So I don't dwell on her comment and change the subject. "I'm off to pick out more items for the house."

"Oh, that's wonderful, Fleur. I can't wait to see everything you do to it. It's about time that beautiful place was made to shine." Mrs. Northgate lets down her silver hair before adjusting and pulling it back up into a clip again.

"I'm just grateful Adam is able to help me. He's been a blessing for someone like me—I'm renovation challenged." I snort.

"Adam? Adam Parker?" she asks, her face contorting into an expression somewhere between curiosity and concern.

My jaw drops open as I attempt to answer before realizing—

"I don't know his last name. I met him at the home improvement store about a week after I got here. He came to the house to check it out. Said he was the handyman around town."

"Adam Parker," Mrs. Northgate says matter-of-factly.

"He's been really helpful. Sounded like he needed the work too."

"I'm sure he does."

I narrow my eyes at the sweet old woman who's not acting so sweet at the moment. Obviously, I'm missing something.

I help myself to a bottle of water Mrs. Northgate keeps on hand for housekeepers and the young groundskeepers. Mr. Northgate utilizes high schoolers instead of keeping a full-time gardener or maintenance personnel. Usually, they've commandeered all the beverages for themselves in this summer heat.

"I'm hoping I can at least determine the countertops," I say, smiling and trying to get over the awkwardness at the topic of Adam.

She nods, then turns to continue mixing the pecans for another round in the oven while I hunt for my time sheet.

Finally, I end up clocking out right after the first guests arrive and drive across town to the home improvement store. I pull into the parking spot and immediately flip down the car mirror to pinch my cheeks and dab on some lip gloss.

You're being ridiculous.

Maybe so. But the truth is, I like how distracted I am when I'm with Adam. There's always something to talk about or renovation decisions to be made. Falling into conversation with him is easy. What's even easier—ignoring the pain and hurt I'm feeling.

Like clockwork, my phone dings with another message from Chris.

Answer me, Fleur.

I glance at the others before that.

So, you left?

Are you coming back?

Where are you?

Can we talk?

How do I speak with him? How do I talk to the man who ripped my heart out and beat it to death with the heel of the college girl he was screwing behind my back.

I smack the wheel, anticipation over seeing Adam now gone—another moment stolen by Chris and perpetuated by none other than me.

My fingers find the rubber bands on my wrist, and I roll them each between my thumb and forefinger. The smooth elastic is soft and pliable but meets resistance as I draw it taut. They hover there, above my arm, before I let them snap. The distinct sting bites into my wrist as I release the two bands. Angry, raised red welts appear instantly.

Only a tiny amount of pain for distraction.

There's always the need for distraction.

Especially in the last month.

A knock on my jeep's window spooks me and I jump. My elbow bumps the horn for a short beep that draws the attention of people in the parking lot. Adam's muffled laugh through the glass softens the instant panic, and I give him a light wave before opening the door.

"You scared me."

"Sorry about that. Didn't mean to distract you."

My gaze snaps to his, and I hold his deep brown eyes as I swallow at his words. He tilts his head, bringing a hand up to graze my elbow.

"Hey ... are you all right?" he asks.

"I will be," I say.

He winks, tossing a thumb in the direction of the sliding double doors. "Let's go then."

Chapter 6
Fleur

In a blink of an eye. That's how fast the next two weeks pass.

With Adam working on the kitchen renovation multiple days a week, along with weekends, I've spent ample time with him. And I don't mind.

It's amazing—the work he's done in such a short few weeks. Although I'm pretty sure the farmhouse is his only job right now. Still, he's put in long hours with me. The kitchen is almost finished, and last night we were able to enjoy a pepperoni pizza sitting on my new granite countertops. The white with speckled black stone complements the shaker-style cabinets painted in a soothing cream, and I couldn't stop the giddy giggle that bubbled out of me when they were installed.

The asphalt driveway squeaks under my tires as I reverse out of the B&B parking. Ordering the dishwasher is on my after-work to-do list. It's one of the last items we need for the kitchen renovation. The butcher block was installed on the island this morning, and Adam also hung the new pendant lighting. Having opted to keep the kitchen sink—which turned out beautifully—and refinishing all the cabinets instead of replacing them, I've saved money. Which I've needed because I'm paying Adam much more than I had originally told myself I could.

Practically skipping into the home improvement store, which has now become my second home, I head back for the appliances. My new refrigerator and stove were delivered last week, and it's felt like a luxury to finally have a kitchen to operate out of in the mornings.

After spending the next thirty minutes looking at and ordering a dishwasher, I'm finally ready to head home and see Adam's progress. Already I picture his rolled-up flannel and sharp grin as I enter the door, having decided on a dishwasher. He seemed awfully worried about me doing dishes by hand.

A hankering for coffee gnaws at me. Which is odd because coffee at 4:00 p.m. is not something I usually do. However, I'm five minutes from Adam's favorite coffee shop, and the thought of giving him a coffee *and* delivering him the dishwasher news feels like an even greater win.

After passing several local businesses with trimmed hedges and keystone pillars, I pull into the two-story coffee shop. Several advertising flags ripple in the wind outside, telling passersby they sell more than coffee—they sell milkshakes, too.

The shop has an aged patina to the iron windows, and the bricks, weathered by the elements, look sad and defeated. A single wooden door with a glass window sits on the right-hand side of the building's facade, but it's riddled with stickers from tourists' travels, making it hard to see inside.

A bell chimes when I step through, and the aroma of coffee melts away much of my exhaustion with a promise of energy. It's welcoming.

The sound of beans being ground fills the small space as I step in behind a couple of customers. Exploring the walls, my gaze falls to a large map on one of them. Red pins scattered across the world mark where patrons have come from. All making the trip into the distinctive coffee shop during their visit to Ruin, Mississippi—odd but pretty wild all the same.

There isn't much seating downstairs, but past the ordering counter, stairs ascend to the second floor. Voices and soft chatter drift down from above, and I assume that's where people relax while enjoying their drinks.

An older woman is ahead of me in line, and when my phone rings, she turns to offer a smile—giving me an unhindered view of the burly man in front of her.

Large, hulking shoulders twitch under a black leather vest and white T-shirt. I freeze, swallowing the thickness in my throat. The young girl behind the counter hands him a drink and his muscles move with a fluid motion as he takes his coffee.

"Thank you."

My eyes widen when his low, gravelly voice glides over me. And it's like the whole shop hears the tone of those two words.

His hair is pulled into a half bun that tilts to the side as he pays the woman in front of him. Her face is pulled taut, worry pulsing in her neck. Is she uncomfortable? And the way his shoulders shake ... is he relishing it?

My phone dings again and it's like hearing one of those red pins drop on the concrete floor. There's no other sound. The whole shop is quiet aside from the few unknowing conversations above. I scramble to silence my phone, praying it's not Chris at such an inopportune time.

The man's head swivels to the side, and I'm able to catch a glimpse of dark blond scruff covering his sharp jawline, but he doesn't turn fully just yet. Images of the group of men in the bank knock around in my mind, and when I lift my head and catch his profile, I know it's him. The man from the bank; from across the street that day.

Now is the time, I chide myself. Leave. Run. Go.

After what Adam mentioned about these people ...

But my feet don't move. Won't move. The oddest desire to see his face up close glues me to the tiled floor, which I've come to realize is sky blue, cracked, and scuffed from the steady flow of town traffic.

I hug my purse to my chest as the man takes a few dollars to put into the tip jar.

It's as if it happens in slow motion—which is unfair. He pivots, offering the older woman a faintly amused smile, his lips not fully stretching into one. Then he notices me, and any hint of a smile disappears along with my desire for coffee.

His nostrils flare as his eyes narrow on me, tracing around my face and glancing quickly down and back up my body again. Sunburst eyes meet mine, the hues of blue and greens mixing with the blackness growing in his gaze.

He stalks toward me—no, the door.

I move away, closer to the counter and toward the lifesaving caffeine.

His shoulder grazes mine as he passes, and I shudder out a sigh when the bell rings and the door slams shut.

As if on cue, the coffee shop comes alive again teeming with life like this strong storm of a man didn't just blow in and destroy me in seconds. Who is he?

He's one of them, you idiot.

The black vest, broody behavior, and the reaction from the locals in the shop all tell me the same thing. What it doesn't tell me—I rub where his body collided with mine—is why my skin tingles even after he's long gone.

Chapter 7
Him

I hate new people coming into the town. Even more, I hate it has to be a beautiful woman. The guys have already started eyeing her.

Recognizing her from the bank, I couldn't stop but stare at her in the coffee shop. Fear exploded in her gray eyes, and even with her light blond hair pulled over her shoulders, I saw them shake.

The town wasted no time informing her of us.

I snort. I'd expect nothing less.

I head to my motorcycle and gulp down the rest of my coffee, now tasting bitter on my tongue. I toss it into the nearby trash can.

Lifting my leg, I throw it over to straddle the leather seat, then pull on my gloves before my phone rings.

"Yeah."

"Are you prepared for a drop today?"

I sigh, looking back over at the coffee shop while memories of the woman's freckles that dust her nose and cheeks distract me. I stiffen, and my grip tightens on the handlebar.

"Ten p.m.," I say, then hang up the phone.

Before I can rev my bike to life, my phone rings again. It's Darrin.

"Yes, Boss."

Chapter 8
Fleur

Adam has moved on to the master bathroom, having demolished it completely last week. He's since added new drywall and shower backer. Took me all of three minutes to pick out the traditional white subway tile for the shower and the black hexagon for the floor.

Last week, I went to the thrift store again after River messaged me a picture of an antique dresser that needed some love. She told me her vision of making it into a bathroom vanity, and I immediately had to look at it.

"You could add a vessel sink on top, a round bowl, and you would only need to remove part of the drawers for plumbing," she said.

River, I've come to find out, has an eye for design. Her mind thinks of some of the cleverest uses for the donations brought into Double Lucky's.

Grateful isn't a strong enough word to describe her late-night answers to my questions or her willingness to look over my photos of the deconstructed house to get her opinion.

Today is no exception. River walks into the bed-and-breakfast in a whirlwind to pick up a load of donations Mrs. North-gate has for her. Guests have left a wide variety of items behind: coats, hats, books—after a certain time unclaimed, they get donated to Double Lucky's.

After I help her pack the bed of her truck, I take my break for lunch, and we sit on the back porch overlooking the property.

The ducks paddle across the well-manicured pond. And Mr. Northgate rides around on his side-by-side, digging up bushes that haven't quite made it in the heat of the summer.

"So the motorcycle club that's in town ..." I let the words hang between us. I know from my brief interaction with Pam they are *not* a motorcycle club. But they dress like it. Act and intimidate like one, so it's the easiest way to segue into getting some information.

River eyes me. She waits for the rest, but I don't continue. Crossing her legs, she looks over the hedges of the back porch and toward the wooden deck extending into the water. Adiron-dack chairs sit nestled on the end. It seems like she picks one and stares at it.

"They aren't a club. And they aren't all bad. I know this town, especially Adam"—she rolls her eyes—"will say other-wise, but many of them got caught up with Darrin or hooked on his product."

Her gaze flits up to the cloudy blue sky and her eyelids close briefly. With a trembling chin, she turns to me and swallows.

"My brother," she says, her head hanging down. "They call it Jackpot around here, but the world knows it as Fentanyl. He's been addicted for four years now. Worked with Darrin for two."

"And Darrin's a dealer?"

She snorts at my question. This feels personal, too personal.

But gosh if I don't want to know what kind of town I'm living in. Call it self-preservation.

"Darrin's the kingpin. Drug lord. Narcotrafficker. Heart breaker. Bastard incarnate. Whatever you want to call him. According to my brother, he's one of many in a large distribution network spanning from D.C. to California."

She sniffs, and a tear drips down her cheek. Possibly pain for her brother and brokenness outline her quivering chin.

"I'm sorry. I didn't mean—"

"It's fine. I'm used to people around town knowing. What's one more?" She wipes at her face with the back of her hand and offers me a sad smile.

"Why don't they just arrest him?"

She shakes her head. "It's complicated. He's surrounded and well insulated. Darrin never moves drugs himself. He focuses on the underground casinos and gambling circuit within this town, which is how he has so much control. People need more money for drugs, he loans it out, and then they're in debt with him. Even the mayor enjoys gambling at his underground establishments. So they aren't exactly pressed to kick him to the curb. If they ever could."

"And local law enforcement?"

"Also on Darrin's payroll. My brother has mentioned seeing our sheriff at several of Darrin's establishments." She sighs.

"Someone, somewhere has to have these people on their radar. Don't they?"

"You'd think so. But honestly, Darrin has roots in this town." River's eyes flutter as if she's trying to bat away memories. "He grew up here but never went to our public school. Never had any friends. He's wicked smart, though, and it's serving him."

I study River and can't help but guess there's more she isn't telling me. She's already offered more information than anyone else, and I don't want to push my luck by asking for more.

Her hair flickers in the breeze, and the pained expression on her face makes me want to change the subject I so casually brought up.

"Is Double Lucky's yours then?" I ask.

Her down curled lips turn up into genuine joy. "Yes. My grandmother willed it to me when she passed. I used to help her in the shop growing up. It was my first real job. It's how I met Darrin actually ..."

And I failed to change the subject ...

"He used to come into the shop with his mom once or twice a year. She was a single mother raising two little kids alone. My grandmother gave her a significant discount on any clothes and toys for the boys. She always told me there was no profit worth watching other people struggle. I've carried that with me."

I smile. "Sounds like she was an amazing woman." Both sets of my grandparents passed before I was seven so unfortunately, I didn't get to connect with them much. Listening to River recount her grandmother's vision for the store and her philosophies about giving when you can—it's refreshing. Is anyone truly selfless anymore these days?

Future pictures of my parents offering sound wisdom and advice to my kids shuffle through my mind. I only hope that someday, despite my brokenness, I can offer the same to my children.

✳ ✳ ✳

It's raining as soon as I walk out of the grocery store. I slump, letting the bags hang low as I watch the sheets pour down.

When I finished my shift at the bed-and-breakfast, my errand for the day was grocery shopping. Finally, I'm able to fill my fridge with groceries for cooking meals in my farmhouse.

Thunder cracks and the awning I'm huddled under snaps in the storm's wind. An engine revs and several motorcycles drive by, causing a shiver to distribute between my shoulder blades and down my spine as my thoughts move from my conversation with River to the unfortunate need to get these groceries home.

Dodging the rain is impossible as it pelts down my back, and I pop open my trunk to load everything. That's the easy part.

The drive home not so much.

Navigating through the rain and the cover of night in a town I barely know is challenging. Slick wet roads pull at my tires. I clutch the steering wheel, knuckles clenched tightly around it.

Bright lights pull close behind me. Too close. Glancing in the rearview mirror, I'm blinded by white spots that speckle my view of the road. My heart races as I slow, pulling over to the side of the road. A large red truck slows down behind me before swerving around my jeep and speeding past.

My shoulders relax, and I pull back on the road to find my way home. My recent conversation with River has made me paranoid.

I turn into my long, curved driveway. Normally a mix of gravel and red dirt, I can almost feel my tires sink an inch or two. The drive is now a mud pit. The jeep sloshes through and fights for traction to the house. Streams of rainwater barrel down the sloped pathway to my farmhouse, making for the road's culverts.

Warm lights shine from the porch, and I smile, thinking Adam must've tackled the outdoor lighting today. I had texted him after being spooked by my lunch break conversation with River and asked him to make outdoor lighting a priority.

Letting out a breath, I park as close to the house as I can, and Adam runs out with a jacket over his head. As if I can't get out of the car fast enough, I fumble with the handle, but he beats me to it. He yanks the door open, and I'm greeted with a smile that slices through the chill of the rain.

"Hi. Bit wet out, huh?"

"It decided to rain as soon as I left the grocery store." I smile up at him.

He moves the jacket to hover over me when I step out. "I'll get the bags. You can go inside."

"And let you have all the fun in the rain?" I wink.

Wait—am I flirting?

His grin widens as he tosses the jacket to the ground. "Ah, she loves the rain. Good."

Is he flirting?

He holds my stare, but I divert mine to the side like I expect someone to be watching us. We make our way to the trunk, where we each grab as many bags as we can load onto our arms, then hobble to the kitchen and dump the bags on the counter.

Laughing, I wring out my hair. Drops of water bead down my back, the crisp coolness doing nothing to counteract the heat pooling low in my core as Adam smiles at me.

I'll admit there were times during my relationship with Chris I appreciated another attractive male, but I never let it go any further. It didn't fester in my mind. But these new feelings of attraction—after I thought I'd never think of another male that way for the rest of my life—feel foreign.

He reaches up to strip his shirt off and my breath hitches as his creamy bare chest stands out in front of my stainless-steel fridge. Instead of continuing to ogle him, I busy myself by digging through the groceries for the cold items while Adam tosses on another shirt he has stashed in his tool bag. Snagging the oat milk, I push past him to the fridge. Seconds later, there's warmth behind me.

"Here." He hands me the sticks of butter I purchased and all of a sudden, I'm having trouble remembering why. I slide them into their spot in the drawer and turn to find Adam stepping into me. "Fleur."

I close my eyes, wishing the sound of my name on his lips washed over me, beckoned me ... but it doesn't. My eyelids open as he tilts his chin inches from my face. I try backing up, avoiding this, but it would put me inside the open fridge.

Lips descend toward me, and as they graze mine, I lower my head, looking at my soaked sneakers. I wiggle my toes. Embarrassed.

"I'm sorry," he says, taking a step back.

His apology draws my attention. I like him. Sincerely. He's been a good friend for the month we've been working together. Why am I turning away from him? This would be a good thing for me. Right?

"No. No, Adam. I'm just ... I'm fragile right now. I was in something long-term." It never felt right telling him details about Chris, and I'm not sure I have the energy to explain right now.

"Totally understand. I'm being unprofessional."

Somewhere, in some remote I-haven't-been-touched dark alley of my mind, I scream at myself. *Give him a chance.*

I hold his gaze and press up on my toes to kiss his cheek. "I like you, Adam, our friendship. I'd like to go slow."

The look of disappointment lifts from his frown and his eyes sparkle with hope. "Yeah? Because I'm crazy about you."

I bite my lip, the corner of my mouth lifting.

Then I wait. Wait for the fluttering to come at his words. It doesn't. At least not before the next words are out of his mouth.

"Let me take you to dinner. Please."

I nod, wondering if my heart is just as lost as I am when I drive in the rain. And unfortunately, my rubber bands snap more than usual tonight.

* * *

"Chris came by the house yesterday."

I pause, letting the sheet I'm tucking into a perfect hospital corner fall. Pink floral wallpaper garners my attention as I adjust my earbud. I'm sure I've heard my mother wrong.

"Came by?"

"Asked where you were and if you were okay," she says flatly, and I catch myself almost sitting on the freshly pressed sheets. Cotton laundry softener tickles my nose as I press my palms into my eyes.

He should've asked if I was going to be okay before he cheated.

Snarling, I grab the sheet corner yanking it taut before tucking it into place, then move on to the next.

"I'm sorry, Mom. He's been calling me, and I haven't had the heart to answer."

"Do *not* apologize for that weasel. I told him exactly how I feel about what he did."

I cringe at her words. Not because I don't appreciate her standing up for me, but because I know how close they were. Our families too. High school weekends were spent with him over at my house, both our parents taking turns driving us to dates before we could ourselves. When we graduated and purchased our own place, they'd come over for Sunday dinners and barbecues. He was like a second child to her. A son she never had.

"D-did you tell him where—"

"Absolutely not."

"I'm going to tell him. Talk to him, I mean. But I need to find my footing first." It's true. Reliving the moment I found out my almost-decade-long relationship was a farce has kept me underwater. Drowning. The only clarity I had at that moment was enough to leave. And here, the only clarity seems to be when I'm focused on renovations.

"You don't owe him anything, Fleur Jacobs. Remember that. But he looks worn down—older. I think he wants to make sure you're safe."

I clamp my mouth shut, not wanting to say something spiteful. Because bitterness has been my friend; a constant companion for the past couple of months.

Replacing the fluffed pillows on the bed, I chop them before taking out my turnover checklist and double-checking everything is ready for the next guests. Mrs. Northgate mentioned they're a newlywed couple. Go figure.

"The house is getting there. You and Dad would love it. I'll let you know as soon as it's finished so y'all can come down for a visit."

She chuckles in my ear. "Y'all? Oh boy, Fleur. We would love that though."

I roll my eyes, but I can't wait for them to visit. Pretty sure they've been fighting the urge to hop on a plane and come down themselves to help me. But I've told them I need to do this on my own. Not counting the numerous phone calls to my dad, of course.

Adam has helped in that area. With the master bathroom almost complete and the new drywall going up in the living room this afternoon, the house is closer than I'd ever thought it'd be.

Costs more than I have, though.

I tried to cut down on labor by helping, but when the bills for tile, drywall, appliances, and lumber started rolling in, I knew picking up more hours here at the B&B was necessary. The credit card debt I've incurred is ... shameful. For some reason, I couldn't tell Adam no.

"Listen, Mom. I have to finish up a couple of rooms before I head out for the day."

"Okay. Love you, sweetheart. We miss you."

I catch a sniffle on the other end of the line and my heart sinks. They weren't prepared for my leaving either. When I approached them with my choice to run to Ruin, they thought I might have lost all my marbles. Which may have been the case. Though I was dead serious, and I believe it pained them to know they weren't everything I needed in that moment. But, as the amazing parents they are, they put my wants before their own and asked what they could do to make it happen.

After cleaning a room with particular wrappers and toys scattered all around—the couple obviously unashamed about their activities—I empty the fresh towel bin. Folding them is therapeutic and often my mind wanders while I stand there. My thoughts escape to my upcoming dinner date with Adam and the almost kiss in my kitchen.

Is it too soon?

I'm not naïve. My heart is a mess. What I told him is the truth. I'm fragile.

After patting the newly stacked tower of towels, I lock up the supply closet and head downstairs, appreciating the sweeping curve of rich polished wood beneath my fingertips.

Clanging from the kitchen gives me pause before I ease the

swinging door open, its effortlessness due to Mr. Northgate keeping it well oiled.

Mrs. Northgate fumbles with a kitchen cabinet hanging by a damaged hinge.

"Can I help?" I ask.

She jumps, the white cabinet face dropping to the counter. The color clashes with the black granite. The monochromatic colors in this kitchen surprised me the first time I entered, considering the rest of the bed-and-breakfast is more traditional. However, it's grown on me.

"Darn it," she mutters, then wipes her hands on her apron, moving to stir a pot on the stove. I glance at it as I walk over to the cabinet mishap, the steaming blueberries and sugar making me salivate.

Mrs. Northgate bakes desserts for all her guests as they check in. She leaves cookies, cakes, or pies out on the wet bar with a stocked mini fridge. Guests help themselves, and it's always devoured by morning.

"Looks like you might need new hinges. These look broken."

She nods, a smile poking over the wrinkled lines around her mouth. Her hands flutter to her hair, smoothing her chaotic strands back into her bun.

"I'll have to get a handyman to come take care of it. Mr. Northgate is too busy with the property."

"Oh, want me to ask Adam to stop by? I'm sure he could fix this quickly," I ask as I move to the time sheet I have to submit for the end of the week. There's only a slight discomfort when I volunteer Adam to fix the hinges. We aren't an item. But he *is* a handyman. I shrug, mostly to myself, but I meet Mrs. Northgate's eyes.

They're preening with neutral disinterest.

She stiffens, rolling her shoulders back. Her normally soft, inviting demeanor has been plucked away, right off the hinges like the cabinet.

"No need. I'll get someone to tend to it."

I stare at her. Flour is tossed on the counter as she dusts an area and plops homemade pie crust down. What feels like the violent beat of a drum is actually her wooden rolling pin attacking the dough. Guess it's a blueberry pie for the check-ins this afternoon.

This is the second time she's gone weird on me about Adam. I'm missing something. Unfortunately, I hate confrontation, and I like my job too much to push back. Maybe he had a job here and they didn't like his work. Or had a disagreement about something.

Either way, my shift is over, and I rise, smiling at Mrs. Northgate as she shoves flattened pie crust into a dish.

"Have a good night, Mrs. Northgate."

"You too, sweetheart. Thank you." She grins at me, shooing me out of the kitchen as I linger, flummoxed by her whiplash expressions. Homesickness settles in the pit of my stomach at her "sweetheart". The name my mom always calls me, no matter my age.

Practically jogging to my car, I jump into the front seat. Reaching for the radio, I turn on the local station and back out of the side parking lot reserved for the Northgates and any staff. I *was* looking forward to my date tonight and seeing Adam. Part of me wants to be proud I'm going and working to put Chris behind me.

But the way Mrs. Northgate seems to freeze up when I mention his name ...

I'm sure that in a small town gossip runs wild, and perhaps grudges linger when you interact with the same handful of people every day. She'd warn me about anything unsavory, right?

Chapter 9
Fleur

Thirty minutes. That's all the time I have to get ready for dinner.

Dashing up the front porch steps, I nearly bull-doze past the freshly painted porch. It was impossible to finalize a color, and I spent three hours at the paint store before finally settling on Greek Villa, a creamy white.

I drag my hand over the freshly sanded wood now a milky color. Images of early morning coffee in a rocking chair, watching the sun morph above the horizon, while the neighbor across the street bales his hay stream into my mind.

I glance at the fields surrounding my little farmhouse that are visible from all three sides of my porch, not another house in sight. Country air dances around me with a mix of grass and the soft, sultry night smell. I let it wash over me, closing my eyes to inhale the peace and quiet.

The house I had with Chris, his house, sat in a tiny commu-nity inches from a four-lane highway. Each night, I fell asleep to the hum of traffic or the neighborhood block party. There was no porch. Only a stoop Chris and I used to sit on with our morning coffee before I'd get tired of waving to the twenty people walking their dogs or running before their morning commute to work.

I sigh and peer around at the empty porch. Outdoor furniture is next on my list.

Dashing into the house, I sprint to my bedroom, stripping clothes as I go, and quickly step under the spray of the shower. It's bone-chilling cold, but I don't have adequate time to let it warm up. Within minutes, I dart around my new master bathroom, blow-drying my hair and tossing on some makeup. Stepping back, I shrug. Guess this is acceptable.

I've let my hair hang long, framing my face and hiding the pearl studs in my ears. Deciding on a peach-colored summer dress with cap sleeves, I slide it up and over, eyes snagging on the claw-foot tub and smiling.

It was a splurge. Vintage cast iron coated in porcelain. The all-white tub with its ornate claw feet that curve outward like the talons of a fairy-tale creature. It's timeless, especially with the gleaming chrome fixtures. Even though now it's sitting on my credit card.

However, the bath I sank into last night, propped against the end while I texted my mom—worth it.

※ ※ ※

Adam asked me to meet him at the restaurant. Apparently, he has some work to do up until our date. Honestly, I'm glad. Mentally, I'm not sure I could handle the whole pick-me-up-for-a-first-date thing right now. At least this way it feels like I'm meeting a friend for dinner.

I pull into the quaint restaurant described online as "Ruin's novelty delight with classic Southern cuisine." But the building is quite weathered and bland. Mostly wrapped in browns and greens, the building's only color is planted in the hanging flower baskets adorning every other porch post.

After a quick glance around for Adam's truck, I sit back, content to scroll through some of the socials I've been actively avoiding.

That's the problem with breaking up with your high school boyfriend after nine years. Our entire friend group is shared. Or ... *was*. When I left, I effectively removed myself from it. Not that I wanted it that way, but it seems they've picked a side.

Tina is pregnant, and Sarah is engaged. All within the two months since I left. No one texted me. Both their significant others are best friends with Chris, but Tina and Sarah were *my* two closest friends in high school. I thought I'd at least hear from them.

A glaringly pristine white truck pulls in next to me and Adam raises a hand in my direction. *Huh. I thought his truck was red.* In fact, I clearly remember the dirty mud flaps and toolbox in the bed of it.

Gathering my purse and courage, I push out the door. Adam rushes to grapple with the handle, intent on finishing the job. It's not necessary, but I let him shut it when I'm out and standing in front of him.

"Fleur, you look ..." His words trail off as he reaches for my shoulder to give it a squeeze.

I peer up at him. His clean-shaven face and his deep earthy eyes drink me in. He's in classic blue jeans and a light green V-neck—not much different from his attire when I've seen him before. *Am I overdressed?*

"Not so bad yourself," I say, pulling my arms in to wrap them around my middle.

He gives me a cheesy grin and guides me to the double doors.

When we step through, I realize I am, in fact, wildly over-dressed. Locals fill the rickety wooden building dressed in jeans and work boots. Checkered tablecloths mixed with the aroma of home-cooked comfort food transport me to a time of diners and handwritten menus.

Adam and I draw attention with the first few steps we take to be seated. All eyes in the room feel like they are on us as a young woman leads us to our seats.

She rattles off the nightly special. Fried catfish with collard greens and something else I miss. The bread pudding for dessert is the last thing I catch before she dashes away for our drinks.

"I'm sorry. I haven't been on a date in a while. I'm rusty," Adam says.

I blink up from my perusal of the collection of iron skillets hanging on the wall and tilt my head in his direction with a smile. "Rusty? We just sat down."

"I should've pulled out your chair."

"That's okay, Adam, really. Have you eaten here? What's good?" I pick up the menu and study the rows of delicious-sounding food.

"I have, but nothing compares to my mother's home cookin'." His accent grows every time he talks about home.

"I'm sure."

"Even at thirty, I'm still wandering home for good food. But if I had to choose ..." He scans the menu. "I'd have to go with the tried-and-true catfish. Comes with hushpuppies, but you can sub that out."

I'm not sure I've had fried catfish before, although I'm excited to try.

Our drinks are delivered, and we both place an order for the special before we chat about his day.

"Did you have a nice day at work?" he finally asks.

"I did. I was able to talk with my mom a bit while I turned over several rooms for the weekend. Mrs. Northgate is having some issues with her cabinets, and I think—"

"I see."

I pause, mouth half open to continue, but Adam's gaze is staring past me. The urge to rub the ear he seems to be focused on is strong.

"Do you know them well? Mrs. and Mr. Northgate, that is."

His spine snaps straight, gaze narrowing instantly before softening. "I guess you could say that."

That's it? That's all I get. It's like I'm a ping-pong between two stubborn paddles. I tell myself I'm not entitled to any information or drama. Perhaps it's best if I don't understand ... but then again ... "You know—"

"So, Fleur. How does an amazing woman, such as yourself, find herself in Ruin, Mississippi, of all places?"

I blink. "Actually, I—"

"Well, well, look who it is." A slithering, ear-grating voice interrupts my attempt to be honest and divulge that I'm a broken heart in need of repair.

Adam's eyes jump to the three men standing beside our table. Dressed in dark jeans and leather jackets, they all sneer down at us. One man isn't even concealing his side-holstered gun. I suck in a breath as Adam addresses a man with gold teeth.

"Blitz."

Is that his real name or ...

"Fancy a dinner out tonight, Adam?" the man asks. His patchy gray hair places him most likely in his forties. The gold in his teeth spans the entire bottom row, and my gaze flits to his black hoop nose ring before flicking back to Adam.

His face is flush. Defeated, lifeless eyes bob down to his menu, his right hand fidgeting with the fabric menu cover. He works loose a string to roll between his thumb and forefinger.

The entire restaurant has slowed, the hum of conversation sinking to whispers. Expressions tense around the room as they regard the three men. One of which, a younger man with buzzed blond hair, has a to-go bag full of food containers under his arm. The other bald man, who looks semifamiliar, shoves his leather-gloved hands into his black jean pockets.

A brittle laugh volleys back at us from Blitz, and he flexes his fingers at his sides. "No answer. Guess that's pretty typical of you. Letting others solve all your problems, pay—"

"We get it," Adam snaps, then immediately folds into himself.

Blitz's eyes tick to the side, sliding over my face and down my body. My muscles tighten, flinching as he reaches forward to tap twice under my chin, lifting my gaze to meet his.

I can't speak. Can't smack his hand away. I'm frozen.

"And what's a pretty thing like you doing with him?"

Background laughter from the other two men slices through the silence in the room. I hold his stare, but the icy blue peering back at me feels shattered—fuzzy. In fact, I'm pretty sure the room is spinning.

"All right, Blitz. That's enough. I've got people to feed here," an older woman with a raspy voice hollers from near the kitchen.

"Just saying hi to an old friend, Deborah." He smirks at Adam and licks his lips at me.

"Yeah, well, take your food and head out. It's on the house."

Blitz finally diverts his gaze from our table and looks back over his shoulder at the tiny woman. "It's always on the house."

She flicks her hand in his direction, so casually that it makes me wonder if they're frequent customers.

With one last sneer at Adam, all three men turn to the doors and exit, the air in the room finally returning. Taking a deep breath, I glance at Adam. His head is buried in the menu like he hasn't already decided and ordered.

"Are you okay?" It's the only thing I can muster. Adam looks like he got steamrolled into oblivion and while the rest of the guests work on amping up the conversation and taking back their night out, Adam looks ready to throw in the towel.

"Yeah," he squeaks, then tries again. "Yeah, yeah. Fine. Just assholes being assholes." He clears his throat and takes a sip of his sweet tea.

The tone of our dinner date changes. We chat about the summer weather, and he fills me in on the upcoming town activities, which seem to be the highlight of the small town's life. Personally, I'm looking forward to the farmer's market.

Periodically throughout our meal, Adam studies me, then glances back at the spot where the three men stood. Like he's trying to decide how rattled I am from this strange encounter.

River said many of the townspeople know some members of this "organization". So I can't hold it against Adam that he does. It's a small town. Everyone knows everyone. However, it's his shame-induced expression that fuels the war within me. That keeps questions leeched to the tip of my tongue. *What was all that about?*

When our meal is finished, our server comes by with the check and Adam gives her his card.

"Thank you for dinner. I have to admit, I think I've been converted to a fried catfish lover."

"Ah, just wait until you have my mom's. She and my father do a large frying for the Fourth of July. Barbeque, homemade french fries, catfish, coleslaw, and other sides. It's practically a community event. You'll have to come."

I smile.

"Adam," the waitress says, "I'm sorry, but the card was declined."

"Oh, shoot. Here, try this one." He reaches into his back pocket for his wallet and pulls out another card. The waitress scurries off.

"I have cash. Do you want me to—"

"No," Adam says, a sharp bite to his words. "I mean, no, Fleur ... shit, I'm sorry."

He drags a hand through his dark slick hair, tousling it into a mess before resting his chin in his palm and propping his elbow on the table.

"This one isn't working either." The server pops back up. She's obviously uncomfortable telling him. Her lips are pressed together in a thin line, downturned into a timid frown.

Adam's eyes narrow on her, and his brow furrows into deep lines harboring annoyance. "I don't have another card."

"I've got it tonight, Adam. Please let me." I pull out my purse, wanting to put this young girl out of her misery. She looks between Adam and me before I hand her cash. "Keep the change. Thank you so much."

Adam doesn't say much, walking me to my car. I haven't been on a first date in, well, forever, but I'm trying not to let one experience ruin what I know about him. He's always been kind and hardworking, even if it's in an eager way.

Reaching my car, I turn to say goodnight, but salty lips suddenly meet mine. Soft and tender, he pushes me into my jeep door, deepening the kiss.

My mind whirls as his hands fly to my cheeks, holding me against him. His tongue darts out, seeking entry, but I ... I can't.

I pull back, panting at his sudden fervor, and search his

eyes. Dark with desire, he allows his hand to linger on my cheek, thumb caressing over my heated skin.

"I had an amazing time with you. I hope we can continue this."

Stunned into silence, I can only offer him a closed-lip smile. Flashes of Chris and the ache of a broken heart cling to me. Claws embedded so deep I fear yanking them out. Or perhaps ripping them out for Adam would leave gaping holes he wasn't qualified to heal. Would anyone be?

"Safe trip home," he says before planting a chaste kiss on my cheek and walking around to his truck to climb in. His tires squeal off, leaving me standing there.

Hands shaking, I manage to pull out my keys and unlock my door. I sit in deafening silence, fingers tracing the rubber bands at my wrist and the spot on my lips where his mouth suddenly met mine.

I glance over at the empty parking space next to me. His truck *definitely* used to be red.

Chapter 10
Fleur

The rumbling of a motorcycle pulls me out of my thoughts mid-scrub down of the jacuzzi tub. Purple foam slides down my pant leg, and I drape the microfiber cloth over the spout, quickly fleeing the tub. Cold tile meets my feet. I learned quickly that cleaning the large tub took me getting in the thing as short ole me could only lean across half of it.

I slip, barely making it to the window overlooking the narrow employee parking lot to see a man getting off his motorcycle. His head is covered with a glossy black helmet reflecting the nearby trees. He stomps around his bike toward my car, and I angle myself, pushing up on my already tender toes to peek farther out.

Tilting his head to the side, he looks at my license plate, then bends down to get a better look.

Umm. What is he doing?

Turning, I bolt out of the bathroom and spring to the stairs. This man wouldn't vandalize my car, would he? Most of the town's people have been welcoming, but I wouldn't put it past some to hate outsiders enough to want to drive them off.

Mrs. Northgate ascends the steps, smiling at me as I dart past.

"I'll be right back!"

Each tread comes quicker than the last. I jog past the entryway, passing the blueberry muffins Mrs. Northgate has already set out. Through the kitchen, I shove the back door open and fly through the river-rock driveway. Only now I realize I still don't have my shoes on from when I was cleaning the tub.

Skidding to a halt in front of the man's motorcycle, I throw my hands up, my annoyance getting the better of me. "Can I help you with something? You're taking too keen an interest in my car."

He stiffens, rising to his full height and turning around slowly. I cross my arms, glaring at the man while both of his hands meet his helmet and lift it.

Dirty-blond hair falls around his neck, leather jacket zipped to cover it. With each inch he pulls up, the more my heart pounds. Scruff is revealed as the helmet moves past his chin, and when his hazel eyes come into view, my heart nearly stops.

The rest of his hair, wavier than I've seen it before and damp with sweat, falls around his face.

Cold eyes meet mine.

It's him. The man from the bank. From the coffee shop.

His gaze moves from my face down my body and to my feet. "Have something against footwear?"

His voice is raw and rough, and I blink. "What? No, I was in the jacuzzi—listen, why are you near my car?"

"Curious about the newcomer in town."

"You're curious," I deadpan.

He shrugs.

I snort. "Just leave it alone."

It's an accident I speak so freely. So to shut myself up, I chew the inside of my cheek, worried I've pissed off whoever this guy is. There will *never* be a time I want to be on this man's radar or his boss's.

He stands there, black jeans hugging thick muscled thighs. Boots, also black, kick outward as he leans back, his large arms folded in front of himself.

Observant of other members in town, I've noticed this man dresses more like he's in a motorcycle gang than the others. Often in black and gray.

I spin on my heels, wincing at the rocks pressing into my socked feet.

"Is there a name that goes with that mouth?"

I pause. Back still turned to him. Over my shoulder, I glance at his smirk. Sinful and smug, his smile widens at the annoyance I'm working hard to convey. Biting my tongue, I ignore him, stepping back inside to finish my rooms for the day.

Laundry means I'm staying later than normal this evening, and I keep going to the windows to look out at the dark blue motorcycle still sitting in the employee drive. The driver, however, is no longer there. His helmet rests on the back of the leaning bike. Kickstand propped out, the large beast is in the way of my vehicle. The reasons why he has parked there bother me the rest of the afternoon, and I'm convinced I'm going to have to plow over the bike to leave.

When I finally get to my time sheet to clock out, two figures working at the pond catch my attention. Mr. Northgate moves large bags of mulch from the side-by-side. However, it's not what he's doing that causes my hand to skip as I write down my eight hours. It's who's with him.

That man.

My mind scrambles to reconcile what I'm seeing. Is he

helping out here? Worry has me flipping through the other employee time sheets, searching for any names I don't know. An invasion of privacy, for sure, but panic affects my judgment. There are no other names I don't recognize. The handful of employees who work here are mostly young high schoolers working part time during the school year and full time in the summer. I know most, if not all of them.

Mouths open with laughter, Mr. Northgate loads up the man with several bags, which he hauls to the landscaping by the pond's dock.

I think I'm seeing things.

Stumbling over a dining chair, I stub my toe and fall into the window I'm leering through.

Nice, Fleur.

"You okay, sweetheart?" Mrs. Northgate's humming voice strides into the kitchen.

I jerk away from the window and shuffle the time sheet papers away from me. "Yep. Clocking out. Do you need anything else?"

She studies me, clearly curious about my run-in with the glass.

"Well, if you're up for it. I could use the Fourth of July decorations pulled out of the garage. The bins aren't heavy, just the flags for the guest driveway."

It's such a neat idea. She told me about how for years they've lined each side of the drive with mini American flags and put red, white, and blue lights on the large oak trees that tower in the front yard. Framing the house, those trees highlight every beautiful angle of Old Hillside. Christmas can't come soon enough, as I anticipate their lights for the holidays being even better.

"Sure. No problem. Are they labeled?"

She nods, going to the window to look out at Mr. Northgate and the bulky man obsessed with jeeps.

She smiles, warmth flooding her expression. Her eyes gleam at the two men working, and I want to warn her. I'm sure she's heard of the drug lord who runs around this town with his men. But, at the same time, maybe she hasn't, and this guy can't be up to anything good by working here. Can he?

I open my mouth to ask or say something—I'm not entirely sure. But I end up biting my tongue. Instead, I stalk out the back door.

Within the garage is an abhorrent amount of holiday bins scattered among all the other odds and ends. Lucky for me, the Fourth of July bins are not only labeled but color appropriate. Red, white, and blue.

The problem? They're buried under twenty years' worth of Christmas decorations.

I sigh, starting at the top and pulling each bin off the others. Five rows down and I'm breaking a sweat. The summer heat mixed with zero air conditioning in the garage causes pools of sweat to move down my temples. It's even dripping off my nose and into my mouth. *Gross.*

The next bin I reach for is a hundred pounds—it must be. I can't muscle it down and it's going to fall.

It's falling—

I yelp, moving backward with a large bin barreling down toward me. Arms burning, I lose my grip and—

Relief.

The weight is suddenly gone, and my body slams into a large form behind me. I startle, turning to see his muscled chest at eye level while *he* stares down at me. One hand above his head, he holds on to the bin, keeping it from falling on me and also from breaking.

I realize I haven't moved from where I'm plastered at his

chest and I shake myself out of the stupor, ducking under his arm. He extends up to grab the other side of the bin and moves it down, stacking the box where I have piled the others.

No words are uttered between us as he moves to another bin and lifts it down for me. I'm stunned into paralysis. The black leather jacket is gone, replaced by a T-shirt. Sweat lingers underneath his black tee, the darker patches growing larger along his back each minute he stays in the sweltering hell pit.

His hair is pulled up into a bun, the hair at his temples sticking to the skin there. I'm no better. Mascara comes away from underneath my eyes when I wipe where the sweat and heat have melted my makeup off.

Ten bins later, the Fourth of July decorations are free, and he turns to look at me, lifting the collar of his shirt to wipe at the beads of sweat clinging to his upper lip.

"Thank you," I mumble. Unable to look at his face, I pretend to count the bins of decorations, my finger jabbing in the air, but I lose count after one.

He grunts in response and sulks out of the garage. Not long after, the engine of his motorcycle roars to life.

When I finally make it back to my car, pit stains and all, there's no bike blocking my path, and I can't help but wonder why he was here at all.

* * *

Showering after a long, hard day at work is glorious. Showering after a long hard day of work in my *new* master shower ... even better.

Many nights I prune under the steady spray. Thinking

about Chris and how foolish I seem for it. It's funny how he's the one who screwed up, yet shame shrouds me.

Tonight, though, as the warm water spews around me, my thoughts drift to a different man.

I wrap myself in a warm towel and pull on some jeans and a T-shirt. Even though it's 8:00 p.m., Adam called me on my way home, asking if he could bring some drinks and food over.

Initially, I hesitated. Dinner. The kiss. The moment his lips met mine plays over in my head, and I search for the right words to describe my discomfort. But the thought of cooking after the grueling day I had is *definitely* not ideal, so I told him yes anyway. Still a yes person, it seems.

So I opt for jeans instead of my pajamas, planning to sit and relax on the porch.

After cleaning up the living room as best I can, despite the exposed drywall and the paint samples sitting out, there's a knock on the door.

Opening it, Adam stands there, a pack of beer and wine spritzers in hand.

"Hey," he says, leaning in to kiss my cheek.

"Hi."

"So I grabbed the drinks but figured we could make food here."

I deflate.

The last thing I want to do at almost nine at night is cook food, but I grit out a smile and hold the door open. "I'm sure I've got a frozen pizza or something."

Sure enough, there are several frozen pizzas in my freezer. Pepperoni feels like a safe choice, although not my favorite, and I snag one to pop in the oven. Adam digs around the drawers to find a bottle opener, and he cracks open a beer and wine cooler.

He leans against the counter, one hand in his pocket, watching as I tear down the cardboard pizza box for recycling.

His perusal floats over my face and down my body, and heat licks my cheeks.

When I can't take his staring anymore, I suggest, "How about we sit on the porch?"

It's the only time during the summer you can enjoy the porch without the sun baking your clothes to your body.

We move to the new porch, and contentment flutters through me as I sit in my rocking chair, gazing across the wide front yard and over at the expansive hayfields across the road.

When the mosquitoes decide to join us for dinner, I lean forward and light a few of the bug barrier candles I have scattered around. It's the only way to avoid being covered in welts and bites the next day. One might think to screen in the porch, but there's something about having an unhindered view of the surrounding landscape that speaks to me.

"I helped Mrs. Northgate pull her Fourth decorations down today," I say, taking a sip of the sparkling berry spritzer. Surprisingly, it's delicious.

"Oh, yeah. They usually have a cool display."

I nod and swig another.

"I told my mom you'd be coming to the family barbeque." He smiles, reaching for my hand and fumbling with my fingers. "I know how it sounds, but trust me, it's a community event."

I wince, hoping those thoughts weren't plastered on my face. "I'm looking forward to it. What should I bring?"

"Anything you'd like. My parents do the catfish, pork butts, and brisket, as well as all the fixin's. But then everyone else brings side dishes and desserts. There's food for days."

I ponder that, a slight pang in my chest at being far from my parents. I've already been saving my vacation time up for Christmas. I'm going to make sure I'm home for that.

"It sounds nice. I'm excited to come." And I am. It will be nice to meet more people and do something more community-focused besides the constant hours at the bed-and-breakfast or working on the house. Hopefully, in the next two weeks, I can come up with something to bring.

Lights flicker down the road. They're obvious in the pitch black. The porch lights only illuminate the front yard and offer mediocre highlighting of the surrounding fields. But these lights are bright.

Stark white dots act as beacons in the night, and two other lights come into view behind it. They move closer while the crunch of the dirt road and the roar of motorcycles creep toward us.

Adam goes still, his face ashen as he watches the slow-moving vehicles inch down the road.

"Is it just me, or are they getting slower?" I ask. But as if in answer, the vehicles ease up in front of my driveway.

"Go in the house, Fleur."

I stand but don't move. This is my home, and I will not be scared off my porch by a couple of cars and motorcycles. We don't even know who—

"It's them. You need to go inside."

"Them?"

In an attempt to appease Adam, I shuffle back a few steps as the car slows in front of my long driveway. It wraps in the front like an S, but I'm able to make out a black or darker-colored car. The two motorcycles flank either side of it, and they ... sit there.

Do these people have nothing better to do?

I pull my damp hair into a bun and march to the steps.

A hand circles my waist, and Adam hauls me back. "Don't, Fleur. Let's go inside."

"Why? They can't just sit there."

"They can. Trust me."

Trust. It's getting hard to do that in this town. People avoid these men like the plague. Content to let Darrin create drug addicts and capitalize on their gambling addictions. River's eyes when she was talking about him, them—fear splintered out, making her whole expression tight and nervous. And that was only *talking about* them.

My chest is heavy as I think about this town that seemed so appealing online, but in reality, I'm starting to think Google needs to add a disclaimer to the town map. It should read: charming, quintessential small town riddled with drugs and motorcycles.

Adam opens the door, hand placed on my lower back to push me into the house. Twisting my head, I crane to get one last look as the bikes rev and the car speeds off in a cloud of smoke. The pungent smell of rubber burning and acrid exhaust fumes catch on the breeze and slam into us.

Time on the oven continues to count down, and within the next three minutes, Adam and I are sitting quietly at the peninsula eating our undone pizza. Then he's leaving with the promise to see me this weekend and that he looks forward to taking me to his family's home in two weeks.

Later, after repeatedly checking the window to ensure they're gone and triple-checking my locked door, I finally nestle into bed. Unfortunately, I can't help but wonder if *he* was out there.

My mind returns to my earlier shower and the man who occupied my thoughts. It wasn't Adam.

Chapter 11
Fleur

The fruit salad sloshes with a wet slap up and over the festive bowl I purchased specifically for this barbeque. The road leading to Adam's family home weaves through meadows and cotton fields, the red dirt bordered by wildflowers and patches of unruly grass.

Fine layers of dust settle on my jeep the farther I drive and I'm starting to wonder if we're even in the same town anymore. Rustic wooden fences mark the boundaries of farmland, the occasional tractor in the field harvesting a hay crop or tending to livestock. The scent of fresh country air carries into my car through the cracked windows—and I thought *I* lived far out.

Adam lives in town, and I can't imagine moving from out here in the peace and quiet to be near Main Street. But he says he's close to people for business, which makes sense.

A few more miles on the dirt road, and I drive up on a massive field with rows and rows of cars. All of them are meticulously parked. People emerge from their cars, all carrying dishes or coolers. Smiles pull across their faces as if they have been waiting all year for this event.

I park in a neatly lined row of other cars and gather my items. Since all the other people are wearing shorts and T-shirts, I'm starting to wonder if this summer dress was a good idea. When a breeze kicks up and blows the back to wave like a flag, I'm sure I made the wrong decision.

Following the sea of people, I grin at a few familiar faces I've seen around town. As I approach the driveway across the street from where I've parked, the potent fragrance from three large magnolia trees lingers in the air. And when I move with the crowd up the gravel drive, I'm blown away.

Adam mentioned his family owned an old plantation home, but this is—

Weathered white columns, bearing years of patina, line the expansive porch. The exterior of the home is painted a bright yellow that reflects the warmth of the Southern sun. Large windows, adorned with delicate shutters, flank either side of the front door. Red brick lines the walkway up to the stained oak double doors that are wide open and inviting guests in.

Well-maintained gardens surround the home with several different pathways canopied with ancient oaks and towering pines. When ushered through the front doors, the polished hardwood floors creak delicately, and I snort, thinking about how mine sound like a squirrel stubbed his toe.

But ... wow. This home is breathtaking.

Both sets of French doors are open, leading from the rear porch to the lush gardens. In the center of the yard, a large white tent stands, with several bounce houses for the kids set up on one side. Cornhole games are arranged along a narrow strip of grass between the towering hedges and the tent while lively guests challenge each other to games.

I'm slightly overwhelmed by all the people. Adam wasn't lying when he said it was practically a community event.

I follow the tantalizing aroma of smoldering hickory and

mesquite BBQ down to the rows of tables covered in fine linens supporting all the dishes the guests brought. Tables and chairs, also lined with crisp linens, have mason jar centerpieces holding mini-American flags propped up in them. Red, white, and blue table confetti is sprinkled over each of the twenty-five-plus tables. The amount of work that must go into this ...

Warm hands wrap around me, and a quick kiss is placed on my cheek. Adam turns me around, taking in my outfit, and his smile widens.

"Blue. I like it. You look beautiful."

I roll my lips in, trying to hide my reaction to his compliment. "Thank you. Where should I put this?"

My bowl is sticky from the bumpy ride and sloshing of fruit, but I lift it in offering anyway.

"Here, let's find a spot for it."

We walk past sizzling stacks of ribs, succulent brisket, and perfectly charred vegetables. Pasta salads, tossed salads, potato salads, and coleslaws take up two entire tables, and I place my fruit salad in between the ten others.

"Let's get you a drink."

Adam leads me to the bar, which is in a whole other part of the gardens I didn't even see. Three bartenders are filling drinks for the guests and a large chalkboard sign has a photo of a special Independence Sparkler drink made specifically for this event.

How can I pass that up?

"What can I get y'all?" the bartender asks.

"I'll try the Independence Sparkler," I say.

"And I'll have another beer. Same as before. Thanks, Erin."

Erin, a petite woman with short hair, smiles and moves to start working on our drinks.

"What do you think? Fireworks start after dusk, and I have a prime location for them." Adam elbows me.

I smirk. "You take all the girls in the back of your truck to watch the fireworks?"

"Nah, just the ones I like." He beams at me, and I lean into him as I gaze around the party.

"Here you are." Erin places the Independence Sparkler on the bar.

The drink is a rich indigo blue, with a layer of white cream on top. The smell coming from it reminds me of coconut. On top of the cream is a puree of strawberry, and I'm slightly in awe of this patriotic drink.

"Hey, sweetheart." A familiar older voice croons. Mrs. Northgate and her husband approach where we're standing at the bar.

"Hi, Mrs. Northgate. It's so good to see you both outside of work."

"Oh, I know. It's usually hard for us to leave, especially during a business season like this. But we don't have any new check-ins tonight, so we can be out for a bit."

I nod, taking a sip of my drink. Blueberry bursts in my mouth, followed by a creamy coconut and the sweet tang of strawberry. I don't taste much alcohol, but having this many people here with gobs of fireworks coming later—it's probably not a bad thing.

Adam hasn't said a word, and his eyes are focused on his sneakers.

"Adam." Mrs. Northgate acknowledges. A fallen smile twitches across her lips and the lines in her face are etched in pain. "We'll see you at work tomorrow, Fleur. Good to see you here, dear." She extends her hand, rubs my shoulder, and gives it a loving squeeze.

I dip my head as they walk away, enjoying another sip of my cocktail—or at this point, it might just be a mocktail.

"Adam, what's the deal with—"

"Adam!" A woman jumps up and waves. Her dark hair is long, with subtle threads of silver. Although her eyes are light, her features are familiar and sharp. There's no question—this woman is Adam's mother.

"Mom. Great party as always." She comes up to him and pulls him in for a hug. She lets her gaze move down over his red T-shirt and khaki shorts.

"Festive," she deadpans, and I let out a chuckle. Her cream-colored dress is stunning, definitely something a hostess would wear. "And you must be Fleur. I have to admit I've heard more about you from my son than the town gossip, and that's saying something."

She offers Adam a wink and he rolls his eyes.

"Your father is around somewhere. Probably getting ready for the fireworks. And I think your brother is combing around here as well. Probably trying to avoid helping out. It's so nice to meet you, Fleur. I hope we get to sit down to chat later."

"You too, Mrs. Parker."

"Oh, please, it's Fran." She scurries off on tiptoes to avoid her heels sinking into the grass, and I smile as she prances along the food tables, socializing and hosting.

I turn to face Adam. "She's sweet."

"Yeah, she's my biggest supporter. My dad, on the other hand ..."

He takes a swig of his beer, a far-off look in his eye.

"So what's your favorite part about growing up here? On an old plantation, I mean?"

"Hosting all the parties." He chuckles. "It was nice. In school, all our friends wanted to come out to our place to ride four-wheelers, swim, or play a game of football. As we got older, my siblings and I would have bonfires and parties. It was an easy spot to hang."

He leads me as we walk about the gardens. More blooming

magnolias scent the path and crepe myrtles burst into colorful hues of lavender and pinks. We aren't the only ones enjoying the lush gardens. Many of the guests are mulling about and sipping their cocktails before settling down for dinner.

"Adam." A deep, baritone voice from behind us causes me to stop in front of some beautiful white azaleas. Adam sighs to my right and pivots.

"Dad. Get all the fireworks squared away?"

"I did. And who is this?" His dad's tone is clipped and borderline rude, but I smile and extend my hand.

"I'm Fleur. It's nice to meet you, Mr. Parker."

He shakes my hand once, then lets it fall. "You're the new girl in town? Bought the old farmhouse."

I think those were questions, but he says them so matter of fact, I'm unsure.

I nod. "Yes. I hired Adam to help me, and he's been great. It's getting close to finished." I might be paying for it for the next four years, but at least it's almost complete.

He grunts, and I narrow my eyes at him. This man is the total opposite of his wife in every way. Personality and appearance. Although I catch his brown eyes, and it's in those I see Adam. See where he resembles his father.

"I'll see you around." He nods to Adam, then addresses me. "Nice to meet you, Fleur." He steps around us and continues on, hulking form taking up the entire garden pathway.

Adam lets out another sigh. As if he's glad the encounter is over with and they can go back to ignoring each other. "How about some food?"

* * *

My plate is piled high with catfish, pulled pork and every type of salad there is on these tables. I also grabbed three fruit kabobs full of red, white, and blue patterned fruit, which I admired, and then subsequently was annoyed I didn't think about doing something like that. My sloppy fruit bowl will have to do. Honestly, I think I'm the only one who touched it.

The food is delicious. We sit with a few guys Adam knows from different contracting jobs, and I meet their wives, who all seem excited about the renovation of the farmhouse and have asked if they can stop by for a tour.

Midway through our meal, a tingling sensation on the nape of my neck causes me to shiver and I glance up to see ... *him.*

Talking to Mr. Northgate, the man chuckles, and I shiver, really hoping it was the cross breeze through the tent. But his eyes jump around the tent until they land on me like he was alerted, too.

Great. Caught staring.

The man's glance moves to Adam and then back to me before he finishes his conversation and starts to move in this direction.

Goodness. Why is he even here? I run reconnaissance through the tent and surrounding areas—I wonder how many of Darrin's men are here. How many are part of the town? He's halfway to the table before I decide I need more fruit, and I jolt up, effectively knocking my knees against the table and sending Adam's beer tumbling to the ground.

"I'm so sorry. I'll get you a new one." I reach for the bottle and Adam's fingers meet mine.

He notices my shaking hands and his brows furrow at my face. "Fleur, what's wrong?"

"Adam."

My eyes flutter closed at his firm tone. A mix of sensual grit and terrifying dread.

Adam jumps to stand, meeting the man chest to chest. His dark wash jeans hug him tightly, and his navy-blue shirt is the most color I've seen on him.

"Going to introduce me to your ... friend?" He sneers at the last word and my knees shake. This is ridiculous.

Adam's mouth suddenly doesn't work because he swallows several times, eyes almost pleading with the man.

"I'm Fleur." I cross my arms in front of my chest to avoid extending a hand in greeting.

The man's mouth twitches, and he looks at Adam, who says, "Fleur, this is Liam. My brother."

Wait ...

His brother? I stare, slack-jawed at this large burly man, but then I see it. His mother's hazel eyes and his father's blond hair with an imposing form. They *are* brothers.

I blink. Then blink again. Adam tilts his head back like he has found something on the top of the tent's ceiling.

"You have barbeque on your face," Liam says to me, and my eyes widen. I duck my head down, embarrassingly wiping at my mouth with my hand. When I glance back up, Liam has sauntered off to the food table, and I turn, gaping at Adam.

"*That* is your brother? I thought he was—"

"Please don't. It's complicated."

I slowly nod, my gaze flitting back to Liam, who catches me looking. He raises the spoon of something and makes an exaggerated point to dump three spoonfuls on his plate. I squint at the bowl and realize it's my fruit salad.

Chapter 12
Fleur

A t some point, I get roped into the bounce house with a bunch of kids—pretty sure I've become the babysitter for several parents while they get a drink or two.

Harper, a three-year-old little girl, has stuck to me like glue in the inflatable kitty castle, and I have thoroughly enjoyed making sure the older boys in here don't knock her over.

After I unceremoniously met Liam, Adam said he needed to go help his mother with a few things inside. That was twenty minutes ago. Since then, I've gotten more exercise in this bounce house than I do in a normal week.

I'm only slightly embarrassed.

Harper's parents come back, and I follow her out of the bounce house, trying to keep my dress from sticking to my legs with the static electricity. I scan the groups of people for Adam but don't see him and decide to use the restroom inside, hoping to spot him along the way.

The house is more immaculate inside. Antique furnishings mixed with the modern style give me endless ideas for my little farmhouse. I float around to each room, running into other guests also admiring the traditional interior design.

In my hunt for the bathroom, I pass several rooms. A grunt sounds from one partially ajar, and I step closer.

"—instead, you got a new damn truck. Did you think I wouldn't notice?" The voice yelling is pure gravel, and it twists at my gut.

"I-I didn't ..."

"Think. You didn't think. You're a selfish prick."

There's another grunt, and I can't take it anymore. I push the rest of the door open, and my eyes widen.

Liam has Adam pinned up against the wall, feet an inch off the ground. His hand is fisted into his shirt as he growls up at him. His eyes snap to mine at the same time Adam's do. But while Adam's are burdened, Liam's are bright with rage, seething so deep it's as if I can almost see into his soul. His nostrils flare at my presence.

I step into the room. It's an office or library of some sort. A chair is knocked over next to a desk, but despite that, book-shelves line the back wall and everything has a place. My guess is they don't use this very much.

"Is everything okay?" I ask, turning back to where they're staring each other down.

"Fleur, sorry. Just a bit of a disagreement with my brother," Adam says, trying to play it off. He offers me a smile while Liam lets go of his shirt.

Adam moves to step forward, but Liam shoves his palm into his chest. He hits the wall with a dull thud. Unspoken words pass between the two of them, and about when I decide I should leave these two to themselves, Liam steps back. He stalks to the door, eyes locked with mine as he pushes past me while a chiseled shoulder gently knocks me back.

He doesn't stop, though, only keeps going.

"Are you okay?" I move to Adam, who has since leaned back against the wall. Wallpaper engulfs his head, the blue birds looking like they are nesting in his dark hair.

"Yeah. I'm fine. Like I said, just a disagreement."

"I thought he was part of Darrin's group ... but your brother?"

"It's complicated."

And that's the second time I've gotten that answer today. I fold my arms in front of myself.

"Listen, Adam, I need to—"

"But yeah, he's part of Darrin's group. Working off some debt." Adam's pupils seem to go cloudy, and he rubs his forehead. "He's part of Darrin's trusted circle."

"But—"

"Stay away from him, Fleur. Please."

There isn't anything in me that wants to get involved, but I'd be lying if my interest wasn't piqued. Why this feud between brothers?

"Is he addicted?"

"No, no. It's not like that."

Tell me what it's like then.

I fidget with my two rubber bands, fiddling with the need to pull at them. To gather some control back, snap it back into place. Adam thankfully doesn't notice my ministrations and moves to pick up the tipped-over chair.

The air in the room grows uncomfortable. I'm not quite sure how to put my finger on it, but fleeting tingles rattle my belly. Like someone is poking me over and over saying, *trust your gut. Trust your gut.*

The problem with that. I used to trust my gut. But my sixth sense obviously missed a few waving red flags if history is any indicator.

"I'm not sure I'm up for the fireworks tonight," Adam says,

reaching for my hand. He rubs his thumb over the back of it, smoothing over my knuckles. "Would you hate me if I went home for the night?"

"No. Not at all. I get it. I'm probably going to head home myself."

He leans down, feathering his thumb across my cheek. "Happy Fourth, Fleur."

"Bye," I whisper back as he leaves the room.

I end up walking myself back to the car. Dusk settles in with a delicious golden hour, the bright sky turning into warm hues. Perfect weather for today. Cool air whips through the dwindling cars, and having left my fruit salad bowl behind, my hands feel empty.

The sound of several cars rolling down the dirt road captures my attention, and I turn to see two black sedans pulling off the side of the road near the house. Three motorcycles pull out of the driveway, and I recognize the one bike from the bed-and-breakfast.

Liam.

The back window in the first black car rolls down, while Liam pulls his bike up to the side. Grass tickles my ankles as I continue to my car, every few seconds looking over my shoulder at this little meet.

"It's not like that." Adam's words from earlier ring in my head.

It sure looks like that. How did Liam get mixed up with this crowd? His family seems loving and Adam determined to keep away—it has questions bubbling up to the surface.

I reach my car and unlock it. Soaking in the last of the dipping sun, my eyes flit to the revving engines across the field one last time. Both cars make a U-turn and trail off back down the road, while two bikes flank their side. Liam's bike idles, and squinting, I can see him stare down into his helmet. His head swivels around, looking straight at me. My breath hitches, and I wrestle with the door handle, yank it open, and jump in.

Cool leather meets my skin as I rest my forehead on the steering wheel.

This town will be the ruin of me.

Chapter 13
Liam

The drive to the compound is shit. Traffic from the party makes the ride three times as long. Then add having to watch out for drunken assholes, even more so since I'm on my bike.

I'm not worried about something happening to me. I'm more worried about my Harley. Cost me more than I'd ever admit. I let the town think it's bought and paid for by Darrin and his operation, but I purchased it myself.

I ease onto the compound, which is accessible from a dirt road off the Natchez Trace. A long scenic travel corridor that stretches from Mississippi to Tennessee.

The back road winds around through the woods enough that tourists or passersby would simply think it was a road that leads nowhere.

But nestled back here—well, more like concealed—is the compound entrance. It's a rugged place with several ruined buildings housing many of the workers strung out or using. Darrin doesn't put too much effort into those living quarters.

The clubhouse and the trusted circle, however, are a different story.

I snort at the term clubhouse. Darrin hates being referred to as a motorcycle club, but with half the men riding hogs and an organizational structure like one—it's damn close.

The large oak and pine trees surrounding the gated entrance cloak the moon. Brilliant bursts of colors occasionally pop into view above the towering branches from those still celebrating the Fourth. And I wish it would end.

Pulling past the gate, I guide my bike to the clubhouse. Darrin requested I swing by before returning to my cabin for the night.

The clubhouse is a large two-story building that serves as the hub for our operations, meetings, and eating. Honestly, the whole place smells like drugs and engine oil. The communal firepit sits off the back porch of the clubhouse, although while some may think it is a nice bonfire for bonding, it's far from the case. Darrin has a sick obsession with branding people.

The horseshoe seared on the side of my ribs burns with the memory.

Luckily, my assigned cabin sits a good distance from the clubhouse, and I do my best to stay away from this place as much as possible.

A buzz in my back pocket tickles my ass as I pull my bike into park and swing off.

Received.

Deleting the message, I stride to the double doors.

"Have fun at Mommy and Daddy's?" Blitz's oily voice seeps into my ear. He stands to the side of the double doors smoking a cigarette.

I scoff. "Same shit, different year."

He snorts in laughter that turns into a wheezing cough. "See that brother of yours? Heard he had a new piece of ass."

My nostrils flare and Blitz narrows his eyes at me. Steeling my expression, I grunt in response, yanking open the door.

He's an idiot, my brother. Bringing a woman into his life. Enjoying the perks of having everyone else clean up his mess. He may only be two years younger than me, but he's acting foolish.

When I walk in, several of the guys hover around the meeting table. Darrin's dark brown hair is curled and wet as if he just got out of the shower, and it indicates he's over this day like the rest of us.

"We have several shipments coming in from the border this week. It will be all hands on deck to get it moved out. I don't want it here long." He blinks, those mismatched eyes looking at each of the guys.

The men nod. The warehouse on site allows us to consolidate and distribute. Most of the product goes into the hands of local dealers, but we have a few trucks we move product in for out-of-state transport. Darrin procured three United States Postal Service trucks modified to conceal product. We've never once been stopped.

"In other news, we caught a snitch. Found an undercover cop snooping around. Y'all know how I feel about cops." Darrin holds out the S so it hisses from the tip of his tongue.

"What'da do with him, D? Make an example out of him?" Snape chuckles. Snape is a hound, always sniffing for blood.

"No. That would draw too much attention. Gave his name to our friends down south."

Hollering and fists on the table distract me from the pit growing in my stomach. Silently, I'm praying they don't ask about Adam.

Pounding on the front doors of the clubhouse pauses the meeting, and Blitz runs in, saying we've got a junkie at the gate.

This happens. A lot. The town's people get hooked on Jackpot and the dealers are squeezed for information. Ultimately, the compound location is given away, and they rummage through the woods, looking for a fix.

Darrin stands, his tall form striding to the front doors before the rest of us. There are six of us in this trusted circle. Micah is the only one with more brains than muscles. He's Darrin's little brother and he handles all the finances, so he doesn't live on the compound. He's a treasurer of sorts—but again we aren't a motorcycle club.

Reaching the gate, we see the man. His hands shakily grip the secure fence, attention darting to each of us as we approach. He tries to claw his way in, reaching through each post. Plastering his head to the gate, he smooshes his face there, pleading with us.

"Let me in. I-I-I can pay. I'll pay."

Darrin steps forward. "How did you find this location?"

The man blinks rapidly, eyes working overtime as he tries to remember.

"J-Jace. He told me he was out. Had to get some from the compound. I followed him out here."

Darrin's cold expression hardens even more as he steps forward, taking the man's face between his thumb and fingers through the iron bars. He moves the man's face up and down, inspecting him. "And just what would you do for a hit?"

"Anything, man. I'd do anything."

* * *

91

It's a little past midnight when I finally make it to my cabin.

Darrin decided he'd let the man in, give him what he desperately craved, and then told him there was an upcharge for it being a premium on-site product. It took everything in me not to snort during his tirade. That's Darrin, though. Uses what you crave, what you seek. He gives it to you, then pulls the plug, expecting loyalty in return, or charges what you can't afford. If you can't pay it back, you're in debt to him. For the long haul.

The cabin is quiet. Undisturbed. It's not the traditional Adirondack Mountain cabin you picture when planning your winter vacation, full of serene views and tranquil gentleness.

No. This is a rectangular box.

Sided in traditional rough-sawn lumber with a humble front porch, it houses one bedroom and one bath. With a minuscule kitchen and a decent-sized living room, it's nothing special. But good enough for me.

Honestly, I'm not sure how Snape lives in his small cabin with his woman. My large body barely fits in between the damn doorways, let alone trying to share the space with another person.

Most of the men here aren't in committed relationships, but there's a constant supply of women on the compound. Many looking to trade intimate moments for a hit of the latest batch that came in. A few have girlfriends, but even then, if Blitz wants one of them, he takes them. No questions asked. Call it the perk of his position as next in line. The only time he backs down is if they're married.

A couple years ago, a guy named Cider found out another guy on the compound was sleeping with his wife. Cider killed him. And at that point, new rules were instated about marriage and messin' with another's wife.

Stepping through the door, I move to turn on a low-light

lamp in the living room before removing my boots. They are large, clunky things needed for riding my bike and occasionally beating the shit out of people. As is part of my job as the enforcer.

It's only part of the work I do for Darrin, though. When I first started with him, after I was allowed in the compound, I had the rookie jobs. Cleaning up blood, unloading shipments from the border, or sobering up the guys after a long night. Since then, Darrin has trusted me more and more. I liaise between Darrin and the dealers often. I go to them. Check their count and their stash.

In the corner of the cabin, near the door, is an old coat rack my grandfather made me, and I fling my black leather coat on it. He gave them to all three of us grandkids a few years ago for Christmas. He doesn't have much time for woodworking anymore, but the deep cherry and smooth lines make it the only nice piece of furniture this whole place has.

The couch is an old burgundy leather from Double Lucky's, and the recliner is from my father's shop. Everything I used to own I sold to come here four years ago.

Wood paneling wraps the kitchen, and I installed open shelving with reclaimed wood instead of upper cabinets. The light pine lower cabinets are full of knots, and most needed replacing when I moved in. Then two years ago, tired of all the wood, I replaced the butcher block countertops with a precut piece of granite.

Sliding a cast iron skillet from the lower cabinet, I place it on a burner before kicking the stove twice to turn it on.

I grab five eggs from the refrigerator, which is usually what I reach for most nights as a midnight snack. They splatter in the sizzling pan and the heated butter pops out to sting my skin.

I don't flinch. Only stare at the eggs as they cook, exhausted.

Blonde hair and gray eyes flicker in my thoughts from this evening. My mother kept going on and on about how lucky Adam was that he'd found someone. Him being such a "good boy" and all, he deserves to have a "nice woman".

I snort and my eyes slide around the dimly lit cabin and over the knitted Afghan folded neatly on the couch. If only my mother knew.

Fleur, though—her narrowed eyes at me. They dilated in fear and widened in apprehension when she found out I was Adam's brother. He hadn't told her. Probably for good reason.

But that fear melted into something ... more. Furrowed brows and deepening lines in her expression—curiosity. Like she had a million and one questions to ask, and I can be sure Adam won't answer them. If he tries, they'll be lies.

I flip the eggs. Yolk spills out of one, creating swirls of golden yellow in the curved pattern of a horseshoe. Scowling at the eggs, I stab the others, violently breaking each one until they're seared through.

Mismatched plates are all I have, and I reach up for a blue one with red speckled dots and slide the snack onto the plate. Starved, it takes two forkfuls to devour them, and I clean up in a hurry, craving sleep.

But before I can shower, I take out my notebook and draw those eyes. Glistening silver in the sun but storm gray in the clouded day. They claw at my mind, and I draw. Dumping out the vision of how they widened in fear, yet also detonated with irritation when she saw me today. Who is this woman? And why am I drawn to her?

When I'm finished, I pad into the single-person bathroom and twist the shower handle to near scalding. The blistering burn doesn't even register with me anymore.

I feel nothing.

Chapter 14
Fleur

B arbeque invades my thoughts for the entire week since the Fourth of July community event. Some of the best-smoked brisket I've ever had.

Adam said his mother told him I was welcome anytime, and that she'd be happy to smoke more meat for me. I'm so obsessed with the food. I almost took him up on the offer right there on the spot.

With some additional work projects and my own farmhouse slowly entering the finishing stages, I haven't seen Adam much since the Fourth. It may be for the best. He was rattled by Liam being there. Questions distract me when I talk with him and threaten to blurt out of my mouth. What's the deal with him and his brother? Why is he being secretive? Probably not the best move on my part if I hit him with an interrogation.

Today we have three new check-ins at the bed-and-breakfast. All the rooms need to be turned around. The Floral Room, The Art Room, and The Writing Room are three of the five here at the B&B; each one decorated to live up to its name.

Dusty pink wallpaper with an explosion of unique flowers

line the wall of—you guessed it—The Floral Room. When I first cleaned the room, I wondered how anyone could stay in the room without going batty from the wallpaper, but the more I'm in it, the more peaceful it feels. Soft, muted pastel colors create an enchanting whimsy.

In contrast, The Art Room is bold and brash with straight lines and dark frames housing art I'm not sure I've seen the style of before. The room has a masculine tone.

The Writing Room is bland in comparison to the other two. Matte white walls with white linens and furniture. One piece of art hangs on the wall that says: *Start with a Blank Slate.* The blank walls are void of color. Very blank.

As I scurry to the laundry supply closet to gather towels for the new rooms, the smell of chocolate wafts through the house. Mrs. Northgate is baking her dessert for the bar, and I secretly hope she made extra. She mentioned deciding between chocolate pie or fudge. Either way, I'd be happy to sample anything she cooks.

I scramble through my cleans. Spraying and wiping, disinfecting, then spraying and wiping some more. Surprisingly, cleaning often gives me a sense of relief from the loneliness. The out-of-control feeling abates when I'm knee-deep in toilets or fresh linens.

Voices from downstairs signal the first new check-ins have arrived, and I quickly close all the doors after the final mints are placed on the pillows. After dumping the old linens and towels down the chute, which I still find oddly satisfying, I head down the stairs to start some of my tidying of the main breakfast area.

Careful to stay out of the way—I don't want to scare away the guests with my frizzy hair and tired eyes—I take the back service stairs. They aren't very wide or grand in opulence like the front steps leading down into the main foyer. Nope. These are narrow little buggers with stained old carpet the color of my reddest lipstick.

I pass stacks of books and new linens still in their plastic pouches. Travel-sized shampoo and lotion from an old brand the bed-and-breakfast used to stock sit inside baskets lining the steps. It's like Russian roulette. You never know what could bring you down.

I dart off the last step that leads into the kitchen and walk right past the back door filled with Mr. Northgate's work boots and a pile of items that need to go outside.

When the back door opens unexpectedly, I startle, falling backward into something that topples over with a loud splintering crash and rattles through the kitchen. I squeeze my eyes shut.

Please don't have broken something important.

Please don't let it be expensive.

"Goodness, Fleur. I'm so sorry. Are you all right?" Mr. Northgate's friendly voice is drowned in concern. I open one eye, looking at him and wincing.

"You frightened me. I'm so sorry, I—" I turn around to see a pile of sweaters and coats on the floor. But I grimace at what's underneath. A beautiful oak coat rack is now split at the top. Several pieces lie around the main post, and I slap my hand over my mouth. "Oh no!"

I'm on my knees in an instant, reaching for the pieces and cradling them in my arms like an idiot.

"What was that sound?" Mrs. Northgate pushes through the swinging kitchen door from the other side of the room, and her eyes widen.

"I gave Fleur I fright, I'm afraid. Walked straight through the door as she was walking past."

"I'm so sorry. If you tell me where you got this, I'll have it replaced."

"Don't be silly," Mr. Northgate says. "It was an accident."

"Besides," Mrs. Northgate chimes in, "Ed made that." Thankfully, her tone doesn't hint at being upset, but something more like pride laces the timbre of her voice.

My eyes drag over the smooth finish and the beautiful details. "You made this? Well, now I feel even worse." I pull my hands over my face, rubbing my forehead. Mr. Northgate chuckles as he kneels to examine the breaks.

"Don't. I made a bunch. Gave them to family and friends— all that. Looks like I can easily repair this. Don't sweat it." He gives me a sweet smile, his dark brown hair peppered with gray falling in front of his face as he leans down further to inspect.

"Broken things can be fixed," Mrs. Northgate singsongs as she pulls chocolate fudge out of the blast chiller.

Can they?

I hope they aren't only talking about the coat rack.

✿ ✿ ✿

It's late by the time I end up leaving work.

Wind whips the leaves across the road. They dance and tumble into my headlights before disappearing into the darkness surrounding the Natchez Trace.

During the day, the Trace is picturesque, and the fifty-mile-per-hour speed limit creates a leisurely drive. Bicycles and hikers are often on the road, exploring the historical sites along the way that veer off into the numerous hiking trails.

At night, though, it's different. There are zero lights, and towering trees line the two lanes weaving through the state. An eerie tone settles on the road. Few cars drive the Trace at night, trying to avoid the chance of hitting a deer or falling asleep at the wheel. But it's the fastest way home and I'm tired.

Movement to the right of me brings three deer hopping across the road several feet in front of my car. I lift my foot off the gas, slowing down to make sure there aren't any more.

When I determine there are none, I step back on the gas. A sudden burst, a pop, then a hiss scare me, and I jump, swerving to the right. Gasping, I fist the wheel and jerk to the left, correcting my loss of control.

No. No, no, no. Crap. Adrenaline shoots straight to my chest and my heart thumps rapidly.

The car wobbles as I slow to a stop, pulling off on the nonexistent shoulder.

Closing my eyes, I take a deep breath, hands shaking, still clutching the wheel.

Flashlights aren't something I typically keep in my car, but with several late-night hardware runs for Adam and the all too scarce lighting around this town, I came to the conclusion keeping one in the glove box was a necessity. Reaching across the console, I fumble with the glove box and open it to retrieve the flashlight.

I step out of my jeep, darkness only broken apart by the stream of white from my flashlight. The air is thick with silence, and the night has swallowed the expected nocturnal noises. Creepily absent. Lovely.

The shadow of my car is cast along the road as I move around, inspecting my tires.

I deflate—or should I say my left front tire has.

Squatting down, I move the light along the rubber until I come across the large nail sticking out of it.

"Damn it." I whack the light against the spot where the nail punctures through, and I shake my head when the light flickers.

A twig snaps from deep in the trees and I freeze. Suddenly,

my mouth is dry, and I tense as I look around before standing on shaky legs. Heading back for my car, I lean in over the driver's seat to snatch my phone from my purse.

No service.

Great.

Another well-known fact about the Natchez Trace—cell phone service is about as shotty as the restrooms. My shoulders slump as I look around the empty road and void woods. There's nothing around here.

All the tricks to get a signal don't work. Waving my arm in the air. Marching my phone across the road and walking several feet in each direction does nothing to give me those bars I so desperately need.

Resigned, I step back to the car and comb through any knowledge my father tried to impart to me when I learned to drive. Because learning to drive wasn't gas, brake, and stay in your lane. No. It was a full-fledged breakdown of the car parts, oil changes, and spare tire equipment I'd be stupid not to have in my vehicle.

I dig around, attempting to locate the jack, when two lights reflect off my car mirrors.

Thank goodness.

Turning on my heels, I watch as a car barrels toward me, going much faster than the well-patrolled speed limit posted. The relief I was feeling for a moment sprints away, and I'm left with the roiling of unease as the car slows to where I stand.

Lifting my hand over my eyes, I squint at the car still blaring its lights in my direction and count four silhouetted bodies inside. The phone in my back pocket is useless right now, but I pull it out anyway, the weight of it offering a false comfort.

All four doors open, and my gaze jumps first to the driver, whom I don't recognize. His hair is dark, but as he strides forward, it takes on a red hue, his sharp nose moving with his head as he scans me from head to toe. A sneer seeps across his mouth, the beer belly he sports jiggling with each chuckle.

"Well, boys, look what we have here. You havin' car trouble, sweetheart?"

The nickname grates in my ears. The nickname my mother gave me and that Mrs. Northgate uses frequently sounds vile on his tongue. Another man rounds the front of their old beater Chevy. He tugs at his leather vest and raises his chin at me.

I recognize him. The man from the diner with Adam. His name was some sort of football move—

"Blitz," another man calls from where he's climbing out of the back seat, "I claim this one, man. You got the last one."

Blitz. That's his name. It's as if he realizes he's seen me before at the same time I pin his name down because his mouth lifts into a wicked grin.

"Hey now. This here is Adam's lady friend." He snorts.

Beer belly scoffs and spits on the ground at Adam's name. I back up, eyes flitting to the two men standing in front of me and getting distracted by the other two emerging from the back seat.

I hold up my phone.

"Thanks, guys. But I'm all set. Just called someone to come help. Appreciate you stopping, though." I throw as much sweet crooning into my words as I can.

"Baby, I don't think you understand," Blitz says, adjusting the bulge in his pants as he walks toward me. "There's no cell service out here. I doubt you called anyone."

I slide around the break light, walking backward to my car. Blitz laughs, his oily wheeze skidding around me and destroying any hope they'd leave.

Narrowing my eyes on him, I turn to jump in my car and drive off anyway, tire be damned. But a hand snatches my hair, pulled back in a convenient long ponytail. He yanks and I yelp, tears stinging behind my eyes.

"Blitz."

The deep rumble of *that* voice vibrates through me, and I know it. Liam.

"What?" Blitz barks.

"That's not very hospitable of us. She's the new girl in town after all."

I strain to see over my shoulder as Liam stalks toward us. His footsteps thud against the pavement with every formidable step, black jeans and T-shirt matching his black boots.

His broad shoulders twitch as his thick-set frame prowls forward, and he slaps a hand on Blitz's shoulder, squeezing. Blitz lets go of my hair, and I can finally turn around fully to face them.

Liam's hair is pulled up into a bun, eyes narrowed on my cheeks. He glances toward my car, surveying it with a self-assured gaze. With each tick of his jaw, I swallow, and he tracks the movement. Brawny arms cross in front of himself, projecting dominance the other men seem to respect and acknowledge. Except maybe Blitz.

"Well?" he asks.

"Well, what?" I snap.

Liam's mouth flinches tight at my tone.

"You didn't answer Trip's question. Are you having car trouble?" His stance screams nonchalance, but I don't miss the way his eyes continuously scan our surroundings.

"Me? No. I love sitting on the side of the road with a nail in my tire in the dead of night."

Liam's mouth tightens further into a straight line, while Blitz laughs.

"Liam, she'd be a feisty one. Let the guys have some fun."

He motions back to the other men, but Liam doesn't even glance at them. He holds my eyes as if he is memorizing them.

"Get back in the car, boys," Liam demands.

They all grumble and curse him while obeying his command. Trip yells back before he gets in the car. "Well, at least let us watch!"

My eyes widen, and my knees quiver. Liam's nostrils flare as he jerks his head around and yells at them to move it. Stepping forward, he towers over me, and I back up into my open door. My cavalier comments in sarcasm were not the best choice, and I'm regretting them at this exact moment.

As if he realizes my panic, he rolls his eyes. "Don't look at me like that. Where's your spare?"

I blink. "My spare?"

"Did I stutter? Your tire. Where is your spare tire?"

"In the cargo area. Underneath, I think."

Liam moves to the trunk and pulls out the jack and lug wrench. He brings both items to the front and squats down, his muscled thighs straining his jeans as he shuffles around. How does a man like this end up with thugs like that? I look back at the car as one of the men lights up a joint and licks his lips at me. *Gross.*

"Fleur." Liam's voice startles me. "Hold the light for me."

He works to loosen the lug nuts, then places the jack underneath the car and lifts it until the tire is off the ground. He moves methodically, pulling off the tire and placing the spare on the wheel bolts and tightening.

When he's finished, he stands, body grazing past me, and I jolt back. He chuckles, setting the flat tire down with a single hand and wiping his other on his shirt.

"My brother must have told you some dark things ..."

Because I'm jumpy around him?

I scowl. "No. Your thugs back there told me all I need to know about you."

Liam's shoulders stiffen, his jaw working back and forth. "What did Adam say, Fleur?"

I'm confused. Why does he care?

"Said you were working off a debt."

He snorts. "Guess that's about right."

"It's not about what Adam said anyway. It's the reaction of the town, the stories about what you all push and sell. You're thugs, plain and simple."

I'm shaking. Questioning my decision to answer him without any sort of filter.

His pupils darken, and anger radiates from his heaving chest. He bends down, grabs the tire, and I catch a glimpse of black ink peeking out from beneath his shirt, hovering above his belt line. He moves to the trunk and tosses the tire in with zero finesse or care before striding back to the car and opening the back door.

He pauses. Glaring eyes meet mine. "Fleur, don't drive on the Trace this late again."

Chapter 15
Liam

The trip outside Ruin took me two hours. My meet was the second dead drop this month, and despite the long trip, riding the Trace let me reflect on our run-in with Fleur here two weeks ago.

I haven't seen her since.

Glancing down at my fingers on my right hand, drawing pencil residue streaks across the outside of my pinky. Evidence of a painful week.

I started in high school. A talent I apparently inherited from my mother, whose watercolors hang in most government buildings in Mississippi. She told me once it was her escape, a haven from the world of motherhood and the emotional drain it took on her. Her own parents had paid for her lessons while growing up and it paid off. She was brilliant—is brilliant.

If only she were proud her talent passed to me instead of Adam. It's him she wishes she had that connection with. Not me.

I've been drawing more than ever this week, compelled by my run-in with Fleur and her mouth, but perpetuated as a way to clean my soul. In the years I've worked for Darrin, I've been more and more complacent. Each time the boys harass a woman for a "good time"—despite my attempts to interrupt. Each kill. Each shipment. All of it goes against my nature.

That's the thing about selling your soul; no matter the reason, it comes at a cost. A debt to a higher power that none can repay.

The audacity of her to speak to me like she did—shit. That's the first thing Blitz informed Darrin about when we returned to the compound that evening. All about Adam's new friend and how feisty she is. Still didn't hide the fact she was nervous, terrified even. I saw each shiver. Her knees trembled, but she masked her fear with casual glances toward the car, where some of the most dangerous men at our disposal waited. And they noticed.

I could almost see the wheels turning in Darrin's head, although he didn't voice them out loud, about Fleur. His silence is even more intimidating than words. Thin lips formed a line, brows furrowing as Trip and Blitz both went on and on about the girl.

It crossed my mind to call Adam, to inform him Darrin caught wind of her name, but the ache of bitterness kept me from dialing his number. He never did truly grasp what it was like to lose something.

A snarl leaves my lips, flying into my helmet as I correct my bike from almost crossing the centerline. The need to get back drives me to run twenty over the speed limit. What I don't need is Darrin asking questions.

Dusk settles over the remote compound as I pull in. Four box trucks are backed into the warehouse, offloading a recent shipment. But this is more than I originally anticipated. Twice the amount I had accounted for. Twice. Shit.

Snape waves me over to the clubhouse after I park. The

weather is cooler this evening, but a nervous energy heats my body, enough that I need to remove my jacket.

The compound is buzzing. It's more than the typical high we get when a new shipment comes in to be divided out to dealers. This is different. More predatory, and I can see that in Snape's eyes as I near him. The gleam in them is haunting.

"Whatch'a say, Snape?" I ask, ready to blow past him into the clubhouse kitchen for a beer.

"Boss is fixin' to send a message."

I pause, one boot raised over the door's threshold. "When? Who?" I snap my gaze toward Snape, who licks his lips the way he always does when someone is about to have their ass handed to them.

"That guy from a few weeks ago who showed up at the gate. He's been taking what he's supposed to be dealing."

I snort. "How? He can't possibly take everything he's supposed to be dealing ... he'd die."

Jackpot is almost fifty times more potent than heroin. The irony that a drug offering powerful relief for those with terminal cancer can also be so lethal isn't lost on us.

Respect the product.

Darrin's words.

But Jackpot is more than highly addictive, it's lucrative. Cheaper than other opioids and easier to smuggle because small amounts are so powerful. The baggies of powder our dealers carry are about equal to a brick of cocaine with the same profit margin. Losing one or two customers to an overdose isn't detrimental to the bottom line.

I've never done the stuff. Never plan to.

"Not sure. His girl is in on it too. Pleaded for his life just an hour ago as Darrin beat the piss out of him," Snape says.

Damn.

Shrieking sounds from the warehouse, and a chill runs

down my back. I steel my face before eyeing Snape, who sighs. "At least Darrin said he'd let the girl *work*. You up for a show?"

No. Never.

I shrug. "We'll see."

We both stride over to the hulking, run-down warehouse. It's one of the better ones, though. Most facilities used to parcel Jackpot are rat-infested cesspools.

The building is long and rectangular. Rusted metal coats the whole thing. Several bays for trucks to load and unload line the back, while a single point of entry funnels everyone in that direction, easily secured or picked off if you aren't supposed to be there.

Reaching the door, the female's yelling gets worse, and I brace myself for what I'm about to witness.

Blitz and Goff stand on the inside of the door. Both of them watch the scene unfold. While Blitz is a trusted member, unaddicted to the Jackpot that flows so freely from this place, Goff is not so lucky.

He's been addicted for several years, accumulating more debt than he can possibly pay back. Always taking drugs or borrowing money from Darrin to gamble or buy a hit. Darrin didn't demand he deal, though. No, he's let him work around the compound. His softness with Goff irritates many of the men, but Darrin pretends not to notice.

Goff's gaze is pinned on the young lady. Streams of mascara blacken underneath her eyes, which are wide in fear as another man holds her elbow. Goff is no doubt thinking of River, his sister. Perhaps wondering if he'll ever go too far and put her in the position this woman is in.

I scan the warehouse. The packers are still working. Most of them don't even glance up from where they weigh and measure out the powder into convenient bags, each designated for specific dealers.

A loud thud, as if concrete itself connected with a skull, rings out. Darrin's fist coils back for another strike. The man who came crawling, pleading to Darrin the weeks prior, is now riddled with black and blue circles. Hair disheveled, he steps back with a limp, making retreat difficult. Darrin follows his every move.

"You stole from me," Darrin says, his voice quiet and unfeeling. A predator sizing up his prey. Those deep mismatched eyes harbor so much pent-up rage and emotion as he scans the man's body, searching for weak points to inflict the most pain.

"I'm s-s-sorry. I can't help it."

"I've given you a chance. You came here searching for a fix. For a high that only *I* can give." Command laces his voice as it thunders throughout the warehouse, reminding everyone exactly who runs and owns this operation. "I provided that, and you ... you squandered it."

A far-off look in Darrin's eyes catches my attention. But as soon as it's there, it's gone. Blinked away and offering no mercy.

"No," the man pleads. "I promise I won't do it again. I'll sell triple. I'll, I'll—"

Darrin grabs the back of his head with his fist and the man jerks, trying to free himself, but Darrin holds fast. The female is crying, full-fledged tears now. Whether for her man or for the drugs she'll now have to work for instead of freeloading, I'm unsure.

Darrin reaches down to unsheathe a knife from his waistband, and the man's eyes widen in terror. A wet spot appears on his light-washed jeans as Darrin drags him toward the packers. Large containers of fine powder line the stainless-steel tables, getting ready for weight checks, but before that—bags. Large bags of Jackpot, sizes I've never seen before. I stiffen at the knowledge. So much. There's so much.

His knife splits one, powder spilling out. Goff and Blitz both jerk in surprise. Each for different reasons. Blitz sees the wasted money while Goff sees the wasted high.

All the while, Darrin sees the perfect ending.

He shoves the man's face down.

Down into the bright white powder piled in the bag, the slice made big enough for his thin nose and mouth.

Silence invades the warehouse. Packers have retreated from their stations. The woman has dropped to her knees, head hung low. There's a silent scream etched over her mouth and her eyes are desperate, heavy.

Muffled sounds are the only noise echoing in the metal building. Grunts and slaps to the table sounds around the man as he struggles to breathe, nose pushed into the deadly powder. His fingernails scratch and claw at the steel. Fighting. He's fighting, but it's for nothing.

Darrin stands over him, his muscled arm holding his head in place over the large, opened bag on the table. Nostrils flared, he doesn't even look down at the man struggling for his life. He meets the stare of every man in the room. Connecting with their eyes in declaration.

This is my house. My power. My operation, he silently seems to say.

The man's arms begin to slow, weakening as he aspirates the Jackpot. His head jerks from side to side and Darrin's hand presses harder, his fingers digging into the man's scalp.

The scene is violent and, in a sick way, poetic.

A squeaking sound shatters the silence as the man's arms slide off the table, going limp at his sides. It's only then that Darrin looks down at the man, and he turns his head. Red and purple splotches decorate his face through the white powder covering it. Eyes unseeing and open. Darrin stares down at the man with zero emotion. His mouth turns into a nonchalant downward curve, and he shrugs, rolling his shoulders.

"Goff, deal with this. Blitz, put the girl in the clubhouse."

Neither of them moves.

"Now!" Darrin barks. "All of you, back to work." Packers jump into action, pulling out their chairs and aligning themselves back on either side of the tables. Scales start weighing, bags are packed, and shipments sorted.

I move to Darrin, treading carefully with the hatred in his expression. "Where's this shipment headed?" I ask.

Darrin raises his chin. While Darrin meets my height, he's all lean muscle—thinner. The hallows of his cheeks are more gaunt than I've seen before. He ignores my question.

"We have security items to discuss. Raven, another drug lord across the state line in Alabama, is encroaching on our territory. We meet in the clubhouse in an hour."

I nod, a swallow working its way down my throat. Spinning on my heels, I turn to the door and leave the warehouse. Fresh night air slams into me, and I gulp it down while power walking to my cabin.

Each step is quicker than the last. Stars overhead shine through the trees, speckles of constellations and far-off wishes never granted. Never for me.

Despite the cooler summer air and the breeze kicking up through the trees, sweat beads on my upper lip and I swipe at it. Week-old stubble grazes my hands, and I bat away another drop of perspiration dripping down the side of my temple.

Plowing into my front door, I slam it. My breathing becomes heavier, and a strangled choking noise wrestles itself from my mouth. I cover my lips, taking several steps forward, and stop at my small drawing desk.

In one fell swoop, I toss the materials there. Hands destroying the neatly arranged cups of items and filled pads.

Charcoal sticks and drawing pencils clank to the floor while sketch pad papers float in the air. They dip and glide as sketches disappear in the dark cabin and cover the wooden floor.

I stare down at them. Ash-colored eyes stare back at me, boring into me until a sour, bitter tang in my mouth drives me for water.

I fill a cup and down the whole glass in two gulps, then place the empty glass in the sink and rest my arms on the counter. My gaze flicks to the door of the cabin, then flutters closed as I take a deep breath in through my nose and blow out. My stomach churns, but I steel my grimace, striding back to the door.

Pencils crunch and charcoal breaks under my boot, and I spare one last glance. My boot print stomps out those silver eyes before I stalk through the door.

Chapter 16
Fleur

"So you and Adam are ..." River asks, placing several oranges in her reusable bag. We move away, on to the next booth ripe for the picking.

I'd seen signs for the Ruin Farmer's Market for a month or two since I moved here and always wanted to go. Finally, a Saturday arrived when Adam wasn't working at the house, and I committed to going. Unfortunately, he had something else to do today.

But it was the perfect opportunity to have River over to the farmhouse to look at the progress before she drove us to the farmer's market.

It's everything I imagine a small-town market to be, and I have to bury the feeling of wanting to capture this in a photo.

Held in the library's parking lot, local farmers, vendors, artists, and more have tents set up here. People roam freely over the array of homemade items. Even the local coffee shop has a table, the aroma of freshly ground beans overpowering many of the smells.

Piles of heirloom tomatoes, plump fruits, and crisp heads of lettuce are all plucked from their stands by a large number of community people, and it's almost like a race to see who can get the most before noon. I swear the whole town must be here.

River picks up a woven basket next to the table of hand-crafted soaps I'm currently sniffing. She eyeballs me, not forgetting I haven't answered her almost question.

"Adam and I what?" I ask, stalling to answer.

She rolls her eyes at me. "Oh, come on, Fleur. Are y'all together or what?"

Together. I hate that word. I was together with Chris for nine years.

Being together didn't stop him.

I pause with the lavender and thyme soap to my nose and immediately place it back on the table. I don't do lavender. "We haven't exactly had that conversation. Right now, I'm enjoying getting to know him. But I just got out of a long relationship that ended badly. I'd have to have someone sweep me off my feet in order to move on so soon."

"I see," she says, paying an older lady for the basket.

Glimpsing her expression, lips tucked into a thin line and eyes darting around like she can't decide where to look, I ask, "Do you know him well?"

"Adam?"

"Yeah."

"Not really. Not anymore. My brother does, though. They used to hang out a lot together. But where my brother stepped into the Jackpot world, Adam steered clear. Don't think Liam would let him if he tried."

She smiles, rubbing her arms as a rumble rolls past the road lined with the tents, and several motorcycles pull into the parking lot. I glance around. Everyone's fixed on the group of five men, each on their bike. One by one, they return back to their work as if this is something they're used to. River, however, keeps her attention locked on them.

Her eyes are somber and her lashes wet with tears. She stares and stares, blinking only once.

The men get off their bikes and load up a few pre-purchased crates. Crates of fresh produce mostly. In awe, I watch as these large burly men gather food and strap it to their bikes as if they were tricycles with pink baskets carrying their precious dolls or stuffed animals.

A person whips by me, and before I have time to realize River has moved, she's halfway across the parking lot, determined. With each step, she emphasizes her march, her long legs stomping toward the men.

One of the brawny men—cause aren't they all—spots her and turns in her direction. He taps his hand over the arm of another man, and he too looks at River charging at them. They both laugh while scouring her body.

Slinging my reusable bags full of my own farmer's market finds, I jolt into a brisk walk to follow, catching up to her as she asks, "Where is he? Is he here?"

She hasn't asked anyone in particular, and she scans the tents and crowds where a few of the men have walked off. The two men who saw her coming step into her, towering over her.

River is tall. Well, taller than me, and I'm about average. For them to stare down at her like she's a bug under their obnoxiously large boots ... well, I'm not sure it matters. She meets them stare for stare.

"River. Finally decide to give me a shot?" a tall younger guy with a dark goatee and greasy face says.

She glares at him, while townspeople pass by, ignoring the conversation.

"Bug off, Tilt." But her eyes soften after her snap back.

They flick down to the parking lot gravel, and she kicks at some pebbles before eyeing them again. "I just want to know ..."

"River." A loud voice booms from several feet away.

I gravitate to that voice, motivated to find it. Seek it out. My legs suddenly feel off balance when my gaze lands on him. I find myself holding my breath as he strides over.

Thundering legs take massive steps in my—our—direction, erasing the distance. With each step, the hairs rise on my arms and around to the nape of my neck.

Liam's black boots and black jeans are standard, but his dark red flannel catches me by surprise and my eyes widen when it blows open, exposing a gray V-neck. All of his long hair is down today, the wind blowing a few strands in his face, which he promptly pushes away. Two rings and a leather bracelet wrap his wrist on the hand he moves to the back of his neck.

I can't move. Can't focus.

Why does someone like him have to be so attractive?

Liam stops in front of River, with me slightly to the side. His focus is wholly on her, like I'm not even here. He's rugged and intense, but that doesn't stop his sharp expression from lessening when he sees her.

"He's not here," he says.

She sniffles, and I move a hand to her shoulder. The movement snags his notice and when his gaze drifts over to me, he bristles.

What the ...

He shifts on his boots, the deep treads leaving marks the size of a bear paw in the pea-sized gravel.

"Fleur." He grumbles my name in a short tone, his posture going more rigid when he says it. If that's even possible.

"Liam. Tell me, please, how is he?" River brings his attention back to her. She's folded both of her hands around her mouth and nose as if she's whispering a prayer to them. I can't help but notice her trembling hands, and I glare at these assholes, who have her brother so wrapped up in addiction he won't leave their side. Won't get help in order to have a better relationship with his sister.

"He's okay, River. I'm watching out for him," Liam says.

The snort that comes out of my mouth actually burns the back of my throat, and a wave of heat rushes through me at his words. Watching out for him? In what universe did he think *he* was watching out for anyone?

He returns the sentiment with a sluggish grunt of his own. It's unnerving and my breath hitches when his glare pins me in place.

"Thanks, Liam," River says. She tilts her head to the rows of tents we have yet to look at. "Let's go, Fleur. I see Mrs. Nell, and I need to tell her about the antique set we just got at the shop."

She marches back off the way she came, her hands swiping under her eyes.

Liam holds my stare for a beat before I turn, ready to dart behind her and finish my shopping.

Deft fingers wrap around my wrist with a tingle that seers along my skin, and I shiver. I search for the source, down to where a large hand circles my arm.

Liam's teeth grit together. Clenched so hard I can hear them grinding among the market's chatter. I pull hard, but he doesn't let go.

"What ..." I rasp, my mouth suddenly dry and unable to form words.

"You need to stop." Liam growls at me. Growls.

"Stop what?" My cheeks are red. I just know it by the way my face feels like it's burning.

His fingers move briefly over the two rubber bands nestled

on my wrist. His gaze goes from them to me, and his jaw twitches. "Just stop. You know nothing about us. Comments and snide remarks will get you killed."

I flinch at his words because he's right. I'm not being smart. My heart picks up speed and I swallow, and he tracks the gulp.

I can't stand it, though. The look of longing in River's eyes as she talks about her lost brother. Except that's the thing. He isn't lost. He lives here. He's alive. Choosing to live a life buried in Jackpot and working for a man seemingly untouchable. It's not fair, and it makes me angry.

I pull at my wrist again, whimpering when he still doesn't release me. Quick, shallow breaths make it feel like I can't breathe. *Are my toes numb?*

"Okay," I say, tugging once again, and he finally lets me go. I take a few steps back as soon as I'm released, my eyes glued to his. I rub at my wrist where his fingers set fire to my skin. The pads of my fingers trail over the rubber bands there, and I twirl them between the tips.

Liam lowers his head to one side, studying me. Feeling the summer Mississippi heat, I reach back and flick my hair over my shoulder, letting the cool breeze caress my neck where drips of sweat make their way down my back.

"Where's Adam?"

My lips part, taken aback by his question. Although, I made no move to leave when he let me go. Maybe he thought I wanted to talk, which I don't.

"Working," I snap, and the corner of his mouth twitches. "What are you doing here? I didn't realize motorcycle gangs frequented farmer's markets."

"We aren't—" He pauses, suppressing another growl. "Picking up supplies for home."

"And where's that exactly?"

He gives me a look like he can't believe I'd asked that question. Because ... well, because he most definitely wasn't going to tell me. I flash him a smirk in return, but it fades just as fast when I remember what he told me about snide comments. I'm guessing annoyed facial expressions count?

"Hey, Fleur." River runs up to me, panting. "Mrs. Nell is going to come look at the bedroom set at the shop. Do you want to come? Or if you're not finished, I can swing back by and take you home."

"Oh, um, yeah, swing back by. I still have a few more tents to check out. Take your time. I'll be fine." I offer her a sweet smile and she turns to Liam, her gaze volleying between us before turning on her heel.

Liam steps backward, eyes lingering on what appears to be my nose, then he takes another step back. And another. Each one with his concentration still on me. I squirm under his stare, my heart stammering. But I raise my chin, turning to the several rows of tents I didn't get to check out yet.

Walk away, Fleur. Do it.

I have to give myself a pep talk. I'm not sure why I want to linger. To observe him in this awkward element. My body resists leaving even though my head is complaining that I move.

At first, it's a shuffle, but then, as my feet get farther away, it practically becomes a run. I sprint to the tent I left off at and don't look back.

※ ※ ※

River dropped me back off at home about an hour ago, and I managed to shove the excessive amount of produce I bought into my fridge before pulling out a frozen burrito. I know—the irony isn't lost on me. Honestly, though, I was drained. Not only from the beating sun that could cook chicken wings on the sidewalk but emotionally.

To go from a solid feel-good morning with a friend, to unease prickling my senses and churning my gut with my interaction with Liam. Unfortunately, that still didn't stop me from getting mouthy.

What is it about him? He makes my skin crawl, but I'm not sure it's in the icky wrong way. I shake my head, intent on running a bath and enjoying the basket of fresh oranges I bought.

My jaw falls open.

Crap.

I turn the bath water off and rush into the kitchen, my braid whipping me in the back as I slide to a stop.

Damn it. I left my basket of oranges on the ground at the farmer's market. I told myself I was going to set them down to give my aching arms a rest while I waited for River to come back, but I must have forgotten to grab them.

After digging around for an apple instead, I pad back to my bathroom, stripping off the jean shorts and white tank top I wore today. White wasn't the best idea as I purchased and sampled berries. Dark red and blue juice is splattered across the shirt, and I toss it into the ever-growing pile of laundry I haven't tackled. It's the one area of the house that hasn't been finished yet, so I've been slacking on it lately.

I wash up and take ten minutes to relax before climbing out, slide on a pair of overalls, and redo my braid. Long hair during renovations has been a pain, so I've been keeping it tied up most of the time.

A knock sounds at the door, and my pulse skips at the sudden noise—I'm not expecting anyone. I toss the ChapStick I was applying into the top drawer and dart past the box in the hallway from Michigan I have yet to open.

The front door is original to the house and there's no peep-hole, so I throw open the door to find Adam.

His dark hair is combed back, not the typical tousled look he sports when he's working and running his hands through it. A light green V-neck hugs his lean build and in his hand is—

What?

He's holding my crate of oranges. The ones I'd left at the market.

"Hey! These were just sitting at your front door. Did you leave them outside?"

Did I leave them outside?

No. "I didn't. I left them at the market by accident."

"Oh, well, River must have dropped them off for you," Adam says, moving past me with the crate and into the kitchen to set it down on the island.

More tingling blazes up my spine, and I shiver despite the unbearable heat. I peer both ways down the dirt road, over the hayfields that ebb and flow across the flat country terrain. But it's then I hear it. Over the clinking of ice into a glass from behind me. Over the wind hitting the new chime I purchased last week. Over the rustling oak leaves in the front yard.

Faint and in the distance.

The rumble of a motorcycle.

Chapter 17
Liam

I hate oranges. I've hated them since I can remember, but seeing the way Fleur picked out each sphere. The way she cradled the bright fruit in her hand before deeming it satisfactory for her crate—made me want it.

Why I'm compelled to draw the vile fruit is beyond me.

In fact, I hate blondes. Blondes with braids. Braids I want to wrap around my fist and yank. Yank that perfect tan body to me.

I tried to ignore her when River first approached. Pretended not to notice her until it became glaringly obvious and then ... then I lost the battle.

Hell.

I'd watched Fleur from the time she twirled around and ran from me.

Good. I'd thought.

But I made it all of two steps before seeking out her long braid, loose and hanging down her back. That mouth. Her attitude.

Stupid and reckless.

She doesn't understand who she's dealing with. And I'm positive Adam hasn't told her—won't tell her. His own self-preservation, or maybe his pride, won't let him.

I shrug, shading in the shadow of the orange sitting in a crate.

I told myself to leave the oranges alone, let them get run over by a truck or perhaps be taken by another person. But no. She'd left them there. So instead of strapping my share of the produce for the compound on the back of my bike, I ditched it with Tilt and strapped the crate of oranges to it.

I hate that I'm attracted to her. I hate that I want what my brother has. Or does he? I'm not sure she's his. Knowing Adam, he's inserted himself into her life, liking the fact she has renovations to accomplish on that farmhouse.

The farmhouse I lingered at.

I stood at the door, peering at the old refinished wood, wondering if she heard my bike approach. It took me two whole minutes to decide if I should knock or not.

I didn't.

I plopped the crate down, picked up the one orange that bounced out, and tried to escape down the stairs while I slid the disgusting fruit into my pocket. I was already down the road when I saw Adam's new truck pull into her place in my bike mirrors.

I don't even care.

The buzz of my phone causes me to darken my shade too much and I growl at it. Pushing up from my seat at the dining table, I rip the phone from my back pocket.

It's Darrin. He wants a meet in the clubhouse in twenty minutes.

Organizing my charcoal sticks and pencils, the ones I salvaged from the floor the other night, I slide them into the container. The plastic container was the *one* thing my mother

123

gave me in relation to my drawing. Everything else I've had to figure out myself.

I shove the papers together into a stack and move them to the rest of my drawing paper before stalking into the kitchen to wash up and grab a glass of water. The pipes groan when the water turns on and the faucet spits before a steady stream finally dumps fresh, cold water into the glass.

Faster than normal, I guzzle the water, tasting the slightly metallic tang that is unique to the compound. I'm hungry but keeping Darrin waiting isn't an option.

Shaking my head, I leave the orange casting a shadow on the granite, which causes my hand to twitch at my side with that need to catch the perfect light on paper. My leather jacket hangs on the coat rack, and I pull it down to wrap around me. I swallow, do up the zipper, and take a deep breath as I head for the clubhouse.

The Break Room sits toward the back of the main clubhouse area. It's not what you think when you picture a break room for the average office. There isn't a vending machine and free drip coffee with a few round tables and chairs. No. The name Break comes from something else entirely.

It resembles a lounge. Black leather couches and chairs stand in the room. Muted lights highlight a long stainless-steel bar fully stocked with all the liquor and beer you could have the hankering for. Usually, one of Darrin's lackeys is behind the bar. Working for money he's ultimately going to return when he buys his Jackpot.

Two poles stand straight on each side of the room, each occupied by women dancing. A cool summer breeze from the cracked windows blows Blitz's cigarette smoke into my face before it's sucked back out into the night air. He watches the woman from the other day wrapped around the pole with a smirk on his face. His legs are spread wide as he relaxes back on the couch, hands palming his thighs.

Tears stream down the woman's face, her black hair snarled. She's violently shaking as she's forced to work. Forced to dance to pay the debt her now dead boyfriend incurred.

"Going to take off that coat, Liam? Stay awhile," Blitz says, his back to me as he groans out something inaudible, inching closer to the pole. "Or do you not want to show off that new sleeve you finished the other day? Jay told me you finally had it completed."

He snickers, and I turn away.

The tattoo sleeve was one I started five years ago with a good friend. The original plans I had for the piece morphed into something different over time, but I finally decided to finish the beast on my right arm.

"I'm shocked you care, Blitz."

Several of the ladies walk around in their cut-off shorts and ripped tees. Their job here is to bring drinks to the guys or service them in other ways.

Most of the men won't commit, though. They prefer to take their pick of the handful of women always hanging around.

Darrin has this rule. Unless you claim a woman by marrying her, there's zero tie to you. Any of the asswipes here can take and use as they please. That's why Snape married his old lady. Didn't want anyone else with her, so he claimed her.

Claim. As though another man's claim is the only reason to keep your hands off a woman. Disgust roils in my stomach with every tear that drips down that girl's face.

Many women here enjoy it, though. Food, shelter, and drugs—all for free. They're usually better off than if they were outside the compound.

One of those women, Roe, sways her hips to the music, eyes lingering on me. She moves down the other pole in the room, opening her legs offering an invitation, but I'm not interested. Neither is Darrin. Haven't seen a girl in years who can turn his head.

Another girl, young from the looks of it, brings me a beer. Her light brown skin, lighter than Darrin's, glimmers under the soft light. Her eyes are bright blue when they meet mine, not yet torn down by this world, by these men.

"Snape said this was your favorite," she says.

I take the beer, the pads of my fingertips relishing the cool sweat dripping off the bottle.

"Thank you."

She retreats to the bar and slides in next to Trip, who wraps her in his arms.

"Liam." Darrin's voice breaks through the haze of music. He's propped up in one of the leather chairs, elbows leaning on his thighs. The ring on his pinky finger glistens with an emerald-colored stone that appears surprisingly feminine. His eyes bore into me as I stride over, taking a sip of my beer. The chilled alcohol slides down to ease the burn in my chest.

"What's going on, D?"

He snorts, then motions for Blitz, Snape, and Trip to come over as well. Roe twirls on the pole, and she bends over in front of Darrin's face. He glances away.

"Alabama is going to be a problem. Their dealers have been spotted on our turf. They're poaching our users across state lines."

"Let's take them out," Snape says.

I shake my head. "Gotta be smart about it. Are they feeding into the national shipments? Don't want to go to war with those contributing like us."

Darrin leans back, the chair creaking as he settles deep into it. "They're a new player. They aren't part of the national relationship. The Cartel isn't dealing with them like they do us. I talked to a brother in Chicago, and he's sending me their formula for it, dirty." His blue eye shifts over to me. "There's demand there. Even more so outside of Ruin and surrounding Mississippi. We have the means."

Blitz practically salivates. "Make our product better, D. They won't even want the Alabama shit. Plan B is we kill them."

I stiffen. Dirty Jackpot means the powder will be cut with other potentially more harmful substances.

"I've secured a small shipment of weapons from New York for this exact reason," Darrin answers.

I bite my tongue so hard it bleeds. But that still doesn't stop me from asking, "New York?"

"Luka Morozov."

"Oh boy." Blitz cackles, downing the last of his growler. He wipes at his mangled mustache with the back of his hand and lets out a belch. "Never thought we'd go as high as the Mafia."

There's no way in hell I want the Mafia involved in this business.

"Is that a smart idea?" I ask.

All three heads snap to me, and I level them each with a stare. Folding my arms across my chest, I shrug.

Blitz snorts while sticking his hand down his pants and I narrow my eyes at Darrin, who kicks him in the shin. He tries, unsuccessfully, to stand up straight.

"It's a small shipment. An insurance policy. This will make us richer, boys." Darrin raises his glass and we each do the same, most of them sloshing over the side and landing on the already sticky floor. "To getting lucky," he says.

I take my sip before turning to toss my bottle in the trash. It lands with a loud clank against the bottom of the barrel. "I'm off to bed. Need to check on dealers early in the morning."

Darrin rises, extending his hand to mine. "Keep me posted on tomorrow."

I nod, taking his hand in mine, and he pulls me in for a slap on the back. It's a hug. The big baby.

Pulling away, I smile and raise my hand to Blitz, who is going for round two with a different girl. Snape yells something about the music needing to be louder, and I step out of the room as the bass rattles the clubhouse. It fades as I exit the building.

A few men work to clean up the firepit area. Many of the packers are leaving the warehouse and returning to their bunkhouses for the night until they start all over in the morning.

The Mississippi night air is humid. Thick and sticky, as if I could pick out the moisture by hand. Dampness settles in my nose, the earthy notes mixing with the stench of body odor from the men passing by. Tilting my head up to suck in a fresh breath, I eye the full moon. The rocky and cratered texture pins me with memories of the dimpled peel of the orange on my counter.

I hate it.

Chapter 18
Fleur

Four Months Ago

Traffic in Grand Rapids is disgustingly congested at times. After spending the afternoon with my mother shopping, my feet are tired, and I want to curl up with a cup of coffee. Snow still dusts the roads, and despite the glaring sun and blue skies, the temperature barely made it past forty degrees today.

The plan was to meet my father for dinner downtown, but both my mother and I were over the day.

While driving out of the city, I call our favorite pizza place in Rockford, planning to surprise Chris for dinner. He's been working from home today even though it's a Saturday. He won't admit it, but he's throwing as many extra hours as possible into his schedule. I think he's saving for a ring. At least I hope he is.

My heart flutters at the thought, and I glance down at my left hand that grips the steering wheel. Nine years. We celebrated nine years over a month ago, and while I thought we'd be married by now, I'm content with our life.

The house we purchased sits on a busy road in a small community. Both Chris and I have talked about moving before having kids. Unfortunately, the housing market where we live is awful and interest rates are too high right now to consider purchasing another house.

It's hard, though. Our friends from high school, the group we always surround ourselves with, are slowly getting married and settling down. Logically, I know it's not a competition to see who can end up in a secure marriage and pop out babies the fastest but ...

I pull into the pizza shop, noting it's busier than normal. Probably with others who have been running errands all day, not wanting to cook either.

The owner, Rob, pins me with a judgy look when I pay for the two pepperoni pies. Pretty sure he remembers we picked up pizza only five nights ago. I flash him a grin and shrug my shoulder.

Raising my hand to open the door, I head back out to the parking lot. The pizza in the car makes my mouth water so I slide open the top of the box to pick a greasy pepperoni off the top. It's official. I eat too much pizza.

Most of the time, I can get away with bringing leftovers into work. However, Chris's mom often makes snide comments about our takeout. I believe she's looking for me to make home-made meals for her son.

It wasn't my plan to forgo a four-year college after high school, but Chris bought his house right after graduation, and we didn't want to start our life in too much debt. When the opportunity to work for Chris's parents presented itself, I jumped in with both feet. I enjoy my job, though. Mostly, I deal with customer service for them, but I feel like part of the family.

This job is something I can do with my high school diploma and still have time to devote to learning photography. Chris gave me my dream camera last Christmas, and I melted at his thoughtfulness.

Our little community sits off a four-lane road, but the kids are still outside, playing as if in their own little world while their parents sit in the driveways, sipping drinks. I smile at them as I round the corner to our home.

The plants I have in the two cream pots on the stoop are twigs now, having been destroyed by winter. The siding needs a good power wash, but the front door is inviting.

I pull in behind an unfamiliar car, grateful I grabbed two pizzas in case Chris has his buddies over. The black Ford Focus has a GVSU sticker on the rear window and I rack my brain, trying to remember who we know from Grand Valley State University.

The pizza warms my hands as I walk to the door, fumbling with my keys. Trying not to drop the precious pepperoni is my only goal as I wrestle to pluck the right key from the ring, but I manage to open the storm door, then the heavy wooden one.

"Hey! It's just me," I call out, dropping my keys in the bowl on the island. I set the pizzas down and yank off my coat, then toss it on the mini church pew that doubles as our entryway bench. It was a flea market find and I'm slightly obsessed.

I don't hear anything, and I glance into the living room, noticing an unfamiliar black coat tossed on the couch. I spin, searching the house. It's not large, so I'm not sure where he would be.

A sound comes from the back of the house—from our bedroom. I squint at the closed door and an odd sensation wriggles up my spine as I pad toward it.

The shower is on. I can hear it from the en suite despite the closed doors. Brows furrowed, I push into the bedroom. The bed is still made from this morning, but a pink purse lies sprawled out on the end.

I gulp.

Chris's laughter sounds from the bathroom, muffled by the sound of the falling shower. I turn toward it. Steam wafts under the crack between the door and the bedroom carpet.

A pit forms in my stomach as I inch forward, my hand hovering over the door handle.

"Right there, Chris. Don't stop." A high-pitched female voice mewls.

I freeze. Heat flames in my cheeks, and I can feel the blood drain from my face. My mouth falls open as I stare at the door. Embarrassment and shame have me taking two steps backward, my eyes still glued to the bathroom, where Chris lets out another grunt.

He ...

He's ...

I turn, stumbling into the bed, my face planting next to the pink bag and the waft of—what the hell—lavender? Numb, I push up, bolting for the bedroom door, my head taking one last glimpse toward the bathroom. With one quick jerk, I slam the door to the bedroom behind me.

Our bedroom. Our haven.

He was my first, and he was going to be my only. Forever.

The confusion from that first flash of the bag on our bed is eroding and I'm falling. I run to the door, shove my feet back into my boots, and I dart out the door without my coat.

The first tear blindsides me as I lean on my car door, trying to take in breaths. Pressure and pain crush my chest, and I clench my teeth, determined to get out of here.

He ...

He was ...

I back out of the driveway, narrowly missing the mailbox as I swing back on the street. The last thing in my rearview mirror is that damn sticker.

I'm so naïve. I'm so stupid. How did I not see this?

I grip the wheel, shock shaking me to my core. I can't stop fidgeting. My heart pounds while every car on the road is a blur around me. Through the crippling ache in my chest, I manage to avoid a complete breakdown.

What do I do? Why did I just leave?

I should've stormed in there. I should've knocked on the door. I might have done ... something. Anything.

Why does it feel like I did something wrong? I went from bringing dinner home to my future husband to feeling like a stranger in my own house.

My muscles are taut as I stare straight ahead, speeding to the safest place I know.

I'm utterly devastated.

A text message flashes across the screen on my phone, but I can't bring myself to read it. Ironically, I can't even bring myself to feel rage at this moment.

My childhood neighborhood comes into view and instant relief floods through me at the sight of my parents' vehicles there. I fumble out of my car, my knees shaking as I reach the front door. The cold temperatures dip lower as the sun sets over the horizon, and I shiver while I knock. It's pathetic and weak, just like me.

How did I miss this? My thoughts vacillate between trying to search my memories for red flags and disbelief—maybe I misheard?

The door opens and my dad stands there.

"Fleur?" he says. "What are you doing here? Sweetheart, what's wrong? Where's your coat?"

My dad's voice soothes the panic bubbling in my chest, and it eviscerates the hold I have over my tears. A sob bursts from my throat. Followed by another, then another.

I fall forward, the scent of my father's aftershave bringing me home. I shudder as he wraps his arms around me, and I release a flood of tears on his sweater.

※ ※ ※

Present Day

I stare at the box on my kitchen table. The memories of that day are still fresh in my mind when I look at it. My dad held me, broken, for hours after I arrived at my parents' house. My mother made coffee, and I worked through what I was going to do.

My whole life was in the house. Wrapped up with Chris.

As much as my mother told me it wasn't my fault, that he's the asshole, I couldn't help but feel the need to run away. Far away.

I spent that abysmal night ignoring every phone call from Chris and searching for a place to disappear. One result yielded the *Top Ten Smallest Towns in the South* blog post, and after scanning the photos, I found Ruin.

Old Hillside was the only place in town to stay and when I clicked over to their website, they were hiring. It sealed the deal.

Circles. That's what I walk around the table as I stare some more at the box. When I walked up to my front porch with the brown package sitting there, I had a feeling about who had sent it. Took three hours for me to bring the box inside, and it's been in the front entryway for a week now.

He doesn't have my new address, so it took me a minute to realize I had my mail forwarded to this address through the post office. I guess he assumed it would get to me.

I left almost everything behind. Tossed a few items into a duffel bag that my mom went to retrieve for me. There was no way I was going back into that house. But it left me starting over.

I don't want to open it. The mirror in the corner of the room captures my reflection and I pause, sighing. The box needs to go. Adam is coming over later today. For the first time in several weeks, he's coming over to chill and watch a movie. He's been busy and unavailable lately, but I told myself in August I was committed to moving on. Or trying to.

Sliding the scissors through the tape on top of the box, a hum of peacefulness slithers through me. Maybe I need this. This will be healing.

Relaxing, I pull back each brown flap until I'm peering into the top of the box.

A letter sits on top of my black camera bag, and I roll up the sleeve of my cardigan to fiddle with the rubber bands. They instantly ease my anxiety. A tear takes off down my face and I snap a band, closing my eyes at each sting. Allowing the pain to ground me, to pull me deeper, shifting my worry.

The envelope has his handwriting on it. My name is in all capital letters because that's how he writes. I swallow the lump in my throat while removing the letter.

I can't do this.

The pads of my fingers skim the soft paper and I turn it over in my hand, flipping it several times while I mull over what he could have to say.

A knock sounds at the door, and I shove the letter back in the box, then move the whole thing to my bedroom. The front door opens as I shut my bedroom door, and Adam strolls in past the hall.

"Hey!" I say, tucking my hands into the back pockets of my jeans as I come back down the hall.

He doesn't answer me, though. Instead, he sulks over to the couch and plops down, letting out a deep sigh.

That's new. Usually, Adam is impossibly upbeat.

"You all right?" I ask, moving to kneel in front of him. His hair is disheveled, and his head hangs low. When he lifts his face to look at me, I gasp.

A large black and blue shiner bruises his left eye—the lid swollen. Dark circles camp underneath his eyes, the paleness of his skin creating an even starker contrast between the coloring.

"Adam, what happened?" I grip his knees and peer up at him. His eyes are dull and his face gaunt.

"Nothing. Had a run-in with a few of Darrin's men." Defeat shines in his eyes.

"Did you call the police?" I ask.

"No."

"Why not? Gosh, they can't get away with randomly punching you in the face." I pull at his arm. "Let's go right now. I'll drive."

"Leave it alone, Fleur," he snaps, and I narrow my eyes at him.

I don't want to leave it alone. This is getting out of control. I hesitate before standing and go to the freezer for a bag of peas. There's more going on here. Somewhere in the back of my mind, I understand that.

I slowly turn back to the living room, watching Adam type out a message on his phone. He doesn't want me to know and I'm not sure why. But I can relate to the struggle. It's the same way I don't want to tell him the man I loved found me replaceable. It's embarrassing and stirs the insecurity around in my stomach.

Tossing the peas in the air twice, I sit next to Adam, curling into him on the couch, and I press the frozen veggies to his eye. He wraps his hand around mine, holding it as I hold the peas to his head.

"Thank you, Fleur." He gazes at me, and I squirm under his study. I offer him a smile but jolt up.

"Coffee?"

"Sure," he says, leaning back against the couch and closing his eyes.

I piddle around with the coffee maker for longer than I need to while watching him out of the corner of my eye. I can't seem to shake the roiling sensation fluttering through my belly.

After fixing both cups of coffee, I snuggle on the couch and toss the remote into his lap. He scrolls through the app and picks out some action movie, and I settle in taking sips every few minutes or so.

We're about halfway through the movie when Adam pulls me farther into him, rubbing my thigh. Tingles spread with each of his smooth touches, and I try to convince myself I'm ready for this. He's been understanding about my reluctance—even though he doesn't know why. I want someone to want me. Need to feel something other than humiliation. But am I ready to edge past our status of friends?

Don't balk at this.

I nuzzle into his side, my head finding the crook of his arm. I smile up at him, and that's when he moves. Tilting my chin up further, he leans down and presses his lips to mine. They are soft and subtle. A rush of blood to my head makes me dizzy as his kiss deepens. His tongue presses into my mouth and he moans. I meet his kiss, opening my mouth to him, searching. I want those fireworks, something to hint at the fact I'm moving on and it's worth it.

Adam positions himself so he leans over me, and stroking hands roam up my side.

The ache to feel what he's feeling grates at me, and I chase it. I press back into him, wrapping my hands around his head and tugging at his hair. He groans at my fervor, moving his mouth from my lips to my neck.

I can do this.

Adam rips away from me panting, his eyes pinning me. "Fleur, I want so much from you."

I reach up to pull him back to me but pause. With my nose in the air, I sniff. Adam's brow furrows, turning his face in the direction I'm smelling.

"What's wrong?" he asks.

"Do you smell smoke?"

Chapter 19
Liam

Stepping out on my front porch, the compound is a madhouse. The sun has finally set, and I can see the firepit roar to life for the evening. Several men dart to their bikes, and I'm missing something.

"Hey, Trip. Where's the fire, man?" I yell as he runs to his green Kawasaki.

He turns, running backward as he yells back, "Not there yet, but there will be at your brother's girl's house." He snickers at that and turns.

I blink, fear slowly pouring into my veins.

What the ...

In two steps, I'm off the porch, running to the clubhouse. I meet Blitz coming out with a backpack.

"What the hell is going on?" I demand.

"Liam." Darrin's voice booms from behind me, and I turn to find him with his leather jacket on and the keys to his car twirling in his hand.

"Darrin. What's going on?"

"We're making a move on your brother. He's been at each

establishment for the past several weeks, racking up more and more debt. Don't think I didn't notice the new truck." He strides forward, lowering his voice. "There's only so much you can do, Liam. Or would you like me to pay a visit to your grandparents?"

I stiffen, fighting the urge to cast my fist in his face. Like hell he'll go to my grandparents. I could kill Adam. All he had to do was put his head down and work hard, but he can't even do that.

Shit.

"What's your plan? I won't allow you to hurt him."

Darrin's eyes meet mine. Blue and brown hold my stare, and he doesn't even blink. Disgust rolls off his nose and he narrows his stance, spitting on the ground next to me. It doesn't faze me. I step up to him, and he meets my chest with his.

"I'm sending a message. Adam will pay for his stupidity. Don't get in my way, Liam."

"Let me come with you."

"No. You're too close to this. Stay here. Don't step out of line."

He turns to walk away. My hand twitches at my side with the desire to run to my bike. I yank my phone from my pocket and text Adam.

Where are you?

I pace the sidewalk to the clubhouse. Torn between my duty and my brother.

Damn it.

I run to my bike.

Chapter 20
Fleur

As soon as the word smoke is out of my mouth, the fire alarm goes off. Thick and gray it pours into the living room from down the back hallway. It's not even coming from the kitchen.

I jump up from the couch, rushing toward the smoke. Where the hell is that coming from? Did I leave a candle burning?

"Fleur!" Adam shouts, but I move anyway down the hall and to my bedroom. Plumes of dark smoke climb the walls, and I turn exactly as the crackling of wood sounds. How did it start here? And so quick—everything is catching so fast. The gray smoke turns into a glinting orange fire that rages over my head-board. It's hot, and I turn on my heels and run to the kitchen. I smack into Adam and he grabs my hand.

"We have to get out."

We take off to the front door, and I grab my cell phone off the table before we spill into the front yard. I gasp at the sight of my newly renovated home. Flames rapidly consume the walls, the reflections shimmering in each of the windows. The white wood siding turns to black with each lick of flame.

The smell of rancid smoke and burning wood invades my nostrils and I choke back a cough.

"Fleur, we need to leave. Come on." Adam pulls at me, but I can't move. I'm paralyzed by the sight of all I poured into this home falling around me. Beams crack and pop, with the heat getting hotter and hotter.

"We need to call the fire department." I fumble with my phone, tears threatening to spill faster than I have the hands to wipe them away.

A chuckle scares me from behind, and my phone flips out of my hand. I turn to see five men walking toward the house from the road. Behind them, their cars and bikes sit, and I let out a whimper.

No.

Adam steps up to them. "Did you do this, Blitz? Did you seriously—"

Blitz delivers a punch to the side of Adam's head, and he goes down. Sprawled out on the grass, he moans in a cry of pain.

"What the hell is wrong with you?" I scream at the men before falling beside Adam. Blood seeps from his nose as he tries to get up. Spitting, he rolls over, and another fist lands on his stomach. The sound of air rushing out of him makes me shiver and he coughs.

Wincing in pain, he grits out, "Fleur ..." I think for a moment he's going to tell me to run, to get out of here. Instead, he continues, "... help me."

Fire rages all around us, reflected in each of the men's eyes as they stare down at Adam. I reach for him, but—

"Take her," someone says. I jerk, turning to run, but a yank to the back of my shirt has me flying back into large arms. They wrap around me as I claw at the sweaty skin gripping me tight. He lifts me off the ground, and I thrash.

"Leave her alone. This is about me. This—"

Another blow to Adam's face has me flailing until the man loses his grip and I fall to the ground. The grass under my hands feels like a fresh spring of cool water compared to the heat blazing at my back.

Run, run, run, I tell myself, scrambling for purchase against the slick green. I slip, the tug on my ankle pulling me back down before I can fully stand. My foot kicks out behind me, connecting with a man's face. Refusing to turn to look, I crawl, panting and struggling not to collapse. Smoke fills my lungs, and I cough, trying to suck in another breath.

Too close. Too close to the blazing fire.

My hands clench around the grass. With large fistfuls, my fingernails dig into the dirt as if that will anchor me. Boots step into my vision, and I let out a wail as I'm torn up by my hair.

Crying out in pain, I reach for my head. A man's face hovers in front of mine, and I can almost taste the stench of his breath in my own. I clutch his wrists, trying to remove his hands from my hair. The scream lodged in my throat finally erupts as he spins me around and places me in a headlock.

More crackles and pops sound from the house, and I turn to see the roof cave-in before the man drags me backward down the driveway. Adam's body lies on the ground by my favorite oak tree. Unable to make out if he's moving or not, I shriek, calling out his name, but there's no response. The other four men turn from him and follow to where I'm being heaved toward a vehicle.

A man with silver teeth gets in my face and cups me between my thighs.

"I can't wait to play." The silver in his mouth widens into a large smile, and I flinch, clinging to any extra energy I can.

Lunging forward, I try to escape the headlock, effectively cutting off my air supply. I suck in a breath, gasping for air.

"No! Let me go!"

My mind is a muddled mess between fighting back and trying to understand. I can't make sense of what's happening. Why are they taking me?

Thoughts of Liam flash in my mind, and my eyes flick around to each man as they load themselves on their bikes, looking for him. He isn't here. Why would he allow this to happen to his brother?

The car door opens, and I'm turned around, glimpsing one last look across the hayfields rustling in the night wind. A faint light moving down the old service road flickers through the field. It's a single light, and I narrow my eyes watching a lone motorcycle barreling down the field before it stops abruptly. Too far away for the men to see as they try to load themselves and their supplies back into the car.

A hulking figure jumps off the bike, letting it fall to the dirt, and whips off his helmet. Liam's blond hair falls around his face, and I make out his hand swipe back through his hair.

Asshole. Who lets this happen?

Someone shoves at the back of my head, and I'm pushed into the car. My nose smacks into the other door, and with a crunch, blood gushes over my lips. I fight the urge to throw up as the warm metallic liquid seeps into my mouth. I move, huddling to one side of the car, and I reach for the other door handle before a sharp searing pain stabs into my leg.

The cool window cradles my lulled head. My cheek smooshes against the side of the window. My eyes are heavy, slowly closing with each heartbeat. I find the strength to shift my head, looking at the hayfield once more. Liam turns, the shadows of the night engulfing him. Away. He turns away.

I slowly drift and my body sways. The high of the drugs lifts and drops me like the swell of the waves on the ocean.

My mind flicks to the unread letter with my camera Chris sent. The words I'll never read from him. Was he sorry or did he only want to wish me well? Images of flames ravaging the envelope, ash replacing where my name was scrawled across the paper scroll in my mind.

I will never know.

* * *

Sweat drips on the concrete, and each drop speckles the dust-coated floor. *Two, four, six,* I count each one as it rolls off my face.

Pain was the first thing I felt waking in the cell. I must've been tossed in. Right onto the concrete floor covered in dirt and grime because with each breath, I grimace. My ribs are bruised.

When I first opened my eyes, I couldn't see anything but a white haze. But slowly, as I blinked and squinted through the cloudy blur, my surroundings became clear. Panic surged at first, especially when I saw I was alone. My thoughts immediately went to Adam lying unmoving on the grass outside my burning home—did they kill him? Is he okay? Please be okay.

I cried for what had to be an hour before I couldn't anymore. Emotionally, I'm drained, but more than that, physically, I'm struggling.

A rickety cot is tucked into the corner. One pillow and a thin blanket bunched in a ball sit on top. Both are so dirty that I'm here on the floor, tucked into myself.

I face the back wall, three of which are solid gray concrete, while the fourth is all bars. For a minute, I thought this was a bad dream or I had awakened onto a movie set about pirates.

Rust decorates the iron bars, the lock is the only section that doesn't seem to be withering away. Like it's been well oiled and cleaned for easy, quiet access.

I shudder.

I'm in shock. At least I have the wherewithal to understand that. Right?

The dull ache in my thigh has gotten worse. With each shiver, each jerk of movement, I wince at the throbbing from the needle puncture. Luckily, it seems whatever they injected me with is almost out of my system.

My tongue sticks to the roof of my mouth. There isn't any water in here, no food either, but I'm dehydrated. A headache rages behind my eyes, which are now swollen from my endless tears.

However, crying won't help me get out of here. And I've realized it won't do me any good to kick and scream. I'm locked in a jail cell—I'm not going anywhere.

So I take advantage of the fact I'm alone in a darkened cell. No one is here with me or interrogating me. *Rest*, I tell myself. Gather strength. It does no good to risk further injury trying to break out of iron bars.

Remaining in a fetal position on the floor, I work the problem in my head.

Clearly, it's them. Darrin and his crew. What will they do with me? Is it because of Adam?

A slick oil pools in my gut, coating my stomach with an acid burn that churns the more I dwell on what their plans may be. Memories from the night on the Trace, their faces and remarks, replay vividly in my mind. All of them except for Liam.

Ugh. Him.

The image of Liam rolling in on his motorcycle but

choosing not to intervene flashes through my mind and I scowl. Who lets this happen to their brother? Or me, for that matter.

Granted, he doesn't know me, but we've talked. He helped me change my tire on the side of the road, for goodness' sake. He and those men could've taken me then if they wanted to. So I go back to, what has changed now?

The cell is quiet, save for the loud drumming rain overhead. I'm not sure how I can hear a rainstorm below ground, most likely in a basement, but I do. The rich, damp scent of fresh rain mixes with the mildew stench I'm breathing so close to the concrete floor.

Between the myriad of smells and my pounding headache, I want to throw up. I huddle together, despite the wicked heat in here. The humidity plasters my shirt against my skin, and I'm keenly aware of how gross I am.

I reach up, swipe at my caking makeup, and pull my hand away, inspecting it. Ash flakes on my fingers as I rub them together. Running a hand through my hair, I pull down the strands to find more white ash. I fight more tears with every fleeting thought of my home.

It's only a house. I repeat to myself. *It's only a house.*

But the words do little to curb the sinking feeling in my chest. It was my fresh start. Something for *me* in the chaos of my life in the last several months. I stare down at my empty hands. And now it's gone. Burned down to ash and charred wood.

My wrists still sport two rubber bands, and I sigh. They both stick there, calling to me. I'm out of control again. My life is literally out of my hands. I pluck the strings, playing myself a tune of pain over and over until my wrist is raw with raised meat-colored welts. The sting bites into my flesh and I breathe easier.

A clanking sound gives me pause, and I jerk up to sit, sure

to keep my knees tucked into me. The concrete wall is cool against my back as I move to lean against it. The sound of metal screeching makes me want to rip my hair out as it grates at my pounding head.

A large, tall man with a long beard pulled into a ponytail saunters down the dimly lit hall. The two other cells across from mine rattle with his thundering steps. He steps into the light and his soulless dark eyes lift to mine, studying me. Gut large and round, he chuckles and the sound slithers through me.

I know that sound.

I lift my chin to get a better view. He's familiar. One of the men who stopped while I was on the side of the road and gave me a hard time. More like gave me a very clear picture of what he would do if he got his hands on me. And right now, he's standing outside my cell with the same focused and leering stare plastered on his face.

He fumbles with a key in his hand, turning it over between his grease-stained fingers before sliding it into the lock. A smug twitch lifts the corner of his mouth. He looks at me as he slides the key in, and he licks his lips when it clicks. As much as I dreamed of those bars being unlocked for the past hour, I want nothing more than to slam them shut, blocking him.

Feeling along the wall, I rise, using the chilled stone for support. My knees wobble, threatening to buckle as the ear-screeching sound of metal bars opening echoes off the cell walls.

I press my back to the far wall, as far from him as possible. But it's no use. There's nowhere to run.

"W-where am I?" I stammer, my voice cracking from my dry mouth. The words are sluggish and tumble from my lips in a slow slur. I tense. Perhaps I'm not as recovered from the injection after all.

"Doesn't matter where you are, darlin'. Only matters what you're going to do while you're here," the man says. His voice is laced with poison, and his tone hovers above a whisper but grates in my ears as if he yelled it out.

He stalks for me, and I shake, eyes widening as he reaches out to grab my arm. Pressure is immediate as he grips me. Each pad of his finger squeezes there, leaving bruises in his wake.

I yank on my arm, faltering when his vice grip bears down even harder and pulls a scream of pain from me. Stubby fingers grab my chin, the smell of cigarette smoke lacing them. He strums my lips, coaxing my mouth to open for his pointer finger, but I bob my head from side to side, trying to avoid his disgusting hand.

"Boss wants a word with you. But he didn't say I couldn't play first."

I growl, angling my knee to try to deliver a kick to his groin, but a chilling laugh snakes its way through the cell. I wiggle, trying to remove myself from between him and the concrete wall I cling to.

"Leave me alone!" I topple forward, no match for his weighty form.

He slides a hand into my hair, grips it, and yanks my head back. I wince in pain, letting out a shriek.

"Not sure that's what D meant when he said to get the girl."

A scream lodges itself in my throat and my breath catches with that voice. *His* voice.

The brawny man pivots to look behind him, giving me an unobstructed view of Liam. Casually, he leans against the bars of a cell across from mine while he studies his fist. Two rings reflect the minuscule light and the oddest thought of how he could possibly fit rings over his hefty fingers enters my mind.

Both of Liam's legs are kicked out to the side, and he rests there. But I catch the flex of his muscles, the jerk of his biceps as they tighten when he opens and closes his fist. His hair is rumpled, matted on top from where I'm sure his helmet has been. The black V-neck molds to his upper body, the outline of his pectoral muscles pressed against the fabric, and I blink finally looking at his face.

He looks bored.

His eyes meet mine and he smirks, looking faintly amused by his buddy's handsy behavior.

"Darrin didn't say I couldn't sample the goods first. Get out." The man snarls, his lip curling in disgust. Liam interrupted his attack, and I hold Liam's gaze, silently pleading he won't leave.

Don't go, my mind begs.

Liam doesn't say anything while he pushes off the bars and strides into my cell. Folding his arms in front of himself, he tilts his head in my direction, seemingly disinterested.

"Probably want her clean before you touch her," Liam says, eyes racking over my body in revulsion.

I swallow the nausea, heat flooding my face at his mention of my current hygiene. It's not my fault I escaped a house fire, fought on the grass, and was hauled off and dumped into this awful cell. But as much as indignation flares, I can't help but exhale a short sigh of relief when the man roves his inspecting gaze over me and scrunches his nose. With ash tangled in my hair, dirt smeared across my face, and makeup sagging in streaks, he must finally reconsider.

"You're right. Patience always makes it better." He sniffs, rubbing his hand back and forth over his nose. "But I'm first, Liam. Don't pull rank."

"She's not my type," Liam clips out, not sparing me a glance. "Better see what Darrin wants with her before you start making plans, Trip."

Not his type? Good. I don't want to be his type—arrogant jerk. Fighting the drop in my chest, I tremble when Trip forces me to him, pulling my shirt by its front collar. The strength of his pull causes me to slam into him, and I nearly throw up at the smell of his body odor and the scent of stale chips on his graphic T-shirt. My hand grazes the sweat-slick hair between his too-short shirt and hanging belly, and I try to flinch away, but he holds fast.

"Let's go, beautiful." Trip's hand comes to the back of my neck, gripping there, and I yank away. On instinct, I knee him in the groin and duck when he tries to grab me. Darting for the open cell door, I make it two feet before a muscular arm spans the width of the opening.

Tendons and veins spread the length of his arm and I freeze before colliding with him. Trip uses the pause to yank back my hair and another whimper of pain leaves me. Out of the corner of my eye, I watch as Liam's nostrils flare briefly while he focuses his gaze on the upper corner of the hallway. I try to catch his attention and fail.

I'm not sure why. I've only interacted with him a handful of times, but in this moment of uncertainty and fear, he's the only person I remotely know. I was at his parents' house, and they aren't people I'd associate with this insanity for one minute. My eyes flutter to him, seeking an ally. But he avoids me altogether, and I'm on my own.

Forced through the door, I'm pulled through the narrow hallway with another three cells lining the hall to the double-door entrance. Liam follows, fists clenched at his sides. With every shove from Trip, I try to angle my head back to see him. His chin is raised and he scans ahead as though on the lookout for something to jump from the shadows.

Through the doors, a darkened ramp ascends gradually

before it zigzags back and up even farther. Lights flicker and the cement foundation blocks break into drywall halfway up.

Trip opens another door and I squint at the bright light.

A dining hall? What is this? It's like a high school lunchroom. Round tables are scattered throughout the vaulted room with plastic chairs circling each one. I'm so confused. My brows furrow as I try to slow, to figure out where I am, despite each press behind me.

Is this a school?

We pass a kitchen hidden behind a stainless-steel serving buffet with rolling doors operated by a chain dangling to the side.

At first, it's eerily silent. The white lights reflect through the windows, blocking my view outside. Up ahead, the illuminated hall dims, and a neon sign above another set of double doors is lit with the word *BREAK* and the word *ROOM* scrawled like graffiti next to it.

Quickly, the surrounding atmosphere grows heavy. Bass pulses from the room, rising louder with each push. Trip licks his lips, his eyes hungrily trained on the door like he's starving for what's inside.

The overpowering smell of smoke and sweat seeps out, and as we reach the door, I have to swallow the bile rising in my throat because of it. It's pungent and strong, masking even the suffocating odor that wafts off the man jostling me closer to his side.

He pulls me close when the door opens into the room.

No. Not a room.

I'm struck with the sheer size of what lies behind these doors and what's taking place.

The "room" favors the square footage of the first floor of my house, with a makeshift bar in the back. Rustic wooden shelves stack behind the stainless-steel counter. All lined with liquor, some lean slanted, and most of them asymmetrical. Two rows of back bar refrigeration units are on each side, stocked with a variety of beer.

But the bar only holds my interest for seconds before it wanders to the two stripper poles. Each is positioned perfectly in the room so no matter where you sit or stand, you can see. Mismatched chairs and lounge couches are placed around the space, the focus on one large leather chair in particular.

Smoke billows across my face, and I turn to see the man named Blitz sitting with his back sunk into a couch while a woman straddles him. He flicks the cigarette in his hands as he's focused on me.

It feels like slow motion, watching the embers drift to the tile floor. Light in this room is barely existent and the tiny ashes scream into the darkness.

With his heavy lust-filled stare, I instinctively step back, running into the belly of the man clenching my neck. Trip chuckles and runs a finger up the side of my arm.

"Don't worry, darlin'. I'll take good care of you." He whispers his vile words in my ear and I shudder, teeth aching from my tense jaw.

I avert my eyes, counting more than twenty men in the room, all of whom are nursing a drink and fondling a half-naked woman. Tears threaten with each passing second, and I wrestle with the severe desire to slump to the ground and sob.

What have I gotten myself into?

Trip maneuvers around the space, dodging occupied chairs and full couches to drag me toward the corner of the room.

A handsome man sits in a deep, black leather chair. Tight dark curls hug the top of his head, but it's the one blue eye next to the bronzed brown that snags my attention. Trip kicks the backs of my knees and I stumble forward, the hard floor stinging bone.

I keep my head hung low but don't miss the black boots that step into my peripheral. Following the black jeans up to his blond hair pulled back into a bun, I watch Liam's jaw work back and forth. His eyes look past me at the darkened windows drawn closed.

"Meet Darrin, sweet thing," Trip says, kicking my feet currently tucked under my bottom as I practically kneel before this man.

Under my lashes, I peer up at Darrin. He slides forward out of his chair, leaning both of his forearms on his thighs.

"So this is the woman Adam has been pursuing."

I flinch at the man's words. They're smooth and quiet, and instinctively, I compare it to the rough voices I've experienced from this group so far. He rubs his forehead between his eyes with his middle finger, head tilted to regard me.

"Please," I say. "Let me go."

I'm not sure why I plead with him. It's probably futile.

A laugh sounds behind me and Blitz, who has since finished with his girl, steps over to me. "Never going to happen." He reaches down to grab my chin and yanks my face to the side so I'm looking at him. Instead, I gaze past, eyes landing on Liam. I narrow my focus on him, irritated this is Adam's brother and blood. Disgusting.

I must take him by surprise because for the first time, he meets my glare and I catch the slight rounding of his eyes before they flick to where Blitz has his hand on my chin.

Then his fingers slide farther down reaching through my shirt.

"Hands off, Blitz," Darrin says, still watching me. I squirm under his study. "Fleur, is it? Funny, he never mentioned you while he's been at my establishments the past few weeks."

Darrin's eyes drill into me, and I focus past them on the curves of the chair and the dips in the cracked leather.

I'm confused, but I press my lips together fighting the urge to ask. Adam doesn't come here, does he?

"How's his new truck looking these days?"

An immediate brisk cold sensation crawls up my arms and settles behind my neck. New truck?

Anger snaps any of my resolve and I blurt out, "What does a new truck have to do with burning down my home and kidnapping me?" I muscle as much disdain to mask the terror coursing through my veins. When Darrin quirks a brow, a small thrill runs through me, similar to when I pulled those first rubber bands long ago.

I sit back on my heels, slumping farther to the floor. "Is Adam okay?" I ask. Because as the words from Chris's unread letter invade my mind, so does the image of Adam lying face down on the grass in front of my burning farmhouse. I want to make sure he's okay.

"That depends. He's had the privilege of people paying his debts for too long. Buying a new truck with his gambling money instead of paying his debts other people"—his eyes flick to Liam—"are paying for won't fly with me. *You* are collateral."

I try to look around me, the thrumming music picking up speed with my rapid heartbeat. Collateral? The word rolls around silently on my tongue. I'm nothing. No one.

"It seems everyone has a price to pay for Adam. Including you."

Chapter 21
Liam

4.5 Years Ago

"Want to go grab some donuts?" Ford asks.

I snort. "Could you be any more stereo-typical?"

He shrugs. "We haven't graduated yet. Heard you're top of the class when it comes to criminal profiling. Who would've thought? All those muscles and you're a wonk." He chuckles, throwing a punch into my bicep before flinching away.

I laugh. "I'd tear you apart in hand to hand any day."

Ford rolls his eyes, the bright green piercing in the sun. We had early morning training, and by early, I mean 3:00 a.m.—practically the middle of the night. We move toward the parking lot, intent on coffee and sustenance. Fuel for our worn-down bodies.

"Meet you there?" Ford asks.

"Sounds good."

I climb in my car and Ford powers up his bike. The bitter chill of south Mississippi isn't really a chill at all. Compared to

Ruin, located so far north it could pass as a Tennessee town, the gulf is much more enjoyable. Although the humidity and heat never bothered me like it does my family.

Guess that's why I'm here.

Ford gives me a wave and drives off behind me, the rev of his bike rumbling through the sitting cars. Someday, when I can save enough, I'll get one. The freedom Ford talks about when he brings up his rides with his brothers is enough to make anyone crave a bike like that.

On the way to the coffee shop, my phone rings and I glance at it, smiling. My mother rarely calls me. It's mostly my father. But when she does, it's usually to vent about my sister.

"Hi, Mom."

"Liam?"

The smile on my face falls immediately at her panicky tone. "Mom, what's wrong? Is everything all—"

"Liam, Adam's missing. He isn't answering his calls. Each one goes to voicemail. Your father has been out looking for him but hasn't had any luck. People we've talked to say he's been hanging with some new people, but I don't know who to ask or what to do. I'm afraid this is your sister all over again—"

"Mom, Mom. Calm down. How long has it been since you've talked to him?" I don't have the heart to tell her that he's a grown-ass adult and may have decided to hook up with a girl for a long, extended weekend somewhere.

"Days, Liam."

I sigh. "All right. I'll leave right now. Should make it in by evening."

After hanging up with her, I text Ford to let him know I have to pass on donuts and coffee. Then I speed off north to Ruin.

* * *

Sixty percent of the bricks on River and Goff's sidewalk leading to their front porch are cracked. Counting them is an easy distraction as I wait for River and Goff to get off work.

Both of them have worked since high school, and fortunately for me, Adam still runs in their circles, so I'm banking on them knowing something.

After I returned to my mom's and had a conversation with her and my dad, Goff's place was the first stop in my search for my brother.

Car lights flicker as an old Honda pulls into the driveway. It's Goff's car, but he has always been willing to pick River up from work since the death of their parents.

I raise my hand in a wave as they both grin at me. Probably because it's been months since I've been home. With training at the academy extending into most weekends, time off isn't a luxury I have.

They both exit the car and stroll up the sidewalk where I stand.

"Hey, man, what's going on? Long time no see." Goff reaches forward for a handshake and I take it, offering a firm pump up and down before sliding my hand back into my pocket.

River eyes me, her brow scrunching. "What's wrong?"

"Have either of you seen Adam? My mom called me worried because she hadn't heard from him in a couple of days. I figured I'd check in with y'all first."

"I haven't," River says, her gaze turning to Goff and waiting for his answer.

Goff pales a bit before reaching a hand up and rubbing the

back of his head. "Listen, man, I haven't talked to him, but I did see him a few days ago." He shuffles on his feet, avoiding my gaze, and I step into him a bit. The front porch lights to their double wide detect my motion and turn on, illuminating the freshly mulched landscaping that surrounds the bricked walkway.

"Goff. Tell me."

"You're not going to like it," he says, and spares a glance at River, who has already narrowed her eyes on him. She looks equally annoyed with her brother and elbows him while tilting her head toward me.

"He was hanging out in Darrin's spaces when I saw him last. A few of us went to play poker one evening and I saw him at the blackjack table."

"Darrin?" River asks, crossing her arms over chest and shivering as she says his name. Her eyes veer off, gazing up at the night sky before she scowls and shoves past us aiming for the inside of her house. "Tell him what he needs to find Adam, Goff. Darrin is ..." She scoffs, her words trailing off as she swipes at her cheeks. With a turn, the front door slams shut.

Stepping up to Goff farther, I lean my face down, leveling him with a stare and conveying my impatience.

"I'll make a few calls and send you the address if I hear anything," Goff says, and I notice his hand tightened into a fist at his side before he unfurls his twitching hand. The signs we've learned in training of drug use slowly start to register.

Damn it, Goff. What are you into?

I nod at him, knocking his shoulder with mine as I step around him. Not five minutes later, after I've left his house, my phone dings with an address for Darrin's local gambling joint.

I've never been one to bet my money. It's always too precious of a commodity for me, especially because, unlike my brother, I chose to move downstate. Never would've pegged

Adam as the gambling type either. As I drive to the location, I wonder what I'm going to say. Can I say anything?

Adam and I weren't very close growing up, not because of any one thing in particular. Our differences in personality and interests always kept us entertained with separate activities. However, our family is an average one, happy to get together and enjoy a meal. There was never a shortage of discussion to be had or jokes to make at each other's expense. We were normal ... up until my sister.

Rocks beneath my tires give way to the large parking lot. I pull into the old diner that used to sit outside the main road into Ruin. It's since been turned into a place for making a buck.

Stories of Ruin's infamous diner-turned-gambling center have spread outside the town. The gas station attendant I spoke with on the short drive here mentioned he'd gone a time or two while pointing me in the right direction.

Secrecy isn't something required, but this established underground gambling ring is not advertised. Word of mouth and hushed whispers attract the patrons eager to turn their luck around. Trust is the real currency here, and any betrayal can be as risky as the games themselves.

I park a short distance away, my walk in the spring night whisking by too quickly as I approach the door before me. It's covered by a black material with zero security or indication I'm in the right place. If someone happened upon this run-down building, they'd be pressed to assume anything was going on here.

When the door opens, neon light filters out, and I wander through a smoke-filled labyrinth. Tables come into view and high-stakes poker games are scattered throughout. Clicking pulls my gaze to the roulette wheel, punctuating the sounds of clinking liquor glasses.

A few people cast glimpses my way, raising a hand in my

direction before going back to their games. Mayor Johnson sits at a blackjack table with the town's sheriff next to him. He leers at his cards before gesturing to the dealer for another hit. No wonder why this place exists with zero consequence.

I move through the room, sliding behind fully occupied seats and mostly full tables to scan the crowd for him. Adam's hair is an inky brown, the exact opposite of mine, although we both keep our hair short. I've always had the hankering to grow my hair out like I had it in high school, but the academy wouldn't be too keen on the idea.

In the corner of the room, with less light than the rest of the space, several people gather. Bags of something are exchanged, and money leaves hands quicker than you can say the word drugs.

I shouldn't be here. Where the hell is Adam?

There's a man pacing at the front of the room, hands deep in his dark jeans, wearing a shaggy leather jacket. A few men flank around him as they scan the tables of diverse characters playing.

Squinting, I get a better look, my eyes narrowing on the man himself. Darrin.

Stiff beneath the few spotlights focused on the tables, I inch around the room, casing for my brother while simultaneously heading for the front of the room. My fists clench at my sides, a subtle reminder to myself to stay calm. The man on Darrin's right turns in my direction, eyes pinning me. I meet the stare.

As I approach, Darrin raises his chin and studies me as if he's curious about the newcomer in his establishment versus concerned.

"I'm looking for my brother," I say. "Friends of ours, Goff and River, mentioned he has been around here lately."

Darrin stands a little straighter. "River?" he asks, and I blink.

"Her brother Goff told me." I chide myself for even bringing River's name into this. From the swallow that works itself down his throat at her name, I have a feeling he knows her.

"And your brother is Adam, I take it," the man standing at Darrin's side says.

"That's right. He hasn't been seen in a few days. My family is getting worried."

A snort rings out from Darrin, and he wipes the back of his hand across his nose. Several tattoos entwine his fingers with some ink disappearing underneath his jacket. I've only begun my arm sleeve, but Ford is already trying to talk me into my thigh as well.

"Your brother is here, down the hall. Would you like me to take you to him?" A smirk twitches at the corner of his lips.

I nod, following Darrin to another dimly lit hallway. Both of his men walk behind us as we make for the last door on the right. With his hand hovering over the door handle, Darrin peers back at me, his gaze appraising.

"Don't try anything stupid. Blitz, my right hand, is not so forgiving."

I blink, unsure why he's telling me this. Honestly, Adam better be in severe trouble for this charade he's put our family through.

The old door, which I'm assuming was a back office for the diner's owners at some point, squeaks open. I narrow my eyes immediately at the figure sitting slumped against the back wall.

There, Adam sits, head hung. Crimson leaks from his nose in a steady drip, and heated anger courses through my veins. What the hell?

"Adam," I bark, stalking toward him. However, a large, burly man steps in my path, flashing gold teeth at me with an intimidating growl. I'm no small man. In fact, where Adam is lean muscle, I'm bulky and large. Titanic was a nickname in high school given to me by the football players who always wanted me on their team. I preferred to have weekends to myself or with my sketch pad instead of suiting up to plow people over on grassy rectangles.

"Get out of my way," I growl up at the man and after a quick flick of his eyes to his boss behind me, he steps aside.

Crouching down next to Adam, I say his name once more.

His face lifts to mine and I internally wince at the jagged position of his nose and the fresh cut above his eye.

"Liam, what are you doing here?" His words are slow, mimicking his blinks as he looks from me to Darrin. His eyes widen with realization. "You need to leave."

He continues to mumble those words as I place a hand over his shoulder. The slightly less meatiness of his shoulder makes me curious about how long he's been here. Have they kept him here the whole time, or did they move him?

I stand to offer a hand to my brother. "We're leaving," I spit out, making sure my voice is loud enough to be heard by everyone in the room.

Adam visibly flinches and the man named Blitz lets out a disgusting laugh.

"Unfortunately for your brother, he cannot. Owes me two hundred thousand dollars with interest." Darrin shuffles farther into the room and I step closer to my brother. Irritation at his predicament doesn't lessen the responsibility I feel toward him.

"Two hundred thousand dollars?" I ask, seething down at Adam. "What the hell were you thinking?"

"Doesn't even include the inheritance from your grandparents he's set to get. Although, being the local champion of small businesses that I am, I've decided to hold off on collecting my portion right now."

It takes everything for me not to stagger back or place a

hand on the wall. My grandparents built their business from the ground up. And they did it with their grandchildren in mind, having willed the business and the entire property it sits on to all three of us.

My brother gambled away his portion of it? How could he be so flippant about something like that?

Gritting my teeth, I stare down Darrin and his goons. The idea I could have the law here in seconds fizzles as soon as it bobs into my thoughts. Sheriff Easton was sitting next to the mayor. No doubt Darrin has many of the locals covering for him.

"He'll pay you back. Get up, Adam, we're leaving." I reach down and yank Adam up by the elbow, unwilling to be gentle. I'm pissed.

"He can't leave until he pays back the money or decides to come work for me," Darrin spits, his tone becoming more agitated with each attempt I make to walk my brother out of here.

Adam blanches as if he wasn't aware Darrin was trying to proposition him. He opens his mouth, and the dried blood from his nose cracks across his top lip.

"Let me play. I can win it back," Adam pleads.

Furious, I wrench his elbow out and he lets out a whine. Play? He wants to try to gamble his way out of the very mess he dug himself into.

"No," Darrin and I say at the same time. Darrin smiles at me, the corner of his mouth twitching while he studies me again. It's creeping me out, particularly with his different-colored eyes.

"H-how long do I need to work for you? I don't have the money to pay you back," Adam asks.

"Six years."

Darrin lets his words hang there in the silence of the room.

Even the tree limbs scraping the office windows outside seem to stop their ministrations.

Adam cowers behind me, and my protective instinct roars.

"Six years? That's insane. Give me a couple of months and I can come up with the money," I say, glaring at the smug look on Darrin's face. But he shakes his head with almost a knowing glint in his eye. What's this guy after?

"I can't do that. You see, those who don't pay their debts to me either have to work it off for the determined amount of time or pay. You won't be leaving here until you do. And any attempt to rush my men ..." He glances at the two guys wrapped in leather jackets at the door, who both swipe the bottom corner of their coats aside to reveal two large pistols.

"You, however, may leave whenever you'd like. You owe me nothing."

I look at my little brother. The thought of leaving him here is not an option, and something tells me Darrin knows it. Is he a fool for gambling away his money to the point he borrowed from Darrin? Yes. Do I want to beat him to a pulp with my own hands for putting our family through all this worry? Yes. That doesn't make me want to leave him, though. He's my family. I'd do anything for him.

"I'll pay the debt," I say. Darrin's eyes widen only a little before he smiles. Adam's arms go slack in my grip, and he turns to stare at me.

"You have two hundred thousand dollars?" Adam asks, gaze searching my face. I don't miss the slight inhalation and rush of joy that emanates from him before it disappears, replaced by worry.

I fidget, looking over the room. The walls are wallpapered with an ugly striped pattern, and a metal desk is pushed into the corner. Other than several stacks of papers and two chairs, the room is empty, save for the full weight of my decision.

Darrin lets out a *tsk* and my eyes snap to his. He raises his chin in acknowledgment. "No," he says, "he does not."

"But then how—" Adam starts.

"Six years. You owe me your life and loyalty for six years. After that, the debt will be paid."

Blitz's laugh slithers through the room, landing at the base of my neck, and I reach up palming the raised hairs there. "Who knows, D. He may just enjoy our world."

We leave with my promise to meet Darrin tomorrow, and I cringe as I make the drive to my grandparents' house with Adam. I dictate how everything is going to happen, and he doesn't fight me on it. Probably too stunned to disagree even if he wanted to.

We're keeping our parents out of this. I'm taking him to see my grandparents not only to get him cleaned up but also because I demand he tell them. To be honest about how he gambled away his portion of his inheritance all on cheap thrills and a dopamine hit.

The tension in his twitchy face means he doesn't want to, but Adam doesn't have to spend the next six years of his life having sold his soul to the devil. The least he can do is apologize to them.

We spend the night filling in our grandparents, and my grandmother takes Adam to get cleaned up while my grandfather sits pointedly across from the kitchen table, his gaze fixed on the pond in the backdrop.

"If there was something I could do ..." he says. It's not a question, more like a wish. As if he flipped a penny into the water to make it.

"No," I answer flatly. One grandson already pawned away part of his legacy. I wouldn't—couldn't—take more from them already.

My grandfather doesn't say anything else. He only stands

and places a hand on my shoulder, offering it a knead before moving out of the room. Before he reaches the door, he turns back. "You're a good man, Liam. Don't lose sight of that." His tone is even and unwavering, and once he's out of the room, I snort to myself—the realization of what I've done dawning on me.

"Not for long," I mutter in response.

* * *

The text messages from Ford keep filtering in, but I ignore each one.

> Where are you, man? Want to grab a beer?

> Dude, you missed a hell of a night!

> You sick? We had insane tactical training today. They say tests are happening Friday.

> Yo where are you? No one has heard from you. Can you at least tell me you're okay?

> Screw you, Liam. They officially kicked you out of the program. Hope it's worth it.

I ditch my coffee cup in the trash as I delete the message thread and open the email from the academy, officially dismissing me from the program. I sigh, the weight of this making my shoulders slump.

A car approaches and Darrin rolls up next to where I wait outside the Ruin coffee shop.

"Get in."

Chapter 22
Fleur

Spiral coils dig into my back. The impressions they leave are barely inhibited by the thin blanket I laid over them.

I lay there staring at the ceiling after they returned me to the cell several hours ago, considering the information Darrin shared.

Images of Adam pressed against the wall at Liam's hand flicker behind my closed eyelids. His anger was palpable that day, and now I comprehend why. I'd be furious if I had to work off someone else's debt for six years while they were out buying new trucks and still gambling their money away.

Is that what he was doing with all the money I paid him?

Adam made it clear from the beginning he was struggling financially. In what world is he going to come up with the new amount he owes? And for me—I'm not so sure.

A warm tear drips from the corner of my eye and slides down my temple into the arm tucked behind my head. I'm so stupid. Are all men hiding dark parts of themselves? Using me for their own personal agenda until something better comes along. Perhaps it's just me. I'm gullible.

I snort and worry with the rubber bands at my wrist.

The echo of the hallway's door rattles the iron bars keeping me locked away, and footsteps sound down the hall—the stride of whoever it is long and heavy.

I scramble up, pressing my back into the wall where the cot meets cement. A weak hiss escapes my mouth as a broken spring scrapes my back.

Liam's towering figure steps into view. His hair is pulled back, and his eyes dart to the cot, then to the five-gallon bucket they sent me back here with. It's the only place I have to relieve myself and I've done so, despite having no food or water. Because there's no lid, the smell wafts through the cell and he wrinkles his nose.

Heat floods my cheeks. *Like I had a choice*, I want to yell at him. Instead, I drop my gaze to a cup in his hand.

He squats down into a crouch. Using one hand to steady himself, he grips a bar, and despite being half his height, he still demands presence and space.

The grating of metal on the concrete floor snaps my attention from his impressive body to where he pushes a metal cup into the cell.

My eyes flick to his and I catch him watching me. He gestures with his chin to the cup on the floor. "Water."

Before the word is even fully out of his mouth, I fly off the bed, drop to the floor on my knees, and snatch the drink off the floor. My head pounds and the dryness of my mouth I've managed to avoid dwelling on, rushes back at me. I don't care how half-human I look. I gulp the water down. It's cold and refreshing. The water works its way down my raw throat, quenching my thirst and settling into my empty stomach.

All too soon, it's gone. And I set the cup down on the exact ring of condensation where it was placed before.

He's studying me, still crouched low, and I suddenly realize how close we are. A muscle in his jaw ticks, and I shuffle back, my movement pulling him out of his thoughts, and he stands.

I open my mouth to say something but snap it shut. What do I say? Thank you? Absolutely not. I don't care how loyal of a brother he is. It's clear he now enjoys his position in Darrin's world. It's his actions now, not what he did four years ago.

Liam turns, but I catch his gaze flick to the upper corner of the hallway, opposite my cell, before his back is to me and he strides away.

When the door closes, I make my way to the bars, using them to pull myself up. Squinting, I make out a small red dot. It's blinking. I release the bars, backing up until I run into the wall.

A camera.

Was he trying to point it out to me? Or did he instinctively look at it?

Moving back to the cot, I lie down, testing my tongue in my mouth. That wasn't nearly enough water. Feels like I'm chewing on glass with how parched I am.

I turn, making sure my back is to the camera, needing to block out whoever is lurking behind the lens.

I shiver. What the hell am I going to do now?

✳ ✳ ✳

A door slams and I bolt awake. Zero light filters down here and the hours are beginning to blur together. I'd fallen asleep ticking through mental checkboxes, unsure what my next steps would be.

Even if I somehow managed to escape this cell, I have no idea where I am. Regardless of that, Ruin is crawling with Darrin's men. Mr. and Mrs. Northgate are probably the only ones I could flee to. I'm sure River would help me, but I know her brother is involved and she might not want to risk pushback.

Footsteps once again sound in the hallway. This time they're hurried and I clamber to sitting. The man named Blitz comes into view. His lofty body is more monstrous in the weak light.

My eyes flit to the camera, noticing the red light is no longer on, and my stomach roils. I swallow, catching each movement, each twitch or lift in his face as he stares at me. Holding my gaze, he pushes a key into the iron door, and when I hear the click, bile rises in my throat.

The door swings open and I stomp down a whimper as I stand, keeping my chin high. A repulsive grin stretches across his mouth, and my eyes narrow on a black piece of food between his teeth.

Allowing the door to screech shut, it slams, the noise causing me to jump despite it being anticipated. He steps toward me, palming himself.

"D says to leave ya alone until Adam pays up, but the boss has left, and I'd like to get my fill." He snickers, a cruel smile falling in time with his eyes as they morph to undress me.

"Where's Liam?" I ask, backing into the corner of the cell, utterly helpless.

"Busy," he spits.

My eyes dart back and forth between the camera and the door, willing the light to turn on again.

"W-where is your boss?" *Distract him, Fleur. Think, think!*

He snorts. "Had to leave town to meet with the Cartel leader. Guess who's in charge?" He moves to me, grimy hands reaching for my already ripped shirt. His hand yanks the fabric down and a sharp tearing noise echoes off the walls.

My shirt falls away, exposing my nude lace bra underneath. His eyes drop down, combing over my body, and when he drags a finger across my chest, I smack his hand away.

He retaliates, grabbing my wrist and smashing it against the wall. I scream, as he takes his other hand and helps himself to a handful, and I reach to smack his other hand away. He holds it down along his thigh and rubs my fisted hand there, moaning into my ear.

Too much cologne invades my nose as he licks my cheek and I jerk.

"Please don't."

I buck and twist to get free. It's no use. The weight of this overgrown, dreadful man pins me in place.

"Blitz."

My eyes pop open, following the voice and releasing a sigh of relief when it's Liam. I'm not sure why.

"Back off, Liam. Get the hell out," Blitz says, bringing my downed wrist to the other trapped beneath his palm above my head. He grips tight, using his now free hand to fumble with the button on my jeans. I buck again and Blitz hisses. "Yeah, you like that, don't you."

I growl, almost going feral with terror and rage at this point. The clinking of another key opening the iron bars barely registers in my attempt to throw Blitz away from where he has secured me to the wall. Glancing over, Liam comes in, holding my eyes, but I flinch when I see his cold stare.

"Blitz. Darrin said hands off," Liam says again.

"I'm in charge right now," Blitz responds as he shoves a hand over my stomach.

"No," I whimper.

Liam halts Blitz's hand, holding fast, while Blitz tries to yank away.

"Get off. Just because you can't have her doesn't mean you need to hinder my fun."

They scuffle, Liam pulling back on Blitz until the pressure from where he's pressed his body into mine abates, and I can finally suck in a deep breath of stale air.

"Easy, man," Liam says calmly. He doesn't look at me. He keeps his eyes trained on Blitz and laughs while patting him on the shoulder. "Trust me. My brother's sloppy seconds aren't my thing. I don't want D pissed off, is all."

His comment washes over me, and I ignore the sting his words cause. Sloppy seconds? Whatever. He can call me the worst names on the planet if it means this beast of a man stays the hell away from me.

"Darrin isn't going to care." Blitz spits on the floor near Liam's boot. "I don't appreciate you always interruptin'. She'll be dead when Adam doesn't pay up anyway."

I freeze, my eyes darting down to my bare feet. Dead? I thought Liam covered Adam's debts.

Blitz huffs past Liam, deliberately slamming his shoulder into him as he barrels out of the cell and into the hallway. The door slams with a thud.

My gaze moves to Liam, and I find him already staring at me. His jaw clenches as he takes in my tattered appearance. I wrap my arms around my uncovered torso, the lace bra allowing the chill of the damp room to prickle goose bumps along my arms.

Liam's face is stone. I can't read him at all, and I study his eyes, which seem to be the only thing I can look at right now.

"Dead?" I rasp out, unable to hold his eyes any longer. I move to the cot to pick up the puny blanket I was given and drop it in front of me to cover myself. He follows each movement, his chin lifting to meet my inquiring eyes. "I-I thought Darrin said your work for him paid Adam's debt."

Liam grunts and spreads his legs wide, arms crossing in front of him again. He likes this position, I've noticed. Oftentimes, people have tells when they're uncomfortable. This might be his. The fists Liam's hands are clenched into have a strange black soot on them, and it draws my attention until he answers me.

"Six years is what Darrin required for Adam's first debt. He's since acquired more."

I blink. More? Adam went back to Darrin and dug himself into another debt hole even after his own brother took on the debt? That's ...

I'm still working through the thoughts in my mind when Liam strides over to leave the cell. I nudge off the back wall, reaching out to grab his arm. He turns, forcefully knocking me back while his searing gaze towers over me. Vulnerable, I flinch.

"I-I ... thank you," I say. When his brows knit together in confusion, I add, "For stopping him. Thank you." I sniffle those last words, my eyes welling with tears as the trauma of what almost happened to me in this disgusting cell fully takes root.

"Don't get used to it," Liam grunts. With those callous words hanging in the air between us, he locks me back in my cell and leaves.

I spend the next several hours wrapped in my dirty cell blanket and crying into my pillow. I'm uncomfortable without a shirt, and with Blitz's looming "dead" words echoing in my head, I can't sleep. Muffling each of my cries and screams into my pillow, I try to stay strong. Try to pull myself together enough to think of a plan.

Help from Liam would be ideal. He always seemed nicer when we interacted outside of this place. *You aren't outside anymore, Fleur. You're collateral.* I reprimand myself for thinking Liam was anything different.

At some point, I fall asleep, waking the next morning to another creaking sound. Panic surges and I listen for footsteps coming down the hallway, but there are none.

Whoever it was must've been leaving. Thirsty and hoping for water, I roll off the cot to hunt for the stainless-steel cup I've been given a few times. I practically groan with appreciation when I find it sitting inside the cell bars filled to the brim.

Reaching for it, I pause on a folded shirt next to it. The soft cotton fabric slides through my hands as I pinch a portion, rubbing it between my fingers.

I grab for it, spreading the V-neck shirt in front of me. The gray shirt is an extra-large, and I bring a hand to my belly, relieved to have something to wear again, even if it'll hang down past my knees.

Dropping the blanket I've cocooned myself in, I pull the shirt over my head. Cedar and charcoal envelop me, and I purposely pull the corner of the V up to my nose, inhaling the scent. It's warm and clean—the only two things that matter to me right now. The intoxicating scent is a happy accident.

Faster than the last time, I down the water in two gulps and close my eyes, relishing it. The anxiety of whether I should be rationing it blooms in my gut. What if I don't get more until tomorrow? I downed the whole thing. Would it have been better to take small sips throughout the day?

I tell myself the next cup to show up in my cell will be different.

As the day moves on, I determine I can, in fact, tell when night falls. Despite being in a windowless cell, the slightest dimming takes place. Similar to dark clouds blocking out the sun on a clear blue-sky day. The growling in my stomach also indicates the end of another day with limited water and zero

175

food. I'd like to know how long they are giving Adam. Does he even know?

As the already backlit cell morphs into further dusk, another clicking sound from the hallway's door sounds, and I glance down at the empty cup. It's rare for me to have two cups a day. Unease prickles back up my spine again, my shoulders sore from the constant tension held between them.

I sense him before I see him. Each heavy footfall echoes between long strides where the boot meets the floor. Liam peers at me through the bars, his eyes catching on the shirt I'm wearing. His nostrils flare in the briefest of moments. Still staring at me, he backs up until his back hits the empty cell across from mine, and he sinks to the floor.

His legs are pulled up and bent, allowing his arms to drape over each kneecap. Both of his hands come together to twist the rings tugged over his fingers. I stare at him, and he meets my gaze with a faintly amused smirk on his face.

For the first time in this exceptionally quiet cell, loud thumping music sounds directly above me. And as if on cue, Liam purses his lips and raises his chin, leaning his head back so it smacks between two of the cell bars behind him. He closes his eyes, the rapid movement of his chest slowing with each breath.

I squint, eyes darting back and forth between him and the hallway that disappears out of my line of sight.

What the heck is he doing?

Chapter 23
Liam

I can feel her eyes on me.

The look on her face as she watches me sit on the floor outside her cell would be almost comical if it weren't for her messed up situation.

Damn it, Adam.

This is the last thing I need to be dealing with right now. With Darrin being out of pocket for a while, I've been afforded a significant opportunity, but leave it to Blitz to get in my way. Took it upon himself to open the clubhouse for a Friday night party, and without Darrin here, I don't trust it not to devolve—a whole new level of debauchery.

Many of our dealers are on the compound for the weekend, picking up Jackpot and the levels of alcohol mixing with it concerns me. While my first thought should be on the job I need to do, I found my thoughts drifting to Fleur and the last time I had to make an appearance down here. Blitz can't keep it in his pants. He has to have the newest shiny thing. The fact he mentioned killing the girl is unhinged. Darrin isn't one to support this, but his trip for an undetermined amount of time has me on edge. Leaving Blitz in charge is a mistake we'll pay for.

Fleur doesn't deserve this. The crew has always had it out for Adam after Darrin allowed him off from his previous debt, even though I'm paying the price. I'm afraid Fleur will be next, and I'm not sure what to do.

I peek out of one eye to find her still standing, arms crossed over her chest and eyes trained on my hands clasped together between my legs. I severely underestimated the decision to give her one of my shirts. The fabric hangs low, the V coming between her breasts because of how large it is on her. Better than the lace bra she was left with after Blitz attacked her. I wanted to gouge his eyes out for even looking at her. She is pure light, and the thought any of us looking at her might taint her soul scares me.

"What are you doing?" Fleur's soft feminine voice soothes some of the turmoil rolling around in the pit of my stomach, and I crack my other eye open.

"They never play the music I like." I keep my voice low, cold even. While the camera's red light is off, I know for sure it still works. I've watched her, curious how she's doing. I watch her toss and turn, never truly getting adequate sleep. Whenever the guys ask me what I'm doing, I make excuses about ensuring she doesn't escape—like she actually could.

I could never understand why people watch others sleep ... until her. The urge to draw her assaulted me until I could no longer watch the live footage. It's creepy and wrong. She's interested in my brother, and I've effectively aided in capturing her.

"So you came down here to pout?" Her hissing tone nearly breaks my frown, but I grunt. I didn't expect this feisty disposition from her. Perhaps the glimpse of brokenness reflected in her eyes was wrong.

When I don't answer, she snorts, moving to sit on her cot, which doesn't look any more comfortable than the floor my ass is planted on.

"Any news on Adam?" she asks once she has pulled the blanket up and over her shoulders. It's not cold in here, but I've seen her wrap herself often enough to know she does it for comfort. I narrow my eyes as she fiddles with something at her wrist, but I can't quite make it out. A myriad of emotions works across her face as anger mutes her concern and worry. I decide to put her out of her misery.

"He's fine."

Her eyes widen, and she stiffens, sitting taller. "Really? Because he was unconscious and badly beaten when you took me."

I grind the back of my teeth as she lumps me in with the rest of them. As if I didn't break a direct order to risk coming out there, knowing it was going to be bad.

But I *was* there. I hauled Adam up into his truck and drove him to the hospital, then waited around for an update from the doctor and left before my family plowed into the room. My father is the only one aware I was there.

"He's fine," I repeat, and her lips curl in disgust. *Good. Hate me.*

Fleur gnaws on her cheek like she's at war with her mouth. I can tell she wants to ask something else but is fighting it. The fidgeting is driving me up a wall and I sigh, dropping my arms to my side.

"Spit it out."

She glares at me, but she takes a deep breath and asks, "How much does he owe this time?"

"Seventy-five grand. It'd be a lot less if he hadn't purchased a new truck."

She looks down at her lap with her next words. "And ... and what do they think I'll be able to do? Why take me?"

Isn't that the million-dollar question. This screams of Blitz and Snape. Darrin listens to them too much.

"Aren't you and Adam together? I think he'd want you back safe and unharmed," I say, tilting my head to the side to get a better view of her between the bars.

"We hadn't defined anything." She crosses her arms back over herself, and I know there is more there. Are they not truly together?

I don't care. Shouldn't care. But I find myself leaning forward a bit. A pinch of guilt flashes over her face, and I drop it. It doesn't matter anyway. She's here now.

The door to the hall opens and several men shove each other forward, each of them stumbling and leaning against the walls as they trip toward the cell.

"Snape was right. Said you'd be down here." Tim, one of our dealers, lets out a loud snort, followed by what can only be described as a giggle. Three other men, all taller than Tim, saunter down the hall and I hurry to stand, moving to angle my body between the men and the door.

"Awww, Liam. Didn't your parents teach you to share?" Tim swings the key to Fleur's cell around his finger.

I chance a glance back at Fleur, who has shifted backward to the farthest corner of the room. Her eyes seem to cling to mine as if I can offer protection. I both hate it and crave it.

"She's off-limits until Darrin decides what to do with her," I growl. Stepping forward, I cut off any continued progress they try to make.

"But D isn't here. Blitz is in charge." Tim's words are slurred and each one of them is staring past me, leering at Fleur with hungry eyes. I know most of these guys are a drink or two away from passing out for the night.

"How about we grab a bottle from Darrin's private stash behind the bar and finish it off?" I say.

Tim nearly drops the cell key as his eyes widen and a grin plasters across his face. They look at each other and laugh, nodding their heads as they turn around back toward the way they came.

I follow them out, peeking over my shoulder right as I reach the door before passing the threshold.

Fleur's chest rises and falls rapidly, and she moves forward, both hands gripping the bars in front of her. Relief shines in her eyes, and I'm worried about all the things I'd do to see peace on her face again.

Chapter 24
Fleur

I chip away at a crater in the concrete. My nail has whittled down to nothing as I drag it mindlessly over the rough patch of mortar.

Liam hasn't been back since yesterday, which is most likely for the best. I smell. The whole cell burns with every breath I take. The putrid air is stagnant and carries with it a mix of my own body odor that makes me gag. I've run my fingers through my hair in thought and worry so many times it's tangled in too many places.

My stomach rumbles, the gurgle echoing in the silent cell, and I almost miss the thumping music from last night. It drowned out the pains of hunger and the incessant thoughts.

I'm starting to panic—really panic. I half had it in my head they'd let me go by now, perhaps feed me. Each minute that passes stifles my hope, and the words Blitz threatened becomes a bit more real. *Dead.*

Liam's presence last night was a morbid comfort. My gut nudges me to trust him, that he doesn't want me hurt, or want his brother hurt. I cling to that. He gave up six years for his brother. That has to mean there is good in him somewhere. Whether it has been snuffed out is another question.

Halfway through the day, I realize no water has been delivered this morning, and when the door to the hallway opens, two distinct voices filter through. I further realize it is on purpose I didn't receive any water. They're going to move me.

Two men, who were there the night of the fire, approach the cell and unlock it. There isn't any lust in their eyes. In fact, they purposefully avoid meeting my gaze. I grip at the hem of the shirt I'm wearing. *What is happening?*

They move toward me, and instinctively, I back up running into the cold wall behind me. It's pointless, but my body reacts anyway when they grip each of my arms, twisting them around my back and gripping my elbows. My whole body stiffens at their rough touches, demanding me forward.

After a couple of days here, I finally emerge from the cell I've been hidden behind. But, even though I'm out, I feel more vulnerable than I did tucked neatly away. I'm utterly exposed, with no idea where I am.

Shuffled through a door, I'm pushed up a set of stairs, the climb putting a strain on my weakened muscles. Although it hasn't been that long, I can already feel the effects of no food impacting my body. Each step is a chore, and by the time I arrive at the top, I'm dizzy and panting.

We arrive in a dimly lit hallway with a flashing neon sign outside one door toward the end of the hallway. Unfortunately, I'm dragged to the opposite end before I can read what it says. A metal door with red letters stenciled on it reads EXIT, and when the door is shoved open, the damp, humid heat hits me. I shiver. The exact opposite reaction to the sweltering summer night I should be having.

An enormous firepit stands proudly off the side of the concrete patio we've stepped onto. Curvebacked Adirondack chairs are scattered around the pit, and one or two guys sit around the fire sipping a beer. They make an effort to glance up but go back to their conversation, not paying me any mind. This sort of thing must happen a lot for them to ignore a girl being dragged outside by both of her elbows.

Moving my head around to view as much as possible, I'm shocked that this looks like a teen summer camp the way it's laid out. Small cabins encircle the building we exited, with slender lamp posts highlighting the larger warehouses and metal buildings far off in the distance. Several motorcycles are parked in a line to the right of where we exited the building, and I'd gamble this was their main meeting point.

However, beyond it all is the thickening of dense forest pine. A foreboding woods doused in twilight with only thin slivers of moonlight breaking through the tops and rustling branches. It spans all around the camp. The only breakthrough is the gravel road leading to a gate I can barely make out in the stretch between.

We've stopped moving, and one of the men is on the phone as if waiting for instructions. When he hangs up, I'm pushed through the gravel and into the woods. Light from the cabins and fire slowly fades away until my eyes adjust to more of the dark. Pine needles smash beneath my feet, the condensed carpet muffling our footsteps.

The two men weave me through the trees, and if it weren't for their nonchalant demeanor, I'd be afraid they're planning to take me in the middle of the woods for their own pleasure. They're following someone else's orders, however, and I catch them counting the pines as if they're plotting their directions to get to their destination.

The distinct aroma of pine grows stronger the deeper we trudge through the woods. Gnarled branches snag on my legs, and it isn't long before bright light assaults my vision as streams intrude through the ink of night. Substantial-sized flood lights, angled in different directions, illuminate a clearing ahead of us.

Dread coils in my belly, squeezing my stomach into a ball of knots. A group of what looks like over fifteen men stand in a semi-circle around something ... is that a tripod? I swallow.

The two men at my side march me into the clearing and toss me to the ground. Dirty boots step into the rust-colored dirt beneath my hands, the dust of it kicking up into my face.

When I raise my head, I meet the intense gaze of Blitz, who has a sinister smile spread wide across his face. His head is angled down at me, the speckled night sky fanning out behind him, uninhibited by the gap in the trees.

He crouches down, and I find I can't look away from the pride in his face. He knows something I don't.

"Adam was discharged from the hospital this morning," he says, the words smooth and coaxing. "He was informed of your ... predicament and it seems he has vanished." Blitz clicks his tongue and gestures around us with his hands. "Seems he hasn't had the proper motivation yet, has he, boys?"

He doesn't look at me again. Instead, he stands, moving out of my vision. I scan the group of men for Liam, searching for him as if he could offer me any salvation. But I don't see him. He isn't here. I land pleading eyes on each of the men, most of them meeting my plea with a snarl or a wicked smirk. A few offer me a slight frown, as if they're thinking of their sisters in this moment and are worried about what might happen with me.

The sound of damp dirt being sliced through next to me beckons my attention, and I turn to find a shovel pushed into the earth, it standing tall beside me.

"You're going to dig for him. Dig your own hole six feet deep," Blitz says from behind me, but I don't turn to look at him. Tears sting my cracked lips as they fall down my face. I don't cry out or scream, but inside I'm screeching. "Turn the camera on. Let's show Adam what his girl has to do. If he doesn't pay, she'll end up digging her own grave."

For a moment, I wonder what they would do if I sat here and didn't move. Didn't placate their twisted ways for money they probably don't need. What if I didn't play their game, refused to dig my own grave?

I don't move.

A few men murmur something I can't hear, while Blitz moves into my vision again and yanks me up by my hair. I yelp at the prickling on my scalp, and Blitz throws down a handful of my hair to the ground, the blond strands almost looking white against the Mississippi red dirt.

"It would be a shame for Mom and Dad to also pay the price for Adam's stupidity." My eyes widen as he rattles off my parents' address in Michigan and gives me a toothy smile. He shoves the shovel into my hands and pushes me into the middle of the clearing, where all the men leer around me.

I press a hand to my belly, the rolling nausea ruining my resolve. "Please," I beg. I'm not above it at this point. This is torture.

I haven't eaten in days, but I swear I can taste the grits I had for breakfast several days prior in the back of my throat. I'm going to be sick. My nails dig into my free hand's palm, and I claw at myself, stabbing mini half moons in my skin.

Despite the heaviness of the late summer air, a gust of wind brushes past me and I suck in a breath. The humid air dries my parched throat, and I cough.

"Dig!" one of the men yells out, and a few chuckles rise into the quiet night air.

I whimper, and scan over everyone again, seeking Liam out. They land back on Blitz, who curls his lips in disgust, a knowing look indicates he's aware of who I was searching for.

My heart thumps wildly in my chest. My ribs are caving in, smashing my lungs until I can no longer breathe.

I can no longer breathe, but I lift the shovel and slice into the earth anyway.

* * *

The clink of the steel on each rock vibrates the handle and sends a shockwave up each arm. The shirt I'm wearing is drenched in sweat and I've made it less than two feet into the ground. Each stab into the body-sized rectangle is met with resistance as the top dirt turns into red clay, hard and gritty.

Only two men have left the circle surrounding me, claiming boredom and aching to get back to the multitude of women around here somewhere.

I listen intently, trying to focus on snippets of their conversation like that may somehow help me.

It's not.

They're talking about their next lay and shipments from down south. Two things that do nothing to help my fractured spirit.

"Dig faster." Blitz comes over, checking that the red light is still lit on the camera recording my progress. Footage meant to encourage Adam to pay up.

If he hasn't paid yet, he isn't going to pay. I want to be mad at him. In my mind, I call him a lazy coward, but in reality, why would a man who's known me for only two months come to my rescue? Why would he care about me when he allowed his own brother to pay his debt price—with his soul.

"I can't," I hiss out. Sweat and tears mingle together to

swamp my face. "The ground is too hard for me to move any faster."

Snickers rumble around me as I focus back on the hole I'm digging. While it's true the red dirt is hard and unyielding, I'm also stalling. Every few minutes, I get the urge to chuck the shovel and bound into the woods. When I think the men are distracted enough, I count down from ten, but usually around the number three, they have refocused their attention on me. I've tried over five times.

Another hour passes and I want to fall in exhaustion. I've had no food or water, which means zero fuel for this pointless torture. I lean into my shovel, eyes rolling back in my head as I sway, trying to gather my strength and bearings.

Through my hazy vision, the men part, and my breath catches as Liam strides into the clearing, moving quickly. Both of his arms swing at his sides, reflecting the long strides he's taking toward Blitz. Hair pulled into a bun exposes his severe expression. Lips pulled taut into a scowl, his eyes narrow on where I cling to the shovel like it's my lifeline instead of the tool digging my death.

"Blitz!" His cold tone pierces the enjoyment of the other guys, and they fall silent. "What the hell is going on?" His eyes flick to the camera and he slows, eyes skirting around the outline I've dug in the ground and landing on me. He says nothing as he turns back to Blitz.

"Motivating your brother to pay up. That's what is going on," he answers.

"Not going to do much good if you bury her in the ground."

Reality crashes over me, and warmth seeps through my pants, trailing uncomfortably down the insides of my legs. I lower my head and eyes embarrassed and craving privacy. I'm terrified, and I just peed myself.

Glancing to the side, most of the men are trained on the

exchange between Liam and Blitz. They don't notice my now wet jeans. But when I look back at Liam, his eyes are on me, lowering to my pants. His jaw works back and forth. Heat roars to life in my cheeks and I squeeze my eyes shut, praying the tears don't fall again.

"Who knows," Blitz continues, "maybe we'll all just take a turn to show Adam what he's really missing."

Liam doesn't hesitate. As fast as I could snap my fingers, he reaches behind him and pulls out a pistol, the sleek black metal aimed straight at Blitz's face.

Chapter 25
Liam

I've made the worst mistake. Jeopardized my entire position here by aiming a weapon at my second's face. What a fool I am.

I harden my resolve, staring into Blitz's eyes.

When I got back to the compound from a drop-off, I instantly went down to check that Fleur had water brought to her. I even had a pack of crackers to sneak in. It's no surprise there wasn't a cup in her cell, but what was surprising and equally disturbing was she wasn't there.

Panic surged in my chest, and I banged on each of the six cabins to find them empty. Two guys by the fire outside the clubhouse mentioned seeing a girl dragged out into the woods and I knew immediately she had been taken to the clearing.

The place where people die and are buried. Darrin rarely uses this tactic, and if he's killing anyone, it's never a woman. I dialed Darrin on my way to confront Blitz to ask for permission to do something about this.

He was shocked. I had stunned him with my request. But what am I supposed to do?

We've had average townsfolk and even law enforcement tortured and killed out here. Knowing she was going to be raped and murdered because of *my* brother's actions ... well, I guess I've assumed another responsibility.

Blitz narrows his gaze down the barrel of my gun before peering over the top, meeting my stare.

"You've now earned yourself a punishment."

I don't flinch at his words. "This is over," I tell him, and he snorts.

"The hell it is." He goes to move, but I straighten my other arm up to join my hand tightened around the trigger and he stills.

I glance toward Fleur. She's pissed herself. Her hair sticks to the sweat gleam on her forehead, and her shirt, which is actually mine, is soaked through. Her eyes are red-rimmed and heavy. She's barely holding on. She clutches her shovel, embracing it, to keep from falling over.

This is all wrong. It's horrible what I'm about to do, but I don't know another way out. I take a breath.

"I'm claiming her."

The already quiet clearing becomes soundless. Not even the nocturnal creatures make a peep.

Fleur's brow furrows as Blitz roars with laughter. "Claim her. You can't do—"

"I've already cleared it with Darrin." I roll my shoulders back and lower my gun, planting a vicious smirk on my face. "It's the perfect penalty for Adam. Watching the girl he was vying for marry his brother."

At the mention of marriage, Fleur's face freezes, shock warring in her expression, and she frowns.

"Plus, it saves some space in the clearing. You know we're running low," I add. Tension sweeps away with my carefree comment and the men laugh. Nausea thickens in my gut.

Blitz chuckles but pulls out his phone and brings it to his ear as he steps away. "Boss ..."

His words trickle to the side as I turn to Fleur. I expect to find relief in her eyes, considering her fate, but she glares at me, wobbling with her fatigue. I glare back at her. I don't need this. I did this for her. For Adam.

"Darrin says he's approved this. I've been instructed to bring in a minister first thing in the morning. Take her, clean her up. God knows she needs it." He turns to address Fleur. "Liam saved his brother yet again. You'll marry him in the morning. As is our tradition, claiming means you're his unless he decides to share."

He smirks at his comment and a primal urge to growl at him hits me out of nowhere. I'm not sure how I'm going to explain this is how we do things here. That Darrin and Blitz resemble cult leaders over drug lords. Not to mention claiming her requires a branding no one should be subjected to against their will.

It's not my problem. I did what I needed to.

"Get this cleaned up," Blitz says to some of the guys, and they automatically jump to obey.

Now comes the part I'm dreading. Saying I claim Fleur was the easy part. The hard part is everything that follows.

I turn toward her, exploring the long blond strands sticking to her face. The dark circles under her eyes are so intense it looks like she was in a fistfight.

Food, water, a shower, and sleep. That's what she needs right now.

Fleur watches me as I approach her, still propped up on her shovel handle. I don't think she has the strength to hold herself up anymore. When I near her, she flinches, nearly tumbling to the ground. I reach out to steady her elbow—she's shaking.

With my other hand, I take the shovel from her.

She stares back at me, those gray eyes probing me with unspoken questions. I can tell she wants to know what's going on. Why I'm doing this. Can she trust me?

I don't offer her any answers. I can't. Instead, I pull her toward me and gesture back over toward the cabins, prompting her to follow.

She does her best, but I notice every few steps she stumbles over the thick pine needles or downed branches. I grit my teeth and tighten my fists at my sides to keep from reaching back to grab her—I can't be seen helping her. This is meant to be a punishment for Adam, nothing more.

Blowing out several huffs of frustration, we finally leave the surrounding woods and move along the gravel pathways toward my cabin. Women shriek and giggle from the clubhouse, seated in the laps of men around the fire. I manage to catch Fleur's horror as she watches the languid party taking place after her traumatic experience. For me, it's another day.

I slow as I approach my one-bedroom cabin, grateful this one is farther than the others. Some of the men are known for sneaking around, not overly thrilled to be following Darrin's rules of claiming.

I run through everything in my head as I jog up the steps, glancing behind me to see that Fleur has slowed. Still shivering, her eyes flick from side to side and over the cabin. It's not much, but it's home. I've had to make it mine.

First on the agenda, a warm shower and clothes. I'm going to have to take her into town at some point to get new clothes that fit her. Given her farmhouse is currently ash in a field, she's going to need a few things. Get too little and she's uncomfortable, get too much and the men will think she is too comfortable. The balance of this game is already mentally taxing, and I haven't even married her yet.

Unlocking the door, it squeaks when I swing it open and

move to turn on the light. I can feel her at my back, her warmth seeping into me. Leaning against the wall, I kick my boots off and motion her inside with my hand. She hesitates.

"The warm shower is *inside* the cabin, Fleur. Not on the porch."

She narrows her eyes at me, but they falter as she shuffles inside. I shut the door and ignore the living room and kitchen to march straight into the bathroom.

It's small, featuring a shower-tub combo and an obnoxiously short vanity. Ripping back the dark green shower curtain, I move the handle to hot and let the shower warm. There are only a couple of towels under the vanity, but I snag one and set it on the toilet seat. After checking to make sure there's soap and shampoo, I glance back at the front door.

Fleur hasn't moved a muscle. She stands straight, arms clasped to her front, eyes roving around the homely living area.

"Shower is on. Everything you need is in there. I'll grab you some clothes from my room. Unfortunately, until we can get you some new ones, you'll need to borrow a shirt and sweats from me."

Fleur doesn't answer. I track a single tear falling from the inside corner of her eye as it drips down her nose. She looks lost.

"You're alive, Fleur. Get in the shower."

A hand smacks her tear away and she scowls at me while slowly moving to the bathroom. Once she steps in, she faces the rectangular medicine cabinet mirror, and her eyes widen in horror.

She doesn't look bad. I'm not sure Fleur could look bad. But her eyes are bloodshot and so heavy they look swollen, and red dirt is slathered all over her face. While she studies herself, I gather an old T-shirt and the smallest sweatpants I own and set them on the toilet next to her towel. I realize quickly she won't have a new bra and underwear until we can go into town.

"Fleur. Get in the shower. Then you need to eat."

She startles when I speak. Playing with the hem of her shirt, she opens and closes her mouth several times as if she wants to say something. I wait for what feels like an eternity before she finally says, "I can't lift my arms."

It takes me a moment to fully understand what she's saying. Her voice is so thin, torn by her screams and pleas. But it finally registers. She spent hours tonight digging in hard-ass dirt and her arms are spent. She's got nothing left.

I step to her, holding her eyes in a silent question. She nods, and I move my fingers to the bottom of the stained shirt and lift the fabric off her. The lace bra from the last time I saw her sits on her pale skin, while several bruises mark her body from, I'm assuming, her struggle at the farmhouse and the metal cot. I don't let my eyes linger on her, even though I want to. She's in such a vulnerable position, and I don't want her to get the wrong idea. She blinks at me when I don't instantly move, then I turn to leave and shut the door.

The shifting of the shower curtain lets me know she's gotten in, but it's quickly followed by short whimpers growing into long, drawn-out sobs. She tries her best to silence her cries, the muffled sounds muted, but this is a small cabin. You can't hide anything.

The charcoal pencils sitting on my desk call to me, and I trace my fingertips over some paper before I flick it away and storm out the door.

Echoing laughter from the clubhouse manages to filter toward the cabin, but it's better than the ugly sobs causing my stomach to knot.

For twenty minutes, I stare at the stars. They're dull, and the dark of night settles over the cabin like some kind of omen.

Fleur being here is ... wrong. She shouldn't be here, let alone with me.

I push to stand, noting the noises coming from the cabin closest to mine. Most of the men had a great night tonight if the roaring laughter and sounds of pleasure echoing through the compound are any indication.

I walk back through the door and listen for the crying I was so desperate to escape. It's gone, the cabin is utterly silent. Turning each of the three deadbolts to lock the door, I also draw the simple ivory curtains shut.

The fridge is currently empty aside from a few items, so I'll have to make a trip to the grocery store when I take Fleur to pick up some items she needs. I mentally run through the canned soups possibly in my cupboard while switching off the cabin porch lights.

Turning, I freeze.

Fleur stands in the living room, hair wild and wet. Droplets from her long hair drip down the shirt I gave her, and the pants she's wearing barely stay up despite the fact she rolled them several times.

She stares at me, gaze flicking to the three locks on the door. Her gray eyes, like the stars, are dull and lifeless. Her face is clean, free from the dirt and grime of the past couple of days, and I had almost forgotten about the scattering of freckles dusting her nose and cheeks. But now that I can see them, I'm wondering how I could ever forget.

She glances at the couch, and with a lean ever so slightly, her eyelids flutter. It's as if she's imagining how it would feel to sit on the soft love seat after days of sitting on concrete, and she's drawn to it.

"Why don't you sit," I say. "I don't have much. But I'll heat up some chicken noodle soup if that works for you."

As if on cue, her stomach rumbles and she wraps her arms around her middle and nods before shuffling over to the couch.

Sitting straighter than a rod, her gaze flits around the cabin space. She pauses when she gets to the coat rack my grandfather made, and she spends even longer studying the sketch of the forest framed above my desk.

In three strides I'm rifling through the cabinets, searching for the canned soup. After placing a pot on the stove, I empty the can's contents and stir, making sure the soup is plenty hot. The fanciest bowl I have is a speckled blue one, but I pour the soup in there and then grab a spoon. I take the dish to where Fleur is still frozen on the couch.

Milk crates make up my coffee table. It was a project I did with my grandfather in high school, which he kept stored away in his garage. When I moved back to Ruin, he pulled it out for me. It's sturdy enough, I guess, so I set the bowl down on it and extend the spoon to her.

She blinks but reaches up to take it, carefully leaning over the bowl to bring the first taste to her mouth. Her throat works the soup down, her eyes widening a bit before her slow pace melts away into a small frenzy. She eats so fast I'm worried her stomach won't be able to handle it, though I say nothing.

In no time at all, the spoon clinks in the finished bowl and she wipes the back of her hand across her mouth.

"Sorry," she says, redness creeping up her neck and blooming over the apples of her cheeks. "I was really hungry."

Pain settles deep in my gut. *You could've done more for her. You should've done more.*

Rationally, I know I did what I could in the parameters of my job and position within this place. I can't afford to compromise myself, but it doesn't feel good. What's another black spot on my soul?

Instead of answering her, I nod.

She frowns. "I don't understand," she says, her voice less raspy than earlier.

There isn't anything that follows her statement. It's implied, and I don't know how to answer her questions.

"Essentially, I've claimed you. We use that term here with some of the women who marry into the group. Keeps most of the men and dealers from sniffing around a woman and offers protection."

Her brows knit further together, and I know I'm not explaining it right.

"Men marry the women they want to stake a claim on." I try again, but her expression moves into a frown. "It was the only way I could think of, in that moment, to get them to leave you alone. It'll also piss Adam off, which considering his current issues with Darrin and the guys, will keep the guilt of anything happening to you off his conscience. He doesn't need that."

"I see," she answers.

I didn't realize I was squatting so close to her. One hand on the love seat arm, I move back, pull out a kitchen table chair, and slide into that.

"And if I don't want to marry you?" she asks.

I snort. "You'll marry me if you value your life. This works, Fleur. Trust me."

"Trust you?" A sarcastic laugh trickles out of her mouth. "Trust a bunch of law-breaking druggies who kidnapped and almost killed me. Trust *you*?"

Her voice cracks as she wipes her face. Being lumped in as a law-breaking woman-beater on drugs triggers me, and I snarl. Jumping up, I knock over the chair as I move to the kitchen for a cup of water.

Let her think what she wants. Let her.

I gulp down the water and steel my emotions, glaring at

her. "Trust me, I'd rather not marry you, either. I did this for my brother." Disgust curls at the ends of my mouth, and I meet her icy stare and raise an eyebrow.

She breaks our stand-off first, sitting back on the couch and pulling her feet up. Part of me wants to tell her I'll take the couch. That she'd sleep a hundred times better in my bed, but I doubt she'd agree. I'm sure a comment like that would scare her and she probably wouldn't sleep anyway.

"I'll get you a blanket and a pillow." I march down the short hallway to the linen closet outside the bathroom and pull out one of my grandmother's quilts and an extra pillow. When I return, Fleur isn't there. The faucet in the kitchen turns on, and she fills a glass of water. My chest tightens watching her in the kitchen, but I stomp it down, laying the blanket and pillow on the couch.

"I'm going to hit the shower and head to bed myself." I turn to go, but her voice stops me.

"And in the morning?" she asks.

"In the morning, we get married."

Chapter 26
Fleur

Last night is a nightmare I can't shake.

Claimed. Like some sort of ritualistic bride being led to slaughter. I can't argue that it's better than dying, but the idea Liam stayed my execution like some sort of hero is disconcerting.

He was mad on the way back to his cabin last night. Fists gripped at his sides, and each time I'd fall or trip, he'd huff in anger.

Barbaric jerk.

He pitched this as a way to make Adam pay—taking what's his. Blitz barely bought it, and I'm unsure Darrin is truly on board. Part of me worries when he returns, he'll decide that all of it isn't worth it and put a bullet in my head for causing too many issues. Because at this point, that's what I am. Adam didn't morph out of the shadowed trees last night, willing to pay up so they'd let me go. No, he's nowhere to be found.

Pounding on the cabin's door wakes me, although I can't say I was sleeping too soundly. The couch is a thousand times more comfortable than the cell's cot and I couldn't be more grateful for the reprieve my back got, but every little sound made me flinch. Each rustle of leaves outside, the sound of footsteps striding through the gravel pathways to other cabins, or the slightly heavy breathing coming from the only bedroom in the cabin and the man behind it. They all caused my heart to jump into my throat.

This morning is no exception. I bolt upright at the pounding but quickly turn into the back of the couch, my back exposed to the living room, when I hear Liam stir. Pulling the quilt, which smells an awful lot like cinnamon rolls, up to cover half my face, I steady my breath as Liam lumbers out from his room. I listen as the door whips open and a man stutters before Liam pushes him back out.

While the cabin is warm and homey, it's not soundproof and does not block out the noise of their camp.

"... what the hell are you doing pounding on my door this early?" Liam's voice quietly yells.

"Blitz wanted to make sure you still had the girl and were ready for this morning?" The second man's voice is muffled through the door, as if he's farther away. Liam most likely chased him off the porch.

"She's tired. You'd be too if you slept on a concrete floor worried for your life, then made to dig your own grave. Get the hell outta here before I bury you in the clearing myself."

"But—"

"Get."

I can almost see the sneer on Liam's face as he barks out the last command as he would to a feral dog.

My mouth suddenly dry, I fling the covers off myself and move to grab the same glass I used for water in the middle of the night from the kitchen counter. Every time I woke, I went to get a glass. My body did it unconsciously as if it was preparing for another several days with so little. The groan of pipes sputters out some water, and I gulp it down, then rinse out the glass and set it back where it lived all night.

The door plows back open and Liam steps back in. I freeze, staring at him across the counter through the living room and straight to where he stands at the front door. Shirtless.

Black jeans hug his lower half, while the work of art on his bare chest is displayed on his muscular top half. Ink drips down his chest on the right side, rolling into a full right arm sleeve. The left side of his chest and arm are blank, with the exception of what looks like a scar, and I can't help but wonder if he has plans to cover those too. His hair is tousled and snarled from his night's sleep, which makes it look like he didn't sleep much better than I did. Dull gray and blue underline each of his eyes, and when I finally meet his stare, he's looking at me, confused.

"Sorry if that woke you."

"It's fine. I'm not sure what time it is anyway," I say, shrugging my shoulders and removing my gaze from him in favor of the door he came through.

"Clock is right ..." He points behind me and I turn to see the round manual thing ticking furiously. It's 7:00 a.m. "Blitz most likely has already blackmailed a priest to come to the clubhouse, so we should get ready."

I snort, looking down at my clothes. Well, *his* clothes. I have these sweatpants and an oversized shirt. Can't get ready—not that I want to.

"Trust me. It's going to be five minutes and not pleasant. Shower if you want or freshen up. I'm going to get dressed and we'll walk over."

Trust him. I shake my head at those same words spoken to me last night. His calm demeanor is eerily and utterly terrifying. "How can you be so cavalier about this? I'm sure getting married to a random stranger isn't something you planned for either."

"I always do what needs to be done." He marches back to this room and shuts the door while I stand there wondering how far I'd make it if I ran through the trees to find a road out of here.

Blitz's threatening words for my parents quickly dispose of that idea. Plus, the thought that maybe this would keep them from going after Adam crosses my mind. I'm sure it's all Liam is worried about at this point. No matter how angry he is at his brother, they're still family.

Padding to the bathroom, I decide against a shower. There's no one I'd rather impress less than this bunch. Instead, I finger-brush my teeth with some toothpaste I find in the medicine cabinet and swish out my mouth with some water cupped in my hand. I have zero makeup, and I'm grateful my hair seems to be fairly tangle-free.

When I exit the bathroom, Liam is already waiting by the door. Seems he isn't too concerned about what he looks like either. He opted to keep his black pants on and threw on a T-shirt, layering it under his leather jacket, his hair pulled back into a loose bun.

Fiddling with sunglasses in his hands, his mouth drops when he sees me but closes it quickly. Without saying anything, he opens the door and we both make our way down the pathways to the clubhouse.

I squint in the bright rays. It's been several days since I've seen the sun, or any daylight, for that matter. Everything is vibrant and humming with color. A grouping of cabins sits behind us as we leave the area and walk to another building. The pit in my stomach grows with each step I take toward the clubhouse, as they call it. With the large firepit out back, I know I've been held somewhere in that building.

Thank goodness it's too early in the morning for all the men to be up and around, considering I heard them partying until three or four this morning.

I wipe my palms on my baggy sweatpants as we near the building, my anxiety at its peak. Both rubber bands still on my wrist are stretched out, rendering them ineffective for chasing away the restlessness. I'll need to replace them—soon.

The front has a wide overhang made from round wooden beams. This whole place mimics a high-end campground and my brain is having trouble separating the lawlessness of the men and their actions to the beauty and serenity of the place right now.

With one hand on the door, Liam grabs my hand, bringing my eyes instantly to his. His pupils are blown wide—is that fear fighting its way through?

"It's going to be quick, cold, and callous. Don't react," he says.

Confused but unwilling to admit otherwise, I nod, and he squeezes my hand before opening the door. It's not tender or loving, but there's a comfort in it and at that, my brow furrows even more.

We pass through a large dining area and approach a door with the words BREAK ROOM over it. Inside, Blitz stands with several other men in leathers and another man sweating bullets. His Roman collar does very little to hide the damp beads above his lip and the drops seeping from his temples.

As soon as we enter, I'm ushered in front of the priest, with a gun pointed at my head.

I never imagined my wedding would be held at gunpoint. Considering how long I waited to marry my high school sweetheart, this wedding puts a whole new meaning to the term shotgun wedding.

There's no mistaking this as anything but forced. They

aren't even trying to fool the priest which means they must have something on him.

"I-I'm Father Michael," he says. "I'll be performing the vows and witnessing the marriage. I have the marriage certificate for you to fill out afterward."

As Father Michael speaks, he looks toward the gun, terror gripping his expression the entire time he's speaking with us. I'm sure the vows he took are not being upheld at this moment.

"P-please repeat after me," the priest says, and he gives me my first line.

The ceiling starts to collapse. At least that's how it feels. Crushing and suffocating. I'm going to lose it.

"I, Fleur J-J-Jacobs—" The words get caught in my throat, and I fist my shaking hands at my sides. The priest gulps when the gun is raised toward me, and in my peripheral, Liam flinches.

"Say it!" Blitz demands.

I squeeze my eyes shut and grit my teeth to try again. "I F-F-Fleur—"

A hand grazes mine and I glance down to my right to see Liam's closed fist brush mine. He's no longer touching me, but that brief contact—I look up to catch the pleading in his expression. It's fleeting but revealing.

The realization that Liam's actions, however twisted and strange, are all to save my life, gives me the resolve to clear my throat and steel my spine. And finally, I repeat the priest's words without fail.

We aren't turned to look at each other. We only stare at Father Michael in front of us, and I do my best to zone out this painful moment. The irony I waited for so long to be married to the love of my life, and now in a matter of days I'm marrying a stranger whom I don't even like isn't lost on me.

When I say "I do" I almost laugh, but tears find their way instead.

Liam and I move to sign the documents needed and when I hear the click of the gun being returned to one of the men's hostler, I breathe a little easier. That is until Blitz opens his mouth.

"Well, Liam, never thought I'd see the day when you'd claim a woman. Never had the balls to bring any around here. Too afraid we'd steal her away." He chuckles and Liam purses his lips and crosses his arms in front of himself, creating a barrier.

"We done here?" Liam asks. His voice is different from when he spoke with me. It's cold and unfeeling.

"For now. Don't forget tonight," Blitz says, a hunger in his eyes brings a shiver up my spine.

What's tonight?

Liam nods once and roughly grabs my elbow, yanking me toward the door with him. The men behind us laugh and snicker. When I turn back to glare at them, the priest wipes a single tear from his cheek, an expression of remorse and worry mirroring my own.

Liam drops my elbow as soon as we exit the clubhouse like my arm is blazing hot and he's burned himself.

I blink away my fuzzy vision, the intense sunshine glaring off the rows of motorcycles lined up in the gravel parking nearly blinding me. Having to run to catch up to Liam, I fall into step behind him, unsure of his direction but my lifeline anyway. There are zero people here I trust, but maybe I distrust Liam a little less.

"Let's go," he barks at me. Slowing down by a vehicle covered with a canvas cover, he whips it back, exposing an older Ford F-250. It's a mix of candy apple red and burgundy and it's in perfect condition. I trace the silver mirror jutting from the side, appreciating the truck.

Liam must notice because he grunts out, "It's from 1980. My grandfather gave it to me, but I prefer the bike."

I can't help myself and snort. He narrows his eyes at me, his expression unreadable. "I mean ... why the bike? This is gorgeous."

"Just get in."

"Why?" I ask. Liam's jaw ticks at my second question in seconds, and he hardens his face while ignoring me. I roll my eyes and move to the passenger side. My dad would love this. As soon as the thought enters my head, it wipes the smile off my face and replaces the minor excitement I have with the feelings from minutes ago in front of the priest.

My parents. They're most likely worried sick. Gosh, they've probably been calling and calling the phone I don't have anymore. Have they reached out to local police? I'm sure if they do, they'll learn of the farmhouse fire and panic. Will they try to come down here?

I pull at the rubber bands hugging my wrist, twisting and pulling them while I sit in the seat, waiting for Liam to get in. Yanking them back as far as they will stretch, I let the sting ground me and center my thoughts. I still feel. *One thing at a time, Fleur. One thing at a time.*

With another pull upward, I'm ready to let the two bands snap again when the door opens. The creak is loud as if a sheep groaned in a question. I jump and release the rubber bands, covering my wrist, my fingertips scratching the newly formed welts.

Liam stares at my attempt to cover my hands and his gaze drops to where I grip my wrist in my lap. He climbs into the truck, starts it, and pulls down what I assume is the main entrance. We drive through an electronic gate that hums as we drive past. The gravel gives way to the khaki dirt, and the truck shakes over the tiny pebbles beneath the tires.

We must drive a good mile or so before I realize how far out here we are. No other houses or buildings have caught my attention and the sinking feeling deepens. No one is going to be looking for me out here.

Liam is silent, and I'm not sure if that makes me happy or uncomfortable. I slide my gaze over at him and tell myself this is survival. He's now my husband. Words I'd never equate with a man like him. But again, it's for survival.

Another mile or so and I can make out the red octagon of a stop sign ahead. A paved road comes into view along with the Natchez Trace signage. I twirl the white string hanging off my sweatpants around my finger.

"Where are we going?" I finally ask.

"To town. You need clothes and supplies, and I have another stop to make."

"How long will I be here? Can't you drop me off somewhere? Actually, what about the bed-and-breakfast? I'm sure Mr. and Mrs. Northgate would let me stay with them a bit. You can tell Blitz and Darrin I bolted on you."

Liam tenses and slams his fist on the steering wheel. "You think this is a game? You want me to drop you off, pretend you got away? No one gets away from me. They'd never buy it. It's not just your ass on the line."

Part of me wonders if they know why Liam married me. I'm sure they know it was for Adam.

"And need I remind you that those close to you are at risk too? So you'll get some clothes and supplies. Get what you need because most of the women don't get to leave all that often. Unless you're with me, you don't go anywhere."

"Comforting," I deadpan.

He scowls at me, and for a second, I think about what he

gave up for this. Was he seeing someone? Did he have a lady friend around the compound? I squash the thought. Why should I care? He got himself into this mess with this group. But as I say that, a sliver of compassion whittles away my bitterness.

We roll into town within fifteen minutes, and I try to gauge the direction of the compound, but I've always been terrible with direction and have no clue. Passing the home improvement store I've become so familiar with, Liam turns to me.

"Where do you want to stop?"

"Double Lucky's." I spit it out so fast. I've been thinking about it since he told me the plan was to get me more clothes. Perhaps River is working, and I'll be able to speak with her. Or even get some help from outside the town and the local law enforcement that is too lazy to do anything about this group.

He narrows his eyes at me. "You and River friends?"

"Yes." I don't hide it. I'm not going to pretend like I won't say anything to her, and I get the feeling he understands that.

He grunts, but then he moves into the right-turning lane for Main Street and the thrift store. Pulling into the parking lot, my adrenaline spikes. I practically have to walk with my hands on the waistband of my pants because they keep falling down. At least at the thrift store, I can get a wide variety of items.

The town of Ruin does not have a big box retailer. Everything is niche, and if you want to go clothes shopping, your options are Double Lucky's or the hunting store riddled with camo. It takes a good hour to get to a department store from Ruin.

Liam opens the store's one functioning door—the other blocked by a pile of boxes River hasn't sorted through yet. The bell goes off and River's voice pipes up from the back.

"Be with you in a minute."

I want to cry at her voice. It hasn't been that long, but it feels like I've been away for a lifetime.

Liam stands at the entrance, arms hanging down by his sides, but his fists are tight, and I don't miss the rapid pulsing in his neck.

"So what can I help you—Oh my! Fleur?" River bolts through two racks of shoes to embrace me. She grips me tight in a hug, running her hands over my back as if she's trying to make sure I'm real.

"Hi, River," I say.

"I'm so glad to see you're okay. Adam told me about the fire and that Darrin had—" She shakes her head. "Never mind. Here you are. Are you okay?"

I've never heard River talk so fast, but as she does, her gaze shifts to the door and her eyes widen when she notices Liam.

She points at him. "You didn't ... did you?"

Liam nods, and they stare at each other. I'm certain there's a silent conversation between them, and I can't shake the uncomfortable bubbles gurgling in my stomach.

"So did Adam finally get to you? When I spoke with him in the hospital, he said he was making a phone call and had a plan."

I chew on the inside of my cheek and glance at Liam. River looks between the two of us, then down at the sweatpants I'm wearing.

"I need some clothes. The fire ..."

"Where are you staying? Do you need—"

A heavy sigh from Liam interrupts River. "She's staying with me. She'll be fine River. Let this play out," he says.

River's mouth drops open, and she grabs for my hand. "Did he claim you? I thought Adam was coming ..."

I'm not sure what I can say without crying. This whole situation is screwed up, and the only thing keeping me from darting out the back door and hopping on a plane home is the fact that Blitz personally threatened my family. It's not a chance I'm willing to take. I'm not brave. I run away from problems, not confront them. I'll deal with it myself.

The warm gush of tears wells in my eyes and I smack them away, earning a glare from Liam. "It'll be fine, River. Adam didn't come. I'm not even sure where he is. But Liam ... he technically saved my life." I shrug my shoulders but allow the words to sink in. "For now, I need some clothes and a few things."

River yanks the collar of her red T-shirt to dab the corner of her eye, then shakes out both her hands at the same time.

"Whatever you need."

It takes me a good hour to gather several pairs of jean shorts, tanks, T-shirts, and a couple of dresses. River digs through newly donated boxes to find some unopened underwear that will hold me over for now, and she places an order online for me I'll be able to pick up when it comes in.

While I'm grabbing a couple of books and storage for some of my clothes, River approaches Liam at the front and they talk in hushed whispers. I tilt my head, tucking a stray piece of hair behind my ear, trying to hear their conversation, but it's no use. I frown. They seem closer than I thought. Or maybe that's small-town life for you.

"Cash or card, Liam?" River asks, and he pulls out his wallet, then hands over a card without knowing the total. *Must be nice. Drug money at work.*

She rings up my clothes and hands back Liam's card. The urge to say thank you is on the tip of my tongue, but I quickly swallow it. River floats back around from behind the check-out counter and pulls me in for another hug.

"I'm sorry about everything. I'm just glad you're safe and alive. Adam may still come yet," River says, squeezing me a little past uncomfortable. When she releases me, Liam grunts toward the door, and River wrinkles her nose in disgust at him.

"Hold your horses. She's coming."

"Yeah. And I'll tell Darrin you say hi," Liam says.

River's face goes as white as the freshly painted porch on the farmhouse I no longer have. She freezes, narrowing her eyes at Liam before shooing him with her hand.

Back in the truck, Liam starts it but doesn't move. He props his elbow up on the window and rests his head in his hand there, rubbing at his forehead.

I study him out of the corner of my eye. He looks stressed. The fine lines around his mouth curve downward, and his eyes appear flooded with worry. He does a double take when he catches me staring.

"I figure we can stop at the drugstore. Get a few shower and bathroom items. I know you're basically starting over."

"Yep. That's what happens when your house is set on fire." It flies out of my mouth so fast I can't take it back. I'm being rude to the man who's trying to save his brother and help the random girl caught up in all of this. "Sorry ..." I add.

"Don't be." Liam grips the wheel, backing out of the parking lot.

I grab what I need from the drugstore, feeling more comfortable about the days going forward with some basic amenities. I didn't realize how low maintenance I was until I had to replace all my items at once and stripped my needs down to the minimum. I could tell Liam was slightly shocked by how little I walked away with. But I view this as *oh so very* temporary. The moment I can, I'll be leaving this town and my failed farmhouse dreams with it.

We turn down another road, an all too familiar one, and my eyes widen when we pull into the bed-and-breakfast parking lot

—the employee one. Where I had one of my first encounters with Liam.

"What are we doing here?" I ask. I make zero attempt to hide my concern.

"Figure you'd want to check in with them? Let them know you'll be out of work for a bit."

"A bit?"

"It won't be forever, Fleur. I can promise you that." He doesn't look at me when he says this. Only stares out the window toward the massive oak trees in the front lawn.

His words should bring me comfort, and they do in a way. There *is* an end in sight. I'm not sure what the rules are regarding how long one needs to be married before filing for a divorce, but surely a forced marriage won't be contested. *It will end*, I say to myself.

I dismiss the odd sensation probing at my chest and reach for the door handle at the same time Liam opens his.

He directs me to the back kitchen door, which knowing he's been here helping Mr. Northgate doesn't ring as odd. What does seem odd is the way he walks right in. No knock. No doorbell. He didn't even wait for me to walk inside.

I swallow, cautiously stepping in after him. He stops short, avoiding a box by the stairs. I accidentally slam into his back and wobble to the side, arm reaching out to grab the coat rack for balance.

A flicker of recognition passes through me before the realization hits.

Chapter 27
Liam

Fleur puts it together and I almost laugh at her expression. Her stormy eyes narrow at the coat rack my grandfather made, and I know she's made the connection when they burst open, widening while her head snaps to me. She must know the story behind these coat racks then.

She opens her mouth to say something when my grandmother's voice rings out in the kitchen off to the right.

"Liam, is that you? I told your grandfather I heard that truck rumbling out in the—oh, Fleur. I didn't realize you were here."

My grandmother's eyes drag over Fleur, working their way down her oversized shirt, that's mine, and the sweatpants she can barely keep up, also mine. She looks between us, wiping her hands on her apron. The scent of orange scones wafts across the kitchen. Couple that with the rhythmic tick of the grandfather clock in the corner, my eyes suddenly feel heavy. Every time I come over here, I want to nap. Truly sleep because it's something I haven't done in years. This place is home. All things comfort. More so than my own parents' house.

Adam didn't think about Darrin coming after his portion of the Old Hillside legacy. Didn't think he would. But that's the thing about Darrin, he would, he did. I'd do anything for my brother, but I'd sell my soul to the devil so my grandparents could keep their livelihood.

Fleur shuffles behind me as she steps from the back door into the kitchen with familiarity and ease.

When I first heard the new girl in town was working at my grandparents' bed-and-breakfast, I was happy they had some extra help around the place. They've had trouble keeping consistent housekeepers willing to show up and do a job most believe is beneath them. I'm unsure why Fleur escaped to our little town, although I doubt she'd say she's escaped anymore. Although her determination to fix up the old farmhouse while cleaning rooms to do it is admirable.

Seeing Fleur with Pam at the bank, I instantly pinned her as the new girl, and I probably made myself come to town more than usual to get a small glimpse of her. Being able to talk with her in this very parking lot—her with no shoes—gave me more peace in the last four years than my drawing has.

I never had a shot with her, not really. Not with who I'm associated with. Then the town was buzzing with how Adam was helping her renovate the farmhouse and the local gossip mill had them married in the next five months.

Some part of me, maybe the primal part, relishes the fact I've married her and he can't.

"Sit down, Fleur. We've been so worried about you! Can I get you a scone and some coffee? Your parents called here looking for you since they hadn't heard from you. They mentioned a call to the sheriff but got nowhere."

I sneer at that. Of course not. Darrin owns the sheriff. If

anyone thinks there's law and order in this town, it's because Darrin allows it.

Fleur swallows, looking at me with sad eyes. I hate it. When she cried in River's store, I about drove the two hours to the airport and put her on a plane myself, removing her from this ruin of a town. If I didn't have so much riding here, I would've.

"Thank you, Mrs. Northgate. I'm okay. I-I'd love to call my parents to let me know I'm all right. Could I use your phone?"

My grandmother stares at me, and I know what she's thinking already. How could I? The short answer is I paid a debt with my soul and everything I do is questionable these days. It's hard to keep pointed true north. To keep the burn of hell from licking my heart.

"Of course, sweetheart. Here, let me grab that for you. Liam, your grandfather needs help in the garage." She says it less like a fact and more like a command, one I jump at to avoid Fleur's pleading face.

When I walk outside, the picture before me reminds me of when I found Fleur in the garage. My grandfather reaches for boxes inked with scrawled lettering across them I can't make out. It smells rank in here. My nose wrinkles in disgust, and when my grandfather catches me out of the corner of his eyes, he blows a puff of air out through his mouth, the gesture swelling his cheeks.

"I know, Son. Something's dead in here, and your grand-mother tasked me to find it."

I smile at the name he's always called me. While I'm not truly his son—my mother is their only child—our bond is just as strong. Past events made sure of that.

"I can smell it," I mutter, ripping the hair band from my hair and slicking it back to put up again. "How can I help?"

He lets out a chuckle. "Well, I need to get past all these

boxes to find the issue. Probably a raccoon or possum got stuck back here and couldn't make its way back out."

Moving forward to help displace the stacked boxes, my boots thump against the concrete, and when I look down, the outline of feminine flats is still on the dirt-dusted floor. My mind wanders to the woman sitting in my grandmother's kitchen, munching on orange scones and most likely being doted on by her nurturing ways.

Focus, I tell myself, mumbling the word that has been on repeat in my mind all day. This thing with Fleur is secondary.

"So why have you come by?" My grandfather groans as he bends low to wrestle a cardboard box that is darker in the bottom corner, having been soaked by something. I'm not sure I want to know.

"I needed Fleur to stop by."

My grandfather sighs as he relinquishes his box to another pile of stored linens and garden gnomes. It's slightly disturbing my grandmother's affinity for them.

My grandfather's expression morphs into one of confusion. The silver eyebrows matching his hair fold together, creating a deep V, and he tilts his head, searching for more than my few words.

"I married her." It's entirely vague and not enough information, but those three words worm their way into my darkened heart and my chest swells, regardless of the coercion.

Grandfather clears his throat, propping a lanky arm on his waist while the other comes up to rub his forehead. "Is this one of those—those—" He flutters his hand as if willing the word to come to him. I answer for him.

"Claimings. And yes. Adam dug himself into a hole again. Darrin thought taking Fleur would make him pay up. It didn't. Then Blitz got ahold of her ... It was ... not a positive outcome. I stepped in."

"As you always do. Does she know?" My grandfather's words are stern.

"No."

I kick a box off to my right and dive after it when it slides farther than I anticipate.

"Do you plan to?" My grandfather is my confidant and I look up to him in more ways than one. He's more than family. The slinking urge to lie to him is on the tip of my tongue, but I go with the truth.

"Right now, it does no good." My eyes rise up from the third box of gnomes I've come across and land on my grandfather. His wrinkled mouth frowns at me, the deep lines curling down and to the side as he contemplates.

"And what about Adam?"

"What about him?" I bristle at the mention of my brother's name.

"Aren't they an item?" he asks.

The fact is, I don't know. I have a feeling someone wounded Fleur, and I doubt Adam has had enough time to accomplish the decimation of her heart. No. She ran here for a reason. Regardless, she is *my* wife now. That was the whole point.

"Darrin deems it a significant insult to Adam—me marrying her. I pitched the idea as that, but it was to save her life."

He nods as if this makes sense to him, and I wonder if he's truly understanding or if he has no words.

"And your mother? Your father?" Worry etches itself in the grooves around my grandfather's eyes. For the same reason we avoided telling my mother about Adam, I'm assuming he would want me to avoid telling her this.

The thing is, we can't avoid it. It's supposed to get out. It's supposed to weave around the small town, gossiped out of the mouths of the locals, quick and hurried. Surely the news will find my mother.

"I'm sure I'll hear from them soon."

We continue to work, my grandfather grilling me about my plans with Fleur, and I sense he's hunting for any further motivations besides what I've told him. I can't stomach the distraction each time her name is murmured. And the looming anxiety about tonight presses deep into my temples. I knead them.

"Aha! Found it."

My grandfather shoves two boxes to the side, and I glance over his shoulder to find a half-decayed possum carcass. Poor guy. Must've run in while the garage was open and gotten stuck trying to get out. Instead of waiting by the door, though, he buried himself deeper, further blocking his path.

I make a note. Not to bury myself any deeper.

When we're finished in the garage, we move back into the bed-and-breakfast. My grandfather makes straight for the kitchen, no doubt hankering for one of the scones. The half bathroom is off the entryway, and since there aren't guests this weekend, I don't bother knocking.

When I yank open the door, a high-pitched squeak escapes from someone.

Fleur leans over the bathroom sink, dabbing her puffy eyes. While they widen, mine narrow straight on the splotchy pink grazing her cheeks and her red-tipped nose half buried in tissue.

Hell.

"Why are you crying?" I ask. It comes out loud and in a growling tone I try to temper, but it's no use.

Fleur rolls her eyes. Her hand holding the white tissue drops to smack her thigh with a dull slap. My sweatpants are rolled over her hips, the large T-shirt tucked into the side. A small patch of creamy pale skin, unmarred by the Southern sun, peeks through and I curl my hands into fists to keep from stroking a finger there.

She sniffs, and the noise beckons my attention back to hers.

"Who made you cry?" I ask again.

She raises her eyebrows, and those steely eyes pin mine with a deadpan stare. As if to say: *who else?*

Two beats pass and the stare between us lingers. But then Fleur shoves past me, her shoulder barging into my bicep as she steps through the door to stride away.

Once I've used the bathroom, I follow the voices coming from the kitchen and end up propping my body against the doorjamb to take in the scene.

Fleur stands at the kitchen counter, piping bag in hand as she dollops white cream on top of flaky puff pastry. A watery smile lifts away the sadness I encountered minutes ago, but it doesn't erase her swollen eyelids or still wet lashes. My grandmother twirls around her and wipes her hands on her apron while my grandfather sips his coffee and flips through the mail on the table. Past him, the ducks in the pond parade about as if caught up in the twilight zone of happiness.

Annoyed, I shake my head at the warmth that hovers over my chest, but it's quickly chased away with a single text message from Blitz.

> Make sure that old lady of yours is ready for tonight.

Chapter 28
Fleur

My eyes are gritty.

After I sat down with Mrs. Northgate to let her know I'm temporarily staying with Liam and won't be at work for a while, I found myself sobbing on the phone with my parents. Of course they think it's entirely because of the farmhouse fire that demolished all my possessions and hard work in a single night.

When they ask if I'm coming home, I tell them no. That I'm staying at a friend's cabin and I'll be there until I can figure out a more permanent solution. I don't mention Liam, and I don't tell them about Adam. Pretty sure the only information I was able to offer was that I lost my phone in the fire—which isn't a lie.

To give myself credit, the tears didn't start until my mother's did. When she mentioned the trials I'm going through and how they break her heart—it made my own clench with an indescribable ache. Chris was the first major trial in recent months and now this.

I suppose when you're a mother your heart hurts when

your children suffer, so I can imagine her tears were for me, in solidarity. However, they triggered the floodgates, and I buried my face in my arms at Mrs. Northgate's table while she massaged my head. I didn't even have it in me to be embarrassed.

I'd gone to the bathroom to clear my mind. First with several snaps of my rubber bands and then with an entire box of tissues. The cubed box was decorated in a giddy watermelon print that made me want to crush it into a ball.

The cream puffs Mrs. Northgate made for an ill friend gave me an easy distraction. However, Liam's lingering stare while we topped the last dozen with delicious cream quickly scrubbed away any moment of peace. His eyes tracked my every movement around the kitchen to the point I began to feel self-conscious. Maybe I had cream on my face or crumbs in the corner of my lips. But when I swiped at my face several times, my hand came away with nothing. Were it not for the ding of his phone, I'm sure I'd have never gotten relief from the intensity. His eyes dimmed as soon as he opened it and he rounded me up to go.

I didn't want to leave. More tears flowed as Mrs. Northgate gave me a long, comforting hug and a pan of lasagna to reheat.

Those welled tears pooled, finally releasing when I got in the truck, and my head feels as though it's been smothered in sand. A pricking sensation makes me want to pluck out my eyeballs.

"Were you able to speak with your parents?" Liam's voice shatters the roar of the truck, and I nod, unable to look at him.

I count the houses as we pass the neighboring community before riding through town. A little boy runs around his front yard, a young chocolate lab chasing his heels with a stick in its mouth. I smile at the simplicity.

Another couple embraces in a hug, standing by a smoking

grill in their driveway. Ribs? Chicken? What side dishes will they have? I play over the details of their dinner and imagine what it would've been like to cook a meal with the true love of my life instead of the imposter husband seated next to me or the fraud of a man I gave nine years to.

What if I was cherished? What if the man I was with would rather cut off his arms than wrap them around another woman? What if the man I was with demanded nothing from me instead of using me to make a statement? Then maybe I could have a life like the couple in the driveway.

We pass several familiar road signs, and I straighten from my slouch, turning to Liam. "Can we go down by the farmhouse?"

Liam winces, and I realize it's bold of me to want to see the charred remains of the house. But I want to see it before I'm sequestered away amongst the woods and in a one-bedroom cabin.

"Is that really a good idea?"

I shrug, my eyes moving over his beard and past him to the fields outside his window. They've started harvesting the crops already.

He doesn't press me anymore and I'm grateful. We make the left-hand turn down my road. Because it truly was mine as the farmhouse shared it only with hayfields and oak trees.

As we approach, the outline of blackened wood and a crumbling chimney inked in ashy soot stand out. The heap of the remaining farmhouse clashes against the pure blue sky without a cloud of white to offer a reprieve.

Liam slows at the base of my driveway and before he's fully come to a stop, I yank open the door and hop out.

"Fleur!" Liam yells, but it gets lost in the breeze that whips behind my tangled hair. I run toward the house, slowing with each step I get closer.

It may be a trick on my mind, but I swear I inhale a pungent breath of burned wood. Memories of the raging flames assault me, and I run my toes into the front steps of the porch, the only portion that remains.

I close my eyes, chew my lip, and reach for my wrist to pluck away what I can't control, but as I pull back Liam's voice interrupts me.

"Fleur?" He murmurs my name as if he's creeping slowly behind me, attempting not to scare a frightened animal. I release the bands without a snap.

The heat of Liam's palm hangs just above my shoulder like he wants to set it there. But it drops away, the whoosh of air fluttering against my back and producing a shiver instead.

For a moment, I mourn the loss of the would-be touch, but it lasts a split second before it's replaced with relief and the realization of where I'm standing—the charred dirt beneath my feet compliments of *his* people.

Continuing to scan the rubble, I'm half tempted to start digging for anything salvageable. It's ridiculous. I wasn't here that long. Only recently did I start to feel more at home in my newly renovated house and less like a guest. Still, it was my soft place to land after Chris and—I look around the empty fields surrounding us—it served as a peaceful place for the pain. I'd pictured myself here much longer than the time I had.

A snap of a twig near my side makes me jump. Liam's thundering frame slides up to my right, arms crossed in front of him as he looks from the toppled mess to my fractured expression.

"It's not all lost." The warmth of his breath skirts along my cheek as he speaks those words to me. I, however, keep my face forward, willing him to turn away and do the same. His words sound like he's mumbling something profound, when in reality all I hear is false hope.

"I doubt that's in the cards for me."

"And why's that?" he asks.

"Because it takes time, money, and freedom I don't currently have."

Liam's jaw works back and forth before his throat bobs and his fingers, rested on his muscles, flex. He dips his chin, leveling his eyes with mine, and I squirm under the intensity of them.

Unable to stay here any longer, I turn to go, but a calloused hand wraps around my wrist. He doesn't pull. There's only a slight tug that feathers out from the tips of his fingers, pressing into my skin. At first, I divert my gaze to the beautiful oak still standing untouched in my front yard before it snaps back to his. And, as if he noted my expression from his touch, he drops my hand like it singed his own.

I glance down at my wrist, looking for marks to go along with the sizzling burn emanating from my joint.

"We need to discuss tonight," Liam says, his tone no longer soft. I've heard *tonight* mentioned several times. And I'll admit my curiosity is piqued when worry, and perhaps shame, tightens Liam's mouth into a thin line. He doesn't strike me as a person to be bothered by much, yet he looks ... bothered.

I kick at the gravel driveway, a pebble skipping across and into the lawn. "Discuss away."

He blows out a breath and tells me about the branding.

* * *

When the wheels of Liam's truck move from the smooth pavement of the Trace to the rutty dirt road leading to the compound, I recoil. Liam filled me in as we stood in front of my scorched home, and frankly, the irony almost made me laugh.

225

Actually, I did laugh, from complete nervousness and the sheer horrifying act I'm about to endure.

They brand their people.

Their wives and members.

I'm—I'm to be branded.

Tonight.

I lean my face into the rays of sun slowly straining through the tall pines, wishing it were winter so the window would be cool under my cheek. I could use the chill to cope with the raging anger.

Liam explained all members who live on the compound, or have privileged access to it, receive this mark. Apparently, it started when Darrin first had problems with his dealers. With so many of them, and the high rate of turnover, it was becoming impossible to distinguish whose dealer belonged to what drug lord. Reports of shootouts over a deal gone bad would reach his ears and when he went to look at the scene, he didn't know which men were his. Mutilated bodies or minor decomposition made identification difficult.

It grew from there.

He branded all his men with the Jackpot symbol of a horse-shoe. It extends to his private gaming establishments as well, requiring guests to present an obsidian-colored card with a white horseshoe on it to get in.

I wonder if Adam has one of those cards.

Eventually, the brand extended to the women Darrin's men claimed. Easy to identify, yet, also to mark them.

The two scones I devoured at the bed-and-breakfast threaten to make an appearance. Between the churning of my stomach in response to iron searing my flesh, and the constant *dip, dip, bump* of the road, I need to crank the window down.

As I stick my head out to let the warm air topple into my

mouth and nose, Liam turns to me, eyes darting between me and the road.

"It will be over fast."

His words don't comfort me.

I huff out a *humph* and press my head against the back of the old truck's stiff upholstery. Sun flickers above my closed eyelids as we pass between pines lining the road. Fiddling with my rubber bands, my heart pounds beneath my rib cage, creating an ache that won't subside.

"Why do you wear those?" Liam asks.

My eyes pop open and I immediately cover my wrist. I roll my head along the headrest in his direction to briefly meet his glare before he turns back to the road. With his left hand, he grips the wheel while his right lies flat on his bulging thigh. His fingers twitch as if they notice I'm staring.

"Never know when I'll need them," I whisper.

Even though he doesn't look back at me, he drags the lower corner of his bottom lip between his teeth. Pretty sure he's sussed out my lie.

He mumbles a snarl and it's the last sound made between us for the rest of the ride until we reach the compound.

While the towering gate was intimidating before, what's even more disconcerting are the newly stationed guards with guns slung over their shoulders. These men don't have uniforms or tactical gear. They're in blue jeans and black leather coats like most of Darrin's guys. The weapons look abnormal with their attire, and I swallow as Liam approaches.

"I-is this normal?" I ask.

"No."

It's all Liam says as he rolls to a stop before the glinting keypad and card reader. Liam lifts from his seat, reaching into his back pocket to pull out a black card, and he waves it in front of the small square box. As the gates open, he slowly creeps through, leaving his window rolled down.

One of the guards lifts his hand. "Hey, Liam."

"Hey, Collin. New toys?" Liam's voice booms, loud and different than he's been all day. There's a command there but also a sliver of seething disgust. Either way, it stills me and any solace I found with him today on our trip to town is stripped away.

I inch toward my door, the slightest of movements, but the slink over snags Liam's attention and he breaks from his conversation to whip his head in my direction, noting the added distance.

He smirks.

"Darrin returned, and our shipment from New York arrived. Meeting tonight after the marking." The man—Collin—grins at me, yellow teeth promising pain and depravity. I divert my eyes. "Blitz says he can't wait to get his hands on Adam's chick."

I cringe and roll my eyes. Everyone assumes Adam and I were a thing and we—

"She isn't his anymore." Liam's voice is thick like syrup, but instead of sweet, it reeks of bitterness. He rolls up the window as Collin's face pales, realizing his misstep with Liam, who I'm assuming has some authority over him.

We weave through the compound, and I note the several men entering the clubhouse and a few scattered out on their cabin porches. Most of the cabins have motorcycles parked in front of them, but a few have older cars like the one I saw on the Trace that evening.

Liam's cabin sits farther back, in a more secluded area, and I'm already grateful to be kept more out of sight. Hopefully, that also means out of mind.

We park, and the truck door creaks as I open it. While I

slide out, my asleep ass tingles, and I stretch my arms above my head, releasing the stiffness from the ride. The sun glides low behind the trees and the smell of campfire smoke pops any bubble of happiness I had to be out of the truck.

Liam helps me carry the bags into his cabin, and I toss mine onto the floor, surveying the cramped space. With a little time before tonight, the first thing I know I need is a shower. I've been stuck in Liam's oversized, baggy clothes all day, and they're stifling. A good scrub and detangler are long overdue.

I rummage through my things, grabbing my bathroom essentials and the small plastic pouch I keep close. After a quick look, I pick out a pair of cut-off jean shorts and a tank top. I might regret it later if the chill sets in, but right now, I'm burning up.

Liam plops on the couch and opens up his computer, but he ignores it, watching me dig in each of the bags, looking for the bras and underwear I desperately need.

With an "Aa!" I spin on my bare heels and take him in sitting there.

He's leaned back, the silver laptop balanced on his right leg, while his left hand absentmindedly spins the ring on his pointer finger. His gaze lingers on me, steady and unreadable.

"I need a shower. If that's okay." I'm half asking, half not. He'd have to pry my body from the shower at this point because the next thing I'm doing is cleaning myself.

He doesn't say anything. Only gestures to the bathroom and begins typing. Unable to move, my mind shifts to the sleeping situation, and I wonder if I'll be sleeping where his ass is currently planted. I shake my head.

Make it through tonight.

I dart into the bathroom and spend way too long relishing the warm water. Unfortunately, it doesn't last long. After putting on some makeup to feel somewhat put together, I've spent well over an hour in here.

When I'm dressed, my hair damp with water, I open the medicine cabinet. Nail clippers, hydrogen peroxide, shaving cream—I pore over the items while moving the toothpaste off the top shelf to make room for my stuff. There isn't much to give him away, but I notice a small hole in the back of the cabinet. Is that—

Three loud bangs on the door startle me, and I drop my face cream into the single-bowl sink. I snatch it up and toss the jar into the cabinet before I slam it shut and open the bathroom door.

"Yeah?"

"It's been over an hour, and this is the only bathroom in this cabin," Liam says.

I raise my eyebrows at him and offer him a slight shrug, wondering what his point is. He lifts his chin over to the toilet and my eyes widen.

"Oh, right." I gather my ball of laundry from the corner by the tub and bolt out, stubbing my toe on the doorjamb. I yelp and stumble forward, but a large hand seizes my elbow before I go down.

Liam glares at me, his eyes skirting over my scoop-necked top and moving down to my shorts. With a quick jerk, I yank my elbow out of his grasp and turn with my laundry, well, his laundry, and open my mouth to ask where to put it, but the door slams in my face.

Despite the one-bedroom cabin being only one bedroom, there's a tiny stackable washer and dryer in a linen closet, and I spend the next couple of hours washing the new clothes I purchased in hopes of keeping my mind off being treated like a possession.

Liam offered me a drawer in his dresser. And while he

reheats the lasagna Mrs. Northgate gave us, I stalk to his room with my freshly cleaned clothes and nearly melt at the oddly cozy space.

It's simple. A queen-sized mattress atop a rustic log frame bed. It must be cedar, because the closer I got, the more charming the smell. A green and blue plaid comforter is made neatly on his bed while a matching cedar dresser sits across from the foot of it.

Going to my knees, I open the bottom drawer, although I'm baffled it's still full after he said he cleared out a drawer. I try the next. Then another. Climbing the six-drawer dresser until I reach the top drawer that is, in fact, empty.

It's slightly odd he'd give me the top drawer when bending down to the bottom one is probably harder on him than me due to his size. But I make quick work of putting my minimal clothes away. I spy a closet in the far corner of the room but leave my dresses folded in the drawer. I couldn't care less about a few wrinkles, especially out here.

When I'm finished, I join Liam in the kitchen. We each have a plate of lasagna—him eating two helpings and me unable to stomach but a few bites. We don't talk.

It's night by the time Liam and I leave the cabin, and I follow close behind him as he leads me to this barbaric ritual. Still, he says nothing. The comfort he offered in the truck is nowhere to be found.

The air is warm, and it wraps around me but doesn't help my shaking. Stars blink in the sky and there isn't a cloud in the way to disturb them. Truth be told, it'd be a fantastic night for a bonfire. One with marshmallows and laughing friends, not drunk men fondling women and burning marks in people.

With my gaze squinting at the ground, I watch for roots from the massive oak trees. I'm so focused, I don't notice Liam has stopped and I slam into his back.

231

He hisses but turns to address me. "Two other men are getting their mark tonight. It will be crowded." Liam's gaze struggles to keep mine because mine is pulled to the raging fire and swarms of people outside the clubhouse. "Fleur, listen to me. Stay close tonight."

The terrorized part of me wants to bury my head in my hands and weep. Another part, the angry and annoyed this is happening side of me, wants to punch Liam in the face. Stay close to him? That's not going to get me out of being stamped by that psychopath Blitz.

I'm sick of the whiplash with him.

We stalk around the clubhouse, not through it, and smack right into the noisy crowd. Music plays from outdoor speakers, and most of the men have a beer in one hand and a female clasped in the other. I look away, heat rising to my cheeks. This is insane.

The firepit is outlined in cinderblocks stacked four high and the sheer size of the fire roars and crackles over the music and loud voices. A drunk man stumbles into me, his warm beer sloshing up and over his open bottle and onto my periwinkle top. Thank goodness it's not white.

"Well. I'm sorry, miss." He hiccups and leans into my face. The stench of his beer-laced breath along with the vile body odor makes me take two steps back where I'm met with the front of Liam's hard chest. I dart to his side, and when the drunk man tries to pursue me again, Liam grabs my hand and pulls me away. The man yells out a "hey, not fair" before spinning twice in a circle and making for another woman.

When we've moved away from the crowded area, I'm sure Liam is going to drop my hand. However, he doesn't. His palm engulfs mine, holding fast and tight. The rough pads of his fingers rest on top of my hand and with each jolt of movement, they scratch and rub. I'm so focused on the sensation his hand over mine causes, I miss the fact we now stand in front of Darrin.

My stomach sours.

"Liam." Darrin nods. "Meeting tonight after this. She'll go first."

It's instinct that I tug away from where Liam's hand is tightened over mine. I want to run.

He quickly releases me, but I don't move. I can't.

Oh God.

Ohgodohgod.

Blitz raises his hands and claps several times, garnering the attention of the crowd. Darrin steps forward and spews some utter nonsense about their tightly knit brotherhood and how special it is when someone claims a wife. It's all crap, and I stop listening in favor of eyeballing the trees, wondering how far I'd make it.

I don't want to do this. I thought I had this locked down, had my nerves controlled, but I'm afraid I don't. I'm not brave. I'm terrified. Am I built for this sort of pain?

The words Darrin speaks next cause me to shiver.

"Now we offer the horseshoe mark to Liam's new wife, Fleur."

Blitz stalks toward me, a sneer curling his lip, but Liam slaps an arm over his chest, stealing the branding tool from his hand.

My knees wobble and I'm afraid I'm going to faint. I can't do this.

Liam approaches with slow, steady steps. He's so close I have to tilt my head to look into his eyes. He takes my elbow and I glare at him, icy and cold.

"Please," I beg. The reality of the moment is finally setting in.

Liam's eyes dart around to the surrounding men with the

barest hint of concern before his nostrils flare. He leans down close to my ear, his warm breath skirting along the rim and raising the baby hairs on my neck.

"Breathe, Fleur."

I can't. My breaths aren't calm or unwavering. They're a hiccupped mess.

"Trust me," he says, pushing the branding iron into the hottest of flames, the iron rod glowing orange with rage.

My breath catches and I divert my eyes to the nearby pine trees, swaying in the wind. I'm shaking wildly and want to scream. But what good would that do? Probably only give Blitz and the other men something to fantasize about later, so I pinch my lips shut.

Liam moves the iron toward my wrist, using his other hand to turn it up, the underside exposed. His eyes snag on the healing welts already there and he pauses. I don't look at him. It's already taking every bit of my composure to stand here.

Laughter fades in and out, washing over me. The crackling fire draws my attention and I stare unblinking as it licks the night sky. Tears well in my eyes, and one slips from the corner, but I won't let them fall. I continue to gaze at the tip of blue, dancing in the wind.

A rough thumb grazes the underside of my wrist. It's delicate and thoughtful, everything this moment isn't.

Liam shifts the iron, and my eyes follow the rod, finally making out its shape—a curved horseshoe, like a U with tapered ends. I flinch, twisting my wrist, but he holds fast. I search his gaze, desperate for something to anchor me, but his irises are dark, almost black, as he spreads his massive hand beneath my wrist.

"Whatever you do, hold still."

Agony.

Pure agony sears through my body as the hiss of the iron

burns into my skin. I scream in pain but keep my focus on the fire. What should be five seconds feels like a lifetime. When the iron pulls away from my skin, I bite my tongue so hard the metallic taste of blood floods my mouth. The pain. The pain is unbearable.

It takes even longer for me to look down at the new brand when he's done. The new mark glows pink, smaller than a quarter, but placed carefully over the handful of welts.

Cheers, which at first sound like they are underwater, become clearer. Men hoot and holler, clinking glasses and offering smacks to Liam's back. He gives them clipped nods and smirks in their direction.

Tears stream down my face. My wrist is on fire, but all I can think is that when it heals, I'll be able to snap two new rubber bands right over this mark, and it hurts a bit less.

Chapter 29
Liam

Fleur's tears threaten to undo me. I want nothing more than to shove this hot iron into Darrin's blue eye. I reach into my pocket, pull out four painkillers, and dump them into her outstretched hand as she stares at her shaking wrist.

I'm glad Darrin agreed to the smaller one. There are three sizes. The brand on my ribs is the largest, and I can't fathom inflicting that level of pain on her.

I didn't miss the welts already on her wrist, nor did I buy her story about being a Girl Scout and always being prepared with rubber bands shit. She's hurting herself, and I wonder who in the world made her feel like she deserved pain.

A woman hands me a bottle of water and I crack the top, then hold it out to her. Her eyes are clouded over, glassy and wet, and she keeps staring at the new mark on her delicate wrist.

She's so beautiful. Even in pain.

"Fleur," I demand. Her eyes snap to mine, and I swish the water in the bottle and gesture to the pills in her hand. For a minute, I think she might fight me on taking unknown pills, but she surprises me, popping the four ibuprofen into her mouth and chugging half the water.

I guide her to the clubhouse and push through the back door. One of the tables in the dining area has three sets of gauze and antibiotics as a preventative. A set for each of the three people getting a mark tonight.

Tipping out a chair, I move Fleur by her shoulders and push down until she yields and sits. Each sniffle, each wince or flinch punches me in the heart. I'm barely holding myself together.

I work as quickly as possible to wrap her wrist and soothe the painful burn I know she's feeling. When I'm done, I glance around, and realizing we're alone, I bring my thumb up to swipe away a tear plummeting down her cheek.

She smacks my hand away with her uninjured arm and I grab it. The fight still in her makes my chest pound even harder.

"Let go!" she cries. When I don't, she adds, "Please ..."

It's the crack in her voice that prompts me to release her. This girl is addicting. Blows in out of nowhere and infects my mind from day one. It never mattered Adam was interested in her. She was mine from the start.

I lead Fleur back to the cabin to drop her off, then make my way to the warehouse for a meeting. Darrin said because the party at the clubhouse would likely last well into the early morning, he'd like the peacefulness of the empty warehouse to meet.

When I push through the door, the fluorescent lights blind me. Trip, Goff, Blitz, and Darrin wait there in a circle. Letting the door slam behind me, I stalk toward them, absorbing Darrin's assessing glare.

"Fleur did well," he says.

I nod in agreement. He's right. Many of these men scream and babble like newborn babies when they're marked. While Fleur screamed in anguish, it was brief and nowhere near as high-pitched as some of these guys.

"I bet she's crying now, though. Might have to put in some effort for your lay tonight," Blitz says.

I glare at him, folding my fingers into a fist to knock the ever-living shit out of him, but Darrin beats me to it with a loud smack to the back of his head.

Blitz curses but backs away.

"My meeting with our suppliers was quite lucrative," Darrin interjects with a simple sentence that garnishes my attention immediately.

I slowly let my gaze drift to him. "The Cartel? What did they say?" I ask.

Darrin studies me briefly, sliding his tongue along his top teeth. "They're prepared to supply larger shipments of their more potent product. What's even more appealing is their desire to merge the network further."

Ice floods my veins along with an uptick in my pulse, causing my heart to audibly pound in my ears. I hang on to every word—considering it's the single thing helping to distract me from what I inflicted on Fleur mere minutes ago.

Blitz's crude words wedge themselves between the silence after Darrin's declaration. "I'm not working with that bastard from Alabama. The Cartel can kiss my—"

"Unnecessary," Darrin cuts him off, looking at each of us. When he meets my gaze, I focus past him. Steel steps ascend to upper platforms that traverse the entirety of the warehouse. The long tubular lights that hang from the ceiling swing back and forth slightly, and I keep my eyes plastered there.

Eventually, Darrin moves on.

"This network is what we've been working toward for

years. You're all fools if you think we're privileged enough to run our own operation. The Cartel controls us. We ... we do their bidding."

His voice cracks on the last word, the sting to his pride clear in the way aggravation twists his face into a grimace.

"What's that mean for us?" Trip asks.

"It means to be on the lookout. We've just become bigger fish to fry. Every undercover, rival organization, and random tweaker will be looking to sink their teeth into this larger pie." He glides a hand through his hair while a flash of panic contours his face.

Amidst the circumstances of my being here, I've come to know Darrin. In another life, I'd venture to say we could be close friends rather than him being the harbinger that holds my soul. A twinge of sadness ripples through me and I almost feel bad for him. Almost.

Fleur's swallowed cries and spilled tears race to the forefront of my mind, and I stomp out anything that whispers compassion for the man.

Darrin seems to catch himself and his current disposition because he laughs, the sound echoing around the metal building. "This is a good thing. More money, more power, more influence, and"—he looks at Goff, the only one of us here actually addicted to Jackpot—"a better high."

* * *

I move toward the cabin by the light of the moon sifting through the trees. Ear-splitting laughter and cackles pulse through the compound as tonight's festivities are only half over, even at midnight.

Thoughts of whether Fleur will be asleep flit through my mind, and I consider waking her to trade my bed for the couch. She must be tired. Probably scared. Definitely pissed.

I've never kept much on the front porch of my cabin. It's just a small space with a single railing wrapped around it and a few extra feet of room. The only thing out there is a lone rocking chair. Unlike some of my fellow cabin owners, who have folding chairs, grills, and their latest round of empty beer bottles lined up on the handrails, as if they are a prize to be displayed.

That's why the sight of sneakers by the front door halts me a few steps from the porch, freezing me in place. Confused as to why her shoes would be sitting outside, I tentatively approach the door.

Careful not to wake her, I slow, my hand reaching for the door handle.

Whimpers sift through the door, oscillating between short bursts of sobs and long angry-sounding squalls. As if I've been punched in the chest, I struggle to suck in a breath and back away from the door. I can't do this—listen to her cry.

I turn on my heels and nearly trip down the porch steps as I bound into the woods. I want to run, but I fight the instinct and merge into a jog instead. My heavy boots crunch over twigs and scuffle through pine needles scattered in the dirt as I make my way to a substantial oak tree and press my back against its sturdy trunk.

I've lost so much. Given *so much*. Probably taken from too many innocents as well, Fleur being the most recent victim. I hate who I am and who I've had to become to make this happen.

The rough bark bites into my back as I slide down, unconcerned as it scrapes against my leather jacket.

Her face.

Fleur's face, red and agonized, as I caused her physical pain tonight pummels me one disturbing image after another. It's nothing new for me, inflicting pain. I've done it before, but with her, it's affecting me differently. I want to burn this place to the ground.

Jerking my phone from my jacket pocket, I quickly check I'm alone and turn it on. Furiously, I type out the message that's been screaming in my mind since I met Fleur. Since she came into my life at a high rate of speed, plowing into me and jostling me off my own track.

Me: I can't do this anymore.

W: You must.

Chapter 30
Liam

3.5 Years Ago

There's no absolution for someone like me. Not after what I've witnessed—had to stand by and watch.

My truck halts to a stop on the road and I scramble to open the door fast enough before the bile in my throat turns to vomit. I upheave the entire day's worth of food into the ditch on the side of the road. Leaves stick to my sleeves as I push myself up from my buckled position on the ground.

Dragging my sleeve across my mouth, I clamber back in my truck and continue on my path to the bed-and-breakfast. If there's anyone who can help me it's my grandfather.

His history as a state trooper was part of the reason I had decided on the police academy over a year ago. When I was a young boy, he often sat us all down recounting stories of his time and the opportunities he had to be a light for people, serve people. While Adam and my sister may have viewed them as only stories, I took it as a calling. I longed to serve as my grandfather did. Protect innocent life, those who can't protect themselves.

I snort.

This is the exact opposite of that. The charred corpse rotting in the secluded clearing near a field assures me I've failed in my mission.

In search of guidance, I pull into my grandparents' driveway littered with fallen leaves from the oak trees out front. I yank the door open and climb out, careful to slink close to the house and let myself in through the back. The last thing I need is for Darrin to know it was me who ratted them out.

I find my grandfather flipping through a seed catalog at the kitchen table, a hot mug of cider in his hand. I'd been so distracted with leaving my place in a rush, I forgot a coat, and I'm immediately aware of how chilled I am approaching my grandfather.

"Hey, Son. What are you doing here?" Noting my ashen face, he adds, "A-are you all right?"

Worry flickers in his eyes at my disheveled state. I manipulate a chair closer, swinging a leg over it and leaning my forearms on the back while facing him.

"I need your help."

※ ※ ※

"You were at the police academy when you were called home to help with your brother?" Agent Wilson asks.

"Yes."

"And you've been taking his place working for Darrin to save his ass?"

"Yes."

"Some brother you are, man."

I grunt, worried that I made a mistake having my grandfather reach out to his former trooper buddies and get me in touch with the DEA. Agent Wilson comes across as the washed-up surfer dude who dropped out of college in favor of catching the next best wave. His long blond hair, almost white, is epically glaring, and I itch to push my sunglasses down over my face to shield myself.

Although what he says next makes me take every thought back. "I could just arrest you. Make you tell me where this compound is."

"I don't know where it is. Have only heard about it. Only his trusted circle and some warehouse workers reside there. I couldn't tell you," I say, my mouth dry with the lingering taste of bile on my tongue. "But I could find out."

Agent Wilson's eyebrows lift slightly. "We need someone in there. Darrin's group is one we've been watching for a while. We've picked up a few of his dealers but more keep taking their place. He's part of a much more extensive network across the nation. His shipments feed into others."

"Why don't you arrest him? Take down the operation in Ruin?" I'm growing frustrated the more I sit here. I came here to escape this life, not learn more about it.

"It's not about cutting off an arm. It's about killing the whole thing. Taking out Darrin would leave room for another kingpin to take his place. We need information. We need someone deep cover for the long haul."

I hate the way he's staring at me.

"With your law enforcement training and your"—he pauses, sizing me up—"your personal investment in ensuring your brother's safety, I think you know what our position is going to be."

That was my original plan. To follow in my grandfather's

footsteps. Becoming a cop was going to be the way I honored him. Instead, I've become the very person I vowed to take down.

"We'll set up protocols and procedures for dead drops. This is dangerous work. They treat undercover cops and agents worse than any other nark in their own group. My partner was killed three years ago. They removed his head and sent it back to the agency in a box."

I flinch at the pit forming in my stomach, and I want to wretch all over again. I'm going to die doing this.

"I tell you this to make sure it's clear. Deep cover means you are on your own. There's no Hail Mary. No cavalry called in. Nothing. Don't have a wife and kids, do you?"

I shake my head.

"Good. Don't get involved."

This assignment, this mission, it could be my redemption. I just don't want to lose my soul before I get there.

Chapter 31
Fleur

An ache in my neck stiffens any potential movement when I wake. I don't open my eyes. Instead, I clench them, trying to take stock of the gnarly position my head is in. Twisted to the right side, my face is buried in between the back of the couch and where the seat cushions meet it. My shoulders, unfortunately, face the other way.

I need to move. I know I do. However, the thought of peeling myself away from this uncomfortable orientation feels like too much effort.

Adding to the twinge radiating in my neck and between my shoulder blades, my head pulses with a dull throb. It's most likely from an emotional night.

When Liam dropped me off at the cabin, I told myself I was going to rest and stay calm. Unwrapped and glaring at me, my wrist had other plans. What am I going to do with this mark when I finally get free? Cover it up? Wear long sleeves forever?

I stared at it for minutes before letting more tears fall.

I'm not sure how long I cried. Stopping only long enough to brush my teeth and pull on some pajama bottoms. Last thing I remember is forcing my face into my pillow to muffle my weeping. Liam must've been out late because he wasn't home when I finally fell asleep.

It takes me another five minutes to lift myself off the couch, grimacing with each crack of my stubborn spine. I rack my brain for a few stretches and yoga positions from years past and awkwardly attempt those for some sort of relief.

When I get back to a normal life, I need to get in shape. This is embarrassing.

Sufficiently limber, I pad to the kitchen, stopping short when a dark residue on the round kitchen table grabs my attention. I narrow my eyes at the gray-speckled dust and drag a finger through it. Between my finger and thumb, I rub the substance together, watching the fine soot-like material settle in the ridges of my prints.

Huh.

In the kitchen, I wash my hands and pour myself a glass of water, my eyes scanning the cabin. It's eerily quiet, and when I pull aside the window's curtain, there isn't a soul moving about the compound.

Figures. Probably a late night for everyone.

My thoughts drift to Liam, and after using the bathroom, I tiptoe to his room. The door is cracked, and with ease, I push it farther open. A large form lies under the blankets moving up and down with the steady rhythm of his breaths. I linger; creepily so. And even move to see his face smushed into the pillow between his balled-up fists.

He's on his stomach, torso bare, giving me an unobstructed view of his fully tattooed sleeve and a huge horseshoe welt on his ribs. I snarl at the thought of Darrin marking so much of his skin—the pain. A sigh escapes him, blowing a fine strand of hair out of his face then back over his mouth.

The stern expression I've come to associate with Liam has

softened. The edges and sharp lines of his face are muted and dull as sleep has pulled him into a moment of peace—a reprieve from the disgusting world he's a part of.

Unlike my fitful night, he looks calm and well-rested. I eye the bed, jealous and slightly disappointed I'll be on the couch for the foreseeable future.

I shake my head at my intrusion into his personal space, deeply unsettled by my prolonged gaze. Quickly, I spin around and dart out.

I end up showering and getting dressed, tossing on some jean shorts and a shirt. Then I shove my damp hair under a navy baseball cap I don't remember grabbing at River's. She probably snuck it in there for me.

Quietly, I open the front door, looking directly at why I'm out here in the first place.

The rocking chair is one of a kind—quite literally because Liam only has one. Scooting the chair closer to the porch rail, I plant myself in the seat, twirling my feet in the rays of sun warming the porch boards. With each rock in the chair, the stained cabin floorboards creak, adding to the sound of shaking branches swaying in the early morning breeze.

The contrast between last night and this morning is indescribable. Except for one or two people far off near the warehouse, not another soul moves around the cabins.

The bandages on my wrist have started to curl and peel, and I pick at the rolled edges, fighting the urge to unwrap the whole thing and study my new mark.

"We probably need to swap your bandages."

His voice jolts me upright and I drop my legs from soaking up vitamin D.

I turn to see Liam leaning in the doorframe, eyes narrowed on where I grip my wrist. His gaze breaks when I move my hand to the side and he studies my face, lingering on my hat a bit too long.

"Yeah, I was just thinking that. Got any more wrap?"

Liam nods and gestures back toward the inside of the cabin. Slinking out of my sunspot where I'm curled up like a cat, I shuffle back toward the door. Liam doesn't move as I approach. Instead, he glances back toward the top of my head and says, "Nice hat."

I shrug my shoulders and give him a confused look because I have no idea what his problem is with this hat. The corner of his mouth twitches before he steps aside, holding the door open.

"Sit down and I'll get some more bandages," he says.

I do as he says, sliding a less than comfortable chair out from the table and plopping down. My stomach, suddenly triggered by the dining room table, growls loudly as Liam makes his way back to me.

"Help yourself to anything you need in the kitchen. I know there isn't much, but we can stop at a store on our way back here this afternoon."

"This afternoon?" I ask.

Liam pulls out the other chair next to mine, thighs spread wide. He's in black jeans again, with a black V-neck that hangs loose, exposing a bit of his chest. I blink away the unsolicited thoughts bobbing in my mind.

"I have a meeting I need to go to. Should only take a minute, but it's about an hour away. We'll take the truck and get groceries on the way back."

He takes my hand, and I can't help but flick my eyes to his. Although he doesn't look at me, he softly turns my wrist over in his hand, causing goosebumps to spring up along my arms. I jerk away at the sensation of his fingertips over my skin.

"I'm sorry. I know it hurts," he says, face wincing. I almost chuckle at the fact he didn't hurt me at all. That it's his touch generating the desire to pull away.

Awkwardly, I hold out my hand to him again and swallow when his proficient hands make quick work to unwrap my burn.

It's not as bad as I thought it would be. The small horseshoe is a reddish-pink. What I thought would look like welts, considering I have several strips across my wrist already, is indented. The skin feels taut and there's a cloudy pink seeping out around the mark. But overall, it doesn't look bad.

Liam opens a tub of antiseptic and drops a dot on my wrist, using his thumb to spread it out. His touch is featherlight and it goes beyond the horseshoe, grazing over the welts on my wrist for a moment too long.

I pull away again. "Thank you. I can wrap it."

Liam tilts his head, bringing his hand to scratch at his beard. He sucks in a breath, then gives me a tight nod, lifting from his seat in a more graceful move than I'd expect from someone his size.

While I chide myself and attempt to do up my wrist one-handed, Liam clinks around in the kitchen until the smell of bacon whirls around the whole cabin. He sets two plates out and places two pieces on each one with a slice of over-burned toast.

I try to hide my small smile when he curses at the stove before kicking it to shut off. He brings over the two dishes and sets them down on the table, then pulls out the chair next to me.

Some part of me wants to be petty. Wants to swallow the words *thank you*, before they make it past the tip of my tongue. But I also know this could've been much worse for me, and for *that* I'm grateful.

"Thank you," I mutter. And because I'm an idiot, I add, "Do you think River was right about Adam coming back?"

His expression moves from passive to immovable and stone-cold before I can finish my question. He pins me with a stare as he finishes chewing the strip of bacon in his mouth. He wipes his hand on his thigh and leans down close to my ear. The scent of bacon with smokey spices and a woodsy smell gathers near me.

"Do you want Adam to come back?" Liam asks, his voice lower several octaves.

The sound kindles something deep in my belly, dangerous and reckless, and no doubt something I shouldn't be feeling. I consider his hazel eyes, undeterred by his clear and blatant stare.

"I want to know he's okay," I answer.

"He's fine." Liam finishes his toast in two bites. "Be ready to go in an hour."

* * *

Liam doesn't tell me where we're going, only that it's about an hour's drive and to use the bathroom before we go because there isn't any place to stop. I've come to this conclusion in my own adventures around Mississippi, so I bristle when he addresses me like a child.

The roads we take are all dirt roads zigzagging through wooded areas. The black duffel in the back seat slides with every turn. Admittedly annoyed at every drag and snag of the bag along the bench seat, I reach back to steady it, earning myself a giant reprimand.

"Don't touch it," Liam barks.

I retract my hand, unsure I've ever heard him use such force behind his words before. Snatching my hand back, I practically sit on them, shame flooding my cheeks. What did he think I was going to do, peek?

Outraged at his implication, I flick my gaze toward his. "Don't worry. I won't touch your precious Jackpot. You may not be addicted to *it*, but you're addicted to your position here." I snort. "And you say it's for your brother ..."

He doesn't spare me a look, but the white of his knuckles blanches as he chokes the wheel.

I bite my lip, anxiously chewing it and feeling the void of my rubber bands. With my hair now dry, I tip off the hat and pull my hair forward, thread it into a long braid at my side, then slip the hat back over. I brush the tip of my braid back and forth along my lips as I stare out the window.

Liam's admonishments are the only words he says to me until we finally reach a secluded river.

There's nothing around. The river winds through the woods, and the surrounding trees lean over each side of it as if seeking a secret. The road, more like trail, is one lane and the old truck doesn't do anything to help suspend us from the bumps and dips along the pathway.

Shockingly, the leaves, while not yet turned, have begun to fall and the fullness of the great oaks is less so as we approach the cooler months.

Up ahead, a black sedan sits by the edge of the river, and I turn to see Liam drag a hand through his hair and blow out a breath. As we slow, a figure emerges from the car, and Liam pulls the truck to a stop almost fifty feet away.

"Stay here. Whatever you do, don't get out of the car," Liam says, reaching back for the duffel while his eyes stay straight ahead on the man stomping out a cigarette.

I lean forward, watching as Liam strides toward the man,

bag slung over his right shoulder. His steps are languid and unhurried, but I don't miss the way his head scans from side to side as if he's expecting someone to jump out of the surrounding woods.

My heart pounds rapidly the closer he gets to the man, and if I thought I could hear anything they were saying over the roar of the river, I'd roll my window down to get a better shot at it.

Liam tosses the bag on the ground before the man's feet. Following the bag up to the other man, I notice his jeans are a casual dark blue wash, his shirt is a navy polo tucked into his belted pants. Not the average dealer attire I've come to assume they wear, but what do I know? Darrin's men dress like they're a motorcycle club and technically they aren't. Though I still think they want to be.

Liam's animated hands move through the air as he clearly explains something important. When the man's face turns toward me, I jerk back into the seat. An unsettling punch in my gut makes me want to dry heave. I look out the back window to see if he perhaps was trying to see something else. Nope. He was looking at me.

I shiver. This whole farce is going to end with me in prison for being an accomplice to drug dealing.

Another few minutes pass, and the man from the sedan—a Volvo I finally figured out—lifts the prize from the ground and saunters back to his car while Liam makes his way to me. Well, the truck, I guess.

He looks over his shoulder a few times as he walks less leisurely than before. There's a quick scuffle with a downed tree limb in the pathway before he yanks open the door and climbs in.

Any other time, I'd ask how his meeting went. However, the frown on his face keeps me from opening my mouth. I try, but snap it shut at the sound of his curses while he fumbles with the truck key in the ignition.

"Normally, I take the bike," he says. Those words come so easily, I'm curious if he has a point to them. Then I get my answer. "Easier to conceal among the trees."

"Makes sense."

The corner of his mouth lifts a smidge, and in this moment, isolated by the surrounding wood and compelling nature, I want to see him smile. For a second, I wonder what the harsh lines of his steely brow would look like if assuaged, or worse yet, what they would reveal etched in pleasure.

I shake my head. *Gosh, what is wrong with me?*

"We're about twenty minutes from a bigger grocery store. We should be able to get what we need there." Liam's eyes skirt to mine and heat rushes to my cheeks as I'm afraid the thoughts I had are written on my face. I divert my gaze in favor of the window.

"Yeah, okay," I whisper into the trees as Liam backs up down the single-lane path until he can successfully turn around.

It takes exactly that before we pull into a well-maintained but older grocery store. The brick façade is worn down from stark red to a dull brown, and the metal awning with chipped paint displays the few letters left. IGGLY GLY.

At least this store is larger than the one we have in town. I drag a cart behind me as I peruse the selection of produce, then grab a head of broccoli and some onions. Liam watches me out of the corner of his eye, and the sudden feeling of awkwardness rears its head.

"So, uh, what do you like to eat?" I ask. Goodness, could this be any weirder?

He shrugs and tosses a bottle of ranch dressing into the cart before eyeing the vegetables as if they wronged him. "Not that."

I can't help it. I end up cracking a smile and letting loose an airy laugh.

Liam, whose eyes are scanning the dairy section, does a double take before staring at my grin. His own falls, going serious and skidding away.

"Do you all eat together? At the dining area in the club-house?" I ask.

"What? No. That's just for special occasions."

"Like marring someone's skin with a hot poker?"

Liam swipes at his forehead, a familiar dark smudge of dust smeared between his fingers. Arching a brow, Liam takes a step toward me, the air twisting taut, and my breath catches in my throat.

I bite my lip and look away.

The ring from Liam's cell phone draws him up short, and he pauses to answer.

"Darrin ..." he says, moving down the aisle so I can't hear.

While he takes the call, I gather some oat milk, coffee creamer, cheese, and anything else that sounds good. Honestly, when I saw the dining area, I figured they all ate there. However, it's looking more and more like many of the guys eat within the confines of their own cabins.

I'm not the best cook. Average at best. With Chris, after the first several years of no proposal, I became overly obsessed with convincing him I was wife material. I cooked to the best of my ability, slaving away with false enthusiasm in the kitchen. Pathetic.

I reach for my wrist, but I'm met with the scratch of the gauze and huff out, annoyed. When I get to the frozen section, I grab a random brand of cookies and cream ice cream, all but throwing it in the cart.

My hand is barely out of the cart when the static brush of Liam's arm shocks me. He picks the tub out of the cart and puts it back. Just when I think he's opposed to ice cream, he puts a different brand of the same flavor in.

"This is superior. You almost committed a grievous error." He smiles at me. Full-on smiles at me. I'm pretty sure my mouth falls open in response. For a minute, I almost forget about our circumstances; about Adam, Darrin, and the glaring burn on my wrist.

Almost.

I eyeball the half gallon he replaced, smiling as I murmur, "Noted."

Liam pulls the front of the cart with two fingers as he examines each of the freezer sections. He pulls out some frozen sausage patties and tosses them in the cart.

"So what do you eat?" I try again.

He shrugs, and I pull a few frozen burritos out.

"Eggs mostly."

I snort, and he stops pulling the cart in favor of striding toward me. I back up, but he reaches for the hat on my head and flicks it with his middle finger.

"Find it funny?" he asks.

"Absolutely ..." Liam's nostrils flare. "Not," I finish.

He steps back. "Good." His mouth twitches like he wants to grin again, and I smile slyly into my shoulder.

We continue shopping, each of us putting items in the cart, and I can't help but enjoy the semblance of normal. Because I'm sure when we get back to the compound, life will be anything but.

Chapter 32
Liam

The hat on Fleur is driving me wild.

I didn't have the heart to tell her it was mine. That the older cap with the town's name, Ruin, MS, embroidered overtop a magnolia leaf was mine from years ago. I hadn't seen it in forever, so I was shocked when she had it tucked over her perfectly shaped head. Come to think of it, the last time I remember having it was in my truck. Probably got mixed with the thrift store bags when we brought them in.

If it keeps her wearing it, I'll let her think otherwise.

I push the empty cart back to the return, the groceries piled high in the back seat of my truck. I have never once been shopping with a woman before. Admittedly, I've never found myself in this situation. I've always lived alone, never sharing space with a member of the opposite sex. Here I've found myself married and living with a woman for the first time all in the same week.

The cabin already smells better. Her scent reminds me of pistachio and salted caramel drizzle on an ice cream sundae.

What the hell? I'm probably hungry.

257

I climb into the truck and twist the key. While the engine roars to life, I chance a glimpse at the girl distorting my life as I know it—because I'll never be the same after this.

She's in her own world, contemplating the saturated clouds that are blowing in quickly. Fleur chews at her lip, folding it over her bottom teeth. Does she know how alluring she is when she does that?

We make it onto the main road before the patter of rain starts on the windshield. Sun blocked out in the sky, the last light of the day gives way to early darkness, and my phone call with Darrin eats away at me for the night to come. He's demanded I come to his latest establishment, which means I'll need to bring Fleur.

I swerve to miss another truck I didn't see, and Fleur's eyes widen.

I hate I snapped at her this afternoon, but the samples I stole from the warehouse along with the intel I need to pass along to my handler can't have any evidence of her.

Selfishly, I want to tell her. Maybe she'd hate me less. But I can't toss her in the middle of this investigation and undercover mission. No one can know. My grandfather is the only one who knows my involvement and that's not without its risks.

She's already handling this better than I would've expected. Any additional measure of comfort on her part would be met with suspicion.

A part of me thinks it would help solidify what I'm doing. But the other part thinks I'd be putting her in danger. Even more so if I'm found out.

No. The less she knows, the better.

I need her to act disgusted with me. As much as tugging out her smile heats my blood, I can't be seen as anything other than what I am portraying. That way, Fleur can genuinely say she didn't know.

* * *

The rain tapers off to a drizzle.

Sluggishly, I exit the shower, having spent too much time in there putting off the inevitable, I suppose. With my towel wrapped securely around my waist, I swipe the steam settled on the medicine cabinet mirror and open it to grab my toothbrush. I pause, taking in the array of feminine products piled on the narrow glass shelves before I slam the door shut, trying to shove the torrent of Fleur thoughts from my mind. It's been a week, and already I can't shake her presence.

Having forgotten my clothes in the bedroom, I throw open the door to find Fleur reading on the couch. Her knees are up, toes tucked under her, while she flips the pages of a *Southern Home* magazine that isn't mine. At the sound of the door, her gaze casually lifts, then widens into shock before she ducks into the pages of the issue.

I'm covered below the waist, but the red settling in on the tips of her ears makes me smirk. With a snort, I turn on my heels to pull on my jeans and a ribbed long-sleeve. After wrestling with the bottom drawer to pull out a pair of hidden socks, I finally wrangle my hair up. Lingering in the bedroom, I stare at the bed. I'd prefer to be in it, rather than being summoned to Darrin's latest conquest. It's unfortunate. Even more so because I need to tow Fleur with me.

I move back through the hall and into the living room.

Fleur, who hadn't bothered to change, slaps closed her reading material in favor of standing. Immediately, my attention bounces to her toned legs. I trace every tantalizing curve, my focus dipping to her rumpled shirt drifting above her hip bone.

She reaches for her tattered braid. Pulling out the hair tie holding it together, she weaves her hand through it, letting the style unwind. The long waves of her hair make me pause.

A flash of blond cascading down around my face, wrapped in the plaid of my bed sheets, has me taking a few steps back.

I reach for the bike helmet and, without meeting Fleur's eyes, hand it to her.

"What's this for?" she asks.

"To wear."

She gulps at the sleek black that reflects like a mirror. "We're taking your bike?"

"Yes."

She nods, rubbing her hands along her thighs, beckoning my gaze again.

Damn it.

"I-I, um, I've never been on one before." Panic laces her voice, and her hand instinctively reaches for her wrapped wrist.

She's nervous.

Normally, the small tidbit of information would thrill me, but at the way her face wrings with worry, along with her subconscious reach for a way to quiet the fear—my muscles tighten with an otherworldly desire to touch her. I flex open my closed fists, trying to quench the need.

"Trust me, Fleur."

✳ ✳ ✳

Darrin's new establishment is at an old dry cleaner. It's rather ordinary in order to avoid arousing suspicion. The building is warped and splintered, the siding a muted yellow that reminds me of piss in snow. The metal roof has been neglected, and the faint outline of the old business name is barely visible.

When we first pull up, I immediately want to take Fleur away. Several men, dressed in their leathers and smoking cigarettes, loiter around outside in the back. Women in scantily clad outfits hang all over them. One of the women's hands wanders over the man's shoulders she's practically climbing. I don't even need to remove my helmet to see her behavior is off. Most likely Jackpot.

Darrin isn't looking to get rich with these underground card games and gambling rings. He wants people in his pocket—favors owed to him. He wants users around to make irrational decisions and those addicted to the game to become addicted to something far more powerful. These places are conduits, funnels to trap. Nothing more.

When I finally maneuver the bike into an inconspicuous spot and shut off the engine, Fleur's hands drop away from where they'd been vice-gripped around my waist. With each rev of the engine or sharp turn, her hold would intensify, sending heat rushing through me. Something about her being at my mercy.

I turn, reaching my gloved hands up to unfasten her helmet. Her hair puffs out when I rip the helmet away, the static feathering out individual strands into the air. For a moment, I take the opportunity to study her through the tinted visor of my own helmet, having not yet removed it.

"Look who it is," a voice shouts from the back entrance. Fleur's hand bolts to my arm, her fist twisting my leather jacket as her eyes find the source of the shout. Barely do I keep my mouth from twitching upward at her slight shift in my direction. As if I'm the one to protect her from these buffoons.

She'd be right, though. I am the only one standing between her and this awful life.

Eventually, I remove my helmet and raise a hand toward Larry, Darrin's bookkeeper.

Dressed in khaki pants and a blue checkered button-down, Larry isn't the sort of guy you'd think you'd catch at establishments like these. With his wide-rimmed glasses and ever-changing bowtie, the guy reads more church-going frat brother rather than someone who'd run in Darrin's circles. He doesn't live at the compound. Actually, he's the only one besides Micah *allowed* to live off the compound even though he has privileged access to everything Darrin knows.

Darrin believes if something were to happen to our hide-away in the woods, keeping Larry out of the mix can only bode well.

"Hey, man," Larry says, cozying up closer to my bike than I'd like. "Haven't seen you come out to the tables in a while. Finally decide to try your luck?"

I sniff, wiping the tip of my nose with my thumb. "Darrin wanted us here tonight. Gotta good crowd?"

He knows I don't gamble. Not after what went down with Adam. Shockingly, Darrin never made me feel as if I had to. Most of the six don't mess with it, same as we don't mess with the Jackpot.

"Yes. We do." Larry grins. He rolls back on his heels, shoving his hands in his slacks, letting his gaze scan Fleur.

"This is Fleur. Fleur, this is Larry." I offer introductions but nothing more.

She nods at him, while he gives me a side pat on my shoulder twice, then winces when his hand is met with my solid muscle. Rolling my eyes, I gesture to the door and Larry leads us.

I linger, waiting for Fleur to step with me. My hand grazes the small of her back, and she sucks in a tiny breath before moving along in the direction I guide her.

Managing to dodge most of the guys at the door is a feat, but Larry is usually one to deter them. They don't have the patience for him and his ever-growing obsession with the numbers. The wide berth they give us is more than I've ever been afforded before, and I take advantage, ushering Fleur in without their wandering or prying eyes.

A few of Darrin's men stand in the front acting as security for the evening, but step aside when they see Larry and me.

A thin layer of dust and grime coats the windows, but the floors are clean, and the smell of smoke-drenched clothes cancels out any musty odor.

The space opens into lines of tables, all filled with people. Blackjack, poker, casino war—table after table of card games litter the vast space.

There's resistance from Fleur as she stops, taking in the sight of each filled table. Women slide through, carrying drinks and Jackpot on trays, dealers stand, keeping eyes on each player, and Darrin sits, lounging in the back on a black leather chair.

A man in front of us winks at Fleur before pinching the ass of a woman walking by.

Fleur's wide eyes look at me, and I lean down, letting my mouth graze the soft rim of her ear. "Trust me and follow my lead."

She isn't going to like who I am tonight.

I inhale and plaster a smirk on my face before making my way back to the guys.

Darrin watches as we work our way toward him. He gestures a hand to another leather chair beside him and Blitz. I take it, leaving Fleur to stand. Confusion teeters on her brow until she notices the other women around the group also standing. Most of them have a hand or two stroking leisurely. An arm, a finger dragging on a thigh—sensual touches to appease the lazy men in their chairs.

Fleur tucks herself between me and, unfortunately, Blitz's seat. She angles her body in order to scan the floor. Sheriff Motley sits at a Texas hold'm table and enthusiastically waves in our direction. I nod then sneak a glance at Fleur who's clenching her fists tight, eyes narrowing on the sheriff seated next to the mayor.

It's impossible for outsiders to truly comprehend how embedded Darrin's reach is in town. Questions are often raised by newcomers. Why doesn't the sheriff arrest him? How come the mayor doesn't take back his town?

The answer—well, the answer is simple. Boiled down to one word. Corruption.

From the look of faithlessness on Fleur's face, she's realized how deep the well really goes.

"Yo, D. Why were we called here tonight?" one of the men asks.

I don't catch who it is, and their voice is drowned out as I'm watching Fleur scan the crowd. Is she looking for someone?

After several seconds, I finally catch up to the conversation going on around me, and I realize that we were, in fact, told to come here. All of the six, and even some others, from the looks of it.

"Four dealers have turned up dead in the last few days," Darrin says.

Silence.

In the immediate area around us, no one speaks. No one breathes. Four dealers?

"Dumped in town. All baring the horseshoe. I've IDed them. All shot at point blank range."

Fleur fidgets. Similarly, the other women do too.

"Is it Raven?" I ask. Raven is the drug lord from over the state line in Alabama. We've had territory issues before considering our dealers work in nearby circles but murdering four of them ...

"I believe so," Darrin continues. "Our meeting with the Cartel, the joining newer networks—they're threatened. More potent Jackpot means more business for us and less for them."

Blitz growls next to me and Fleur jumps in response. He finds it funny and chuckles, running a finger from her knee up her thigh. I steel my face, trying to look as impassive as possible while my inside is screaming to shove his hand in a meat grinder for touching her.

Fleur leans away and his hand drifts back down to the arm of his leather chair, smiling as he stares where his fingers touched her.

"Let's repay the favor," Blitz offers to Darrin, his eyes finally moving away from Fleur's short shorts. A building full of half-naked women and he still has eyes for Fleur. Rage simmers beneath my skin and I itch.

"I already have," Darrin says, swirling a glass beer bottle in his hand. My gaze snaps to his and I smirk in approval. Or at least I try to convince him of my affirmation. But deep down I'm struggling not to demand an answer to why he's decided to start a war with Raven.

This muddies the water. I'm supposed to be passing along information to my handler about the Cartel and the bigger network. That's the information they need. Getting sucked into a border war is dangerous and not what the DEA is looking for right now.

Internally, I'm strategizing. How can I redirect Darrin's attention? How can I keep my mission in play? Can I keep Fleur safe if this happens?

"Cheers to that," Trip says and lifts his drink in the air. His boisterous words seem to lighten the too tightly wound group of men. The women begin their movements again, and several men motion for new drinks to be delivered to them.

Two beers are delivered to me on a tray, and I thank the woman, putting on a show of admiring her for Darrin, who's staring at me, but I'd rather cut off my own limbs than touch another woman. I turn and hand one of the bottles to Fleur. "Here."

"I don't like beer," Fleur says unapologetically.

A snicker from across the wide circle of men in chairs has me grinding my teeth.

"Drink it anyway," I demand.

Blitz makes a crude joke about him saying the same line to a woman last night and the guys erupt in laughter, me along with them.

She flinches and takes the bottle in her hand but doesn't bring it to her mouth. She studies me, her lashes blinking a few times as if she's trying to figure me out. I say a silent prayer she'll forgo an attitude with me. These men would expect me to do something about it.

Fleur snorts and shakes her head, looking away as she blinks through the tears in her eyes.

There's nothing I want more than to grab her hand in this moment. To run my thumb across her soft knuckles and tell her this isn't me, that I'm playing a part.

Would she even believe me?

As the night trickles on, the women are more careless about where they're lounging. Some sit on the arms of the chairs, and others have been pulled onto the laps of the men near them.

Those on the floor grow louder as the night progresses. Drinks flow freely, and shouts of winners and losers escalate, prompting Darrin to get involved several times.

Fleur's still standing straight, shuffling on her feet, and I'm sure she's trying to relieve the pain. After one too many sways, I grab for her, yanking her down on my lap.

She yelps and her spine stiffens when she lands on my leg. With both hands on her waist, I torment myself by moving her closer to my hips until she's nestled between my thigh and the chair.

The leather groans as she struggles to right herself upright, but I clamp my hands on her hips and hold fast. I reach up, finding the back of her neck. I squeeze only enough to garner her attention, then bring my mouth to her ear.

"Relax," I whisper. "Trust me."

She shivers and fights against my hold. When I release her, she springs back, glaring at me. I smirk, then pick a blackjack table to divert my attention to, unable to bear the pain reflected in her expression.

There's no relaxing for Fleur as the night goes on. She remains wholly vertical, unable to slouch into me, much to my dismay. The only time she's jostled is when my phone rings. I lift my hips to remove it from my back pocket and the movement effectively slides Fleur further into me. Her cheeks burn red when her hands fumble with my chest, clawing to right herself again.

I check my phone with a smug smile on my face, only for it to die when I see my mother calling. It's about that time. She's heard, verified, and now processed the news, I'm sure. Two clicks and I've ignored her call, sending her to voicemail.

After tucking my phone away, I glue my hands to the thick arms of the chair in an attempt to keep from touching Fleur. I can't help it; my body hums with her this near. With each shift, she causes me agony of the best kind. My heart pounds so fiercely I can feel it pulse in my fingertips as if in time with my need to splay my hand across her thigh.

Trip, who arrived later with a new girl in tow, takes Blitz's seat while he's pants down in the corner. He leans close. "Trade you for the rest of the night?"

Trade. As if these women were baseball cards. It's gross and disgusting. One more reason why I never brought a woman around during the past four years. If you don't claim them, these men have no boundaries. Even with me married to Fleur, the attempts are nauseating. Darrin mentioned they assumed since the marriage was forced, I'd be bored already. Ready for a refresh.

While there's absolutely no way I'd ever trade Fleur for the night, I take my time answering. I purse my lips, rubbing my chain between my fingers as if I'm truly considering it.

Fleur looks as if she could vomit, her expression sour as Trip lets his gaze linger on her with an obsessive, unyielding intensity.

I bring a palm down, kneading her thigh in his line of sight.

Her legs are smooth, and I relish the goose bumps that flare to life once my fingers spread over her muscles. My hand is large against her petite frame, but there's something right about it being there. I don't move it away.

I raise my chin to Trip, who's staring at me, practically panting like a dog for a new toy to play with. "I think not," I say.

Trip whines, sucking back the last of his bottle before he reaches out and grabs the new girl. She playfully yells his name and bats his hand away, but the look in her eyes is pure terror.

Fleur looks away, tears in her eyes. She reaches for her wrist, where two new rubber bands sit. I don't outright look down. I stare ahead, nodding in conversation to something Darrin is saying. But out of the corner of my eye, I watch her pull them back.

Roughly, I clasp her wrist before she can let them snap. Still, I don't look at her.

Adjusting my fingers, I tighten my grip until she no longer struggles against it. Her gaze burns on the side of my head. I can feel her ire radiating and consuming, but still, I don't look at her. And I sit that way for the remainder of the night.

Chapter 33
Fleur

Time moves impossibly slow here. It's only been three weeks and it feels like three months. I beat my head on the table to pass the time some days. At least that's what it feels like.

After that night at the gambling place, my interactions with Liam have been ... strained. I don't want to talk to him.

I've tried to reconcile the man who stepped in on behalf of his brother with the man cackling at stomach-churning jokes. Or the fact he sits idly by as men and women drown in a high around him, sinking so deep their heads lull to the side in a state of unrepentant bliss. How do I harmonize the man who stepped in to save me with the Liam I experienced that night and the other nights since then? Because, yes, we had to go again. Then again.

I'm not sure I'll ever be able to make the two mesh, but when I get out of here, even after intense therapy, I'm not sure I'll be able to forget.

Each evening was the same—copious gambling and drugs, drinking, and women. Both times Liam pulled me into his lap, content to let me shelter there. To be honest, I've become grateful for it. Watching the other women *service* the men or Darrin's crew pawning them off to high-rolling players—

Despite my apprehension with Liam, he'd safely tucked me away in his lap. His calloused, inky hands stretched over my thighs and hips. I'm not traded or told to do anything I don't want to. And for that, I'm thankful.

My days on the compound are mostly spent on the cabin's front porch. Occasionally, I brave the compound and walk around while Liam isn't here. I've found early mornings are the best time to explore as the other men living here don't seem to stir before 11:00 a.m.

Liam's warned me about venturing too far from his place and having ridden with Liam to town and meetings a few times, I know how away from civilization we are. Getting lost wandering around the woods isn't something I want to happen. So I stick close. Mulling about the cabin, reading, watching TV, and very rarely, going with Liam.

The only TV is in Liam's bedroom, propped up on a stand sitting on the dresser. I've taken to camping out in there, especially when it rains, binge-watching trashy TV.

The warmth and comfort of his bed have, on occasion, lulled me into a deep sleep. My body relishes the softness of his bed over the lumps of the couch. Liam has offered, more than once, to switch with me; for him to take the couch while I sleep in his bed. But pride is a poor character trait of mine, and I've learned to be content with my afternoon naps wrapped in his masculine-scented down comforter.

The point is, I'm bored, and I eagerly look forward to the times when Liam says he has to leave the compound. I'm expected to come with him, and I gobble up each trip.

River texted Liam a couple weeks ago, letting him know my orders where delivered to the store, and we made a trip into town to pick up those desperately needed items. He even took us to a hole-in-the-wall catfish house where I gorged myself on fried catfish, hush puppies, and coleslaw until I was sick. We didn't talk while we ate, and the town's people gave Liam a wide berth, their whispers of our marriage making their rounds.

I still ~~don't~~ can't have a phone, so Liam has on occasion lent me his. I've fed my parents the same lie about an issue with my account and how they're having trouble connecting a new phone therefore I'm using a friend's. It's irksome and I've reached out minimally because of it.

I'm slightly concerned I'm going mad. Literally.

Sometimes, at night, I wake in a cold sweat as if someone's watching me. I never open my eyes, but this cabin and the woods are playing tricks on my mind.

I think about Liam way too much. Find myself wondering what he's doing and getting anxious when he isn't home before I fall asleep for the night.

Today's different, though. He's home before lunch and in the shower while I make myself a turkey sandwich.

My thoughts flicker to his thundering body hissing under the heat of the shower spray, and I blink them away while returning the mayonnaise and mustard to the fridge. As it shuts, I catch the door and take out the ingredients again to make one for Liam.

It's not something I do. I don't cook for him, nor do we typically eat together, but he's been offering up as much privacy to me as possible these last few weeks, and I ... I have a strange desire to know if he's okay.

If there's anything I've learned about Liam these past few weeks, it's that he works himself to the bone. Exhaustion rides his face; the weariness sunk deep in his eyes.

The only drawer for silverware is to my right, and I open it, then reach for a knife. My gaze snags at the random pencils sitting there, and I linger, staring at them before shaking my head and closing the drawer.

After cutting his sandwich in half and adding some chips to the plate, I study both lunches side by side and wipe my hands on my shorts, nervous I've crossed some line.

When the door to the bathroom opens, the loud squeak makes it impossible to miss. Liam saunters into the living room, moving to skim through some papers on the small desk he keeps nestled in the corner of the room.

I clear my throat and he whirls around. Water droplets still drip from his wet hair, hanging around his face. He's tightened up his beard, the scruff shorter than I've seen it since I've known him. My gaze drops to where both his hands slide into his blue jeans—wait, blue jeans?

Confused, I narrow my eyes but remember the plate before I can ask him what's going on. I lift it, quirking my lips to the side. "I made you a sandwich. Not sure what you like on it but figured since I was making myself one ..."

I let the words hang in the air between us. The shock on his face is somewhat disconcerting. Did he not think I was capable of doing something nice?

"I like anything. Thank you. Haven't had a turkey sandwich in years." He moves toward the kitchen and my knees almost wobble at his scent caressing my nose. Wood and pine wrapped in a fresh spring rattles my insides as he takes the plate I can't seem to relinquish from my grasp.

He cocks his head to the side and studies where both our hands linger on either side of the plate.

One heartbeat passes, then two before I finally let go, embarrassment lacing my cheeks. A slight twitch at the corner of his mouth begs for my attention, and I back into the counter, distracted. My blundering earns me a smile and I chew on my lip and reach for a chip off my plate.

Liam moves to the table, sliding his plate over the pocked and pitted wood. He pulls out his phone, turning it over in his hands several times before sitting down and turning to me still standing.

"I, uh ... my mom called," he says. "Again."

I don't say anything, unsure where he's going with this.

"She wants to have us over for dinner tonight."

My mouth drops open. "She does know the situation between us, right?"

Liam bounces a fist up and down over his knee while pretending to inspect a chip in his other hand. "My mother doesn't know about Adam or what happened. My father and grandparents kept it from her. At the time, they ... they thought it was the compassionate thing to do. Keep her from knowing what Adam's involved in."

"And does she know about you?" I ask.

"Yeah. She knows. Tries to avoid talking about it. Probably thinks the worst about me already. Now add the town's gossip surrounding us—my brother's girl."

I bristle. "I'm not."

Frankly, I'm getting sick of all this talk as if Adam and I were practically walking down the aisle already. I was upfront and honest with Adam about my fragile state, the one I'm running from.

Liam's eyes move over my face, surely noticing the tension there, but he regards my lips so intently. My tongue darts out to lick my bottom lip, and he snaps his gaze back to mine. The silence extends between us, and Liam looks as if he wants me to say more.

"I was in a long-term relationship before I moved here. I told Adam this when he wanted to explore *things* between us."

Liam's jaw tightens but he softens his stare. Can he read

what's written all over my face? The hurt, the ache of pain thrumming through me.

"Did he hurt you?"

"Who? Adam? No, he—"

"The man you were in a long-term relationship with. Did *he* hurt you?"

I swallow, the knot in my throat painfully unbearable. I don't want to talk about this. For him to see how broken and tarnished I truly am.

I shake my head. "Uh, no. Well, not physically."

It's all I offer. Because some days it felt like Chis drove a knife into my heart. It felt like I couldn't breathe. That suffocating weight in my chest has lessened as the weeks and months have ticked by, but it still ... hurts.

"Sometimes it's the emotional pain that scars us the deepest," Liam says, studying where I've moved my fingers to toy with the rubber bands on my wrist.

My breath hitches and the sting I know too well prickles behind my eyes. How did this conversation get so off course? I don't want to be vulnerable with him ... do I?

"Fleur." Liam's voice towers over me. It's then I look up to see he's moved directly in front of me, his hand gripping my wrist where I've unconsciously pulled both bands taut needing to snap. "Fleur." He says my name again, gently lowering my hand to my thigh. He doesn't let go of my wrist. He simply cradles it, featherlight strokes tickling the most sensitive skin there.

Stepping back, his warm touch disappears as I move out of his grasp.

"It won't be pretty, but my mother is a good person. This"— he motions between the two of us—"is going to be hard to explain."

* * *

A warm glow descends around the open fields and road we're on. Silhouettes of sizable oaks shadow the tall grasses swaying in the early evening breeze. Deep yellows and oranges dye the sky, and the last of the setting sun's rays flicker behind the trees.

The hum of the truck along the rough pavement, coupled with the settling dusk, almost lulls me into sleep. It's only the clink of the wine bottle jammed into the side of my door keeping me awake at this point. Liam thankfully had a bottle shoved deep in his cabinets. My mother would be ashamed if I showed up as a guest empty-handed.

I have no idea what to expect from this dinner with Liam and his parents. Well, maybe that's not true. If it were my parents learning of my marriage through the town's gossip lines, this dinner would be an intervention.

After Liam explained how his mother was deliberately kept in the dark about Adam, and the lengths he, his father, and grandparents took to ensure she was unaware of her son's issues —this dinner feels like a disaster already, and we're still twenty minutes from arriving.

The road winds in the familiar way it did when I drove to the Fourth of July party. I sigh. That day feels so far away now. So much has happened. With September slowly giving way to the awkward fall heat intent on gracing the South, time is both slowing down and speeding up.

Ringing out my hands, I clench the yellow sundress I picked out on the clearance rack at River's shop and squeeze it between my fingers. I do this several times, only to realize I'm effectively wrinkling the dress. The smattering of tiny flowers dusting the pale yellow aren't something I typically gravitate toward, but the dress reminded me of the farmhouse and the yellow haze that set over the property each morning as the sun rose.

Liam is quiet, no doubt wondering how tonight is going to go as well. Every few minutes, he'll slide his palm up and down his blue jeans or fidget with the pulled-back bun in his hair. He's apparently opted for zero music because the only sound is the whoosh of the truck plowing down the empty roads.

Diverting my eyes from Liam, I glance out my window—
Are those?

I bolt upright from my less than ladylike slouched position and paw the window to lower the glass. Wind whips my hair, tossing pieces over my face, catching in my lashes, and sticking to my freshly glossed lips. But I see them.

Wildflowers seep through the surrounding field and a cluster of daisies bloom at the edge of it.

I suck in a breath, head practically out the window to get a better view of the picturesque flowers illuminated by the dipping sun over the horizon.

Even the light chuckle beside me doesn't pull my gaze from them.

The whipping wind slows, and I realize it's because the truck is also slowing.

Liam pulls over, straddling the red dirt and the crunchy road shoulder. I turn to him, already getting out, and my eyes follow as he walks around the front of the truck, moving toward the field.

His ample intimidating frame weaves through the delicate daisies, creating a mouthwatering picture, and I watch enraptured as he leans down, selectively searching for three flowers. After picking them, he gathers the flowers, their white and yellow petals standing out against his dark blue pants. They

277

hang loosely at his side as he strides back and swings open the truck door.

As he climbs in, I study him. The light on his face in this moment. Did he really just—

His eyes meet mine, bright with tenderness as he extends the flowers out toward me.

I glance at them, then back at Liam. Taking the flowers is natural, but the shiver down my spine as my fingers graze his knuckles is not. My breath gets caught in my throat. I work toward a swallow and my eyelids feel even heavier than they did before.

"It would've been too dark to stop on the way home," Liam says, shattering the silence and anticipation tugging between us.

All I can do is nod.

Running the pad of a finger over the white petals, they're smooth and pristine beneath my touch. I pull my bottom lip between my teeth and whisper, "Thank you."

He pulls back on the road as I stare at the three flowers tucked into my palm. How can this man do what he does, be who he is, and still show this side of himself?

It takes another ten minutes to finally pull into the driveway of his parents' flawless home, severing the lightness I was basking in a moment ago.

"We're here," I say more to myself than Liam, but he answers nonetheless.

"Yeah."

Liam's tone is clipped, and he sighs, moving to exit the truck while I set my flowers on the dashboard and grab the bottle of wine stuck in the door.

The columns flanking the edge of the porch are bigger than I remember. Two containers spilling peachy pink Begonias flank each side of the double front door. Additional pots of ferns weave between the wooden rockers lining the length of the porch.

Heavy footfalls clamber up the stairs behind me, Liam's boots imposing and disturbing the serenity of the evening.

I look over my shoulder and he pauses, shrugging his shoulders.

Suddenly, I wish we'd prepped for this. This awkward dinner, and no doubt appraisal of whatever sham his mother and father think we're running. I sense describing exactly how it happened isn't in the cards for tonight, the wickedness that almost occurred in the woods that night several weeks ago.

Liam passes me and raps his fist on the door twice.

Not walking straight into the house is definitely a tell of their relationship. With my parents, I usually opened the door and poked my head in, hollering a "hello" before kicking off my shoes and raiding their pantry for the best kept snacks. Liam's uncertainty as he scans the house leads me to believe he'd never consider doing that. He's a guest here. A stranger.

There's a slight twinge of pain in my chest at the thought of all he's done for his family, for his brother, only to be treated as if he's the black sheep.

A few seconds pass, and we stare at the walnut-stained door in silence before it opens. Liam's father greets us, a tight smile curving on his lips when he sees his son. He nods at Liam and says, "I would've warned you if I knew."

My heart rate spikes. What's he talking about? I swivel to observe Liam, whose face has paled.

"Hey, Fleur," his dad says to me. "Sorry about this."

I'm stunned into silence, for what, I don't know, but I manage a "Hi" in response.

Mr. Parker extends his hand into the house, stepping back past the propped open door. An invitation to come in.

Frozen, I don't move. It's only the warm, gentle push

against my back that ushers me in. The ghost of Liam's hand lingers on the small of my back much longer than it's actually there.

Not now, not now. I scream at my body to gather its wits.

Once inside, the smell of eucalyptus wafts passed us and I inhale the scent, missing the homey smells from my candles and room sprays. The cabin isn't gross, and it's taken to smelling better in the few weeks I've been there, but it's immune to feminine scents, it seems. Nature and the woodsy scent Liam strides around with permeate the building. I've gotten used to it though, and when I lie on his bed—

A soft voice from the kitchen beckons us, and we're led through a wide hallway, a white staircase on the left, into an open white and marbled kitchen. Farmhouse style and utterly beautiful, this kitchen surprisingly is like a larger version of my own before it was burnt to a crisp. I narrow my eyes at the cabinets, and I cringe thinking how Adam must have helped update his parents' kitchen at some point. His signature is on everything.

"Fleur!" Mrs. Parker shouts, wrangling her apron off and tossing it on the counter. She approaches with open arms and throws herself at me. Stiff, arms pinned to my sides, I suppress a laugh as she squeezes me.

When we break our embrace, she turns to Liam, her smile fading into a frown. "Liam," she says. "It's good to see you."

"You too," Liam responds.

Her tone is pure brittleness and Liam, who tries to keep his face steady, falters. The sadness that flickers in his eyes is short-lived as another voice echoes along the living room walls.

"Hello, *brother.*"

Mrs. Parker darts for the stove, pulling on her oven mitts and ignoring the situation entirely. I'm starting to think it was her who brought him here.

Adam strides toward us, veering toward me, and wraps me in a hug. He breathes a sigh of relief in my neck. "Fleur," he mumbles in my ear. "I was so worried."

Tears threaten behind my eyes. Be it for the fire and our parting the last time I saw him—unconscious on the ground. Or maybe it's the sad fact he was more worried about saving himself than me when Darrin took me. There's even a smidge of resentment. That he would allow his brother to pay his debt, compromising his soul.

I push against him, loosening myself from his grip. "It's good to see you, Adam. I was worried, too." It's not a lie. Those days locked in the clubhouse cell were riddled with fear. Not only for myself but for Adam.

I spy Liam out of the corner of my eye, speaking with his father off the side. A family photo of the five of them from well over twenty years ago hangs above where they talk, and I shake my head at what their family has now become.

In Liam's absence, Mrs. Parker approaches me again. She's wearing a pink blouse with white capris and her hair is down, sufficiently teased.

"I hear you work at the bed-and-breakfast," Mrs Parker says.

Seriously? It's like I'm in the twilight zone. This woman invited us over for dinner, after learning through the town's gossip hens that Liam and I were married. Then she decides to add Adam to the invite list. This woman.

I try to put myself in her shoes. She thinks Adam is her golden boy. Perfectly polished and done wrong by his older brother, who runs with the thugs of the town. An injustice has been done to her son, and while she looks at me with kindness, I can't help but feel she blames me underneath it all.

It looks bad. But if she only knew ...

"I do—did." I shake my head. "Mrs. and Mr. Northgate are the sweetest," I add.

"They'd be happy to know you think that. My parents have always had a heart for hospitality. I'm afraid only my daughter received that trait." She giggles and pats Adam on the shoulder.

The elusive sister and daughter. Her muddy brown hair and bright eyes resemble both Adam and Liam in the family photo, but neither Adam nor Liam talk about her.

"Is she local?"

"Oh no, she's off hiking the western part of the US. She has a heart for adventure." Mrs. Parker's face falls at her mention of that, and I decide not to let on I don't know her name. There is more to this story and I'm not sure it's my place to pry.

A bell chimes in the kitchen and Mrs. Parker backs away, around the hulking island. "Chicken's almost done," she singsongs.

With Liam still in hushed discussion with his father, I lean over to Adam and ask where the bathroom is. He smiles and points down another hallway lined with beautiful watercolor paintings. One after the other of what has to be the same artist's art repeats down the hall until I find the third door on the right.

The bathroom is small but appears to be plucked straight from a magazine. Light blue walls that swirl like the sea brush up against cream wainscoting, wrapping the space housing a toilet and pedestal sink.

Mindlessly, I let the hot water run over my hands after using the facilities. I stare in the mirror, wishing for all the world I could run back to the cabin. Confrontation is not my thing, and my body demands I run. However, for reasons I can't explain, I hate the thought of Liam being here alone to shoulder this burden.

Maybe it's some messed up forced marriage derangement.

I told myself I'd leave Ruin as soon as I'm able to get out of this messed up crazy, but there's a twinge of unease when I think about leaving Liam. He can't have very many years left here. What will he do when his time is up? Will he move on? Try to find someone to share his life with—

I shake my head.

A drawing behind me catches my attention through the mirror and my focus narrows on the familiar building set in a rustic frame. I whirl around, unconcerned with my damp hands now dripping all over my dress.

It's the cabin.

Liam's cabin.

The drawing is beautiful. Sketched with detail I've missed in real life. The whole drawing is void of color, shaded with charcoal or pencils—I'm not sure.

One would think a million cabins look the same, but it's his. The way the lightly shaded areas are directed from the west. The bulky oak tree sitting on the right-hand side, roots deep and broad; I trip over them even from a distance away. The one rocking chair lonely in the corner of the porch where I've spent most of my mornings seated. It's his all right.

What strikes me is the fact it's hanging in his parents' bathroom. Do they know they bought a drawing of Liam's house? I can only imagine if Darrin knew evidence of his compound existed outside of it, he'd be dangerous.

I make a mental note to ask Liam about it.

With one more glance in the mirror and a quick snap to the rubber bands hiding under my cuff bracelet, I open the door to find Adam leaning against the wall opposite the bathroom. Wearing clothes different from what he's normally in, I take in his khakis and tucked in plaid shirt. His dark hair is combed tightly to the side.

I still, unable to move forward as he studies me.

He sighs. It's a long, drawn-out sound that raises the hairs on the back of my neck. "Tell me what happened after the fire?"

What happened? I was under the impression he was informed. Frustrated, I inhale a deep breath through my nose.

"I was taken. Kept for a while. They were waiting to see what you'd do. I didn't know about the money, Adam. Eventually, they took me and threatened my life, my family's life."

Adam winces, but I continue.

"Liam saved my life. Claimed me in a way I guess they respect around there. He pitched it as a way to get back at you, but I know he was saving you too."

Adam's sad eyes morph into annoyance and he snorts. "You think he did it for me? Nah, he took you to use you."

I shake my head. There is no doubt in my mind he was doing his best to keep me safe and protect his brother. "Adam, he was trying to help. Protect you and protect me."

Adam steps toward me, his hand coming to my cheek. "We can fix this, Fleur. I went to see someone, someone who can help me with the money. I won't leave you stuck with him or them."

I rear my head back. Yes, while I'm stuck, I'm also alive and I'm grateful for Liam. There's no way I wouldn't have been sexually assaulted, hurt, and even killed if it weren't for him stepping in.

"Someone?" I ask.

"I'm close to getting the money. I know we only just started, but I care deeply for you. I-I didn't mean for you to get caught up in this mess. I'm so sorry."

His hand moves to delve into my hair, and I try to back away, pinned between the door and Adam. My hands, fisted at my sides, are clammy.

Wrong. It feels wrong.

A growl erupts from down the hall and both Adam and I

snap our heads to see Liam standing there, arms crossed in front of him. His lips are curled with a snarl directed at Adam and I quickly move away from him.

Adam grits his teeth back. "I don't need your bail out this time, Liam."

Liam bristles. "And what? You think I should've left her to her own devices, let them have their way with her, kill her?"

"I'm getting the money," Adam snaps.

"From where?"

"That's none of your concern."

My eyes ping-pong between both men and I hate this. Their feud started before I came along but I'm not making matters any better.

I move back toward the kitchen, hoping I can distract myself by helping with dinner, or better yet, pop the top on the cheap bottle of wine we brought.

Adam grabs for my hand before I make it three steps. "I'm sorry, Fleur. About your home and that I didn't tell you."

I muster a smile even though deep down my stomach roils. "I hope you stay well, Adam."

It's the best I've got right now. I'm not sure what else to say. I'm married to his brother and while his words weren't meant to harm earlier, I *am* actually stuck.

But it's temporary. I look at Liam, the nervousness seeping out from under his cold exterior.

It is temporary, right?

Chapter 34
Liam

I should've known Adam would be here. I'm too intuitive to be blindsided, but like an idiot, I jumped at the opportunity to bring Fleur to my family with *me*. Not with Adam or for a community event, but with me. As if I could be normal. I snort at the thought.

She stared at those daisies as if hypnotized by them, and regardless of the chaos taking place right now, it's all I can think about.

After the confrontation in the hall, Fleur snuck back into the kitchen to help my mother finalize dinner while my brother and I stared at each other in the hallway. Adam's edged smile was all it took for me to see red.

Without another word, Adam moves past me, his shoulder knocking into mine but doing nothing to rock my person. I turn and follow him into the kitchen where Fleur sets forks on the table. Her eyes meet mine full of nervousness and annoyance.

I should've told my mom no. Should've held firm when she practically called crying with a hurt tone for me to bring Fleur over. We've done so much as a family to try to keep her and

Adam's relationship stable, but at this point, the urge to say screw it and divulge all the information we've been keeping—it's on the tip of my tongue.

The dining room hasn't changed much since I grew up. The rectangular white farmhouse-style table still seats eight even though the three of us are moved out. Many memories of my family take place at this table, some good and a few bad. Like the time Adam decided to steal my charcoal sticks and draw on the underside of the table, then denied it with fervor. My father nearly chased me out of the house in a rage until my mother looked at the scribbles and knew it wasn't me.

Adam moves to stand by the double French doors that look out over the backyard.

It's almost like it was a lifetime ago Fleur stood under the large white tent, glaring at me as I purposefully ate her sloppy fruit salad. The shock on her face turned to a glare with a scrunched nose—I remember wondering what other faces I could coax from her.

Fleur brushes past me, attempting another circle of the table with water goblets this time, and the hem of her tantalizing dress falls through my fingers. My middle finger grazes her thigh, and I snatch it away, looking in the opposite direction. I'll pretend I didn't notice the silky smoothness of her skin beneath my fingertip. She'll pretend she didn't feel it at all.

Everyone is quiet, even my mother, who I suspect is now comprehending how terrible of an idea this was, especially with Adam.

"All right, I think it's ready," my mother says as she carries over the barbeque chicken on a platter.

Some childhood favorites are also on the table. Sweet potato casserole, roasted Brussels sprouts, a heaping bowl of collard greens, and some dinner rolls. It's been ages since I've eaten a meal like this.

"This looks delicious, Mrs. Parker," Fleur says.

My mother's tight-lipped smile tells me all I need to know about the way this is going to go. She's concerned about Fleur. The whiplash between her sons.

When we're seated and my father says the traditional blessing, my mother picks up the rolls and holds them tight to her chest. "So, who wants to tell me what the hell is going on?"

Chapter 35
Liam

I count the milliseconds of silence as we all look around the table at my mother. Poised perfectly, she places each dish proportionately on her plate, beginning with the rolls and ending with the chicken.

There's a part of me laughing inside at the fact I'm giving this the time of day. The need to snatch Fleur and leave grows stronger with each lingering stare Adam offers her and with each glare my mother forces in my direction.

My father clears his throat, trying to ease the situation. "I believe they're married to keep Fleur safe at the moment."

Adam shifts in his seat.

"Well, that's exactly the problem, isn't it?" she continues. "If Liam wasn't in with Darrin and his crew, this wouldn't have happened."

My mother turns to me. "Was it worth it, Liam? To align yourself with the scum of this town. Do you know how many families he's hurt? The lives he destroys with his drugs. And you're part of that!"

Fleur's hand grazes my thigh from next to me. Elbows on

the table, I prop my chin in my palm, flicking my gaze over her. Back straight as a board, she's red-faced and clearly frustrated with the situation. Her attempt to console me with contact does something to me.

It's nothing I haven't heard before, from my mother. It's the price I pay to keep her from knowing why I work for Darrin, what the original reason for me coming back to Ruin was in the first place. I take it. Let her think what she will—all for my brother, who'd rather continue in his ways and throw me under the bus, still.

The chime of the grandfather clock in the corner punctuates my mother's tirade. Her eyes dart back and forth between Fleur and me.

"I'm sure Liam was keeping Fleur safe, Mom. He'll do the right thing when the time comes," Adam says, as he shoves a pile of sweet potatoes into his mouth. He's the only one eating, and I ignore the rumble of my stomach.

I narrow my eyes at him, at his tone. His assumption I'll let Fleur go as soon as it's safe or until he's garnered the money owed Darrin is vexing. My nostrils flare in his direction and it takes a gentle squeeze to my knee for me to realize I'm huffing air out audibly.

Her fingers are so small, but the desire they spark as they dance along my leg is anything but. I glance down at her hand still hovering on my knee. Folds of white fabric from the tablecloth brush across her wrist as she keeps her hand there. The light pink nail polish on her fingers is a dichotomy against my dark pants.

"Well, I hope that's true, for your case, Adam, because—"

Fleur's hand drops from my knee, and she tenses.

"With all due respect, Mrs. Parker. While Adam was pivotal with my renovation, we were never an item. I hired him as a contractor, paid him as one. I was upfront with Adam about my past and valued his friendship. As for Liam, I can imagine it was a shock to hear about the marriage through the grapevine, but he came to my rescue. The marriage was ... convenient, yes. But I'll never be able to repay him for what he's done for me."

Fleur holds my gaze as she says this and my heart stutters with each word. With each gulp and bob of her throat, I know she's nervous, trying to keep the information truthful but vague at the same time. But does she mean that? Has her view of me truly changed?

I push the collard greens around on my plate while the warmth curling in my stomach hampers my appetite. Her support and the confidence she has in my motivations are astounding. Especially because I'm starting to question my own.

Did I take advantage?

Can I let her go?

The answer to both is no.

For the first time, I don't feel so alone in this. Agent Wilson would argue I have him, but this has been a one-man show for the long haul, even before I started with the agency.

I can't want her. No attachments; nothing to compromise the mission. But I'm dangerously close to running away with her, to keep her safe.

Adam appears less than thrilled with Fleur's interruption, and my mother ... she looks flattened in her wing-backed chair. I couldn't be prouder.

"Already pitching your angle, huh?" Adam asks me. His fists bunch the tablecloth, wrinkling it in ire. "Having her indebted to you, rescuing her. Is this the sales pitch?"

I chuckle with disdain, and my father tenses at the sound. He knows I'm hanging by a thread.

"I've been upfront with her. Which is more than you can say," I bark.

This was a mistake. My grandfather told me to be careful with the family drama surrounding this, and I waltzed in here like some naive asswipe.

Banging the table, I push to stand, holding my brother's stare. I dare him to continue this. I'll lay it all out on the table regardless of what it will do to my mother. We already walk on eggshells with her regarding our sister. I'm not about to sit here and take this.

Rolling my shoulders, I turn to Fleur, who's gazing up at me. "Give me a minute."

And like the ass I am, I walk out the door.

Chapter 36
Fleur

Pressed against the front window, I watch Liam pace at the truck. He rips his bun out, letting his hair fall before clenching it with his fists.

Mr. and Mrs. Parker are talking in the kitchen while Adam devours the peach cobbler smothered in vanilla ice cream back at the table. None of them hold my interest, my eyes are only on the man fuming outside.

Usually, I'm the one avoiding drama, not interjecting myself in the middle of it. But something snapped in me at the way Liam's mother looked at him. How can a man pay a debt for his brother to protect him, yet receive zero respect? Adam's entitled behavior is disturbing.

My heart aches for Liam. Tightening with each step he moves, it squeezes until I can no longer watch from the inside. I throw open the door and run down the steps to him. Solar lamps line the brick sidewalk, and I'm grateful for them as I dash to the driveway, reaching Liam as he redoes his bun.

"What are you doing?" he asks. Those hulking shoulders

have fallen, and his eyes are black and flooded with a warring I'm not sure he'll ever confide in me about.

I twist under his scrutiny. Antsy, I whip around, noticing the pitch-black night shielding us. Three feet in front of me is about all I can see.

"Done with your pissing contest?" I ask.

"Never."

I throw my hands up, irritation bubbling to the surface. "Are you upset I said something?"

"No," he grits out.

Liam is barely holding on—I can see it. Anger and fear are written all over his normally collected and steeled face. He's letting me see it all in this moment and I recognize it. The desire muddled in with all the rage and fear. My heart rattles in my chest as his savage form towers over me.

His boots toe my flats as he invades the space between us, and I glance back toward the house to avoid the way his eyes skim down my body.

Backing up, I bump into the passenger side of the truck, and he follows me. Unrestrained, the rough pads of his fingers glide up the side of my thigh, catching the hem of my dress. I shudder at his touch. It's light, tender, everything he's not right now.

He stares at my mouth, where my lips quiver, and I smack his hand away. As soon as I do, I want to yank his hand back to soothe the ache building inside me. To knit his fingers between mine and guide his hand to the places I need him. But I don't, and he doesn't try again.

His touch heightens my senses. The large oaks thrash in the wind. Whippoorwills call to each other from some unseen place, and inside me the roar of desire matches what I find in his stare.

This was not in the plans. Not in a million years. This can't happen, this—

His left hand leans on the truck, brushing past my right shoulder, and I suck in a breath at how close he is. Bringing his mouth to my ear, he whispers, "Did you kiss my brother?"

I scowl, tilting my head away from where his warm breath practically licks the side of my face. His brother is the furthest thing on my mind. Why does he care?

As if he can read the question in my eyes, he continues, "Because I'm going to snuff out any memory of him."

His mouth crashes down on mine. Fluttery sensations sweep through my body before I can register what's happening.

The kiss is rough and demanding. Fire erupts and gnaws in my belly as he works to scrub away any lingering trace of his brother. But it's doing more than that.

So much more.

It challenges everything I knew with Chris, the man I thought was *it*. Rewriting what I know.

Liam's kiss is beyond passion. It's raw need and it sends a chill into the marrow of my bones. He pauses to bring his mouth to my chin, nipping me, and I throw my head back into the truck window. He cushions the back of my head before kissing me once more.

I meet him. Every stroke of his tongue and tease of my lips, I give it back tenfold. Pouring out the building attraction ever since I saw him at the bank months ago.

Fisting his shirt, I whimper and immediately regret it because he rips away. Two steps back, and he's panting while he frowns at me.

"Shit, Fleur."

I wince. "Y-you kissed me."

Pressing both hands to the side of the car, I support myself.

This kiss—my knees wobble, weak and utterly wrecked. Ravaged so thoroughly, I'm now a mumbling, bumbling idiot.

He steps forward, a hand lifting to my face but stopping short. Instead, he slides both in his pockets while his eyes trace the narrow curves of my body, lingering where his hand seared my thigh. They then dart to my lips, where the exquisite burn of his passionate kiss brands me.

Gosh, his lips.

"I'm sorry. I'm, I'm being—"

"A brute." My words find their mark and Liam flinches, his head rearing back like I've struck him. Guilt immediately clouds me. I meant it to lighten the mood.

"We should leave," he says, looking back toward the house. What looks like longing and pain lances his face as he squints at his childhood home.

The only thing I brought with me was the bottle of wine, but my parents taught me better than to walk out. While Liam starts the truck, I poke my head back in the house, catching Mrs. Parker at the same window I was staring out. Heat burns my cheeks. Did she see us?

"Thank you for dinner, Mrs. Parker." I grit out a smile and pull the door back closed, then bolt back to Liam like a teen playing ding-dong-ditch. I practically giggle flinging myself into the truck and look at Liam with a smile, but his head is fixed straight ahead as we pull out of the drive.

He doesn't look at me the rest of the night.

＊ ＊ ＊

Several days of gorgeous weather follow the dinner from hell. It's normally still screaming heat at the start of fall in Mississippi, from what I'm told, but these few days of reprieve have been invigorating.

Most of my days have been spent butt parked in the chair on the front porch watching several mail trucks, of all things, pull in and out of the compound's warehouse. While the days have been busy, the nights have been quiet. Normally, the evenings are teeming with drunken parties, but between the constant influx of deliveries and work, it seems everyone has their nose to the ground.

Liam has taken up running, which I'm fairly certain is new. A couple of mornings, I've met him coming out of the bathroom from an early morning run while I'm on my way to pee, having slept like crap on the sofa.

Today I spent too much time lying in the grass next to the cabin, and I'm sunburnt and stiff.

Digging around in every crevice of this cabin, the most I've found for relief is lotion. No aloe to save my life. The sun sets outside the window and I turn to stick out my tongue at the giant ball of gas.

"What'd the window do to you?" Liam shuts the door behind him, his eyes narrowing on my reddened face.

"I have beef with the sun."

"Ah," he says, hanging up his leather coat. How he wears that thing in the raised temperatures around here is beyond me. Stalking in my direction, he reaches up to brush the pad of his thumb gently against my nose. My eyes widen before they blink in rapid succession, and I continue to stare at the vacant spot well after Liam has moved to the kitchen.

Does he realize he touched me? He's barely looked at me since our kiss.

When I finally turn around to face him, his eyes are trained on my backside, a glass of water pressed to his lips.

"The guys are ordering a bunch of pizzas tonight. I ordered

a supreme for us. I'll grab it at the clubhouse when one of the guys texts."

"Uh, yeah. Sounds good. Thank you."

"You don't have to thank me, Fleur."

"Fine. You suck and I don't thank you for the delicious pizza that happens to be my favorite."

Liam roars out a laugh and I have to bite my lip to refrain from squealing in delight at the masculine sound rattling my core.

When his laugh dies, I move toward him. "You should do that more."

"What?"

"Laugh."

Liam frowns, tilting his head to study me. "Not much to laugh about around here."

"Then leave." I sigh. "You have so much to offer, Liam. This shouldn't be the price you pay for Adam. It just shouldn't."

Maybe I could convince him to leave and take me with him. He can't have much longer left here, right? I picture it: us packing to leave in the dead of night, weaving through the trees on his bike and getting the hell out of this town, away from Blitz and Darrin. Would we stick together or go our separate ways? Regardless of what he'd do with me, why doesn't *he* leave?

Liam's jaw ticks and he moves closer to me. The tattooed hand hanging by his side ruffles the string from my cut-off shorts, tickling my thigh. It takes everything in me not to lean in and seek his touch.

"It's more complicated than that now. Hell, you really are burnt." He reaches to brush my hair off my shoulder, inspecting it. I'm unsure if he's purposefully changing the subject, or if he's only now noticed the extent of my third-degree wrestle with the sun.

"You should take the bed tonight," he says.

I roll my eyes. "I'm fine."

"Let me rephrase that ... you *will* take the bed tonight. Should've had you in it from the start."

I bite my lip, looking down at the floor, trying not to laugh at the way he said that or how my bare toes curl against the jagged cabin floor. When I finally gather myself enough to look up at him, his eyes are fixed on me. Storm clouds blur the brightness there and I swallow the trickle of unease—perhaps he hadn't minced his words.

Liam backpedals toward the spot on the couch where I keep my pillow and extra quilt folded and stored. Holding my confused stare, he bends down to grab the pillow, then tosses it at me.

I generally have the reflexes of a baby elephant, so naturally, it smacks my face and falls to the ground while I fumble to gather my arms together but end up hugging empty air.

"It's all yours, Fleur. Put that in the bedroom where you'll be sleeping tonight," Liam says as I bend down to grab it.

Nodding, I shuffle to his bedroom and toss the pillow on the bed, noting the plush puff of sound it makes when it hits. I grin. I may *actually* get a decent night's sleep.

Liam moves to the bathroom for a shower while I finish up folding laundry. It takes me twice as long to fold the towels from the dryer because each warm, fuzzy towel calls for a hug.

With night settled in and the compound lampposts lit, Liam takes off for the clubhouse to check in and grab the pizza.

Dinner with the Parkers the other night made me miss my family. It's rare I go this long without checking in, and while I don't have a phone, I think I could convince Liam a letter would be okay to send.

A desk sits in the living room, directly across from the couch and the coffee table. After standing in the kitchen studying it with a can of sparkling water in my hand, I finally give in and pad over.

It's old, maybe even antique.

My mind wanders to Mr. and Mrs. Northgate, and I wonder if they passed it on to him. The tattered wood is worn and well loved, from the looks of it. I slowly open the single drawer in the front, glancing over my shoulder as if someone may catch me. Liam never said this was off-limits, and I'm only looking for paper and a pencil since all digital options are unavailable to me at the moment.

Luck is on my side. I find paper. It's not lined or anything, and when I pull it out, the weight is heavier than your average computer stock. Running my fingers over the paper, it's slightly textured and I flip through the stack, searching underneath for another option.

Unable to, I grab a few sheets and hip check the drawer closed.

There's an olive-green pencil pouch nestled on top of a folder in the corner and presuming there are pens, I open it, only to be proven otherwise.

Black pencils are tucked neatly in loops, each with a different number stamped in gold across the top. A fine dust coats the inside, and I frown. *Huh.*

I eyeball the pencils, then flick my gaze back toward the drawer a few more times before finally landing on the leather folder—no portfolio.

A corner piece of paper sticks out, and I tug at it, revealing the start of a sketch. There's no making out what it is with only the corner exposed. With another glance at the door, I slide the leather portfolio toward me and before I can second-guess my invasion of Liam's privacy, I fling it open.

Pages and pages of drawings drift out.

I'm stunned motionless.

I stare down at the first one. The medium seems to be something different than the pencils I found. This is a chalkier substance and not as detailed.

There, smudged and buffed out, is the small run-down church on the outside of Ruin I've passed a few times. It resembles one of those large sheds, and fixed on top is a stippled point with a bell. The thing is like a hundred years old and could be considered a historical monument at this point.

I'll be the first to admit I know squat about drawing. Anything creative I've had to work at my whole life, and I don't consider myself a natural at much. Even photography was a pipe dream of mine. However, I recognize the painstaking talent this drawing must have taken, and I'm floored.

Liam captured every detail despite the lack of color. I flip through several more pages of older buildings scattered around Ruin, admiring his work.

The next drawing gives me pause. A few pencil-drawn oranges are piled in a wooden crate eerily similar to those we get at the farmer's market.

I blink. They *are* the oranges from the farmer's market.

A flash of memory hits me. The rumble of a motorcycle taking off down the road after a thump on my front porch had delivered my crate of oranges.

Stunned, I flip the page, only to be hit with another. My throat instantly closes, and a pit knots itself in my stomach.

The point of view is from a camera, and it's looking into a cell.

The cell I was in.

And there, curled up on the barely functional cot, is a figure—me. I grab the picture, pulling it closer to my face as if that will help me understand. I can't comprehend what I'm seeing. He drew me? At my most vulnerable state, he drew me.

Shock gives way to tears and they trickle down my cheek. Every emotion from those days in the cell floods my body.

I knew people were watching me. That the camera provided a way for people to laugh or check on me, but knowing *he* drew me like this. Helpless. Alone.

A loud *POP* echoes around the cabin and I jump, dropping the paper to the floor. Swinging to the front door, I find it's still closed, and Liam hasn't returned yet.

POP.

POP. POP.

I slam the portfolio closed and shove the pencil pouch back against the desk, then take off for a window.

There isn't too much noise out here at the compound. The extent of the ruckus comes from the guys and their parties, perhaps a few noisy shipments. This is sharp and abnormal. While most of the guards at the gate carry weapons, I haven't once heard a gun discharge while here.

But that sound—

Gunfire.

More pops and bangs bounce off the surrounding wood and I peek out the window, squinting to see what's going on. A few men from the neighboring cabins leap from their porches while several figures I don't recognize sneak around. I realize too slowly they're armed and kicking in doors one by one.

For a moment, relief calms me. Have the police finally decided to show up?

But any hope of that dies when a shrill scream from the edge of the compound pulls my attention. I barely catch the curly-haired woman who works around the clubhouse being pulled into the woods by her feet. The man dragging her is unrecognizable, but the long weapon strapped over his shoulder can't be missed.

What the hell?

Racing to the door, I fling it open in time to hear another gurgled cry before she disappears.

It's then the chaos makes itself known.

Unknown persons with weapons dart around while several men from the compound fight back. I flinch with each shot, ducking behind the porch railing, and watch as men shoot back and forth. Another scream tears through the stagnant night air and I whip my head to see a man straddling another woman. Her back is thrown on the gravel pathway, her shirt rides up to expose the chewed-up skin around her sides as she pants and struggles to wrestle the man off her.

A million thoughts run through my head, mainly regarding who these attackers are and what they want. Never would I assume responsibility for these people, the criminals who took me and turned my home into ash. But if there's any injustice here currently, it's this man planning to take what does not belong to him.

I curl my hands around the porch railing, gripping tight enough my knuckles turn white. With a sigh and a deep breath, I dart from my spot, running toward the man.

"Hey! Get off her!"

The man's head darts to mine, and he raises his weapon at me at the same time the girl beneath him bucks. He loses his balance and topples to the stone, cursing. The woman scrambles to get up and I reach her in time to give her a hand. She climbs up my arm, almost pulling me down beside her. We both take off running.

"The ... club ... house," she pants and grabs my arm as our feet dig into the gravel pathways.

Another shot fires from behind me and a man I recognize

from the guard station thumps to the ground. More screams, both from men and women, distract me and I trip over a bleeding arm extended over the pathway.

Skidding on the knife-like stones, I throw my hands out to temper my fall. Rock pieces tear my flesh and blood instantly warms my palms. Slipping, I grapple to stand. The woman halts ahead and turns to find me getting up, but quickly her eyes widen and she takes off running in the opposite direction.

A ping next to me blasts part of the path away, and the cock of a gun freezes my slow crawl. Over my shoulder, the man following us has caught up.

I stare up at him, the barrel of his gun inches from my forehead.

My brain registers very little. Seemingly unimportant facts slither through my mind about how tall he is, or how I've never seen this man in Ruin before. But as he reaches down for my shirt and gathers a fist around it, my thoughts stride to Liam.

Is he okay? Please be okay.

There's more yelling, but the slowing of my breaths and the pounding of my heart in my ears make any words unintelligible. The man above me is red-faced and yelling at me, but I don't hear him as he drags me off the path and into the woods.

Chapter 37
Liam

As soon as the door shuts, I run to the clubhouse to get our pizza. It's been a tradition for several years when we have large shipments ship out. The guys all order from the local Ruin pizza place and two guys make the trek to pick them all up, then toss them in the clubhouse for the rest of the compound to come get. Usually, it's the new guys tasked with pickup, and I don't miss my fair share of those days.

These past few days have been tormenting as I sleep in my bed. Haunted by none other than the woman in the other room, whose kiss has stolen my sanity. I've resorted to running in the mornings to burn off any steam, but it's not helping. No matter how hard I push my physical limits, the need to drag Fleur from the couch and kiss her senseless is unrelenting.

I didn't miss the way her hand, once again, drifted to those rubber bands on her wrist when I mentioned her taking my bed. Her eyes darkened and I fought every primal urge to throw her against the wall and take my sweet time with her. If it weren't for the slight movement in her hand toward those two bands, I may have.

The night air is calm, and even though the cloudy sky blocks most of the stars, the moon is on full display.

In and out with the pizza, that's the plan. I have specific intentions with Fleur tonight and I can't be bogged down with Darrin's overzealous inability to relax.

When I reach the clubhouse, several people exit with their pizzas in hand. Some sit around a small bonfire, nursing a beer and tipping their heads back to gravity-feed their slices.

Trip and Blitz beat me to the door.

"Eh, Liam. About time we saw your sorry ass."

"Yeah, yeah, Trip," I say as he holds the door open for me.

The smell of dough and spicy pepperoni smacks me in the nose as we enter, the pizza boxes neatly stacked by type and in rows on the tables. The guys are huddled around, laughing and chatting, which is different from the typical Friday night party scene.

Darrin rounds the corner, his phone to his ear. A chill spreads up my spine when his eyes meet mine. There could be thousands of reasons for the fury reflected there, but I only care about one. If Darrin ever found out about me, who I am or the information I've passed along, I'd be dead. Or at least I think so. Darrin respects me, despite his beef with my brother. He values me as a loyal member of his crew, so if he's found out I'm undercover—the betrayal will cut him.

Blitz must also read Darrin because he rounds the table and slides his phone into his pocket. Both eyes pin me where I stand, and I note the optional exits to the building.

"What's up, D?" Blitz asks.

"Raven's guys are moving radically. Just had a tip from Fish at his spot and he said none of Raven's dealers are there. Word on the street is they're planning something."

I snort, partly from relief this isn't about me, and second

because Raven planning something is almost humorous. "What are they going to do?" I add. "They don't have any information about our location."

Darrin runs a hand through his tight curls and blows out a sigh. "This world is crumbling into shit. The Cartel is getting more impatient, Raven too bold, and rumor has it the DEA is sniffing around Ruin."

My body tenses, and I reach over to snag my pizza to appear nonchalant. My mind churns through the possible rumors and where they could've come from. I've done everything to keep from compromising this mission.

My behavior isn't the focus right now, though. Darrin's downcast eyes, the way he's pacing back and forth between Blitz and Trip—I don't think I've ever seen him this caged. It's then I notice the black circles highlighting his tired eyes.

Concerned, I back away, trying to make my exit so I can return to Fleur and also check in with my handler. If things are getting hot, I need an extraction plan. Not necessarily for me, but for Fleur.

Spinning around, I make for the door, only to be yanked back by Blitz, who slaps me on the shoulder. "Here, take an extra pizza, man," he says, sliding another box on top of the one in my hands. He offers me a toothy grin, the rot disgusting.

"Thank—"

Glass shatters behind me, and I turn in time to see three men, dressed in all black, clear the remaining glass from the clubhouse windows with the butt of their weapons.

It takes a moment to register the words coming from Darrin's mouth.

"Down!"

I drop to the floor, shuffling behind a table as gunfire erupts throughout the room. Naturally, my instinct is to reach behind me for the handgun I no longer carry. In its place is a military grade knife and I pull it out, turning it over in my palm. This will do nothing against the hardware these guys sport.

Three of our guards burst through the back door, drilling the other three men down before they make it farther into the clubhouse. I scurry to one of the men and rip his gun away from his lifeless body.

More shots are fired around the compound and hair-raising screams come to life in a chilling chorus. I stare down at the man dead at my feet, blood seeping from the four shots in his heart to under my boot where I stand.

So young. He looks so young. A baby smooth face with eager blue eyes permanently opened make me wonder if this kid knew what he was getting into.

A black bandana wraps around his neck, where it was pulled up over his nose and mouth, and I lean down to snatch the cloth.

"Liam." Darrin's voice interrupts my inspection of the man and I jump up to see him being escorted into the back saferooms.

I nod at him. "Orders?"

"Kill them. Kill them all."

I wince and ask, "Information?"

Darrin glances at the black scrap in my hand. "There's no need. We know who they belong to."

Automatic shots fire into the wall beside us, and I dive for Darrin, moving my body on impulse to shield his as six—no, seven more men encroach across the parking lot for the clubhouse. The guards meant to escort him yank us both up but only secure Darrin.

Darrin holds my gaze as they move him to the back room. I nod again. I have my orders and I turn to execute them.

Outside the clubhouse is mayhem.

I allow two seconds for my stunned shock and then move.

Sweeping to the side, I bolt down the pathway. Fear roots itself deep in my gut as I watch men kick in cabin doors, my mind panicking when I think about Fleur left alone and defenseless in our place.

Not once did I show her where I keep my guns hidden, mostly because they sit with all my other materials for my mission. Now I regret it.

There's a click behind me, and I spin in time to see a gun pointed in my face. In one rapid motion, I yank it away, a surprise to the tattoo-faced man, buying me seconds to knock my fist back and slug the black bird inked on his cheek. He stumbles before righting himself and diving for me. He lowers himself enough to knock the wind from me as he plows me into the ground, landing a punch to my nose.

With a loud crunch, blood gushes from my nostrils, the metallic taste hitting the back of my throat. I lift a forearm, blocking the next blow coming for my head, and reach out my other hand to wrap around the guy's throat and squeeze.

I bear down, tightening each finger around the corded muscles of his neck. He claws at my hand, eyes wide with realization. He slackens his weight over mine and I push up, overthrowing him. I hold fast as he bucks, and I climb on top of him to add my other hand to his neck. Within seconds, he goes limp. Eyes and mouth open, his head lulls to the side and I scramble back, picking up his gun.

Screams jerk my attention away from the man I killed to several more men dragging women into the woods. My blood runs cold.

What the hell is this? Kill the men and rape the women—

I slip on the gravel, stumbling back up. I zero in on the direction of my cabin.

Purpose courses through me.

Get to Fleur.

Get to Fleur.

Flashes of those stormy eyes clouded with fear pace through me, and I pick up my stride, sprinting at this point.

A streak of blond stretches over fifty feet ahead of me, but it's her, I know it is. Unease pounds through me and my stomach bottoms out when I see her rush to a man on top of another woman.

"Fleur!" I yell. *No, no, no. Don't get involved. Please don't.*

She doesn't hear me but manages to help the woman up. They turn in my direction.

"Fl—" I'm cut off by the butt of a gun tearing into my back from the side. I topple over, raising my gun to meet the other one pointing at me. I fire three shots, closing my eyes as I wait for a bullet to pierce me as well. It doesn't.

I roll back over, not pausing a second before turning back to where I saw Fleur.

The woman she helped flies by me for the safety of the clubhouse, and I catch Fleur's scream while being dragged into the woods.

Never. Not even in everything I've been through, have I been truly terrified. I growl, tearing off after them and ignoring the responsibility of securing the compound. I pass several dead bodies and a few bleeding women with torn clothes.

If she's hurt ...

If they ...

Damn it!

The wind whips across my face as clouds roll in, and the scent of rain fills my lungs. I suck in deep breaths, sprinting toward the tree line.

Flooded with darkness, the trees mask any light from the compound, and I trip on roots, trying to locate Fleur.

Debt of My Soul

Another scream shatters through the surrounding branches and I follow it.

"Get off!" Fleur's screech dies on the wind. Small drops of rain hit my face as a storm gives way and I pick up my pace, worried I'll lose my sense of direction in the coming downpour.

Two shadowed shapes appear in the distance, pushed back against the night backdrop and fairly hidden between two trees.

"Relax!" the man on top of Fleur bites out a snarl, with Fleur struggling under him. One of his hands palms her head over to the side while a knee holds one of her arms in place on the ground. She fights him, her unpinned hand grabbing for anything she can smack or pull.

I notice her grab a fistful of hair as he leans down, trying to unbutton his pants.

I yell from twenty feet away, and his head snaps to mine. Fleur strains to see me, her expression filled with relief when she does.

The man reaches back, going for the weapon he must've chucked to the side.

Faster, Liam, I chide myself. If he manages to get that weapon before I get to him, I'm—

My body collides with his, and I tackle him to the forest floor. Dirt explodes into my face as we tumble, each of us trying to grapple for the upper hand. Bad luck has him land on me, and his fist connects with my temple. Black dots dance in my vision, almost indistinguishable from the blots of night sky blanketing us.

"Liam!" Fleur screams. My head lulls to the side and I watch Fleur roll over to get up.

"Run! Fleur, run!" I manage to yell.

But she doesn't.

She charges the man, hops on his back, and wraps an arm

around his neck. Like a bug on a bench, he flicks her back, and I hear her gasp as she hits the hard ground on her back.

Growling, I push back up on my elbows to stand and manage to land a kick in the man's groin. He buckles over, coughing. Then before he can recover, I wind back my fist and punch him twice in the face.

Static noise beeps from his back pocket. "Back off. I repeat, back off and roll out."

The man staggers as he tries to stand, and when his eyes meet mine, they widen. No doubt understanding he doesn't have the option to back off or abort.

He turns to run.

Swiping a rock off the ground near my foot, I rear it back and throw. It smacks the back of his head, and he crumples to the ground, moaning in pain.

I wipe the back of my hand across my nose, blood coming away and pain radiating through my cheek. Stalking over to him, he wails while rocking back and forth as if to cradle himself. I barely glimpse the blood trickling out from the back of his head.

"Liam ..." Fleur says from behind me. I ignore her.

He threatened her.

He was going to take.

"Liam ..."

Did he think I'd show mercy?

I don't have enough soul left to show compassion.

"Liam ..." Fleur's plea is drowned out by the crash of thunder around me, her words muddled as if underwater.

The man struggles to sit up. The deep dark of his eyes no longer submerged by lust but with fear. I snatch his shirt and haul him up next to me. Another crack of thunder pierces his cry, and in one fluid motion, I twist, snapping his neck to the side.

"Wait!" Fleur screams again. But it's too late. She smacks her hand over her mouth, and I hold her gaze while letting the body fall with a thump.

Seconds go by while my chest rises and falls in time with the gusts of sideways rain.

Fleur lowers her hand, and it's then I notice the split in her bottom lip. I stalk toward her, intent on inspecting her face at a closer distance.

Up close, the rain soaks her braided hair, mud and leaves caked in it. Her eyes search mine, darting back and forth. Impatience pushes me to step forward until I'm mere inches from her.

She watches me, scanning my face, but it's not in judgment. Each cut she lingers on adds a layer of appreciation deep in my chest. Her nose crinkles when she gets to the blood smeared over my cheek and temple.

"Who—" Her voice comes out in a ragged whisper and dies off before she can continue. She tries again, the rasping worse. "Who were those—"

Gently, and careful not to touch her cut, I press my pointer finger to her lips, silencing her attempt to strain her voice. The warmth of her breath sends heat low in my gut, and I drag her lip down to inspect her small laceration. Her tongue darts out to lick her upper lip, and the fraction of contact with my finger sends lightning sensations ticking through my whole body. I want my mouth on hers again.

The need is so strong I drop back a few steps, lowering my hand to keep from tasting her thoroughly.

This is not the time or place, and the fact I'm considering this after what happened to her is disturbing. *She's safe*, I remind myself. That's what matters. If I hadn't gotten to her in time. If I'd—

I grind my teeth.

"We need to get you back to the cabin. I'll meet with Darrin quickly and return as fast as I can, okay?"

Fleur crosses her arms over her wet shirt, drawing my attention to the goosebumps peppering them. The stare she gives me quickly breaks into sad eyes welling with tears. With a longing look out into the endless woods, she offers me a nod and turns back toward the compound.

Chapter 38
Fleur

W ater splashes out of the tub the more frustrated I get scrubbing the blood and dirt from my finger-nails. The white washcloth is practically pink from the scrapes and minor injuries from my struggle.

When we emerged from the woods, Liam walked me back to the cabin. With a kiss to my temple, he left again, needing to check in with Darrin and work with the guys to start the clean-up, I guess.

I sink down into the water, letting the warmth wash over the many bruises already forming on my legs and arms. A round bruise from where the raged man dug his knee into my side blooms across my ribs. With each movement, I wince.

I didn't plan on hearing Liam until well past the time I crawled into bed, so when the door slams shut, I bolt up, sending more water to slosh over the side. I scramble to get out, but a knock on the door has me freezing mid-exit.

"It's only me." Liam's voice immediately calms my worry, and I slowly sink back into the water. His voice has always brought me some sort of relief and protection, even when I barely knew him.

Instead of moving on, the click of the door startles me again, and I duck in the tub when Liam pokes his head in.

"How are you doing?" He makes special effort to hold my eyes and keep from dragging them across my body.

"I'm okay. You?"

"If you're okay, I'm okay." He offers me a sad smile and moves to close the door.

I'm not sure what comes over me, but the thought of that being the end of our conversation rattles me. "Stay," I beg. "Please."

Liam pauses, his hand white-knuckling the door, and it creaks as he pushes it farther open. He stands there, seemingly paralyzed, but eventually allows the door to click behind him.

"Did you get everything taken care of?" I ask. "And ... do you know if the girl I was with is okay?"

"Yeah. Well, sort of. We lost one of our guards, Sam. The others are getting patched up at the clubhouse now. Fortunately, most of what needs to be repaired can be easily fixed. And Roe, thanks to you, is okay."

I nod and exhale a breath.

Liam shrugs his shoulders and folds down to sit, back propped against the door. I fumble beneath the water with the bands across my wrist. I'm not sure what it is about Liam that makes me feel so out of control yet more emboldened than ever before.

"Thank you, Liam. Thank you for coming for me."

His head snaps to mine and I work to swallow, the lump in my throat unable to slip down.

He scoots forward to bring a hand up to my cheek, and I lean into it, nearly nuzzling him. The few inches of tub and lukewarm water sperate us. I hate it.

Liam's thumb feathers over several of the scratches across my cheek and over the cut on my bottom lip. His gaze shoots down into the water, but it's not in a direction that would heat my blood. No. It's on my wrist, where I fiddle with the rubber bands.

"Who?" he asks.

"What?"

"Who, at some point, made you feel unworthy, Fleur?" His tone is serious, but he keeps focused on my wrist. Embarrassment heats my cheeks as he peels back the layers I've stacked there.

"It's nothing. I—"

"Don't," he responds. "Don't spin a story. I need to know so I can fix it."

My heart gallops, but I draw my hand out of the water, inspecting the fresh welts I snapped when I got back to the cabin.

"I'm not sure," I admit. "I'd done it once or twice throughout my teen years, but it got worse when ... when the man I'd loved for nine years cheated on me in our shower, in our home." Liam's face blurs from my welling tears. A small sob rips from me as the pain from that awful day resurfaces.

Liam doesn't flinch. He doesn't move. The soft look in his eyes prompts me to continue. "I came home and found them in the shower. I panicked and ran out of the house. Didn't even look back. At times I wish ... I wish I'd busted through the door and confronted him. The fact I could've embarrassed him like he did me ... when I heard them ..." More tears rip down my cheeks.

"Fleur ..."

I keep going before he can pity me. "I felt out of control. Nine years spent devoted to Chris—who knows how long it was going on during all the time I was loyal to him. So, I ran away, to a remote place I could feel in control again.

"These"—I motion to the bands on my wrist—"the pain grounds me, makes me feel more in control. It's twisted and weird, but when my anxiety feels unmanageable, this brings me that element back. I'm in charge of my pain. No one else. My trust was lost that day, and I realized how naive I was. Insignificant. Worthless enough for my partner to give up but not have the decency to tell me before he moved on."

I glance up. Now I'm spewing my random baggage at Liam, and it's probably more than he bargained for when he asked.

Rage fumes in Liam's stare and I make a quick effort to shrink back in the water, but I'm stopped short as he grabs my wrist.

Turning it over, he traces the welts and brand with his fingers, drawing circles that tickle with each brush. But then ... then he tugs my wrist to his mouth. He grazes his lips over the sensitive area, and my whole body jolts with a shiver.

He reaches behind him, into his jeans, and pulls out a knife. I jerk back, trying to snatch my wrist away, but he holds tight.

"You say you can't trust anyone, but I know you trust me. You *can* trust me, Fleur."

My breath catches and my heart pounds in my chest as he tilts the tip of his knife at my wrist, sliding the blade beneath the two bands.

"You want pain, Fleur? To feel something? You come to me. I'll give you whatever you need." In one flick upward, the bands sever from my wrist and fall into the tub. After he tucks the blade away, he reaches in and scoops out the remnants of rubber, grazing the top of my thigh as he does.

My tears have stopped dead in utter shock.

Liam stands, then bends down to kiss the top of my head before he exits the bathroom.

I'm left with lightness in my chest and throbbing in my core.

* * *

I wake in a cold sweat. Out the window, it's still pitch-black night, and I sigh, pulling Liam's cover back up over me. Or at least I try to. It's stuck on something. I yank until a massive form next to me moves and I yelp.

Liam startles up, rubbing his eyes. "Sorry. I can't do that couch. I'm so sore."

I smile, but it's lost in the darkness of the room. Reaching over, I turn on the nightstand lamp and sit up to see a shirtless Liam buried beneath the top quilt.

He turns to me and lifts a hand to his forehead to block out the light. Immediately, I'm drawn to the black smudges on his fingers, and I smirk, remembering the sketches I came across earlier. His eyes snag on the corner of my mouth, alight with a playful side I've never seen.

"What?" he asks.

"Your hand. It has black on it."

He snatches it down and shakes it out as if he could fling the dust off. "Uh, yeah. It'll come off."

I'm not sure if he'd ever tell me about his drawings. Or if he'd be upset I poked around long enough to find them, but it's only fair he knows.

"I found your drawings." The sheet up around my chest drops as I sit further up, and Liam follows it down.

"Did you now?" A slight shuffle is the only reaction I get from him.

"You're very talented."

He snorts and looks away toward the cricked TV on the dresser.

"I'm serious." I scoot forward, toward him, noticing him tense the closer I get. One of my hands grazes his forearm, tracing the lines of his ink that swirl into works of art. His muscles contract and relax under my touch and my wild racing heart betrays my thoughts.

His jaw ticks, but he watches intently as my hand continues to stroke him. For the longest while, he doesn't say anything. Crickets puncture the silence out the window and the trees thrash against the back of the cabin, tapering off from the windy storm.

"My mom," he says. "It was always the one thing we had in common. She's the artist of the family and it just so happened I was blessed with her talent as well. Although at times I wonder if she doesn't wish it were Adam."

Confusion must be on my face as I furrow my brow at him because he explains, "Adam is the youngest son. Something about the baby boy and his momma-type shit. They're close, and she fawns over him. Which is fine. Honestly, it never bothered me. But ..." Liam trails off and I find myself clinging to every word.

This man. So selfless and understanding.

I'm an only child, so I can't fathom sharing my parents' love with someone else, let alone two siblings, *and* to accept their favoritism of another ...

"But?" I ask.

"But I guess it was always something that made me feel connected to her. Even as the oldest. Even as she dealt with the loss of my sister and even as she thinks my brother Adam walks on water. Art was our thing. My mother used more watercolor, but she would always appreciate my work. She actually hung one of my sketches in the downstairs bathroom."

The framed drawing of the cabin flashes in my mind, but my brain snags on the comment about his sister. I had no idea. How could I not have realized?

"I'm sorry about your sister. I didn't realize she'd passed. Your mother mentioned her in the mountains, so I assumed ..." I wince as I say the words because I'm truly an awkward person and in the sincerest moments, I manage to screw up basic decency.

Luckily, Liam just snorts and I'm now even more confused.

"She hasn't passed. She left. Ran away six years ago when she was seventeen. Tore our family in two for a season. We finally heard from her about a year after she left when she called to tell our parents she wanted nothing to do with Ruin anymore."

I gasp softly as the briefest tear shines in the corner of his eye.

"I tried to talk with her, to see what happened for her to run off. I blame the boy she was running with—good-for-nothing scum of the earth. Never knew his name, and I couldn't find information on him either."

He shakes his head.

"What's your sister's name? Adam nor your parents ever mention her by it."

"Lily."

Liam shudders as he says her name, and I reach out to grab his hand for a squeeze.

"I'm sorry she left, Liam."

His head falls back to the pillow, and he releases a sigh. "Say it again. My name."

I bite my lip and then offer him a smile. "Liam," I coo.

He laughs. It's rich and haughty, moving through time like molasses on a winter's day.

I stare at his lips, wondering how skilled this man I'm married to is in other areas.

"Why did you draw me in the cell?"

The remainder of his laughter dies off abruptly and he grabs for my hand twirled around the plaid of his quilt. He stares down to where his pointer finger dips up and over each of my fingers methodically. When I think he won't answer, he surprises me.

"I want to draw everything about you. I have from the moment I laid eyes on you. Wanted to know the depth of your pain, the exuberance of your soul, or the simple everyday experiences that bring you joy. The cell was one of those many moments I was compelled to capture."

"Why?"

He sighs and brings my hand to his mouth to delicately kiss each pad of my finger. My blood ignites for him.

"I'm not easily thrown off my track. I have a mission and a job. My life revolves around that. It's what drives my focus. But you ... you in the bank snatched that away. I've never been more pressed to know someone than I have you."

"So I'm a distraction?"

"The best kind," he says and grins.

I lean into him, brushing my nose along the firm muscles of his neck. I inhale, unable to get enough of him. What's happening to me?

I'd never felt this close to Chris, and I was with him for years and years. Everything felt surface-level with him. It makes sense in high school where more adult issues didn't have a place. But as we grew, we never grew into a deep relationship. Maybe that's where we went wrong—or maybe were just wrong in general.

I didn't want to expose myself to him, and Chris, I'm sure, didn't want to reveal his shortcomings and struggles to me. In hindsight, while what he did and how he chose to move on was wrong, I can't necessarily say it wasn't for the best.

"Well, I don't have an artistic bone in my body. You've got me beat there."

Liam snorts. "I doubt that's true."

Now it's my turn to huff. In fact, I'll prove it to him.

Untangling myself from the sheets, I half roll off the bed like a ninja and dart to the bedroom door. Before I'm all the way through it, I grip the frame and turn back to Liam propped up in bed.

His eyes are pinched together in confusion, but the relaxed way he's positioned, hands folded behind his head, leaning against the headboard—I almost hightail it back to bed.

"Be right back," I say and bolt to Liam's desk, where I found the pencils and drawing paper earlier. Before—

I shake my head. I'm not ruining this time with Liam. I'm safe, and I trust him.

After grabbing a sheet of paper and pencil, plus a magazine from the coffee table, I practically skip back into the bedroom.

Liam's gaze immediately goes to the supplies I've collected and a smile breaks over his mouth. He runs his tongue along his back teeth while shaking his head. "What are you doing?"

"Proving to you I can't draw." Feet crisscrossed, I prop my paper onto of the magazine, which is now supported on my knee. "Okay. Don't move a muscle."

"But what if I'm too tempted?" Liam asks, reaching over to fiddle with a piece of hair brushing across my cheek. I bat his hand away.

"Ah, ah. None of that. Let the artist work." I muster as much of a pompous tone into the way I say it, and Liam lets out a bellowing laugh.

He leans back into his position. But instead of looking off into the distance or checking his phone, he watches me intently.

I start with his face. Not overly round, but I draw an oval type shape and call it good. As I study his unruly hair, I focus on capturing its natural waves as I sketch, adding a loosely tucked bun resting on top of his head. I draw some circles for eyes and what ends up looking like a triangle for a nose, then cringe when I realize these particular pencils don't have erasers. Clearly not designed for someone like me.

I spend over twenty minutes working on his face, including the massive muscle that flexes in his neck. Finishing the drawing, I stare at it and chuckle.

"All right. Ready for the big reveal?" I ask.

Liam sits up, scooting closer to me like he's anticipating some epic work of art. Then I turn it around and study his expression.

At first, his eyes are lit with anticipation. Upon seeing said "artwork", his lips fold in and his face tenses like he's trying hard not to laugh. Finally, his expression falls soft, admiring, when he says, "It's not that bad."

I let the artwork fall to my lap and laugh. "Not bad? A two-year-old could've drawn better."

He graces me with another louder than life laugh, and I eat it up.

"Okay. I concede you're not artistic."

I toss the drawing and magazine on the nightstand. "That's all I ask."

Liam laughs, pulls me to him, and kisses my forehead. The joking from seconds ago abates with his tender kiss, and in the silence of the room, I close my eyes while he strokes my band-free wrist.

Liam reaches up to cup my face, eyes searching mine. They

trace the outline of my face like he may be drawing me in his mind, and I catch myself hoping he doesn't ever have to only commit me to memory. I pause, realizing I want more with him.

I tilt my chin up, mouth hovering near his.

He hisses as I brush my lips over his. The rough timbre of his voice whispers, "You're the best thing that's come into my life in a long while, Fleur."

Liam closes the gap between us, pulling me flush to him, and I melt into his arms, protected and safe. With a peck to my nose, he continues over my cheeks before moving to my mouth.

This kiss is slow and unhurried. Like he's savoring the moment before it poofs out of existence.

I want more, *need* more from him. However, he seems content to be as we are in this moment, not taking it any further.

Connection, deep and meaningful, is what I crave. It's what I was searching for when Adam kissed me. And Liam, he blows it out of the water. It feels less like a connection and more like a fusing our souls together.

Chapter 39
Liam

There was a bra on the bathroom floor this morning. I'm not sure why this tidbit of knowledge is still rolling around in my head four hours and a truck ride later, but it is. I've seen a bra or two before. It's just a scrap of fabric. Although the part of me responding at the thought has not gotten the memo.

Thick pine needles coat the path I'm on, and I've counted each step since leaving Fleur in the truck. Something, anything to get my mind off of her in the bath a few nights ago.

More than her alluring body beneath the water, I was drawn to her story. I want to pound her ex's face in the pavement for what he did to her. It's tempting to Google the guy and pay a visit to Michigan—I hear it's nice weather this time of year.

The night turned into pure comedy when she drew a picture of me. It was awful. The entirety of my face was made up of four shapes. But, hell, did it bring me more laughter in that moment than I'd had in years.

Agent Wilson lifts a hand in my direction, a half wave, half robotic movement that makes me wonder if this man spends much time in the field. With the way his eyes keep darting back behind him, I'd guess not much.

This is one of three dead drop and meet locations we preestablished after I took this mission. Scouting areas while under Darrin's supervision was not easy but all three of these give the best cover and are the most out of the way without being questioned for going too far.

"This is the second time you've brought her." Wilson motions to Fleur sitting in the truck.

Her legs are propped up on the dash, feet crossed, and I can practically hear the gum she is blowing into bubbles from here.

Without thinking, I smirk.

"I told you not to get involved." The fall wind crushes his words into a murmur, but I hear them all the same.

"I'm not." I turn to face him, pinning him with a stare I give Blitz most of the time when he pisses me off.

"We got word of what went down several nights ago. Boss man says we aren't waiting much longer."

I freeze, a piece of my hair slapping me in the mouth, and I cross my arms, annoyed. "What do you mean you aren't waiting much longer?"

"It was Raven, right?" he asks.

I fish out the black bandana from my back pocket and toss it to Wilson. He fumbles with the fabric as it hits his bureaucratic suit shirt before spreading it open to reveal Raven's signature "raven" in the middle. To the average person, this is only a bandana with a bird on it, but Wilson and I both know that around the ankle of this bird is a cuff, thick and damning.

"Raven," Wilson says. "How did Darrin take it? Is he rattled?"

"He's pissed. We lost a guard."

"No. Darrin lost a guard," Wilson spits. "It's important to

remember that. Regardless, with Raven's attack, it changes things. The task force believes we can't wait much longer before Darrin spooks and moves his operation."

Move? I raise my brows, looking back toward the truck once again. I catch Fleur watching me, her eyes narrowed on Agent Wilson with such intensity I almost laugh out loud.

"Liam."

I snap my gaze back to him.

"With the attack, we believe the Cartel will intervene. They've invested too much time and money dealing with Darrin, and they aren't to be screwed with. If we don't move soon, we run the risk of them coming in and eliminating everything for themselves. We'll lose our leads into the network."

"Leads *I've* provided over the years," I growl. "Come on, do you *really* think this is the best time?" I take one more glance back at the truck, my ability to stay focused waning by the second.

I've worked for this. To bring Darrin and his crew down with the possibility of giving Ruin its town back, its leaders back. Now, selfishly, I don't want the mission to end. Thoughts of Fleur finally being free from under Darrin's threats on her family should bring me joy. Should, but it doesn't. Instead, I can barely swallow the thought of losing her even though she wasn't ever truly mine, was she?

"It's close, Parker." He nods over to the truck. "We can get her out now if you want. Say the word and we'll pull her into holding. You won't need to blow your cover with her, if you don't want."

I consider it, despite it being the easy way out. I could arrange for Wilson to pick her up, pretending it was right from underneath my nose. She'd be safe.

There's no way I can admit it was an option all this time. Was it? Could I have gotten her out without risking her parents to Darrin's wrath? Is my soul so far gone I twisted this whole predicament to spend more time with her—to know her?

"I'll tell her. What's the timeline?"

"Two to four weeks."

"That's too vague. Do better."

Wilson sighs, running a hand through his head of hair. "That's all I know for now. Check your phone often, if you can, and watch yourself. Darrin isn't going to let anything go unnoticed after what happened." He extends a hand toward me, shakes my hand, and slips a small piece of paper into it. "When the time comes, text the current gate codes to this number."

Without a word, I pull my hand back, new instructions crumpled within, and shove it into my pocket. I turn back toward the truck and work to keep myself from running there—to throw it into gear and whip off to a place where no one can find us.

I need to text my grandparents.

Back at the truck, I pull open the door to find Fleur's elbows propped up on her legs, her head resting on the glove box in front her. Her eyes flutter open as she sits up, grumbling about nearly being asleep.

"Done?" She yawns.

I smile, reaching over to squeeze her thigh. "Yeah, I'm done. Ready?"

"Yes. I'm starving. Can we stop to pick up some snacks on the way home?"

I falter, eyes unblinking as I stare at her mouth and replay the words that came out of it.

Home? Does she think of my cabin as home?

Trying not to let her claim on my cabin get to me, I nod and turn back on the main road. Back toward home.

* * *

My conversation with Wilson was the first thing to disappear from my mind while talking with Fleur on the way back to the compound. She has an uncanny way of making me forget everything going on around me. A distraction indeed.

Watching her take in the surrounding areas around Ruin, her eyes filled with wonder despite the drive being one we've taken several times now. It never gets old for her, which in turn, never gets old for me.

Daily, I battle the desire to tell her I'm in this for the long haul. Annulment of our marriage is not something I want to agree to. But doubt whether I'm the best man for her creeps in, and I question what I could possibly offer her at this point.

Driving around the pines leading to the compound gate, her hand is stuck out the truck window, windsurfing. Her hair, though braided over her shoulder, still thrashes over and around her beaming face.

My phone beeps as we reach the gate, and I check the text while our new guards motion us back through and secure the lock behind us.

I glance at the phone in my lap.

> Be at the clubhouse break room in 10. Alone.

I shift in my seat, annoyed I'm leaving Fleur back at the cabin yet again. This is no life for her. A better man would take Wilson up on his offer.

Fleur says she ran away, but I see something different. I see a woman who ran toward a new life. One without a cheating boyfriend. I see a brave woman, intent on making over a run-down farmhouse because she wanted to teach herself something new. A selfless woman who will do anything to keep her parents safe. This isn't a girl who runs away.

In fact, I'm grateful she wasn't able to confront her ex. Men are notorious for manipulating women. Gaslighting them and making them feel as if somehow their disrespect and inability to remain loyal was their fault. Fleur running out of that house and never looking back gave her two things she needed immediately: distance and Ruin, Mississippi.

I'll admit it worked to my advantage as well.

Pulling into the tiny-ass driveway next to the cabin, I say, "Darrin texted and needs to meet. Hopefully, I won't be long."

She turns from where her gaze is out the window and offers the biggest smile to me.

In my line of work, nothing fazes me anymore. I've learned to expect the unexpected, roll with the punches, and never freeze up in a stunned reaction—but Fleur chucks it all out the window.

Her smile, so different from the terror in her eyes in the cell, punches me in the gut. I don't care what Wilson says, this woman is mine.

"I'm going to make some chili. If that's okay? With the weather changing slightly, I'm itching to hurry fall along."

I chuckle. "This is the South. True fall is a ways off."

She pouts and I reach over to pull her lip down with my thumb. Her eyes darken, which instantly makes me want to say screw Darrin and his cryptic meeting text.

"Hurry back," she says, grabbing her bag of jerky, and hops out of the truck.

After watching her enter the cabin and close the door, I pull back out of the driveway and head to the clubhouse. All is quiet, and I stomp through the dining hall and down to the break room.

I'm not prepared for what I walk into.

The tension in the room is palpable. I can taste it in the first breath I take. My eyes widen at the sight of the three men standing in front of a seated Darrin, Blitz and Trip off to his side.

Raven, his second Drake, and ...

And ...

Adam.

He stands tall, flanking the other side of Raven, his dark hair tussled and longer than how he normally wears is tightly trimmed. Instead of his usual attire of flannel or polos, he sports tan cargo pants and a black tee.

What the hell is going on? Mentally, I calculate how I'd fight my way out with my brother in tow. Are they using him to get to me? Why is Raven even here?

Adam lifts his chin and sniffs, diverting his eyes when he sees me come in. Raven, on the other hand, watches me like a predator sizing up his prey. Except the bastard doesn't know who I am and what I can do.

"This must be the well-known Liam," Raven spits, glancing between Adam and me. "I dare say, you two look nothing alike."

"What is this?" I ask Darrin.

"Raven wanted to stop by for a meeting. Apparently, he has some new employees."

It's then I notice it—the raven tattoo newly inked on his forearm, the skin red around it. Lovely. The first ink little bro gets is under the employ of this drug lord.

This is where he got his money then. He ran to Raven's crew. After all I've done to keep him out of this mess, to settle the score placed against him with Darrin, he turns and climbs up Raven's ass.

Part of me wants to pummel him right here. My family's

relationship is strained because of him—my mother can't stand me, and he's thrown all I've done for him in my face. The other part of me wants to shoot Raven between the eyes for getting his hands on my little brother.

"Wrong move," I say, staring at the bird.

"Oh, please. It's not like you aren't enjoying your position here," Adam snorts, his voice shaky. "You talk like this life you have is intervening for me, but your soul is as good as tarnished now."

He might be right about my soul, but the idea I'm only here for him at this point has sailed years ago. I'm here for a bigger purpose, and Darrin looks at me, the eyes I'll never get used to boring into my skull. At least I *hope* no one truly knows.

"Brotherly spats. Invigorating." Raven speaks like he's from another time and it's eerie as f—

"I doubt this is why you came here, R. Get to it," Darrin snaps.

Raven pulls a hand through his blue-black hair, the hue as if he has an azure light hovering above him at all times. Although his eyes rival the color of coal, the man is ghostly pale. It's a sharp contrast to the deep V-neck shirt he wears, revealing the delicate curves of a lily tattoo inked across his chest.

"I want in," he says.

"In what?" Blitz counters

"Your network. Word around town says the DEA is sniffing close. You need the numbers, D."

A drop of sweat rolls down my back, wicking away at the band of my pants.

"You know I don't have that authority. The Cartel dictates those brought in. They haven't been too happy with you." Darrin smirks and I wonder how he's keeping calm standing near the man who sent men to attack us only several days ago. I, for one, do not have the patience for this game. At the mention of the DEA and rumors circling, I cringe. Our window is closing.

"See, I think you have more pull than you let on." Raven shuffles on his feet, shoving both hands in his pockets. A linked chain dangles from his right pocket, and it clinks with each rock back and forth.

Panic sets in and I swallow the lump in my throat. Raven's desire to get in with the Cartel is not something on our mission radar. He's always been the contender, the rebel to the network. Noncompliant. Darrin always said Raven hated the idea of men from outside the country running things.

"I don't." Darrin says it calmly, but I don't miss the tick of his jaw or the tightening of his fists on the arms of his chair. Rage simmers beneath, and I know he's considering his options at this moment.

Killing Raven would not earn him any favors with Raven's men, and he has many. But I won't let him touch my brother, no matter how stupid he was for pledging alliance to a man worse than Darrin by far.

"Perhaps ..." Raven drawls. "Perhaps I should stop by and have a chat with River. How is she doing these days?"

Darrin stills. His gaze levels Raven, all pretense stripped away.

I've never asked River. Never cared to. However, there was always a taut line that pulled through her when I spoke of Darrin. It's the same one barely holding D together right now.

Whatever the history, Raven knows it.

"I'll reach out to my contact." It's all Darrin has to say, and the high tension is ripped from the room.

"Good man," Raven says, smiling. He looks around, admiring the break room. "Looks like business is good. My men were impressed with your *setup*."

A snarl curls at my lips and instinctively I step forward.

"Liam." Darrin's stand down command is woven in the way he says my name.

Raven continues to bait. "Would be nice to see your new establishment as well. I've always admired your ability to juggle both sides of the business." He chuckles, amused with himself.

Blitz rolls his eyes and pulls his phone out. "Are we through with this shit?"

I can't stand Blitz, but I could kiss him right now for saying what all of us are no doubt thinking.

"Paying customers are welcome anytime," Darrin says as he stands from his seat.

What the hell?

Darrin is not friendly with Raven. Seems like the comment about River has made him *flexible*.

"Tonight then. Show us around." Raven slaps Adam on the shoulder and he flinches. It takes everything in me not to grab Raven's arm and twist until a loud pop fills the room. "It'll give our new guy here some time with his brother and his new *wife*."

Adam's eyes flick to mine and they narrow into slits, all but a growl emitting from him, and he looks down on me in disgust.

I shake my head. I've given everything for my brother, and he hates me for it.

I won't apologize for Fleur, for the feelings I've grown into. She brings new purpose and drive to my life, stretching it beyond a mission, beyond only being good for saving my brother and disappointing my parents.

While I'm unsure about how she feels for me, I've been more balanced than I have in my life with her around. There's nothing else I want to draw—I can't—it's always her. Capturing the light dusting of hair on her arms, or the few freckles on her back that match those on her face. Each detail I cling to and record in my drawings, hoping to retain any and all information about her.

Darrin offers a slight nod to the three men invading our space and with that, Blitz and I bolt from the room. Disappointed in D would be an understatement.

Cicadas punctuate the warm evening, their whirring sound a chorus of annoyance the entire walk back to the cabin.

Inside, it's quiet, and I notice a pan of brownies on the stove, a forkful missing from the corner. After cutting myself a generous square, I hunt the small space for Fleur, peeking in to see her curled up on my bed, sound asleep.

Driven to her, I down the chocolate dessert in two bites and gently sit on the bed next to her. Breaths steady and smooth, her mouth twitches in the slightest movement as I pull a strand of hair back out of her face. She sighs long and hard, nuzzling the pillow.

I don't want to leave her tonight, not again, and most definitely not for the Raven to play a few wimpy-ass games of poker.

I turn from her, sliding my elbows down to rest on my knees, and bury my head in my hands.

Wilson told me not to get involved. Maybe I should've listened.

Chapter 40
Fleur

The bed dips and my eyes flutter open to see Liam sitting closer to me, head in his hands. His shirt, still the same from earlier, is loosened, buttons undone at the top.

I blink away the hazy sleep from my eyes, and my heart crumples at the sight of him hunched over. The impossible need to reassure him makes my hand reach for his thigh.

He's warm, the muscle flexing beneath my touch. He rips his head away from his hands, his gaze trailing down the side of my neck and disappearing even lower.

A sad smile slides slowly into place. "Hey."

"Hi." I smile back. "Everything okay?" I sit up, tucking my hands under myself to keep from touching him.

"I have to go to the establishment tonight. Darrin invited Raven. Adam is going to be there." He sighs. "It's a long, complicated thing, but I wanted to let you know before I left."

Slightly crushed, I move toward him, brushing back some slackened hair for the briefest of moments.

The last thing I want tonight is to be without Liam. Plus,

his slumped posture and downturned mouth at the mention of leaving for the night leads me to believe he's having a hard time with his call there.

"What's wrong?"

He drags his tattooed fingers over his face, scratching at the facial hair that liquifies my insides.

"Adam. He's working for Raven. Apparently, everything I've done to keep him away from this was for nothing."

My stomach drops at his words.

"Liam, I'm so sorry," I say as he stands, moving to the dresser to grab a fresh shirt.

I scramble off the bed, bare feet padding across the floor with a blanket draped over my shoulders. I approach him.

He looks down at me, flipping the shirt in his hand back and forth.

"Take me tonight."

Liam practically loses the shirt. His eyes search mine. "Why?" he asks.

Okay? Valid question, I guess. I want to tell him that I love being near him. It's irrelevant where that takes me. If he's there, I want to be there too. This man has twisted me in knots and he's the only one who can unravel me. I need to hold on to him —it's all that matters.

I fist his shirt, the pads of my fingers burning as they graze the spot above his jeans. The smoothness of his chiseled stomach burns me to my core, and he hisses with the simplest touch.

"Because I don't want you there alone."

❈ ❈ ❈

Liam pulls his truck into a small side street, one block from the establishment. Unlike last time, where he pulled right up to the back door.

Frankly, I'm shocked he let me come after my ridiculous argument. Clearly, he isn't alone here. All the men he works with mill around these establishments along with the string of locals addicted to the high of hearing coins drop and placing bets.

That isn't what I meant, though.

Lately, Liam seems more and more uncomfortable at the compound. He's always looking over his shoulder and stress riddles his face most of the time. I'm not sure how to help him aside from encouraging him to leave, and after Adam threw all Liam's done for him back in his face, I'm not sure why he wouldn't.

The truck's door groans when I open it and my jeans catch as I slide out. Most likely I'm dressed too casually for this place. Last time, the women wore outfits I'm pretty sure I lack the confidence to wear. But I'm here for Liam and truthfully, I only care about what he thinks.

Considering he watched me out of the corner of his eye the entire way here, I'd say my sheer black top with black racerback underneath is on his list of items he approves of.

Liam's hand guides me as we walk the sidewalk, his palm settling into the dip on my back and I shiver.

"You cold?" he asks.

"No." No, not at all. I'm burning up. I have half the mind to sniff under my arms at the amount of sweating, and it's not the Mississippi heat this time.

Wind brushes against the back of my neck and it carries Liam's scent straight to my nose, caressing it to drive me wild. Mother Nature is out to get me. I swear I'll be a sweat-dripping, feral mess by the time I walk through these doors.

What is wrong with me? I've never craved a man like I do Liam and the fact he's *not* touching me much is driving me insane.

The last thing I want to be is a needy burden to him tonight, but I need this man like I need air conditioning in the Southern summer.

When the door opens, the sound of glass clinking and gaming chips tickles my ears, and Liam automatically drags me through the floor to find Darrin and his crew in the back. We slowly pass a poker table where Ruin's sheriff winks at me and raises a glass of not so clear liquid in my direction. I wasn't even sure he knew of me, but I guess he does. Jerk lied to my parents and gave them the runaround when they couldn't get ahold of me. Someone needed to sweep the fire of my farmhouse under the magical rug.

I smirk back at him while breaking away from where Liam guides me, choosing to walk around their table. The players follow my movement, and when I get to the sheriff's hand, I lean over his shoulder and loud enough for the whole table to hear I say, "Wow. Four kings. That's good, right?"

Players at the table laugh, while some fold their hands immediately. The sheriff snorts while twisting his head to glare at me. The whiskey on his breath drives me back.

"Liam. Control your old lady."

I waltz back to Liam with a grin on my face, but it falters when we hit the back seating area. The lights are turned low back here, giving us the perfect view of the well-lit floor like it's a stage. Here for Darrin's entertainment.

In a way, I guess they are. It's all money rolling in.

But that's not why my steps slow and my heart pounds. There, seated next to a man whose skin could very well have never seen the sun, is Adam.

His dark hair is long, straggly pieces jutting out each side and he's leaned back in his chair, nursing a bottle of beer. His eyes find mine before dipping down to where Liam's hand guides me to another leather chair. Most of the guys' women sit on their laps as arm candy, and Liam sits, pulling me down.

I gasp when I hit his taut thighs, the sensitive friction of his jeans rubbing against me. He doesn't look at Adam. Rather, his possessive hands splay wide across my hips, gripping me gently.

My eyes flick to the men around Darrin, all engaged in conversation with each other or shoving their tongues down their companions' throats. Blitz licks his lips when he catches my perusal, and he bites the air in my direction.

I wrinkle my nose in disgust and lean back into Liam, feeling the weight of his chest behind me, sturdy and comforting. Liam's body shakes a bit and when I turn to him, he's chuckling.

"What?" I ask.

"Don't let Blitz get to you," he says, wiping his nose with his thumb.

"He almost killed me."

Liam's smile fades, his expression unmovable, stone-cold, and lethal.

"I'd never let him touch you, Fleur." He snarls at his own words and wraps an arm around my waist, pulling me into him.

My heart catches in my throat at his husky timbre, and my eyelids are suddenly heavy at the press of my body melding into his. My backside nestled perfectly at his hips. The rough prickle of his beard drags along my neck as his warm breath skirts over my ear. "Trust me, Fleur."

He kneads my thigh and I'm desperate for a drink, mouth completely parched. I ache everywhere but couldn't tell you where I need his hands the most.

Roe, the girl I managed to help out during the attack, is a couple chairs down, taking orders for drinks, and I find myself tapping my knee, impatiently waiting for something to suck down. When she gets to Raven, her body strikes a defensive tone.

I'm not privy to much compound information, but I'm genuinely curious as to why Raven is here.

Raven's boots shuffle to the side after Roe finishes taking his order, and I startle to find him staring in my direction. He grins at me, perfectly straight and well-maintained teeth. Unlike Blitz and several of Darrin's men.

"It's Fleur, right?" he asks, holding my stare.

Naturally, I want to look away, at anywhere but at him. However, when I glance at the left of him, Adam's glare is anything but friendly, and he holds a soured look with every sip of his drink. He rounds his lips in slow motion, taking swig after swig from his bottle.

I quickly glance away. "Yeah."

"I know Darrin has a rule about going after a claimed woman, but I don't have such a rule. If you're ever in our territory, feel free to come say hello."

Liam scoffs, and with his movement, I lose my balance and have to shift on his lap. I don't miss his sharp intake of breath.

"I heard D made that rule for a certain someone. Didn't exactly need to ever use it, huh?" Raven says.

Darrin stands, looking down at Raven, the depth of his irritation plastered all over his face. I turn away, Roe finally leaning down to ask me what I'd like to drink. At this point, anything strong should be my choice, but I glance around at the steady increase of drunken placed bets and stumbling women and end up telling her that water will be fine.

Darrin follows Roe down into the sea of tables and patrons, doling out high-fives and schmoozing with the bigger moneymen here.

Blitz takes up his spot of trying to intimidate Raven and his men, but after two or three drinks, a few women rubbing them-selves all over him distract him, and I overhear one of the women asking for some Jackpot.

An hour passes, and Liam shifts underneath me to lean forward. "I'm going to check in with Darrin," he says.

I bite at my bottom lip, nodding while I stand. Liam hovers over me, reaching up to cup behind my head and bringing me forward to plant a kiss to my forehead.

I blink several times, my body swaying with the hot brand in the center between my brows. I clench my stomach and fall back into his seat when he turns to weave through the gaming floor.

Losing sight of Liam, my heart picks up speed, and I find myself tearing at my unpolished nails while watching the town's sheriff throw back his fifth drink in the last hour.

Being here is depressing with the realization that Ruin has no one looking out for the best interest of the town's people.

Another twenty minutes pass and I shrink back even farther into the chair, uncomfortable with the topless women dancing beside Blitz.

A shadow looms over me, and when I glance up Adam moves to the empty seat next to me. "Hey," he says.

I smile weakly.

"I'm surprised you're not out there." Adam tilts his head over to a few tables of all-women playing poker.

"I'm not big into gambling," I say, and he chuckles.

I clench my jaw, exasperated by his cavalier attitude. "Why'd you do it? Why trade one debt for another?"

"Isn't it obvious? For you."

I narrow my eyes at him. I don't buy it for one second. He was free of his debt. Liam made sure of that. And he made sure I was safe. There's zero reason why Adam would need to accept money from Raven unless *he* wanted to. Because it benefited him.

"Adam, I—"

"What is it, Fleur? With Liam it's acceptable he's wrapped in this drug trade, but when I get involved you look down on me ... Is that it?"

There has been a draw to Liam since day one, even before I knew who he was. I'm not sure I can explain my feelings for Liam, especially to his brother, who is clearly irate about this forced marriage.

But that's the thing ...

I'm not forcing it anymore. I want him. All of him, regardless of his associations. Deep down, Liam is loyal and willing to put everyone before himself and at his own expense.

More recently, I find myself less worried about getting out of this mess and more worried about what happens when I do.

"Liam's a good man, Adam. I'm not going to try to pretend I know everything you're going through or unpack the history between you two, but he saved my life, and I ... I care about him."

Adam curls his lip in disgust, eyes flicking above my head. Over my shoulder, Liam stands there, arms crossed with a scowl on his face. Adam rises, stepping toward Liam, brother against brother.

I wonder what went wrong. Is it his mother's favoritism that drove this wedge? The disappearance of his sister thwarting the family's dynamic?

The seconds tick by, the tension between them sucking the air out of the room before Adam snorts and guzzles the rest of his bottle. It slides from his grip and shatters on the floor by my feet.

I yelp, and Blitz shoves off the girl grinding on his lap and grabs

Adam by his shirt. With a raised fist, Adam pulls back and punches Blitz. Liam attempts to grab his brother by the arms, but Adam dodges and turns to shove him, smacking hard against Liam's chest.

"I'm out," Adam says, motioning around him and turning to weave through the tables.

I buckle to the floor, attempting to clean up the broken bottle, but I'm yanked to my feet.

"Leave it, Fleur," Liam grumbles. Then he softens his voice. "We'll get someone to clean it up." He grabs my hand and pulls me into him, his solid form engulfing me. His masculine scent making me weak in the knees.

He pulls me over to the bar area where a few vintage leather stools line the stainless-steel bar top, and he sits me down. The woman behind the bar gives me a glass of water, and she offers me a smile before flirting with some of the other men.

Liam leans into me and his presence overwhelms me.

"I'm sorry about—"

"You care about me?"

We both say at the say time. I freeze, my brain working through how much of Adam's and my conversation he heard. Better yet, why is that what's on his mind after his brother stormed out of here.

"It's not your fault, Fleur. Don't apologize."

I swallow, toying with the hem of his black shirt, wishing I could pull him closer to me. I've been forced to endure his proximity over the last seven weeks and my resolve is whittling down to nothing.

"I know you want better for Adam. I know—"

Liam silences me with a finger to my lips. "I don't want to talk about my brother."

The rough pads of his fingers press gently to my mouth,

and I fight the urge to taste him on my tongue. Another gulp. "W-what do you want to talk about?"

"Do you care for me, Fleur?"

Fidgeting, I chew on my lip, heart galloping in my chest. "More than you know."

There, I said it. Laid it out on the table for him to do with it what he pleases. I never planned on this, especially not in this situation, but I won't be afraid. If there's anyone I want to risk a broken heart on, it's Liam.

His hand finds my thigh and slides up, up, up until he's hooked his deft finger through my belt loop. He's so close, I'm able to map out the gold specks in his sea green eyes. I follow the lines from them down to the scruff of his chin, memorizing the outline of his face.

I need him and it's crushing how deeply I've fallen for this man.

Breathing is impossible the longer he stares. I need air before I'm going to pass out. Scrambling, I fly off my seat, and push past Liam to bolt for the door.

"Fleur," Liam demands.

The stool groans behind me, but I avoid turning around. Two steps from the door, a hulking figure in his leathers steps in front of me, blocking the crisp air outside. I practically whine in protest.

"I need to go—" I start, but I'm cut off by the massive bald head shaking at me.

"Cole. Move." Liam's voice booms behind me, and I flinch as the man named Cole moves from the door. Without hesitation, I push the door wide, letting it bang into the side of the building with a loud thud.

"Fleur." Liam tries again, but I press on, finding the thin strip of brick alleyway between two neighboring buildings, both of which look closed for the night. Streetlights illuminate the light fog settling over the area, and I inhale the rich air like I'm drowning.

Stumbling, I kick a fallen brick, nearly tripping, but a large hand envelops my elbow, keeping me upright.

"Fleur, please."

I spin, eyes surely wild with desire but dosed with guilt and shame. "I need air."

Is it wrong to be feeling this with how we were brought together?

I'm panting heavily, and Liam approaches me, eyes roving over my heaving chest and dipping down to where his hands were glued to my hips inside.

Liam reaches for me, hand on my cheek. He's so gentle. The big, powerful male cradles my head as if it's the most breakable thing he's ever held. "I care about you too, Fleur. More than *you* know."

He parrots my words and I melt. The night is quiet aside from the soft chatter coming from the establishment around the corner. Without a word, I press up on my toes and touch my lips to his mouth.

I shudder at the contact, and I'm swept away instantly in the feel of him. Hands prob at my back, pulling me closer as he deepens the kiss. I drag my tongue across his lips, tasting him and he opens, thrusting his tongue in my mouth. Sparks weaponize my body, and I tug and pull at him as I fist his shirt.

More contact. More, my body seems to chant on top of the thrumming beneath my skin.

Liam pulls away, eyes holding my lips in his sight before glancing around him and where we are.

Dark red brick is behind me, worn and faded from age, and an air conditioner unit is tucked into the window behind Liam. The lighting is faint, but that doesn't stop me from reaching for him, frustrated with his restraint. Afraid he's going to stop, I plead, "I want this, I want you."

"I'm not going to take you against a building."

"Stop treating me like a wilting flower."

He smirks. "Isn't that the literal translation for your name?"

I roll my eyes and respond by dragging my hands up, slowly unbuttoning my shirt with my trembling fingers. Liam's eyes follow each released button, then widen as I shrug off the scratchy fabric. The cool brick behind me barely assuages the burning on my skin. Each nerve ending is on fire. Every twitch in his jaw, every sidestep of his feet—I catch it all, needing it. Needing him.

Stepping into me, he reaches for my shirt. "Put this back on," he says as he attempts to rebutton my shirt. I bat his hand away, but he tries again. Hands fumbling, he shakes as he sneaks a glance down my torso. I smack his hand away harder and push him, growling in frustration.

"Where's the feeling you promised me, huh?" I shove at him again, tears welling in my eyes for absolutely no reason except I want this man with everything I have. It hurts. "What about pain? Pleasure?"

"Fleur, stop. This—"

"Where is it?" I move my hands to the button of my jeans, flicking it open.

Liam's nostrils flare and he steps back into me, capturing one of my wrists and slamming it above me. Thick fingers move to thread between both of mine, pressing them beside my head on either side.

I gasp as my head rolls back to settle on the wall. His mouth hovers to the side of my chin, and the warmth of his breath tickles my ear as it skirts over the shell. I close my eyes, letting my other senses take over.

Trying to swallow the dryness in my mouth, my tongue

darts out to lick my lips, and I hear him hiss. With one hand, the other still pressing mine to the wall, he drags his fingers down over my bare stomach. The gentle touch sends me into a frenzy, and I buck, needing more of his stroking hands. He dips a finger to the undone button of my jeans, tickling and teasing the spot between them.

"There's no turning back from this, *wife*." He moves a thumb over my empty wrist.

I haven't worn the rubber bands since he cut them off a few weeks ago. The only thing that remains is the horseshoe, marking me as Darrin's. It's more than that, though—this mark means I'm also *his*. Liam's.

My core clenches at the thought.

I peer up at him, eyes heavy. There's no second-guessing this. There's not a single reason to stop. I trust Liam and everything he is.

Reaching up, I pull the tie from his hair, letting it fall around his heaving shoulders. Worried lines extend from his burning eyes, so deep I can almost trace them. For a second, I'm concerned *he's* second-guessing this. Us.

"Liam ..." I whimper, and that's all it takes.

His mouth crashes to mine, while his free hand cradles my chin, angling it for better access. He brushes the seam of my lips, and I open for him this time, tasting the beer he was sipping minutes ago.

I run my hand down his back, sculpted muscle tensing as he struggles to maintain control. But I want him out of control. Flutters erupt in my belly as he presses into me, and I gasp, gripping his shirt tight.

I might explode. I need ...

"More," I plead.

He drops my pinned hand, and I immediately go for his belt, clawing at it while Liam drags his teeth over my now exposed shoulder. He nips and teases, making it impossible to focus. I'm trembling, but I've never been so sure of something.

The portfolio of Liam's drawings flips through my mind. The moments he recorded me in his life, needing to commit the memory on paper. Well, I want this one. I never want to forget this. This moment of time in the darkened alleyway. Escaping from the sinister world around us and wholly giving in to each other. It's intrinsic and delicious—I never want it to end.

"I want you to draw this." I moan as he licks and squeezes my flesh. "Us. Together. Here."

He slows, pulling back just enough to read my face, and I chew my lip. He nods, lost in a haze of primal drive. I smile, leaning in to kiss him again and pulling at his bottom lip.

It isn't long before Liam has me, writhing completely and utterly at his mercy. Minutes upon minutes of indescribable pleasure that I never want to end. I never knew it could be like this. And with him, it's passionate and ravaging. He focuses on each breath that catches in my throat, aiming to draw more and more from my lips.

"Fleur ..." Liam whispers my name, and it's such a high, the only drug I'll ever be addicted to is him. He growls my name again, and we fall together.

Chapter 41
Liam

I shouldn't have taken her against a trashy brick building. What was I thinking?

Clearly, I wasn't.

Pure, unrelenting need coursed through my body with her pleas to be touched and I wasn't strong enough to resist.

Every whimper, each sound she made, I devoured, wishing I could keep anyone from hearing her breathy moans but myself.

Her eyes widen when they land on me, taking in what we've done.

I snort internally. Involved my ass. I'm obsessed.

My wife, I say to myself as I stroke her cheek.

Looking around, I help Fleur with her pants while doing up my own and planning the quickest escape to the truck. Darrin will be pissed, but I don't care. Having Fleur in my bed instead of a backlit alley is all that consumes my thoughts. I need more of her, right now.

Fleur worries with her shirt, tucking it into her jeans while avoiding looking at me. "Are you okay? I'm sorry if I pushed too hard ... it's not something I usually do."

"Fleur, look at me." And she does, a blush staining the rounds of her cheeks. That won't do. "You never need to apologize to me. I want your hands on me as much or as little as you want."

The pink on her cheeks deepens to a blazing red and she smiles, rubbing her shoulder.

I check in with Darrin and Goff, letting them know I'm going back home, and I load Fleur up into the truck.

She's content and quiet on the way home, and I wish I could pull her thoughts from her. Head leaned against the window, she stares up at the stars.

She's beautiful.

I want this life with her selfishly. Her in my truck, relaxed. Her in my bed, pleased. Fleur in my arms, loved.

I pause on that word, jerking my head forward.

Shit. I love her.

Pondering this until we hit the gate, I barely hear Fleur ask about food and I end up pulling into the wrong cabin, the one down from us.

When I finally park at the right place, Fleur throws me an inquisitive gaze, her lips twisting into a sweet smile.

"Race you to the shower," she blurts, diving out of the truck.

I chuckle, watching her hair bound behind her head and through the door.

While she showers, I do everything in my ability to distract myself from her. I eat several hardboiled eggs, drink way too much for only having one bathroom, and switch out some laundry I'd left sitting in the washing machine earlier.

After relieving myself in the woods, I come back inside with the itch to draw. Especially after Fleur's request to draw that moment. To occupy the last few minutes with Fleur in the bathroom, my hands trail over the charcoal pieces I have as I imagine drawing the pleasure on Fleur's face. My body hums.

I'm drawn out of my plotting when Fleur clears her throat, and I drop my materials back against my desk to see her standing there in a towel.

"Your turn," she says, and it takes all my willpower not to turn that comment into something more meaningful.

She pads into the bedroom, and I rush through washing away the establishment's stench from my body and finish up getting ready for the night.

I climb into bed next to her, noting how right it is that she's here. Tossing a few pillows to be closer to her, I say, "You're in my bed every night from here on out."

Thanks to her, I'll never be able to have another woman in my life.

She snickers, her hand ruffling my hair. Her eyes ping-pong back and forth between mine like she's searching for something. Before I can ask her, she frowns and plants a kiss to my lips, lifting the sheets to slide closer to me.

She interlaces her fingers with my right hand, her thumb gliding over each of the tattoos across my knuckles. "What do all these mean?"

I smile and nip at her lower lip before bringing our hands up and in front of our faces. The letters on my knuckles spell RIDE.

"I had a friend, Ford. He rode a sweet motorcycle, had lots of tats, and I thought he was the coolest dude ever. He was a couple years older than me, and I looked up to him. Being the oldest in my family and always wearing that title, it was nice to have someone else to lean on, in a way.

"Anyway, he was the one who talked me into getting my first tattoo, and it grew into a sleeve. Most of them are of nature

..." I turn, showing her the forest of pines banded around the top and the mountain range I looked up when my sister sent us the one and only photo from where she ran off to. Fleur's hand slides over the wolf's head, and riverbed with a motorcycle parked beside it.

"Your skin is like a canvas of your drawings. It's almost like you touched the paper and the ink crawled up your arm."

I smile. "I prefer black and white. No color. That's why I draw in charcoal or pencil. Or why my ink has no color."

I shiver when her fingers drag up my left arm. "And do you plan to get this arm done?"

I shift my focus from her captivating lips to where she caresses my tattoo-free arm. The question lingers there. I hadn't thought much about it. It seems like that would be the next step, but as I study my arm, I have a thought.

"I think I might get something on this arm."

I don't expound, and she doesn't ask. Instead, her face falls to my neck.

I massage the drawstring knot of her pajama shorts between my fingers, eyes rolling back as she trails kisses over my bare shoulder. With a hunger in her eyes that rivals my own, she pushes me back, climbing to straddle me. Hell, she's beautiful.

My heart kicks up and I fist my hands at my sides to keep from turning her over and rushing this along. I want her to feel in control—to take what she needs.

Her hair falls over her face, damp from the shower as she presses revenant kisses on my chest and teases the band of my sweatpants with her fingernails. This is punishment for what I did to her earlier, I'm sure.

"What're you doing?" I stutter.

"What I do best. Distracting."

* * *

Fleur is a welcomed distraction over the next week. I haul her into my bed as much as possible, only leaving the cabin periodically to check in with Darrin when absolutely necessary.

The farmer's market is today, and Fleur's managed to bribe me out of bed to take her. Even told the guys I'd drive the truck to gather our pickup instead of stacking the crates on the bikes.

A rush of adrenaline spikes when I catch the view of Fleur in her hat, leaning over to smell the flowers at Mrs. Hinz's booth.

Fleur laughs at something Mrs. Hinz says and I smile. Her hair hangs loosely around her face, contained only on top of her head by my hat that has since turned hers.

Her cutoff jean shorts are driving me insane and anytime she dips out of sight, I panic.

This girl's got me in her crosshairs.

I'm less and less motivated to complete my mission, paranoid about how I'm going to tell Fleur. Selfishly, I don't want this to end. What we've found together—I've never had this.

Knowing Fleur has been hurt in the past, that she was so involved with someone they spent nine years together; I've never had a long-term relationship before. I don't know what I'm doing. I do know I don't want to hurt her. Therefore, I have to find the time to tell her.

Fleur admires a bunch of daisies. Eyes closed and beaming, her nose flares as she inhales, and I shake my head. Each step toward her eases my fixation. When I finally reach her and wrap my arm around her waist, the sharp, consuming need to be by her side dulls.

"We'll take them all," I say to Mrs. Hinz, whose eyes light

up, having sold more in a single transaction than she could've hoped for all day.

Fleur leans into my chest and tilts her head up to study me. "Didn't know you to be such a flower fan."

"I'm a Fleur fan. Same thing." I wink at her, and she sighs. Her body melts into mine despite being in public. People glance our way, but Fleur pays them no mind. In fact, she seems perfectly content with me in public, and I'm in awe of her ability to block out the few disgusted stares. They're all for me, though.

I slide my hand into her back pocket possessively while Fleur takes the bunch of daisies wrapped in brown paper and tied with white twine in her hands.

"Thank you," she says, looking at me through those long, heavy lashes.

We move down a few booths as Fleur looks over the crafts and produce. The smell of barbeque makes my stomach growl, and I have half the mind to grab my wife by the hand and yank her to the nearest food tent.

"I kept them, you know."

Fleur's voice is low and it breaks the peaceful silence between us.

"Kept what?" I ask, confused.

"The daisies you got me the night of your parents' dinner. I stuck them in one of the books River gave me." She fiddles with a few homemade spoon rings on the table in front of her.

I smile, unsure why she's telling me this. To be honest, I hadn't thought much about what she did with the flowers. I assumed they withered away from being in the truck.

"Did you now?"

She gives me a pointed look, but it softens into a serious vulnerable expression. "I don't want to forget this."

"Do you plan on it?"

"No, but what if this is all because we were forced together? What if we're just reacting to something that—"

"Stop." I can't hear this because it couldn't be further from the truth. I had my eyes on Fleur long before she came to the compound. "Do you feel like this"—I pull her hand to my chest —"is forced?"

"No, but how can this feel so right when it was born out of something so wrong?"

"Don't over think it." *Please,* I say to myself.

Pulling her into my arms, I wrap myself around her in the middle of the sea of people milling down the grass aisles and weaving through tents. I press my lips to her forehead. "Trust me, Fleur."

We finish at the farmer's market and load up the back of the truck to head back to the compound. I need to hear from Wilson, but part of me hopes I don't. Instead, I focus on Fleur, and when dinner is over, I strip her down in the kitchen and chase her to the shower.

Her laughter rings throughout the cabin.

Chapter 42
Liam

Itrace circles around a patch of freckles on Fleur's naked back. The sun is just peeking in the cabin, revealing the floating dust around the room.

Sleep evaded me most of the night. Even after Fleur fell asleep, all I could think about was how I was going to tell her about my mission and keep her safe while doing it.

Restless, I sneak out the door and down the hall to the bathroom. A quick splash of water on my face relaxes me, and I stare at the mirror, smiling at the memory of last night. Fleur's hands on me, her body beneath mine, trusting and pliant.

Smile fading, I rip the door open to the medicine cabinet and dig in my hiding spot for my phone. After powering it on, I check for any incoming intel and type out the new gate code I got from Darrin last night. Leaving Fleur in bed frustrated me, but I was able to make quick work of checking in with D and retrieving the newest codes.

My messages are empty, and I slam the phone on the counter, a crack splintering over the glass in front.

Nothing. Not a word from Wilson.

I shove the phone back in the cabinet and pull on my running clothes. Once down the cabin steps, I take off for the woods, skipping over roots and weaving through trees until I burn.

I push my body while running over the conversation I plan on having with Fleur. I need to tell her who I am, and that soon this life for her will be over. Wrestling through it, I rehearse how I want to tell her that once this is over, I want to be with her, and her, me.

My skin tingles as every brush of her lips caressing me replays in my mind. The thought of never having that again, hearing her laughter, seeing her in my damn hat picking out items at the farmer's market.

With a conversation mapped out, I head back home.

Fleur stands in the kitchen, freshly showered, making eggs over the stove. I move to her, wrapping my sweaty arms around her middle, and bury my face into the crook of her neck. She smells divine.

"You're addicting," I say into her shoulder. With a small peck, I pull away to find her beaming at me.

"You're one to talk." Fleur plates me some eggs next to a piece of toast, and we both stand there, leaning against the counter to replenish the calories we lost last night.

The last thing I want to do is ruin our high with a specific conversation, but I never want Fleur to feel like I'm hiding something from her.

"Listen, Fleur. I want to tell you something and—" My phone ringing in my pocket interrupts me. She offers me a smile, before loading our empty dishes into the sink while I pull out my phone.

Darrin.

"Yeah," I answer.

"Warehouse basement, now," he says, then hangs up.

The fact I'm not just playing house somewhere makes me pause. I need to tell Fleur off compound. I'm so focused on sharing my life with her I didn't stop to think how speaking so freely here could be dangerous. I'm distracted and it's showing.

Shaking my head, I round over to where she stands, hands deep in the soapy water.

"D called. I need to shower and head out. Let me take you to dinner tonight."

She smiles, but it fades too quickly. "You don't have to, Liam. I don't expect—"

"Stop right there. We're going to dinner," I growl. What is her hesitancy?

She nods and I turn to the shower.

After I finally leave the cabin and pull open the door to the warehouse, the steady hum of workers bagging product and weighing pickup crates for the dealers echoes off the walls.

Trip and Goff walk around, inspecting, both of them sporting dark circles under their eyes from a late night last night. Goff's hands shake and I know he's fighting getting a fix until this meeting Darrin called is over.

"Hey," Trip calls out. I lift my hand in a wave and move toward them.

"What's going on this morning, guys?"

"D-Darrin's got something big," Goff says.

I narrow my eyes. "Did he tell you what?"

Trip shakes his head, pointing to the basement door. "Gotta go find out."

The basement is not somewhere D likes to host meetings. If it's establishment business or just partying to have a good time, we're at the clubhouse. Product meetings for our dealers or offloading trucks, that's done at the warehouses. But the nasty shit, that's what happens down below.

Smooth concrete turns into rough, pebbled cement on the stairs. Small lights hang every so many feet down and they're all on, meaning a few of the guys are already here. Trip leads while Goff and I follow, the short ceiling brushing against the top of my head.

Uncomfortably small, the stairs narrow into a straight hallway that bends to the right at the end. More lights flood out from the opening and when I turn the corner, my stomach bottoms out.

I stiffen, my mouth suddenly dry but threatened by the instant nausea tossing about.

Son of a—

Goff runs into me from behind, prompting me to move farther in the room, but I keep my eyes pinned on Agent Wilson.

Terror laces his gaze, but I hold it only long enough to assess, then I move, looking around the room. Raven, Darrin, and Blitz all stand there, while a few men I don't recognize line the back wall of the cement room. They must be Raven's men.

"Shit, D. What's this?" Trip says, motioning to where a surprisingly calm Agent Wilson is tied to the metal support beam anchored to the floor. His lips are split open, and bruises pepper his face. I quickly look away, willing myself to act unresponsive.

"Raven's men here found him snooping around the compound last night. He was scouting about a mile out and round."

I clench my jaw, mind working overtime to try to figure out what the hell he was doing out here. Is he alone? This wasn't the plan.

My head snaps when Wilson rattles his chains, trying to sit up farther against the pole.

Raven eyes me, then reaches into his pocket to pull out a badge.

Shit, shit, shit.

"He's DEA," Raven says and tosses the badge at Trip, who fumbles with it in his hand before spitting on it.

"Kill him," Blitz yells, staring at Darrin like it should've been done already.

I keep quiet, eyes flicking back to Wilson. He's blinking erratically, eyes wide. Sweat drips down my back and I can't think. I'm armed, but I'm positive all of Raven's men are as well. The only one not carrying is Darrin for his own screwed-up personal reasons, but that still doesn't give me a shot at fighting my way out of here and securing Agent Wilson.

I shift, slightly, trying to give myself a better vantage point in the room.

Wilson's eyes widen even more, and I realize it's not out of fear, but trying to get my attention. Barely, just barely, he shakes his head and I stop. Swallowing I glance up to find Darrin watching me.

"Interesting, isn't it?" D says, eyes trained on me. My heart pounds. And while I'm nervous for how this is going to go, I'm also annoyed. If they know who I am, they need to say it and stop dancing in circles for show.

But Goff answers for me. "How so?"

"Raven here says he's seen this man before, hanging around Ruin. Says he looked like an insurance salesman or something."

Wilson scoffs, earning a kick in the head from Blitz, who is pure rage and thirsty for blood. He crumples to the floor, and I twitch to check on him. He'd kill me if I did.

Raven steps forward. "Clearly not a salesman. But I

wonder, how is it he got so close to your men, Darrin? It's rather simple, really. You have a mole."

I'm going to kill Raven and his infiltrating ass. Why is Darrin listening to him?

"You're an ass, Raven," Trip says. "We don't have a mole. You're just trying to stir shit up."

Darrin doesn't say anything. He's calm and quiet, and I have no idea what he's thinking. It's almost as if he's checked out.

"What's your angle?" I ask Raven.

Wilson gathers his strength and continues to blink at me.

Ten.

"Oh, Liam. Loyal Liam." I flinch at the cooing words coming from his mouth. "What better way to prove my worth in the Cartel than to expose you."

"What's he talking about?" Blitz bites.

Nine.

Hell.

Fleur.

Damnit, I need to get to her. My eyes flick to the door, but two of Raven's men have already migrated there. My gaze snags on Wilson again.

Eight.

"Is this a friend of yours, Liam?" Raven continues.

I don't react. Instead, I back up, placing space between Wilson and me, and look at Darrin. He looks ... sad. Betrayed. "I don't know what you're talking about." I reach behind me.

"Don't even think about it," one of Raven's men says from beside me.

Seven.

"Tell them. Tell them who you are, Liam. I've had men on you since your bother came to me with his predicament."

My nostrils flare. He did? Was I too distracted to notice a tail while meeting with Wilson?

"Leave my brother out of this."

Six.

Trip laughs. "Liam? A mole? He's one of the six, been here for years. Darrin are you really letting this man take over?"

Darrin crosses his arms, eyes moving over to the wall to ignore Trip's question.

Blitz frowns at his leader's response and he pulls his pistol from his back. He moves to Wilson, aiming the gun at the back of his head. Wilson blinks several more times. I freeze, watching Blitz snicker. "If you're not one of them, Liam, then you won't mind if I kill Mr. Agent here, would you?"

Five.

"You'd kill him before getting any information? Just to see if I flinch, Blitz? Come on, you know me better than that."

Blitz scowls. "You were always too much of a prick, but that doesn't answer my question. If the death of this one here"—he taps on Wilson's temple with the barrel of this gun—"doesn't tempt you enough, what about your sweet wife?"

Four.

"Perhaps I should go get her and have her persuade you to answer. I've always wanted my hands on the woman."

"I'll kill you before you could lay a finger on her," I say.

Blitz laughs. "Oh, Liam, you've got it bad." He cocks his gun and I snap, reaching behind me for my weapon.

"Don't." Darrin's voice is smooth and unaffected—a warning. It's then the three barrels come into focus in my peripheral —guns ready to fire.

Three.

I fist my pistol at my side, each breath turning out faster than the last.

Fleur.

Two.

Damn. I love her, and I wish I'd told her.

Blitz tightens his finger over the trigger and Wilson's blinking finally stops, eyes closing as his body shakes in fear. I lurch forward, and Blitz takes his eyes off Wilson for a second. That's all I need.

One.

Chapter 43
Fleur

I add the last item to the bottom of my list. With the fall weather finally starting to set in, longer pants and shirts are definitely on there.

While tidying up, I daydream about all the fall farmer's markets, pumpkin patches, and hot apple cider Mrs. Northgate let me sample one afternoon as she was perfecting her recipe.

The idea of Liam taking me on bike rides through the Trace while the changing leaves dust the pavement makes my heart skip with giddiness.

For the first time in a while, I'm genuinely happy.

A faint blast sounds from somewhere in the compound, and I frown wondering if one of the trucks had a container slip from its twist locks while loading. I peek out of the front window, not seeing large shipping trucks. Typically, the compound is running trucks late at night so midafternoon would be out.

Backing away from the window, I fluff the couch pillow and glance around the room. Pounding from next door distracts me and about halfway to the other window, a pounding on my door interrupts.

I veer toward the door, opening it to find a man clad in black tactical gear. A helmet is strapped securely to his head, a holster fastened around his thigh, and a long rifle slung over his shoulder. None of that matters, though, because stamped across the black heavy vest are yellow letters that read DEA POLICE.

Instinctively, I back away. Over the man's shoulder, droves of DEA police officers pillage the cabins, pulling men out one after another and handcuffing them.

"Ma'am. I need you to come with me."

I take another step back. No, no, no. I can't. Where's Liam?

A man who yells across the pathway is tazed by an agent as he tries to run away.

I need to find Liam.

The man steps forward. "Ma'am, this isn't a request. I've been instructed to bring you in."

"I-I can't. I need to find someone." *Please let me find him.*

I have to make sure they know he saved my life, that he isn't like the others. He did this for his brother.

"Ma'am." The agent's voice is growing agitated, and he steps forward again, reaching for my arm.

Panic pumps through me and I pull away, only to have his hand clamp down and pull me out of the house. His green eyes clash with mine and I glare at him, clawing at where he holds my arm.

I'm naturally a rule follower, a *don't rock the boat* person. I drive the speed limit. I've never done drugs. Heck, I respect law enforcement, but right now I want to punch this agent in the face.

I'm dragged down the cabin steps but turn back, watching

the door sway in the wind—it's not even closed. I have a sinking feeling I'll never see the inside of it again.

Another home ripped away.

Several packers and dealers are pushed to the ground, handcuffed, and lined up against the side of the warehouse. Roe, I recognize, is crying, pleading with another agent and he points to a spot on the ground for her to sit.

I squint at the sun hovering behind the clouds and want to shout for Liam. I haven't seen him among the others, nor have I spotted Blitz or Darrin either.

"Sit here, please, ma'am." The agent holding my arms guides me into the circle of mostly women.

"Please, I just need—"

"Sit."

I glare at the man again and huff out a sigh while folding my legs to sit. Several agents stand around the group of us sitting here, weapons pulled out and surveying the area. Teams of four raid cabins while a larger group exits the clubhouse.

"Have you seen Darrin?" I whisper to Roe, who has not stopped crying.

She shakes her head. "No. Last I heard, they had a meeting in the warehouse." She sniffles.

"Are you okay? Did they hurt you?" I ask. Because I'm unsure why she is so worked up.

"Assholes confiscated my stash." Roe glares at one of the agents and I blink.

Her stash? That's what all the blubbering is about?

"Have you seen Blitz?"

"Nope."

"Trip? Liam?"

She rolls her eyes at me. "No, okay? I haven't."

I shake my head and turn to try to catch sight of any familiar faces.

"Move, move, move!" an agent yells, and groups of them move, guns drawn into the warehouse. Shots ring from inside and I jump to my feet, attempting to move toward them.

Liam.

A hand grips the back of my elbow and I'm pulled back. "Don't make me put you in handcuffs," the agent barks.

Screaming warehouse workers are brought out. Some wrestle with the agents holding them, others with their heads hung low, resigned to be arrested.

Continued shouting and gunfire erupts from the giant metal building and a strangled cry gets lodged in my throat.

I hope he isn't fighting back. Please, Liam, survive. Survive for me.

Flashes of Liam behind bars for the rest of his life plague my mind, and I wince at the sudden assault of them all. He doesn't deserve to be there, to be locked away for the sake of his brother. He'd argue it's justice and the law, but I know better than that.

Standing here is torment. Listening to the yells and booms from deep within makes me dizzy and I stumble forward.

The agent's hand on me slackens and I take a few wobbly steps.

More agents pour inside and the warm prickle behind my eyes grows with each step. He'll die in this. Darrin probably has them defending him in an attempt to escape.

He'll die.

He'll die and I haven't even told him I love him.

Chapter 44
Liam

I t took me several minutes to understand what Wilson was spelling out. With his fairly swollen eyes, it took a moment to piece together the dot and dashes into the stream he kept repeating.

DEA HERE

When he was sure I understood his message, he moved to counting down.

Wilson quietly clears his throat while Trip and Blitz yell around me. He must have an earpiece in, and they didn't think to check.

One.

When I lunge toward Blitz and Wilson, I tip down the gun pointed at him. A blast sounds from the upper level and two of Raven's guards flock to him, taking the underground tunnel exit out.

"Behind!" Wilson shouts in my ear, and I turn, gun raised to shoot another guard in the chest. Blitz scrambles, then ducks as more shouts and gunshots sound from above.

"Boss!" Blitz yells as he runs for Darrin. But Darrin is

headed for Goff, shielding him with his own body and pushing him into the tunnel behind Raven's crew. They mutter words and with a final shove, Goff is out of sight.

Trip glares at me, reaching to the back of his pants for a gun. I fire at his feet, not wanting to kill him. Any of them. Well, except maybe Blitz. I'd have no problem taking his life for trying to end Fleur's.

"How many?" I ask Wilson as I fumble with the chains securing him to the post.

"Joint task force. Our unit's SWAT and Mississippi's FBI units." His voice croaks and his eyes go wide as Trip's gun takes aim at his face. I drop my work and fire back three more times. Trip ducks behind the entryway doorframe.

"Go after Darrin," Wilson commands.

"Not before I get you out of these." I scowl at the knotted chains and make quick work to undo them, grateful there wasn't a padlock on them as is typical Blitz fashion.

Wilson jumps up, letting out a cry of pain and holding his bruised, or maybe even broken ribs. That doesn't stop him from taking spot at my back.

"I've got your six. We've gotta move. They'll have hit all the cabins and the clubhouse."

I growl, pissed that Fleur is going to be thrust into this confused and disoriented before I've had the chance to talk with her. Hell, I'm confused.

Another shot grazes my leg and I buckle, glancing up to see Blitz firing at us. Trip has turned, his back to us, engaging agents who have flooded the stairwell.

"Some warning would've been nice!" I bark in pain and anger as Wilson and I move around the room, taking cover behind a steel table. Its top is lined with pliers, electric shock wands, and multiple hammers. Guess I know what Raven had planned.

"No time. Chatter in the network places the Cartel here tomorrow." Another bullet flies in our direction and I grunt, flipping the table over. The clatter of tools vibrates off the walls, and I shove the table a few inches at a time. We move, making our way toward the door, shots ricocheting off the turned table with high-pitched pings.

"Darrin didn't know. He didn't mention them coming," I pant. Sweat beads my brow and I turn to take in Wilson, trying to help move the table with his only free hand.

"They were going to kill him. Raven made a deal."

I freeze. I knew Raven wasn't sniffing around for some brotherly feud. He's here to claim this as his.

The guilt of not being there for Darrin these last few months stabs at my chest. I shouldn't feel bad. He made his bed, and he can lie in it. But still, despite how Darrin is involved, his soul isn't forever tainted ... I know it. Probably because I caught a glimpse of his while trying to preserve mine.

Coughs erupt from the doorway where Trip and Darrin stand and a haze wafts into the room, the acrid scent overwhelming.

"Damn it," Wilson says, pulling his shirt over his nose.

A burning sensation claws at the back of my throat and my eyes feel as though I've opened them in a vat of lava. We're farther back, but the gas released in the hall penetrates the room.

Skin tingling with discomfort, I mimic Wilson and pull up my shirt. Trip yells and I peek over the table to see SWAT with gas masks on, pinning him to the wall and cuffing him behind his back.

Three agents dart in the room, one of them with two masks in their hands. Wilson and I jump up. Wilson grabs both and hands one to me.

"Agent Wilson, Agent Parker. Good to see you. Let's get you out of here."

I slide the mask over my face, experiencing the sweet relief of being able to suck a deep lungful of air.

I catch sight of Trip and Darrin both handcuffed and being led up the stairs. Blitz is in front of them, combative. Three agents wrestle him to the top while he tosses out profanities like candy at a parade.

Wilson struggles with the steps, so I lift his arm up around my neck and offer him support as we climb the stairs. The dingy basement falls away to the brightly lit warehouse. It's been totally cleared out of all the packers from only an hour ago and investigative agents have already moved in to bag and tag it all.

Our group moves to the door and the only thing I can think about it Fleur. I rip off my mask, toss it to the ground, and push through several of the other agents filtering out. Wilson tries to keep up, but Agent Hunter takes over for me.

The sun is blinding, and I squint, scanning the area outside the warehouse for Fleur. SWAT trucks and unmarked police SUVs liter the compound. Crime scene tape is already erect around the clubhouse—dread fuels my search.

In a group of unrestrained men and women hovering over by the large oak to the right of the warehouse, I catch a flash of a blond braid whipping around as Fleur combs the sea of people and police. She argues with an agent next to her and he aggressively grabs at her to sit back down.

Possessiveness crashes into me, my chest tightening, and I surge toward her.

Chapter 45
Fleur

My face is wet. Tears stream down my face as I search the area for Liam, panicking when I don't see him.

I've practically been assigned my own agent babysitter, and he won't let me go anywhere.

"Do you know if my parents are okay?" I ask for the fourth time. I'm not sure what's going on, but I need them safe.

The agent doesn't answer me.

Blood catches my eye, and a man who looks vaguely familiar is escorted by. His eyes are swollen, black and blue, and he's half keeled over, but when his eyes meet mine, I swear he recognizes me too.

The wind picks up, whipping my braid into my face and when I bat it away, the man has been lost to the sea of black tactical gear. More police, both FBI and DEA, move boxes and bins into the warehouse, then emerge with full containers and march them onto a cargo truck they managed to back in here.

"... damn pigs! Get your hands off me!"

I recognize Blitz's voice and I follow the sound I'd never

think to want to hear, seeing him wrestled into a SWAT box truck. He's handcuffed and they chain his feet to steel loops welded to the truck bed.

"Blitz!" I yell, trying to get his attention, but the wind carries my voice off, unheard. I move, my babysitter snatches my arm, and I tug and yank, methodically searching the crowds. Then I see him.

Trip.

His eyes are red and dried tears are plastered to his pocked face. An agent leads him to the same box truck as Blitz and I push forward.

"Trip!"

His eyes dart up searching out the voice calling to him. When his eyes meet mine, he snarls, then seeing my frantic search around him, he chuckles.

"Where's Liam?" I yell. But he doesn't answer. Instead, he throws his head back and laughs—laughs until the agent behind him grips his tawny hair and throws him in the back of the truck.

A black SUV rolls next to the SWAT truck and two agents push a man to the back seat. When he looks up, my eyes meet Darrin's. Those dual-colored eyes bright against his dark skin look sad, defeated. He holds my stare for several beats. No malice. No recognition.

They're blank as if he's already checked out.

I don't know the sentencing for an operation this big, but I know prison isn't kind. The thought makes me sick, and I shake off his stare to continue my search, but I don't have to look any further.

Dirty-blond hair, pulled half into a bun dawns my vision, and I skip past the cut on his forehead to his wide eyes as he takes me in.

I gasp, throwing a hand over my mouth.

"Liam," I whisper.

Tears well in my eyes and I can't resist the urge to plow through the group of agents. I bolt, dodging another agent who reaches out to secure me.

"Stop!" he yells, but I don't listen.

I run to Liam, desperate to touch him, to feel he's okay.

He quickens his pace too, and in a matter of seconds, I collide with his solid chest, gripping it for dear life.

"Liam," I sob, at the same time he says my name.

His hand comes to cradle my head, crushing me to his heart. The rapid pounding beats against my ear, and I relish the sound. I count each one, afraid I'll never hear it again.

After a minute, I rip myself away from him, touching his body, looking for any signs of injury. There's a cut on his forehead and a graze on his leg, but he's alive. I glance up at him.

Terror and relief swirl in his eyes.

"I thought—" I try, but the words die as more tears fall.

"Are you hurt?" His voice quivers and I can't handle it.

"No," I whisper and I pull his face to mine. When my lips meet his, my body melts into the safety of his arms. His mouth is dry, and I taste the salty sweat beaded on his upper lip. More tears slide down, the taste mingling with him—

An arm jerks me back, the agent finally getting ahold of me.

Liam growls and my eyes widen as his nostrils flare.

I needed this moment with Liam and now that I have it, I don't want him taken away. I can't have him taken away.

"Liam, it's okay, don't—"

"Take your hands off her," Liam demands, and I flinch, waiting for the agents around us to secure him or cuff him.

But the opposite happens. The hand clenching my arms releases me and I blink.

"Sorry, Agent Parker."

I blink again. What did he just—

"Fleur, listen to me." Liam's words are clear, but I don't understand.

"What's going on?" I ask. I glance around, agents milling about, placing more of Darrin's men into police cars and transport trucks. No one is pursuing Liam. "I-I don't understand."

Liam's thumb caresses my cheek, and I close my eyes, allowing myself to memorize the rough pads of his fingers lingering there. Then I push him away.

"Liam."

"I'm an agent, undercover. My mission was Darrin and his operation."

My mouth falls open as my mind repeats those words.

I'm an agent. Undercover.

The bloody man from earlier approaches and my attention flips to him. Memories of our trips to "deliver" products flash in the back of my mind and I shake my head.

"You were meeting him." I gesture my head over to the man and Liam follows it, nodding when he catches sight of him.

My heart pounds. I'm so confused. "So, all that talk about being here for Adam, your commitment to your brother, saving him—was all that part of your cover this whole time?"

Liam's eyes widen. "What? No, Fleur, listen. I was here for a year because of Adam before I got involved with the agency. With my police academy training and my established connection in Darrin's crew already solidified, it was the perfect mission for me."

"Police academy?" When did he mention this? He didn't. I didn't even know that about him. A pit of nausea tumbles around in my stomach, and I take a step back. "Were you ever going to tell me?"

He reaches for me, but I pull my hand from his. "Yes, Fleur. God, yes. All I wanted to do was to tell you. When you thought the worst of me. When I claimed you. I wanted to tell you that you were safe with me—with law enforcement."

"You didn't trust me."

"No, Fleur, that's—" He diverts his gaze, looking at the agent he called Wilson coming to stand near us. "Give us a minute, please."

"You're needed for debriefing and you need that graze looked at," he says to Liam. The man, Wilson, looks back at me. "Ma'am, I can have one of our agents take you where you need to go."

I flinch. Go? Go where? I glance toward the cabin I called home with Liam, my now husband. Crime scene tape dwarfs it, and I close my eyes, taking a deep breathe through my nose.

As if he's read my anxious thoughts, Liam responds, "My grandparents. She can stay there. Please let me have a minute, man."

Agent Wilson nods and steps away a few feet. I snort at the mere illusion of privacy.

"So Agent Wilson is what ... your handler?"

"Yes."

I press my lips together, pulling them inward and fighting back tears. "You kept telling me to trust you, over and over. But yet you couldn't be bothered to tell me about your mission, your job. I could've helped you. It's not like I was a willing participant here, Liam."

"I didn't want to put you in a compromising situation." He sighs.

"So, you let me think the worst about you?" I bite my tongue at my own words because despite who he was working for, I lost any disgusted thoughts of Liam early on. His temperament and respect for me—he saved my life at his own expense. So why does finding out he's on the right side of the law hurt?

Was this just part of his mission? I'm married to this man. Legally bound.

Liam reaches for me again, but instinctively, I back away. His fingers graze my braid before falling back to his side.

"Agent Parker, the administrator is on the line for a report. We need to debrief," Agent Wilson says again.

Panic laces Liam's eyes. "Listen, Fleur. They're going to take your statement and they'll drop you off at the bed-and-breakfast with my grandparents. Stay there and wait for me. We *will* talk. This"—he motions around to the compound chaos —"is going to take several days to clean up, and I'll need to be deposed and report in."

I shake my head and Liam grabs both of my shoulders gently.

"Fleur, please."

Two agents step up to me. "Ready, Ms. Jacobs?"

Liam hangs his head, stepping back while agents swarm him with work. I'm escorted to a black SUV, and the door opens for me to climb in.

I do.

Once the door shuts, the clamoring sounds of people and vehicles die. Tucking both hands under my thighs, I lower my chin to my chest and cry.

Chapter 46
Fleur

I drag the tea bag back and forth over the top of my peppermint tea, creating mini waves that I watch intently. Even when Mrs. Northgate places a muffin in front of me, I can't look up.

It's been two hours since I was dropped off here and it's already past 10:00 p.m. I was taken to the local sheriff's office where the DEA and FBI had taken over, relieving the sheriff and half his deputies of their duty. I was placed in a long line of mostly women, and after waiting an hour, was finally called into an interrogation room. Even though I was told over twenty times this wasn't an interrogation.

A female agent, Agent Evans, sat across from me with a smile, taking down each detail I provided. From my first inter-action with Darrin's crew at the bank to the farmhouse fire, Adam's involvement, Liam's rescue, the marriage, and my knowledge surrounding it all.

About halfway through my statement, my stomach roared, and embarrassed, I asked for a drink of water. Agent Evans brought me a turkey sub and chips as well.

Tears flowed as I narrated the events of today, and she passed me tissue after tissue as I struggled to detail the raid.

When we were done, she reached over and placed a hand over mine and said, "I'm sorry this happened to you, Fleur. Here's the contact information for a local attorney. I've given his information to several of the women in case they choose to proceed with an annulment."

Annulment.

I mumble the word aloud as I pick the walnuts off a muffin top.

"What's that, sweetheart?" Mrs. Northgate asks.

I sniff and say louder, "The female agent mentioned an annulment."

Mrs. Northgate leaves her post at the stove and comes over to the kitchen table, glancing at where I'm deconstructing her muffin. She taps the table with her fingers.

"Well, is that something you want?" Her eyes dart to my chin, which is no doubt quivering. Tears sweep down my cheeks and I hiccup a sob, splashing my tea with my movement.

"Oh, sweetheart," she says, wrapping her arms around me. "It'll be okay."

Why doesn't it feel that way? Why does it feel like what I had with Liam is crumbling? The unknown of where we go from here is debilitating.

I jump at the back door when it flies open. I'm half expecting Liam, but Mr. Northgate stumbles in. He takes one look at our embrace and walks back out the door with a mumbled apology.

It wasn't going to be Liam anyway. He said his debrief could take days.

I allow my head to flop down into my hands, exhausted.

"Why don't you head up to the North Room and settle in for the night. You'll be able to think better in the morning."

I nod, sliding back my chair and taking my teacup to the sink. When I turn it on and reach for the dish soap, Mrs. Northgate stops me. "I've got it. Up to bed."

I smile. "Thank you."

I have to drag myself up the stairs by the railing and after I'm in the room, I shut the door. With each step to the bed, I shed a piece of clothing. First my sneakers, then my jeans, followed by my pit-stained shirt. When I make it to the bed, I toss back the covers and turn out the light.

The crisp, freshly pressed sheets feel foreign on my naked body compared to Liam's worn, plaid flannel. I reach for my wrist, desperate for control, but only find the raised brand of a horseshoe.

"Liam." His name is a whisper on my lips. I mutter it over and over, the ache drilling deep into my chest until I finally fall asleep.

✳ ✳ ✳

"Is Ruin ruined? That's what townspeople from the small town of Ruin, Mississippi, are asking themselves after a joint task force between the DEA and FBI raided a compound yesterday early afternoon. A spokesperson from the DEA said this was a long-term operation and over forty-five people were arrested. Among them, Darrin Reynolds, Ruin's kingpin rumored to be in with the Mexican Cartel, has been taken to the county jail where he will be incarcerated until trial.

"The compound was located off the Natchez Trace and law enforcement is asking everyone to please—"

Hey! The TV clicks off with a black poof, and I turn to see

Mrs. Northgate standing behind me in the kitchen, remote in hand.

"No need to be watching that when you experienced it firsthand," she says, moving back around to the counter, and cracks an egg into a bowl.

The movement reminds me so much of the way Liam gently smacks his eggs on the counter and empties them into the dish all one-handed. *She probably taught him.*

Images from the news cameras miles away from the compound showed the distant footage of the gates, and I fight the urge to turn the television back on. "Have you heard from him?"

She glances up, grabbing a fork to whip the eggs. Scrambled it is. "Nope. My son-in-law did call late last night, though, making sure Liam was okay. Had to pretend I didn't know anything—not sure how much Liam is allowed to share yet."

I frown. "His family had no clue he was undercover? Only you and Mr. Northgate?"

"No. They didn't know." *That makes all of us then.* Well, except the Northgates.

"Why did he tell you?" I pull out the same chair I was in last night and plop down, craving any information she'll give me.

"He didn't. About a year after Liam went to work for Darrin, he came to my husband, broken and hurting. He'd witnessed things he'd never dreamed of, even as someone who wanted to be a cop. I couldn't stand seeing my grandson suffer for something he didn't do."

I wince imagining Liam alone and terrified.

"My husband is a retired police officer with several acquaintances in the DEA. I pieced together Liam's plan to take his information to the DEA when my husband started making calls. I didn't figure they'd recruit him but looking back, if there was anyone suited for the job it was Liam."

Liam's stony gaze and his hard exterior had been easy to forget as he shared his life with me, opened up to me.

"W-why do you think he didn't tell me?" Gosh, I sound pathetic. Do I seriously think he'd risk an extensive, multi-year sting operation? I understand, I do. He was under no obligation other than to his job. Though, it still doesn't stop the hurt from creeping in. Maybe I wasn't enough?

"I'm not sure, sweetheart, but I know Liam. If he didn't tell you, he had a good reason."

Sweetheart. Mrs. Northgate's name for me brings with it a familiar pain, and I glance toward the phone.

"Mind if I call my parents?" I ask.

"Not at all." She offers me a smile, and I stand, dragging myself to the cordless phone. I dial my home phone number on the way to the back porch, letting the screen door slam behind me.

Propping myself up to look out at the pond, I notice the trees Liam helped plant fully thriving. The landscape is breathtaking.

In two rings, I hear my mother's voice. "Hello?"

"Mom ..." My breath hitches and a sob trembles past my lips.

"Oh, sweetheart—"

That's all my mom has to say before I crack.

Hot tears stick to my cheeks, and I cry. Cry for Liam and the life he's had to live. I cry for me and the betrayal I've experienced threatening anything good in my life. And I cry for us, for the marriage I'm scared is over.

Chapter 47
Fleur

There's no word from Liam the rest of the day or the next morning, and the dread knot twisting in my gut gets larger.

Speaking with both of my parents yesterday offered more support than I knew I needed. I explained it all to them, my mom crying along with me. And when our conversation was over, I felt more at peace than I had since the raid except for the lingering comment my dad made.

"You need to come home, Fleur."

His words rang in my ear all night as I tossed and turned and throughout the morning as I helped Mrs. Northgate prep some rooms for guests arriving today.

It doesn't help she had to rearrange her guest room assignments because of me taking up a room. I tried to tell her I could go to the hotel a town over, but she swatted at my hand while I was tucking a corner into the foot of the bed, telling me to never speak like that again.

It's midafternoon and the biting chill has me grabbing a blanket from the basket on the porch for guests.

Leaves start to wrinkle on the branches, dawning their yellow and red tips. While the back porch is serene and peaceful, the front porch is lively. Squirrels chase each other up the towering oaks, and every so many minutes a car will pass, adding to the wind chimes playing from the post.

A car slows, pulling into the employee drive for the bed-and-breakfast. River gets out, raising a hand at me and waving furiously.

Her tall brown boots crunch through the fallen leaves as she makes her way over to me.

"Hey!" she says. "Didn't think I'd see *you* here."

"Here I am. What are you doing?"

"Mrs. Northgate had some items she wanted me to pick up for the store. Said she was tired of them sitting around."

Funny. She never mentioned anything about items she needed dropped off. I could've done that for her. "Huh," I say.

River walks up the steps and sits on the porch swing next to me. Her eyes rove over my face, and conscious of her study, I tuck a piece of unruly hair behind my ear.

"How are you holding up?"

"Not the best," I say. "Still haven't heard from Liam."

She nods, her eyes glazing over as she looks out across the road.

"I'm sure he'll be a while, but I'm not sure what to do until then. My dad wants me to come home."

Her eyes snap to mine. Are those tears?

"I think you should."

I blink. She does?

"You're blessed to have parents who support you, Fleur. Who want to help you get back on your feet and protect you from the men in your life who can't seem to get it together."

I narrow my eyes at her, unsure if she's truly talking about me. However, I consider her words alongside my dad's. I do want to go home. To curl up on the couch with my mom with a cup of tea, put a puzzle together with my dad. Gosh, I miss them.

My lips pinch together as I shake my head. "The agent who took my statement gave me this."

I pull out the lawyer's business card and run the corner over my thumb back and forth. This piece of cardstock has burned a whole in my pocket since she gave it to me. Mostly with anxious anticipation. Was Liam under the impression I'd contact him already? Did he tell Agent Evans to give this to me as a way to suggest an annulment?

River leans over and plucks the card from my hand. "A lawyer?"

"For an annulment."

She sighs. "You've been through some crap, girl. No one would blame you for taking some time to collect yourself back in the safety of your family."

"It's not like I have anything left here to pack up," I add. I'd still need to deal with the farmhouse property, but other than that ... "Hey, have you talked to Adam?"

Her eyes widen. "Absolutely not. Heard he ran off with Raven's crew."

Guilt gnaws at me when I forget to ask about her brother. "And Goff? Is he okay?"

She nods, offering a sad smile. "He made it out before they rounded everyone up. Told me Darrin told him not to waste his life and made him leave." A tear leaks from the corner of her eye and she smacks it away. "Can you believe that? Darrin," she scoffs.

We sit together, enjoying the silence until Mrs. Northgate brings us the first of the season's apple crisp, and the three of us enjoy simple stories from recent guests, not discussing the events of the recent days for the next two hours.

It isn't until I'm alone in my room with Mrs. Northgate's borrowed computer that I type in the flight information and book a ticket home.

Chapter 48
Liam

"Walk us through your dead drop protocol with Agent Wilson again, please."

I pound a fist on the table, the papers spread over it jostling at the contact.

"I've already gone over it ... twice." I growl.

Six days. That's how long I've been sequestered in debrief, unable to contact Fleur. Meetings piled on top of meetings pack my days, and Agent Wilson decided I was the one best suited to help interrogate Blitz, Darrin, and Trip. Idiots. They definitely don't want to talk to me.

Blitz made that clear this morning while I sat in with the FBI. He spat at my feet and threatened to slit my throat if he ever was released from prison, time served. It doesn't exactly make me excited to join them for Darrin's questioning later.

I want out of here.

"I'd send a message on a secure phone and meet him at one of several locations to deliver that information."

"Always in person? You never left intel?"

"No," I seethe. "Are we done?"

"And your marriage within the organization. Walk us through that again."

I blink, only to stare openly at the scrawny agent across from me asking silly paper-pusher questions.

"She was taken by Darrin's crew, held to send a message to Adam Parker. Blitz was prepared to kill her, or so I assumed, and I claimed her."

"And claiming is?"

"Come on. Y'all have this down already."

"Humor me, Agent Parker."

I fold my arms and slink back in my chair. My knee bounces in time with the clock on the wall—I'm going mad.

"Darrin had a rule. In time, I came to realize it was more to protect the girls brought into the compound, but his rule was if a woman was married in, no other man could touch her. Bro code type deal. Basically, you married a girl you didn't want anyone else to mess around with."

"Interesting. And are you still legally married to Ms. Jacobs?"

I snort. "Considering I've been locked down here until you goons can get your paperwork finished, I'm pretty sure I still am."

"And do you intend to file for divorce?"

I tighten, each muscle locking into place at the word. *Divorce.*

Leaning forward, both arms on the table, I say, "None of your damn business. This meeting is over."

The chair I'm in whines as it slides back, and I stride for the door, ignoring the "Agent Parker" coming out of the man's mouth.

"You know it's protocol." Wilson chuckles as I slam the door shut.

"I don't care. I'm done with this. I hate being in the office."

The Jackson Drug Enforcement Agency offices are old and moldy. Priority for upgrades is low on the list for the small offices of Mississippi.

I'm hours away from Ruin and it's driving me wild not being able to go talk to Fleur.

Agent Wilson follows me to the bullpen where I grab a file folder of paperwork needing my signature off of my temporary desk. Most field agents aren't in the office much, and I've been in here a grand total of two times.

Pausing, I open the desk drawer and pull out my badge. The textured letters are rough under my thumb as I brush it.

"Does it feel weird ... being here, able to converse as Agent Parker?"

Nodding, I keep my eyes glued on the shiny, like new badge and slide it into my jean's pocket.

"Come on, I'll grab you a cup of vending machine coffee before we hit the bunks for the night."

✲ ✲ ✲

A headache blooms behind my eyes and I rip off the shirt I slept in and exchange it for a plain black T-shirt from the drug store.

Since I'm currently stuck in this building until I'm cleared, I had to ask one of the office admins to gather me some supplies.

I swipe my wallet, gun, and badge off the small nightstand next to the bunk and open the door. I glance at the clock on the stark white walls of the hallway: 7:00 a.m.

I wonder what Fleur is doing. I'm sure my grandmother is shoving baked goods down her throat.

The desire to steal someone's phone and call Old Hillside eats at me. My phone's been confiscated until I've completed my debrief and psych evaluations. Apparently, over four years under deep cover makes you more of a risk instead of a loyal agent giving away years of your life.

Hell, bureaucracy sucks.

I use the last of my one-dollar bills to grab a granola bar from an ancient vending machine and end up spitting it out in the trash when it's harder than a rock.

"You're needed in the observation room for Darrin's questioning." Agent Hunter jogs up beside me and slaps me on the shoulder. "Oh, and everyone knows all the food in the machine is expired. Better steer clear."

He laughs and I flick him off, making him laugh even harder. I wander the mostly empty halls until I reach the observation room. Agent Wilson and his FBI counterpart stand there. Two tech guys are set up with their equipment in the corner, ready to read body language and record audio. The see-through window is tinted, taking up the entire length of the one wall.

Darrin sits in an orange jumper, hands cuffed to the table. Both ankles are clasped in manacles as well.

He stares straight ahead, both of those eyes meeting mine even though I know he can't see me.

"That man is creepy," the FBI agent murmurs.

The door to the interrogation room opens and our boss walks in. His silver beard is trimmed short, and his black suit is already wrinkled before lunch.

The questioning starts simple. What's your name? When were you born? He answers it all, but the interrogation slams to a halt when the questions about the compound come into play. Information about the Cartel or Raven, he won't give up.

Darrin's mouth is sealed shut until he says, "I want to talk to Liam. I'll only talk to him."

Figures. But I guess that's why I'm here.

My boss stands, exits the room, and I meet him in the hall.

"We need the Cartel information, names up the chain in the network, and anything he can give us on Raven."

My stomach sours at Raven's name. Yeah, I want Raven's information, too. I nod, rolling my neck and entering the room.

It's the first time I've seen Darrin in a week and the tension is tangible. Although it's not vengeful like Blitz or comical like Trip. No, this is a low simmer of betrayal stewing between us.

I slide the metal chair out and turn it around to sit backward, casual. I'm letting him know his presence doesn't affect me.

Darrin snickers. "You know, I always knew there was something off about you. Guess if it had to be anyone, it'd be you."

I don't respond. Instead, I say, "We need information on the other kingpins in the network under the Cartel's thumb. Oh, and as a bonus, you could throw in what you know about Raven."

The smile leaves Darrin's face slowly, and he sits back, tipping his chin up.

Silence stretches in the room.

After three minutes, he says, "You authorized to make deals?"

I shrug. "Perhaps."

Pretty sure I'm not, but I'm going to run with this.

"I'll give you all the information I know, on one condition. I want unlimited visitation and correspondence with one person while I'm incarcerated."

I blink, confused. That's definitely not what I thought he'd say.

"Okay." I take my small notepad out of my back pocket and click my pen. "Who is it?"

"River."

Yeah, that's *not* what I thought he'd say.

✳ ✳ ✳

It's heaven being back on my bike.

After two excruciating weeks, I was finally cleared to leave with a week's worth of vacation. There was zero hesitation. I jumped on my bike and flew down the highway for Ruin.

Three hours later, I turn down the street of the bed-and-breakfast.

Last week tipped us into November and the thought of Thanksgiving outside the compound with my grandparents—hell, even my parents—is a welcomed thought.

The grand oaks in front have shaken half of their leaves and when I pull up the driveway, my grandfather is raking said leaves into two piles.

He squints at the bike, taking his work gloves off and tucking them back in his pocket. When I lift the helmet off my head, he breaks into a grin, slapping his hand on his thigh.

"Thought you'd never get out of there," he yells as I jog toward him.

Arms stretched wide, I wrap him in a huge hug, a prickling sensation hitting me behind my eyes. The burden of the compound and my mission from the past four-plus years is lifted and I'm lighter, grounded.

Fleur.

She's all I've thought about since the raid. The look on her face getting into the SUV, the way her nose scrunched as if she was holding back tears of hurt. Fixing it is my first task.

I pull away from my grandfather, starting toward the house. "I gotta find Fleur," I say.

A hand wraps around my wrist, and my grandfather stops me.

"She's not here, Son."

I tilt my head, not sure I heard him right. "What do you mean?" She may be out with my grandmother or River. Maybe they went shopping or she's hanging with River at Double Lucky's.

"She went back home about a week and half ago."

Shaking my head, I step back and run a hand through my tangled hair.

"No," I say, swallowing. "I told her we'd talk when I was done. That she could stay here, and we'd figure things out."

My grandfather shifts on his feet. "It may be best—"

"No—"

"—to give her time, Liam."

No.

No.

I don't want time. I've had years of time alone. I want my wife.

I should've demanded to talk with her more. The damn agency. I fist both of my hands, bringing them to my head and resting them over top.

"Did she leave contact information?"

"Liam ..."

"Did. She. Leave. Contact information?" I ask again.

"No. And we haven't heard from her."

I kick the pile of leaves, my mind crazed. Does she want nothing to do with me?

I take off back to my bike, needing to get out of here. I tear down the road, booking it for the open road and watching the speedometer tick up, up, up.

Gone.

She can't be. I need her. I love her.

But what do you have to offer her? You forced her into marriage and kept her in a tiny cabin for the extent of your relationship. Between you and your brother, she's probably tapped out.

The town of Ruin fades behind me and the road opens into hayfields and cotton rows.

You failed. As a brother, as a husband, as a son.

I grip the bike, for the first time understanding why Fleur was so obsessed with those damn rubber bands. I'm losing control. This can't be happening.

She left and maybe my grandfather was right. I need to let her live her life.

Chapter 49
Fleur

One Week Later

I came home about two weeks ago and fell into my parents' arms. My dad even greeted me at the airport with a sign. Not embarrassing at all.

Being at my parents' the next several days was refreshing, then reality set in. I'd left.

Living in the house with my parents is comforting and depressing all at the same time. I think about Liam constantly. I want to know if he's okay, but with each day that passes, the more anxiety takes over about reaching out.

Is he mad I left? Has he filed for divorce already?

I slam on my brakes and swerve to miss a silver Camry and nearly run into a US-131 road sign. Traffic is practically at a standstill and the congestion is exacerbated by the construction that never seems to let up.

It's only six in the evening, and I'm sure traffic will go at five miles per hour for the next hour or so. Though, I can't complain. My dad loaned me his car to use this past week, and the freedom behind the wheel has been welcome.

I glance at my new phone, quickly scanning a message from my mom letting me know they'll be at an education fundraiser tonight and that I'm on my own for dinner.

It was one of the first items I grabbed when I got back home —the phone. And, ironically, it's been obnoxious to have it. Granted only my parents text me, and I've used the email and internet on my phone to take care of business ... like finding a realtor.

I study the next exit and decide to pull off to pick up a supreme pizza to devour by myself.

My chest aches at those thoughts. By myself. Damn it.

Opening my phone, I dial the bed-and-breakfast, letting it ring twice before hanging up like I've done the two previous times. I keep thinking I'll let it ring one more time, but I chicken out.

Throwing my phone in my bag, I wait the thirty minutes it takes to move a mile and a half, then exit the highway, weaving my way through traffic until I reach a familiar sub shop and opt for the closer sandwich instead.

With a turkey sub ordered and tucked securely in my front seat, I decide to drive around. The thought of going home to an empty house is unappealing, so I drive down random streets looking at buildings, restaurants, and homes.

There are no hay or cotton fields. No old homes on acres of land as far as the eye can see. Parking is a joke, and instead of a single local coffee shop, I've passed three different Starbucks within a quarter mile radius.

Who would've thought the temporary town I ran away to would leave a permanent mark.

I roll past a well-lit tattoo shop and my thoughts immediately shuffle back to Liam's muscled arm covered in art. I chew my lip and turn right at the next light before circling back to pull into the parlor's parking lot.

My body moves on its own as I get out of my car and jog to the glass door. It's almost as if I know I'll run away if I give myself too much time to slowly walk. I fling open the door, and the sterilized smell of chemicals wafts out.

A front desk extends out from the wall to my left, with a young girl speaking to another man who appears to be checking out with a fresh bandage on his bicep. There's seating across from the check-in with two red leather couches and a black glass coffee table scattered with magazines. Large frames of pre drawn designs and artwork hang all over the walls, and I walk over to them, scanning the tattoos, searching.

I could get a flower. Maybe a daisy. The memory of Liam stopping the truck to gather the flowers off the Trace for me makes it impossible to swallow, and I quickly dismiss the idea.

One of the pictures is of the Michigan mitten with a heart over where we are in Grand Rapids. Underneath it reads home. *Is* this home for me, though? When I think of home, I don't think of my parents' house anymore. I only think of Ruin. And Liam.

I fall away from the endless options. This was a bad idea.

"Can I help you?" the young girl behind the counter asks. She rocks a red mohawk, and piercings line both of her ear lobes. She has tattoos all over her arms and I mentally think of my virgin skin hidden behind my long sleeves and coat.

"I, uh. I—"

"First time?" she interrupts.

"How could you tell?"

"The look of terror on your face." She giggles a high-pitched laugh, and I smile. "Let me grab Max and he can walk you through everything, so you feel at ease."

He does just that.

Max, a man dressed in black jeans and a white T-shirt, so similar to what Liam dresses like, walks me through it all. The process, the equipment, the sterilization area. Most of the supplies are disposable to prevent contamination, and I honestly feel like this studio is cleaner than my doctor's office.

I lie back in the chair, staring at the florescent lighting on the speckled ceiling. Max's black hair and sun-aged face leans over and in my field of vision.

"So what'll it be?"

I suck in a deep breath and blow out a sigh. "A horseshoe."

Chapter 50
Fleur

Another three weeks later...

B en and Jerry's Milk and Cookies ... check. I cross out the ice cream from my grocery list and move the cart down the aisle, seeing if anything else looks like a good binge. So far, my cart consists of eggs and ice cream.

Doing great, Fleur.

I open the freezer door and reach for a bag of frozen cherries. I shiver, zipping up the coat I had to wear to the store along with my gloves, hat, *and* boots. Michigan is cold and I'm grumpy.

Hence the late-night grocery trip.

There's a ding on my phone, and I fumble in my jacket pocket for the darn thing. When I finally wrestle it out, the notification is an email from my realtor. My heart drops. Standing in the middle of the frozen foods section, I open the email.

Fleur,

Attached you'll find the final signed paperwork for the sale of the farmhouse property. It was a pleasure working with you.

Regards,

Jemma

It's done. I sigh, feeling no less upset than I did three weeks ago when I called a local realtor near Ruin and listed the property for sale. It sold the next day for asking price and now, apparently, has closed.

There's no real reason to hang on to it. I *literally* have no home there. Saying goodbye to the farmhouse was easier than I thought. I'm a whole other person from when I renovated that thing.

Instead of the insecure, heartbroken runaway searching for a love to fix me, I'm now the fearful loser, who ran away overwhelmed by the love that consumed me.

But I still shudder—what feels like my final connection to Ruin is slipping away.

My mind wanders to Liam. Because while I was able to reach out to a realtor to sell the farmhouse, I couldn't muster the ability to call the lawyer. I probe around the back pocket of my jeans, pulling out the now torn business card that, quite literally, went through the wash.

I stare at it before tucking it back in my pants.

"The store will be closing in ten minutes."

I groan at the loudspeaker and look down at my cart. Guess this will have to do.

Turning, I barrel down the aisle. A man up ahead rushes to the only open check-out lane and I freeze.

No, I groan. This isn't happening to me.

Chris rapidly flings his groceries onto the belt, and I stand there.

I wait for the feeling to run. For the loss of control to bubble up to the surface and the itch to snap my nonexistent bands in place to tether me. It doesn't come.

Gosh, I'm so stupid. Why did I leave? Liam's comment about coming to him when I want pain flickers in the dark corners of my mind, and I flush.

I glance down at the horseshoe brand now inked into permanent art and I smile at it. With all I've been through, Chris's affair hurts so much less.

Calmly, I move to the line, standing behind Chris. He's leaner than I remember and frantic as he places pickles, marshmallows, and frozen chicken tenders on the belt behind his other staples.

He looks up as if to shrug at his odd choices, but his eyes widen.

"Fleur?"

I offer what I can only assume is a timid smile. "Hi, Chris."

The cashier glances between the two of us and continues to drag item after item across the scanner.

"I-I didn't know you were still around. Your parents said you left town but wouldn't tell me where you were."

"Yeah, I was down in Mississippi for a bit."

"Really? Would never picture that."

I nod, placing my items behind his on the newly available belt space.

Chris shoves his hands in the pockets of his sweatpants. His face scans mine and moves down my body. Not in an interested way but curious.

"Are you doing all right?" I ask. Because somewhere deep down, despite the hurt and pain he caused me, I want the man I spent nine years with to be okay.

"Yeah, yeah. Going to be a dad actually. Georgia's pregnant." He forces a smile and I'm pretty sure he's panicking inside.

"Ah," I say, glancing toward the belt. "The pickles with marshmallows make sense now."

He chuckles. "Yeah, she's had some pretty funky cravings."

I smile. I don't ask who Georgia is, or if she's the one he cheated on me with. I'm not sure I care. He isn't the man who occupies my thoughts or curls my toes.

"Well, congratulations," I offer.

He tilts his head to the side as if he's confused by my cordial conversation and genuine wish for his happiness. As he turns to swipe his credit card, he asks, "Are, are you seeing anyone?"

I bristle at the question and go to shake my head, before pausing.

"Actually, I'm married."

Chris looks at my left hand and back up like he doesn't believe me. Once again, I don't care. I'm tied to Liam, legally, emotionally, willingly.

A sharp pain in my chest burns and I long for Liam. I need to go back, or at least call and see if he even wants to talk to me since I left.

"Did you get my letter?"

I flinch and distract myself by grabbing a bag of candy from the impulse section that always gets me. Honestly, that letter hasn't occupied much of my thoughts and guilt creeps in.

"Thank you for sending my camera. Unfortunately, there was a fire, and I didn't get a chance to read your letter. I'm sorry."

It's the truth. I'm not about to feed him some lie.

He nods, eyes widening at the total on the pin pad waiting

for his card swipe. He doesn't seem overly pressed to tell me what was in the letter, and I find I'm uninterested anyway.

"I'm sorry, Fleur."

I pause, mid-placement of the specialty cookies and cream ice cream I added to my cart last minute. The kind Liam tossed in my cart telling me was the best, and it was. I'll never be the same. He showed me the potential for greatness. Truly delicious ice cream and I'll never go back.

I blink, wanting to cry. I want him.

If this is how Chris felt about Georgia, or whoever she was...

"I get it, Chris. I do."

He swallows and inserts his card, smiling at the cashier as he hands him the receipt. And while I'm overall glad I had this closure with Chris, my thoughts dwell on Liam.

Chris says goodbye and I wish him best of luck. I toss a twenty at the cashier and dart out of the store without my change, past Chris in the parking lot loading his groceries into a bug.

I don't have time to process that.

When I sling myself into the car, I grab my phone and do a quick search for flights to Mississippi. None for tomorrow.

Damn it. I hit the steering while, eyeing the time. I search Old Hillside, pulling up their number, and my finger hovers over the call button. It's past 9:00 p.m.

I need to wait until morning. It would be rude to call them this late.

I start my car, and it sputters to life. It's an older Ford Focus and the only thing I could afford with my savings after coming back home. I crank up the heat and drive home, making plans to get back to Ruin as soon as possible.

The house is dark when I pull into the driveway. The only

light left on is the upstairs hallway from what I can tell. Gathering my bag, I head to the front porch.

An elongated, startling shadow moves off the front steps, and I yelp. The bag in my hand drops, and the crack of eggs on the pavement is drowned out by the roar in my ears.

A rough voice that goes straight to my chest and makes my head fuzzy booms, "See, now we have to go get more eggs."

Chapter 51
Liam

Fleur is beautiful and currently frazzled. She's stunned into silence, but she could be mute and paralyzed and still be the most gorgeous woman.

"Liam?"

Her voice. I close my eyes and inhale at the sound.

I'm a man obsessed.

After I returned to Ruin, I took my grandfather's advice to wait and give Fleur some space. But after a couple weeks, I was done waiting.

I missed her presence. Her in my stupid old hat. Her in my truck with the window down, the wind flicking her signature braid over her shoulder. I've longed to hear her laughter or listen to her snarky comments. To see her face redden when she's embarrassed or frustrated, highlighting her freckled nose and cheeks.

But nothing compares to those piercing gray eyes that seem to see right through me, down to my very soul. I was hooked the first time she glared at me through her jeep window while I passed her on my bike.

Having Fleur in my life was my salvation, and there is no life without her.

Yep. There was no more waiting. I was going to get my wife.

I had no idea how she would take me being here. I still have no clue, but I know she belongs with me.

Chapter 52
Fleur

Liam is here. At first, I fear I'm seeing things. That my mind has conjured him up from all the memories of him in the grocery store. Like it's a cruel trick and this man is actually a creepy stranger that my brain has morphed into a blissfully unaware daydream.

"Liam?"

"Hi."

Hi. One word and it takes my breath away. His voice is smooth and comforting. My body hums, immediately recognizing him as home.

He takes a few steps toward me, and the streetlight casting a bright light on the sidewalk illuminates him. He's in his staple black jeans and a pullover sweatshirt, not nearly enough layers for the December Michigan weather.

His hair is pulled back in a bun, and I want to run my fingers through his freshly trimmed beard. He looks good. Too good ...

Glancing down at my yoga pants and oversized puffy coat, I'm sure I look ridiculous.

Liam's eyes rake over me, but it's not disgust or anger I sense from him. It's relief. He shivers.

"I'm sure this weather isn't something you're used to," I say, bending down to pick up my bag of now cracked eggs.

A boot comes into my view, and I look up at him. His gaze snags on the cookies and cream ice cream in my bag.

"I'm not cold."

Oh.

Liam reaches a hand down, and I take it, sparks tickling every point of touch. He's right in front of me now and suddenly nothing else matters.

"H-how are you here?"

"Well, fortunately, my grandparents aren't too great about keeping their employee records secure." He laughs nervously, and I'm not sure I understand.

Seeing my face, he adds, "You listed your parents as your emergency contact on your hiring paperwork. I snuck this address off it. Wasn't sure you'd be here, though, and then my flight was delayed, plus a thirty-minute Uber ride ..."

The corner of my mouth lifts. He's nervous. I'm not sure I've heard him string so many words together.

"I realized when I stood out front, I was here too late, and I'd just called for another Uber when you pulled up—what?"

I smile. "Nothing."

We stand there, both our breaths materializing as puffs of cloudy mist. His eyes soften as he stares at me.

"Fleur, I—" A ding from Liam's phone goes off and he glances down. "Shoot, my ride is almost here. Can we talk tomorrow? Please?"

"Wait, you're leaving?" My heart stutters, then picks up pace.

"Yeah. I'm sorry I didn't give much thought to the time." He reaches out, palm delicately cradling the curve of my cheek. Longing pulses in his eyes and time seems to pause. There's so much to say, and I don't want to waste another minute.

"Stay," I whisper. "Stay with me."

He studies me, letting out a deep exhale. He grips my face a bit more fiercely. "You sure?"

"Definitely."

Liam pulls out his phone and cancels his Uber, before following me up the steps to the house.

Quietly, we enter and pad into the kitchen, where I put my soupy ice cream away and toss the eggs. I catch Liam tracking my movements, his eyes disinterested in the foreign house and pinned on me.

"Water?" I ask, squirming under his obsessive stare.

He nods, and I tilt my head, chuckling at seeing his bulky form taking up space in my parents' kitchen. To experience Liam outside of Ruin and the compound makes it all seem so surreal.

I grab us some water and without disturbing my parents, who are probably in bed watching TV already, we head up to my old room.

When Liam shuts the door, I turn and throw my arms out. "Well, this is it. Not much, but I'd been moved out since right after my senior year in high school."

Liam glances around the small room with a four-poster queen bed and two matching white dressers across from it. Under the window is a bench seat with my childhood lovely, Mr. Fluffy, resting there.

"My mom kept the bed for guests, and as you can see, I'm still living out of a suitcase. Haven't even unpacked."

Gesturing to the small carryon with a few shirts and pants, I wince. I'm not sure why I volunteered that information. But, in a way, I want him to know this isn't permanent for me. That

I didn't come here to live and thrive away from him. I'm not sure I ever could.

"Good. Easier to pack when I take you home."

I still, mouth falling open. Home. He wants me home.

"Fleur, listen—"

I hold up my hand. "Wait, Liam let me explain."

Goodness, what must he think of me?

Liam quiets, moving to the bed to sit while I do the same.

"I'm sorry I left. After everything that happened, the very real possibility that this"— I motion between us—"could be over, terrified me. I was swept up in my parents begging me to come home and River's suggestion it'd be a good idea.

"I thought ..." I pause, because the truth is I'm not sure I was thinking about us, or about Liam. I was thinking about me, my own pain, my own needs.

"It's what I do. I run and I'm broken." I hang my head, disappointed it was Liam who had to be the bigger person in this. Guilt gnaws at me. He's being more of the adult in this marriage than I am, regardless of how this came about.

I continue, "I'm *in love* with you, Liam. I think I fell for you the night you changed my tire, no questions asked. I knew you'd protect me. I can't even pretend I'm afraid of getting hurt again, because there's no doubt in my mind—you wouldn't do that. I trust you. With my life and my heart."

That wasn't exactly the speech I entertained on the drive home when I wanted to book a flight back to Ruin, but it's honest and true.

Liam slides closer to me, his hand engulfing mine over the yellow daisy comforter. He dips his head, seeking out my eyes, and I lift my gaze to meet his.

"Fleur, it's okay that you run, because I'll always come find you. It's okay that you're broken because I'll spend each day for the rest of my life making sure we put you back together again."

I swallow, a small sob working its way up my throat, and I cling to each word.

"Unless you tell me otherwise, I'm here. Always."

I lean into him. "When the agent suggested the annulment, I thought back to the day at the bed-and-breakfast, and I wasn't sure what you wanted. It was easier to run than to confront it."

Liam grips my face between his thumb and finger. "I want it to be forever, Fleur. Screw what I said that day at the bed-and-breakfast. I knew I could love you the moment you glared at me across the lobby of the bank. And I *do* love you, Fleur Parker. There's no one else for me. No one."

I pull my lip into my teeth. "Fleur Parker? Kind of has a nice ring to it."

"Of course it does. You're meant to be mine."

My mouth finds his and I sigh at the connection. Feather-light kisses trail down my neck, and he doesn't break for air except to say, "Come home, Fleur. Be with me in Ruin. We'll start over together."

"Ruin?" I moan as his hands trail over my hips. "Is the DEA letting you stay there?"

"I quit."

I break away from his lips, the loss of his touch agonizing. "You quit?"

"I wanted to stay in Ruin and with the loss of law enforcement in the town, there was an opening."

"An opening," I parrot.

Liam grins. "You're looking at Ruin's newest sheriff."

Chapter 53
Liam

The look of bewilderment on Fleur's face is comical, but the things I want to do to her right now are not.

"Sheriff," she parrots again. I reach for her braid, the blond in her hair a bit duller than it is in the Mississippi sun.

"Yes. And I don't have much vacation time, so I'm hoping to convince you to come home, Fleur."

She blinks at me, and I glide my hands up her arm, the texture of her goose bumps thrilling me. When she doesn't say anything, I add, "I rented an apartment in town. Two-bedroom, nothing special, but it gives me close access to things. I plan to build at some point, though."

I run a hand through my hair, worrying that I should've spoken with her first before taking this job. If she only knew how much I would give up for her—

"What is that?"

My gaze snaps to meet hers focused on my hand coming out of my hair. My left hand.

I hold it out for her to see. The new ink band around my ring finger.

"Is that—"

I nod.

Fleur's hand comes to her mouth, and she can't take her eyes off it.

"Liam, this is ... now I need one."

My mouth curls with the thought of Fleur wearing a ring or inking one there. I don't care how, but I want my ring on her finger.

"Now I can say I'm getting my second tattoo."

I nod automatically, as she pushes up to her knees and shuffles toward me. With the tip of her finger buried in my chest, she pushes me back until I'm at her mercy on the bed.

My body sings as she straddles me, her hands pushing my shirt up and over my head. This woman is perfect for me, and she's forever mine.

Wait—

Second tattoo—

Black catches my eye and I snatch her wrist midair. She yelps, but I pull it down closer to my face and brush my lips over it. There, over her horseshoe brand, is a new tattoo. It outlines the pink welts perfectly and I blink, wondering why she'd ever draw more attention to the mark forced on her person.

"Why?" I whisper, dragging my mouth over it.

"Because." She leans her head back, her mouth parted as I reach for her leggings—she has too any clothes on. "Because I never want to forget how much I love you, how I'm tied to you. And there's not a brand in the world that could force me to be married to you when I choose you willingly, wholeheartedly."

I drop her wrist, pulling her down and rolling her over. "I

love you so damn much." My mouth tangles with hers, and I rip her shirt down the middle, exposing her chest where I know she has twenty-four freckles, and I kiss each one. Her hips buck, and I have to slow down because I don't want this to end too quickly.

I have the rest of my life to make love to my wife, and I plan to every night she's with me. There's no debt too great to pay if she's the end result.

Epilogue
Fleur

Three Weeks Later

I spent my first Christmas in Mississippi. Granted, I missed the twinge of white on the ground ushering in the festive spirit, but in this cozy apartment, I wouldn't have it any other way.

Liam and I left Michigan after spending three glorious days with my parents a couple weeks ago, and we were welcomed back into Ruin with open arms. We settled quickly into the new apartment and Mrs. Northgate gave me a small tree to put up in our new space. Liam and I decorated it together and ended up spending the night under the twinkling-colored lights.

The week of Christmas, Liam had a lot of paperwork at the station to wrap up for the holiday, and I helped out at the bed-and-breakfast, putting the finishing touches on the outside Christmas decorations. I've stepped back from my job as house-keeper and have taken on the role of marketing, along with other managerial needs. Even picked up the new camera I purchased to take some photos for the new website we're designing.

Both of Liam's parents came over that evening, and we all sat around the firepit out back, where I listened to Mrs. Parker tell stories of Liam as a kid. They seemed more agreeable after finding out Liam was undercover, but there's still an undercurrent of hurt there, and I hope with time the relationships will thrive.

No one has heard from Adam, but Liam has used his connections to gather information. He doesn't know exactly where Raven's new location is, but he works hard every day, desperate to find it. I'm not sure he'll ever shake the feeling of responsibility for his brother, but with the town of Ruin's safety being his new priority, he's lessened the pressure on himself.

Today, we're headed to the bed-and-breakfast for lunch with the Northgate's. River is also meeting us there.

I stuff some red and green tissue paper into the gift bag I have for River, and Liam comes around the couch in uniform to plant a kiss on the top of my head.

"I'm headed to change and then we should go."

I glance at the clock. "It's a bit early to leave. Weren't we meeting for lunch?"

He waggles his brows at me. "Yes, but I have somewhere to take you first."

Twenty minutes later, we load up into the truck and Liam pulls out of the parking spot.

"Look in the back seat," he says.

I narrow my eyes at his cryptic words but reach back there to find a square-wrapped gift. I pull it upfront with us.

"Open it."

I raise my brows at him. "Demanding," I say, but he smiles, and I rip the paper open, blushing at what I find.

Drawn in charcoal is a black-and-white photo of the first

time we came together. I stare at it. The way he captured the texture of the rough brick I can still feel on my back, or the love in his eyes I didn't recognize then but now see so clearly ...

"Liam, this is beautiful." I trace my fingers over his face and glance up him. This man is my everything and time has nothing to do with it. Nine years spent with a man resulted in heartbreak, yet nine weeks with *this* man, *my* husband, have resulted in bliss. I'll never be happier.

"Turn it over."

I flip the frame and find a key taped to the back. "What's this?"

"You'll see."

I watch out the window in anticipation, the bare trees lending themselves better views of the nature around us. We turn down a familiar road, and I take in the winter hayfields and empty rows of cotton, closing my eyes to breathe.

"Liam ..." I gasp as the farmhouse property comes into view.

Fresh wood walls are erect on a new foundation, and I jump out of the truck before Liam has fully put it in park.

Cold wind bites at my chin, but I barely feel it. Instead, I inhale the fresh pine two-by-fours, and my eyes rove over the PEX piping routed through the walls. Sheathing stretches high up to the second floor and around the sides.

The warmth at my back causes me to lean into the solid muscle behind me.

"Should be finished by spring," he says.

"You were the one who bought this?"

I feel him nod against the back of my head. "I couldn't bear to see it go, not on such a sour note. We can rebuild it and either choose to live here or we can start over somewhere different. The choice is ours."

"I can't believe this." I turn, finding his mouth inches from mine, and I kiss him deeply.

A smile lights up his face. "I was thinking a big yard for kids would be better than an apartment."

I grin. "And what if I want chickens?"

"Then I'll build a chicken coop right over there." He points to an empty spot out back.

"And if I want cows?"

"Then I'll build you a pasture over there." He moves his hand to the side of the house where the property gives way to an open flat grassy area. "I'll give you anything want, Fleur."

I close my eyes while Liam pecks a kiss on my nose, and I melt into his arms, safe and home.

"Come on, let me show you where we'll put the barn."

THE END

Bonus Epilogue

Prisoner # 397564

Dear Darrin,
I hope you rot in prison.
-the person who hates you the most

Dear person who hates me the most,

Hi, River.
-D

THE END

Thank you for reading Debt of My Soul!

If you enjoyed this story, please consider supporting my work by rating or leaving a review. Thank you so much for supporting independent authors like myself.

Playlist

"Two Hearts" by Maryjo Lilac
"Strong" by London Grammar
"Wild Ones (feat. Jelly Roll)" by Jessie Murph, Jelly Roll
"Morally Grey" by April Jai
"Dead Man" by David Kushner
"Burn" by Tom Walker
"Survivor" by 2WEI
"Done All Wrong" by Black Rebel Motorcycle Club
"Poison & Wine" by The Civil Wars
"My Home" by Myles Smith
"Cold Feet" by The Patch
"All That Really Matters" by ILLENIUM, Teddy Swims
"Hurt" by 2WEI
"Love's A Leavin'" by Warren Zeiders

Acknowledgments

The title of this book does more than just name the story—it perfectly captures how this novel poured from my soul, leaving me with a debt I had to repay. This was a passion project. I adore this story. Many elements from the fictitious town of Ruin, Mississippi were taken from my small-town life, and I guess I really did write what I know (with a few exceptions, of course!).

I cannot put into words what it means that you've read this book. Thank you to my readers for picking this up. Whether it's your first book of mine or the third—you've made this job as an author spectacularly special.

To my support team. Wow! I'm so grateful.

Becker, from Jones Novel Editing. Thank you for such a thorough developmental edit. Your feedback was phenomenal.

Sara, Autumn House Editing, your manuscript critique helped me shape Fleur and Liam's story, and I adore your constructive critiques so much.

To my Beta readers: Sarah and Xochitl. Thank you for taking the time to provide feedback and love for the story.

To my editor, Emily. Thank you for your quick work on my manuscript and for working with a newer author like me.

Kelsey, you've proofread three of my books and helped me perfect my blurbs. Your willingness to work with me means the world, and I thank you for sticking with me despite my crazy.

And my ARC readers, you're the force behind this story.

Thank you for being willing to read and review in order to drive Fleur and Liam into the world.

Emily, from Emily Wittig Designs, having a cover designed by you is a dream—I am SO in love with it.

Special thanks to Ali from Dirty Girl Designs. Your special edition cover captured everything I love about this book. Thank you for bringing a SE to life for me.

To my Heavenly Father: all glory and honor is Yours.

Thank you, Joey. For loving me through the hard days. And to my children: your infectious joy makes the stress of indie publishing a bit easier.

To those wondering what's next: you guessed it! There will be books for both Lily and River. Technically, they will be standalones but having read *Debt of My Soul*, you'll have an even deeper insight into the characters.

About the Author

K.P. Haven lives in a small southern town with her husband, three children, and adorable pup. She enjoys slow mornings, reading, and mint chocolate chip ice cream.

For more books and updates:
www.authorkphaven.com